Jump
Madders of Time
Book 2

DL Orton

Jump

JUMP

Madders of Time
Book Two

DL Orton

Jump

Jump is a work of fiction. Names, characters, places, and incidents are the product of the author's imagination or are used fictitiously. Any resemblance to actual persons, businesses, events, or locales is coincidental.

**A Publishers Weekly Great Indie Star
Readers' Favorite Book Award Winner
Indie Excellence Book Award Winner
Indie Book Awards Finalist
International Book Awards Finalist**

"Engaging, Funny, Romantic & Harrowing!"
Publishers Weekly Starred Review

"Exceptionally Well Written & Deftly Crafted"
Midwest Book Review

"Rich, Detailed, Fast-Paced & Intelligent"
Literary Picks

"The Best Sci-Fi Love Story of the Year!"
Panda Books

"Edgy, Literary, Pithy & Refreshingly Naughty!"
E.M. Davis, Senior Editor @ Pressque

**"I was satisfied, exhausted, inspired, and blown
away."**
J. Staughton, Sheriff Nottingham eLit Magazine

Prologue

L ess than three hours ago, Diego Nadales had buried his best friend, said goodbye to the only woman he ever loved, and jumped into a different universe.

His clothes were in tatters. His lungs still ached from the jump. His future had gone dark—and this alternate timeline was no brighter.

The plan was simple: travel to the past, deliver a message, disappear. The odds of it changing anything were garbage. He'd jumped anyway.

Now, the eighty-year-old stood in a thrift store that reeked of mothballs and desperation. Everything in the shop had a history. A couch with a suspicious stain. Lime-green Cisco boots missing a stud. An oak-veneered desk with a bad leg and a past it didn't talk about.

The whole place felt like a mistake.

So did his jump.

This Diego—older, grumpier than the timeline's version— rummaged through a rack of uniforms, each movement slow, like he could still feel Isabelle's hand slipping out of his. He told himself coming here was her idea, her choice. Like that made him less of a coward.

He stopped at a fraying brown UPS jacket and checked the price.

"It'll do," he grumbled, yanking it off the hanger.

The coins he'd panhandled tugged at his pocket like shame. They were barely enough for the jacket. He glanced at the cashier, dropped a pair of scruffy slippers to the floor, and slid his stocking feet into them.

It seems he'd left his money and his dignity back in 2075.

One aisle over, another Diego prowled, unaware he was steps away from himself. In his home timeline, they called him Tego.

He looked good for a thirty-something browsing in a thrift shop. A roll of twenties bulged in his pocket. His cart overflowed: sneakers, shirts, jeans, toiletries—even a suitcase.

He wore a giant orange Stetson stamped with the Denver Broncos logo—swagger incarnate. The black wig under it killed the effect.

He paused at a cracked mirror. Tilted his chin.

"Looking good," he said—then chuckled. "Like Zorro mated with a traffic cone."

He clicked the heels of his ruby-red high-tops. They were back in style, and he'd found two pairs in his size. One he wore now—tag tucked under the laces to pay for later. If he got lucky, he wouldn't need the second pair.

Anticipation rippled through him.

Today, he would see *her* again. He'd waited years for this—for one precious glimpse. Then he would change the future.

Or was it the past? He was beginning to lose track.

He spun, ready to tip his hat to this universe, and froze.

Across the aisle, an older version of himself—now struggling to force a fedora over his wispy gray hair—also froze.

Two sets of brown eyes widened in recognition.

The shop went still.

A radio somewhere blasted "Careless Whisper."

The universe held its breath.

"*Mierda*," the older Diego croaked and tried to dive behind a pile of purses. But his foot slipped, and he landed on his back.

"Less than a day in this timeline," he muttered, "and you've already blown the first rule of time travel."

Tego stepped around the purses, pointing a trembling finger at him. "It's—*you?*"

They each waited for the other to pop out of existence.

When nothing happened, the elderly man frowned. "You're supposed to be at work."

Tego realized the old man thought he was the Diego from *this* timeline. "I'm not *him*. I'm from another universe." He reached out and helped the old man to his feet. "Tego."

"Christ," the older Diego said. "This means there's three of us bumbling around the timeline." He dusted off his pants and tugged the fedora back into place. "It could ruin everything."

Tego suppressed a grin. "Well, the universe didn't implode, now did it, Gramps?"

"It's dangerous. You being here... me being... both of us in one..." The old man's gaze shifted to other people in the store. "The deviations will be enormous, unpredictable."

Tego eyed him with a mix of curiosity and amusement. "Why are you here?"

"Why are you?"

They both stood there, glaring at the other.

A clock ticked unevenly, like time was giving them the middle finger.

They both pretended not to notice.

The old guy huffed. "What sort of name is *Tego?*"

"It's a nickname," Tego said. "Better than being Diego Number Three."

The old man's eyes flicked to the hat, then back to Tego. He scowled. "That outfit screams, '*Arrest me!*' Who are you supposed to be? Rodeo Elvis?"

"This old thing?" Tego tugged on his Stetson. "It's called blending in."

"Maybe in a Western." The old man glanced past him. "Did you leave your horse outside?"

"What about you?" Tego shot back. "You look like Indiana Jones got lost in a nursing home."

The old man grunted and adjusted his fedora. "Subtlety is key."

"A fedora and slippers?" Tego glanced at the man's deteriorating jumpsuit. "Yeah, subtle is the word all right."

From behind the checkout counter, a woman with blue hair fixed them with a glare—probably weighing whether to call security.

Tego cleared his throat and turned away. "Okay, take two. What's your mission?"

The old man squinted at him. "If you must know, I have a time-critical note for... well, *us*. It's from Isabelle."

Tego's grin faded. He stepped closer, still fiddling with his orange hat. "Your Isabel?"

"Yeah," the older Diego said with a dramatic sweep of his arm. "But that's none of your business."

"I am your business." Tego poked him in the chest. "We're literally the same person. So what's in the note, Gramps?"

"Why do you keep calling me Gramps?"

"Because 'Walking Cautionary Tale' was too long." Tego lifted his chin. "What's in the note?"

"Shopping list," Gramps said, clutching his UPS jacket tighter.

Tego blinked. "What, like milk, eggs, and an extra paradox?"

"You forgot regret. Never enough of that to go around." The old man turned too fast and knocked over a teetering stack of metal picture frames, which he caught just before they hit the floor.

Tego barked a laugh. "C'mon, Gramps. We both know you didn't jump timelines for groceries."

The cashier gave them another dirty look.

The old man took a slow breath and lowered his voice. "If I tell you, something terrible might—"

"What? The time stream collapses? Your ticket home disappears? The apocalypse shifts to something particularly nasty?" Tego snorted. "Been there. Done that." He patted his pocket. "I'm here to give Isabel a *jinn* object."

"You are?" Gramps raised an eyebrow. "What timeline?"

"Can't tell you. But it'll fix everything. At least, I think it will." Tego fidgeted with his wig. "She needs to get it tonight."

Gramps narrowed one eye. "Maybe we can help each other. I need to deliver the note to my younger self. Make sure he reads it today."

Tego considered the proposition, then nodded. "That what the delivery getup is for?"

"Yeah," the old man said. "But I do the talking."

"Oh, absolutely." The corner of Tego's mouth twitched. "You're clearly the charmer."

Neither moved—one all gristle and regret, the other still bouncing through life like cartilage was forever.

Finally, Gramps sighed and shrugged one shoulder. "How old are you, anyway?"

"It's hard to keep track with all the jumps. Thirty-something. Close enough to pass as local. You?"

"None of your goddamn business, Slick."

Tego pinched his nose. "Mierda, I hope I'm not this cranky when I hit eighty."

The old man didn't smile. "You are."

"Something to look forward to," Tego grumbled and turned away. "Can we just pay and get out of here?" He pulled a wad of cash out of his pocket. "I'm on a tight schedule to save the world."

"Where'd you get that?" Gramps blinked. "Rob a bank? You some sort of criminal?"

Tego rolled his eyes. "I pawned a strand of pearls. Guaranteed organic." He gave a laugh. "Best option, given the wormhole constraints. You?"

Gramps grumbled something about being a little rushed.

Tego pulled off the cowboy hat and smoothed the wig beneath it. "You're welcome, by the way."

Gramps narrowed one eye. "For what?"

"Me choking down kale and wheatgrass for decades—so you wouldn't look like a raisin."

"Wasn't for me, Sparky."

"Maybe not," Tego said. "But you're still cashing the checks."

Gramps adjusted his collar. "Isabelle always said I was vain—but at least I still got my hair."

Tego shrugged. "Can't argue with that." He tugged a pair of red high-tops out of his shopping cart and tossed them at Gramps. "Can't have you running around in stolen goods."

"Thanks." The old man ditched his slippers and put on the sneakers.

He let Tego pay. What else was he going to do?

The woman with the blue hair scowled at the ten packs of Dodgers-branded underwear, but neither man noticed.

Five minutes later—hats on and one suitcase between them—two versions of the same man waited on a bench at the bus stop.

Gramps adjusted his too-small jacket while Tego fiddled with his sunglasses. The late morning sun was starting to win out over the early autumn chill.

"I'll deliver your note to *our guy*," Tego said. "But in exchange, you have to do something for me."

"What?" the old man said, his brow furrowed. "Murder someone?"

"No," Tego spat out. "Nothing illegal. Just bump into Isabel, drop a puzzle box with the shell into her purse, and hotfoot it out of there. No way she'll recognize you."

The old man took a shell out of his pocket. He lifted his chin at his younger self. "Should we check?"

"Why not?" Tego took out the puzzle box, pushed and pulled some hidden levers, and reached inside. Both men held their breath.

There were no Houdini hijinks.

"Not from the same timeline," they murmured and put their shells away.

Gramps cleared his throat. "How do you know she won't recognize me?"

Tego looked him over. "You have to trust me, *mae*. I just do."

"That's not an answer."

Tego smirked. "I'm not on trial."

Gramps narrowed his eyes. "You talked to her."

"Might have."

"You little bastard."

It wasn't a question, but Tego nodded anyway.

"Before or after today?"

"After," Tego said. "But it was a long time ago."

Gramps squinted at him, suspicion curdling into something sadder. "So how is your shell gonna save this timeline?"

"Not this timeline. *My* timeline. And maybe yours. What comes around, goes around."

"It's too late for my world." Gramps stared at his shoes. "I'm only here because I couldn't say no to her."

"None of us can," the younger man said. He set his hand on Gramps' arm. "But it's never too late. You know how complicated the multiverse can get."

Gramps muttered something about snowflakes in hell.

Tego leaned back on the bench and put his hands behind his head. "And don't act like you're above all this. You're the one trying to deliver a note by pretending to be the world's oldest delivery guy."

Gramps sighed. "It's a simple plan. Direct. Effective."

Tego scoffed.

A bus squealed to a stop on the other side of the street, and people streamed out. The two men watched them walk down the sidewalk.

"Don't even know they're doomed," Gramps said. "Poor bastards."

Both men were quiet, lost in thought.

"What was it for you?" Tego asked. "Pandemic? Bots? Asteroid?"

Gramps exhaled. "Bots, mostly."

Tego nodded. "Those are the worst." He glanced at the old man. "Don't know what it's going to be for us yet."

They both leaned forward, resting their elbows on their thighs.

"What about your Isabelle?" Gramps held his breath, afraid of what the younger man's answer might be.

"Izzy," he said, half smiling. "She goes by Izzy." He swallowed. "*Went* by Izzy. I lost her a year ago."

"Christ. I'm sorry." The old man stared down at his hands.

"Well, you know how it is," Tego said. "She doesn't make it to fifty in most universes."

Gramps pressed his lips together. "Mine is eighty—but dying. I left her alone in Dave's defunct biodome to come here." He expected the younger man to berate him for abandoning the love of his life.

Tego shrugged. "She can be very persuasive." He reached out his hand and set it on the older man's shoulder. "Believe me, I've done worse."

"Let's hope our man in this timeline doesn't screw it up again," Gramps said.

"That's what you're here to prevent, right?" Tego glanced over at him.

He nodded.

"Can I see the note?"

Gramps didn't answer, just stared at the sidewalk.

"Your world can't get any worse, am I right?"

"Oh, it definitely can," the old man said, but handed it over. His heart pounded in his throat as Tego unfolded the handmade paper.

"God, I miss her," Tego said, running his finger across the handwriting.

Gramps snuffed his nose. "Me too."

"Have you factored in the security guard in the lobby—what's-his-name? He was always a hard-ass." Tego handed the note back to him. "He's going to know you're a fake the moment he lays eyes on you." The younger man scrubbed his hand across his clean-shaven face. "What if we leave it in Nadales' car?"

Gramps scowled at him. "Great idea, Sherlock. He won't read it until he leaves work tonight, probably after midnight. My Isabelle will die in vain, and I'll be stuck in this godforsaken timeline until whatever flavor of Doomsday gets me."

"We'll set off the car alarm," Tego said and nudged him on the shoulder. "He'll have to come outside."

"What if the alarm shuts off?" Gramps crossed his arms. "Sometimes it does that."

Tego blew out a sharp breath. "Then we'll trip it again. Or we could wait for the stars to align and hope he reads it telepathically."

They shuffled their feet in near-perfect synchrony.

Tego rubbed his hands together. "Here's the plan: First, we deliver your note. Then, we get a bite to eat, get a room, and change clothes. This evening, we sneak the seashell into Isabel's bag. Tomorrow, we start making money. After that, we stake out the mountain and wait for them to get the spacetime bridge working. Then you use their setup to go back right after you left. Problem solved."

"What are you gonna do?"

"I got a recall coming in thirty days. If I miss that one, there'll be another in a year. And again every five years until I make it home."

"Home?" Gramps muttered. "God help us." But an idea had already started to form—an idea that sent hope and longing pouring into his aging chest.

Maybe he *could* save Isabelle.

They caught the next bus toward downtown, arguing over whose delivery plan was stupider and whether or not the multiverse would survive the other's incompetence.

By the time they reached Gemini Solutions, Gramps was already spouting off about his plan to bump into Isabel outside the law office that evening. Tego tried to tune him out as they climbed the parking garage stairs.

"That's his car," they both said, pointing at a beat-up CR-V parked in a corner.

"Do you think there's a timeline where we drive a Porsche?" Gramps asked.

"Haven't found it," Tego said. He whipped out a pocketknife and walked toward the car.

"What are you doing?" Gramps hissed, hurrying to catch up.

"Getting the door open."

Gramps rolled his eyes, walked to the back of the car, and pulled the spare key off the bumper. He opened the driver's door, hung the note over the steering wheel, relocked the car, and put the key back. "Youth is wasted on the young," he said as he stepped away.

Tego shoved the car with his foot, and the alarm triggered.

The older man muttered something about amateurs as they scurried into the shadows.

Sure enough, a minute later, a harried-looking Diego appeared, jangling his keys. He slid into the seat, silenced the alarm, and froze when he saw the note.

The two displaced versions watched as Diego unfolded the paper, his expression shifting from confusion to shock. He sat still for more than a minute, then pulled out his phone and dialed a number.

The other Diegos exchanged an anxious glance.

"Who's he calling?" Gramps whispered.

"Please tell me it's not the cops."

"Well, if this doesn't work out," Gramps said, "the three of us could always audition to be the new Three Stooges."

Tego shushed him.

Diego's voice floated across the garage. "Hello? I'd like to make a dinner reservation for tonight. A table for two facing the mountains, please. Seven o'clock."

Tego elbowed Gramps. "See? Flawless execution. You're welcome again."

Gramps scoffed. "This doesn't make us friends."

"Friends? No, no," Tego said with a smirk. "We're partners in crime. Big difference."

Lunch was a cheap burger joint with questionable hygiene but decent fries, the kind of place where the tables wobbled and the ketchup bottles looked sticky. But Gramps was in heaven—he hadn't had fries in years. Still, he insisted on sitting with his back to the wall, grumbling about how he didn't trust Tego's judgment.

"Stop fidgeting," Tego said, slurping his milkshake. He'd stuffed the wig in his pocket like a dead animal but kept the Stetson. "You're drawing attention."

"Says the guy with the neon cowboy hat." Gramps speared a fry. "You look like a mascot for the book of bad ideas."

"And yet, my ideas work," Tego said. "Speaking of which, are you ready for your close-up tonight?"

"Yes," Gramps said, though his expression betrayed a flicker of doubt. "You sure she won't recognize me?"

"Relax. This is the easy part."

After lunch, Tego paid for a room in a cheap motel and asked for two keys. As Gramps waited outside, Tego tucked most of his cash into the closet safe, entered four numbers, and shut the door. Tego set the suitcase on the bed and gestured for Gramps to come in. "Help yourself."

The older man croaked out a "thank you."

Until they had a chance to bet on the NFL in Cripple Creek, Tego said they'd need to conserve money.

"How do you remember who wins?"

Tego pulled out a tattered sheet of paper. "The top three parlays should make us a hundred times our money."

Gramps was grateful Tego had said *us* instead of *me*. "How'd you get the list through the wormhole?"

"All-natural paper and organic ink." Tego shrugged. "Same as your note."

"Right."

"But you have to be careful. The ink fades and the paper disintegrates." Tego stuck the list of winners in the hotel safe with his money. "We'll make a photocopy at the library tomorrow. Then whenever we need more cash, we'll place bets. There's a list of stocks at the bottom—on the off chance we need a longer-term solution."

Gramps nodded. "Anything except Gemini."

Tego froze. "What's that got to do with anything?"

Gramps stared at him, realizing he'd violated yet another rule of time travel: don't talk about your timeline. "Forget I mentioned it."

"Sure," Tego said, still looking spooked. "Consider it done."

The old man nodded, feeling exhausted and a bit overwhelmed. "You've obviously done this before."

"A time or two." Tego gave him a crooked smile. "Too many to count, actually."

"This is my first," the old man said. It had come out before he could stop himself.

"Don't worry." Tego placed a hand on the older man's back. "It gets easier. The jet lag is the worst part. I always try to time my jumps to minimize it, but there's no avoiding it."

"Gotcha," Gramps said, wondering what other painful side effects were headed his way.

"And don't lose track of your socks," Tego said. "They're your ticket home." He took his off and stuffed them into the safe. "And don't wash them either. "

"What happens if you wash them?"

Tego shrugged. "They get clean." He picked out a T-shirt and a pair of jeans from the suitcase. "And some of the particles from your universe get washed down the drain. Weakens the anchor and muddies the Peeper. Eventually, the object'll stop working." He pulled on a new pair of socks. "That's why you can't use yourself as a jinn: too much cellular turnover." He yawned. "And never jump with the same anchor twice in quick succession. The second attempt will fail big time. Some sort of time loop splatter."

Gramps didn't know what to say to that, so he just nodded.

The younger man eyed the elder's scruffy face and threadbare jumpsuit. "You can go first," he said and gestured toward the shower. "Save me some shampoo."

The shower was glorious, but Gramps kept it short—and left the best towel for his counterpart. He got dressed and tried not to think of where he'd be if Tego hadn't found him.

Probably in jail.

While Tego showered, Gramps made himself a cup of instant coffee with three packets of sugar. He could barely keep his eyes open. He cracked the dingy window and collapsed into a worn chair. With so many years spent inside a biodome, it was a pleasure to feel the breeze on his face.

Tego put on jeans, checked the alarm clock three times, then closed the curtains. "Get some rest," he said. "After we drop off the puzzle box, we'll make sure she gets to the restaurant. Then we'll grab dinner."

Despite the coffee, Gramps was asleep in a matter of seconds.

The alarm woke them at four.

They boarded a bus fifteen minutes later.

Outside the courthouse, they lingered near the bus stop. Tego slouched against the pole. Gramps shifted in his ill-fitting UPS outfit, fingers worrying the brim of his fedora. The sun was down, the air cold. The old man was glad for the jacket. The orange cowboy hat was back on Tego's head, throwing a shadow across his face.

"This is ridiculous," Gramps said. "We look like the worst buddy cop movie ever."

Tego grinned. "That's the charm. Nobody looks twice at losers."

"I'm too old for this crap."

"Exactly," Tego said, pointing at Gramps' hat. "With that fedora, there's no chance she'll recognize you—as long as you keep your mouth shut. We wait until she's almost at the restaurant—just to make sure she gets there—and then all you have to do is brush against her, stick the puzzle box in her purse, and walk away."

Gramps scrubbed a hand across his beard stubble, eyes locked on the courthouse steps like he was bracing for a bullet.

When Isabel appeared—papers clutched to her chest, hair pulled back, stride fierce and familiar—both men stopped breathing.

Tego straightened. Smiled. Not the cocky kind—the other kind: part muscle memory, part heartbreak.

Gramps gripped the bench. Hard. His heart lurched like it had just remembered how to hurt.

"There she is," Tego whispered.

Gramps exhaled, long and ragged—like surfacing from the bottom of a freezing lake. "She's... still her." His voice was low, barely holding shape. "Headed to the restaurant," he added, hating how loud he sounded, how dumb. "To meet *him*."

Tego gave a soft snort. "The lucky dog."

For a second, neither spoke. Then they shared a look—brief, brittle.

Gramps flicked his chin toward the law office.

Dave Kirkland came barreling down the steps, crossed four lanes of traffic without looking, and climbed into a red convertible with a woman half his age.

Tego didn't even blink. "Some things never change."

They turned back to Isabel.

For five blocks, they trailed her at a careful distance, Gramps keeping to the sidewalk's edge while Tego hung back, whistling a tune so off-key it was practically its own genre.

Isabel quickened her steps, her heels clicking against the pavement, but instead of going into the skyscraper's lobby, she stopped and gazed up at the restaurant.

Gramps looked back at Tego. The younger man shrugged.

The wind whisked a piece of paper down the sidewalk. It caught on her shoe. Isabel lifted it, read both sides, and whirled around.

Instead of taking the elevator to the restaurant, she started walking directly toward Gramps.

For a second, he couldn't breathe.

He looked down at his feet as she hurried past. When he heard her continue on, he adjusted the fedora and glanced over his shoulder.

She was heading right for Tego—and that stupid cowboy hat.

The younger man ducked into an alley. After she passed, the two men shared another look, and Gramps hurried over to him.

"Something's wrong," Tego said and yanked off his sunglasses. "This isn't how it's supposed to go." His hands shook.

Gramps had seen that look before—on soldiers just before the shooting started.

He stepped closer, his voice low. "Talk to me."

"Christ. It must be the Spheres." Tego slammed a fist into the wall. "I should've known that."

"Known what?" Gramps said, his hackles rising. "What spheres are we talking about?"

Tego rounded on him. "It's not safe. She needs to get out of here. Now."

"Out of where? What about the shell? I mean, we could give it to her tomorrow or—"

"No! It has to be tonight. Mierda, it all makes sense now. If she doesn't get it now, it'll be too late." He rubbed his throat. "It might already be too late."

"Too late?" Gramps' voice dropped. "For what, Tego?"

"Her." Tego jammed on his sunglasses and grabbed the old man by the elbow. "Come on. You have to tell her to get out of the city."

They hurried to catch up with Isabel.

"I thought you said I couldn't talk to her." The old man took the puzzle box out of his pocket as he tried to keep up with Tego. "What should I say?"

"Whatever gets her to listen." Tego pressed a hand to his chest like it hurt. "Just... make sure she gets the box with the shell—and then gets the hell out of Dodge."

Gramps looked at the puzzle box like it might explode. "You think she'll believe me?"

"It doesn't matter." Tego looked like he might be sick. "We can't be seen together. I'll meet you back at the hotel."

They were right behind her now.

Isabel's pace faltered. Her heel caught on a grate, and she pitched forward—papers spilling like birds in a gust of wind.

"Go!" Tego shoved Gramps. "Before it's too late."

The old man stumbled forward and steadied Isabel's arm. When he was sure she wasn't going to fall, he crouched down to gather her divorce papers.

Tego watched from the alley, pulse hammering.

As Isabel stood and brushed off her skirt, her gaze locked with Tego's for the briefest moment. His breath caught, and he stepped deeper into the alley.

A minute later, he peeked out and saw his counterpart hurrying back toward the motel.

Isabel called after the old man, but he didn't stop.

Tego shadowed her to The Brown Palace, panic tightening like a fist as she paused to peer at the caged pets.

"Go. Go. Go," he whispered.

When she finally turned back to her car, he let out the breath he'd been holding.

Maybe they'd both make it out alive.

Then a blur tore through the building across the street—steel screaming, glass raining down—before it slammed into The Brown Palace Hotel in a bloom of flames.

The truth hit like shrapnel.

Time travel only ever meant one thing: Payback.

It was a trap, the noose the universe had set. And the rope was already tightening.

Tego ran into smoke.

Into fire.

Into the jaws of what was coming.

Toward her.

Madders' Second Log: Entry 1

Target: Matthew Hudson, Age 51
Nexus: Somewhere in Florida
Chrono Tag: Six Days after Log 1, Entry 29

UN relief flights grounded in West Africa. Food riots in São Paulo exceed containment.

Kirkland Enterprises accelerates media consolidation. NewsCorp reports unanimous support for biodome initiatives. Accounts of civil unrest suppressed as misinformation.

Absence of a functional spacetime bridge in this timeline reduces probability of success to near zero.

The chopper bucks hard, jerking me against the harness. Rain batters the hull. The cabin groans.

Cassie and I are strapped into the belly of a Black Hawk flying across a drowned Florida. She stares straight ahead, lips pressed tight, her hand locked over the chest strap. Eight marines huddle around us, eyes shut, still as statues.

Picasso sits beside me, flipping through images the Peeper captured this morning: Streets carpeted with bodies, eyes open, unblinking. Dogs collapsed mid-stride. Cattle sprawled in fields. Elephants fallen in place, great shadows against the dirt. No bomb craters. No shell casings. No blood. Only silence—and rot.

Whatever killed them moves fast—unseen, precise, efficient.

If the pattern holds, it's already on its way here.

Plague? Bioweapons? Extreme heat? No one knows.

What we do know: the world doesn't end in fire—it stops, and everything falls.

Picasso alerted the White House. They've seen the footage, understand what it means. We're still waiting on a callback. That alone says everything.

He pauses on a photo of a child—limp, glassy-eyed, cradled in the arms of a man too broken to cry. My stomach knots. I press a hand to my thigh—an anchor against the rising fear in my chest.

It's coming. And we've got nothing.

Correction—*we had* nothing until four days ago.

Sam cracked the Einstein Sphere's punch cards months ago and pulled the URL for the wormhole generator. But the project was never found—scrubbed or buried. Dick's people swore it didn't exist. Cassie disagreed. She followed a hunch, tried a few alternate project names, and with Sam's assistance, dug up something the NSA missed. Sabina helped them "borrow" Junior's clearance codes, log into a black site, and trace the project to a government building in southeast Florida.

Once Picasso finished chewing Junior's head off, he moved fast. Cassie took over training the marines. By the third time someone confused a wormhole array with a Wi-Fi router, it became clear: She'd have to go with them.

I knew it the moment the words left Picasso's mouth—and I hated it. But wanting and choosing are different things. You don't argue with logic when extinction's on the line.

We need the spacetime bridge, and without a wormhole generator, we're just taking turns dying.

So here we are—one armed helicopter, eight overqualified door-kickers, and two Hudsons dressed like extras in a low-budget sci-fi flick.

Pretty sure the guy in *Predator* wore the same kit—and he didn't make it back either.

I shift in the seat.

Beside me, Cassie exhales. Her knee bounces like it's trying to make a break for it. I set a hand on her leg. She squeezes it—hard—but doesn't look at me.

Yeah. We're all scared, Pumpkin.

Now we're flying into a different kind of nightmare. Flooded streets. Crumbling towers. Starving people with nothing left to lose.

"Looks like *Mad Max*," Sam had said when he saw the recon shots, "if the desert drowned."

He wasn't wrong.

Picasso swears the looters have moved inland to higher ground.

I hope to hell he's right. Whatever's waiting in that drowned city doesn't give a damn about our mission.

I choke down the jungle-thick dread clogging my throat.

One disaster at a time, Hudson.

I lean closer to Picasso and glance at the photo he's holding. "Say we find the wormhole generator. Then what? Build our own escape hatch?"

He doesn't answer. Just stares at the Peeper image of the dead girl. "It's out of my hands. New director's been appointed." He crumples the paper and stuffs it in his bag.

"What? Bloody hell. Don't tell me they promoted Johnson."

"Hasn't been announced." He shrugs. "But if this goes sideways, it won't matter."

I sit back. "What's your recommendation—assuming we get the bridge tech working?"

"Get Nadales to talk and see what he knows."

I frown. "And if we can't find him?"

He meets my eyes. "Johnson put him in the brig last week."

"What?" I grab his arm. "You locked him up?"

Picasso doesn't flinch. Just shifts his gaze to my hand, like he's deciding if I'm worth the trouble.

"Diego's not a criminal," I say, releasing my grip. "Why didn't you tell me?"

"Not my call," he says. "Right now, I need you to focus on the mission."

"But—"

We hit an air pocket, and the copter drops hard. My gut lurches.

The storm reminds me what little control I have.

None of the statues seem to notice.

I try to imagine us getting back on the helicopter, the wormhole generator packed in the hold. But my mind is stuck replaying the practice run. Picasso instructed us to hit the deck if we heard gunfire. Once down, I had to be prodded to get up.

That evening, after my spectacular performance, Picasso offered to take me off the team.

I'm embarrassed to admit I actually considered it.

"If she goes," I said, forcing the words out, "I go."

And now I get to see if that noble gesture gets us both killed.

I sit on my hands to keep them from shaking and steal a glance at Cassie. She always seems to know what I'm thinking and gives me a quick smile.

Wish I had a tenth of her pluck.

The plan is simple. We get inside. Tag anything that looks remotely useful. Then sprint back to the chopper while the marines carry the goods.

At least that's how it's supposed to go.

Let's hope the wormhole folks didn't build an underground linear accelerator or something—because we're about to walk into it blind.

"Sir," the pilot says, her voice calm. "We're approaching the LZ."

Picasso leans forward. "How's the situation on the ground, Captain Rodriguez?"

"Weather conditions are less than ideal, Sergeant Major. Limited visibility and strong crosswinds due to another storm brewing in the Gulf. I estimate the soup is ten to fifteen inches deep, over."

"Understood, Captain."

"We're also detecting Charlie activity," she adds. "They're following the bird, sir."

My throat gets tight. "I thought you said there weren't any looters?" The words barely land. My brain's already projecting blood on wet concrete and Cassie facedown in the soup.

"Let's hope they're just curious," Picasso says. I'm not sure if he's talking to me or the pilot—or if he's trying to convince himself.

"Rodriguez," he says, "exercise extreme caution while you sit on the nest."

"Copy that, Sergeant Major. Down in two minutes."

"And Captain, be ready to dust off at full tilt."

"Yes, sir. I'll keep an eye on the situation and stand by for your signal. I can have us in the air in six seconds."

Six seconds to get inside if things go sideways? That's not a rescue window—it's a coin flip.

Picasso nods at the newly animated marines. "Do not use lethal force unless you have no other option. Lots of hungry, desperate people out there, and the last thing they need is a bullet."

There's a round of assent—and a couple of expletives.

The men adjust their backpacks, grab their rifles, and line up next to a door. Picasso shoulders an M27, holsters a sidearm, and turns to us. "Stay low and keep moving. Chang and Liszt know the way to the target, so stay behind them." Two guys wave from the front, and the others step aside to let us through. "Once we're through the exterior doors, Garcia and Schwartz will lead you to the lab." Garcia's face is stone, but his finger twitches against the trigger guard. Schwartz winks, probably to cover the same nerves I'm trying to ignore.

"Thirty seconds, sir," the pilot says. "Watch your six."

"Will do." Picasso checks the ammo in his rifle and turns to us. "Until we get inside the building, no talking unless it's mission-critical. I'll be right behind you." He waits for both of us to nod. "And just like we practiced," he says, "if you hear shots, drop to your belly and wait for instructions."

"Yes," Cassie says. "I still don't know why you won't let me have a—"

Picasso cuts her off with a shake of his head. "Not now."

She nods, lips tight, and gives him a look that says she's got six ways to outmaneuver him if it comes to that.

He turns to me. "Are we clear about gunfire?"

"Loud sound," I say. "Get down."

Getting up is what breaks you.

Picasso jostles in behind us, and the cabin seems to shrink. My mouth tastes like metal. My hands are slick with sweat, and we haven't even touched down. Every part of me screams that I'm not cut out for this.

The hatch slides open. Warm, damp air slaps my face. We're still dropping, rotor blades thumping above us. My stomach flips as the light slams into my eyes.

We lurch to a stop on the roof of a hospital. Skyscrapers jut from the water like gravestones. The city is drowned, the ocean taking back what was hers. The air reeks of brine, mold, and rot—nature creeping back amidst the skeletons of human achievement.

I've read post-apocalyptic scenarios. Living one is different.

"Go," Picasso says, his voice low and controlled.

Cassie follows the marines out of the helicopter, jumping onto the trash-strewn platform and splashing across the pad towards the open doorway. I hesitate, and someone pushes me from behind. A squeak escapes my lips as the two men in front grab my arms and set me on the ground like some debutante.

Christ. Get a grip, Hudson.

Someone yanks me forward. I stumble over a painted red cross, head down, and run.

The moment I'm inside, everyone turns and pushes through a heavy door. By some miracle, the lights are still on, and we file down a metal stairway. I lose count as we pound down the steps, turn, pound down more steps. I glance at what looks like a pile of laundry —then the smell hits. Bodies. The stench makes me gag.

Don't look. Just keep moving.

I pound down more stairs, legs already turning to rubber.

Someone holds the door open as we step out of the stairwell into a hallway full of shin-deep, floating plastic waste. The water is warm and slimy, and I wonder what sorts of pathogens are waiting to infect me.

Two of our guys force open an emergency exit while water leaks in around the heavy door.

"Stay behind my men," Picasso says. "Step where they step." We file into an alley, water up to our calves. I follow right behind Cassie.

Overhead, the sun loses out to the clouds.

It's been months since I was outside, and I look up. Skyscrapers float in a sea of muddy water. Drowned palm trees poke out in a long line, their tops empty and lifeless.

"This isn't a parade, people." Picasso's voice has an edge to it. "Keep your eyes on the task and your mind on the mission."

I slosh across the street—rainbow sheen swirling with every step —and catch up with Cassie.

If someone starts shooting, we die wet.

"This way," Chang says.

Cars and trucks sit rusting as we trudge past, the buildings behind them covered in bathtub rings—some higher than my head.

"Charlie's moving with you," the pilot says. "North building. They don't appear to be armed."

"Let 'em watch," Picasso says. "Take 'em out the second they pose a threat."

"They're just people." Cassie stops walking. "Not terrorists."

Picasso doesn't blink. "You do your job, Dr. Hudson, and I'll do mine."

I step in, a hand on her elbow. "Let's go, Cassie."

We step down a curb to cross another street. Water swells past my knees.

Something ripples the oily surface to my left.

My heart jumps into my throat, and the image of Luke Skywalker in the garbage compactor fills my brain.

I watch the ripple come toward us, my throat getting tight.

"Bogey in the water!" I blurt, already clocking a wooden bench half a block away, the seat just above the waterline. I brace for a fifty-meter dash in soaked boots—with Cassie in tow.

"Juvenile anaconda," someone says as I watch the wake moving away from us. "Standard South Florida welcome party."

"Here, kitty, kitty," someone else croons.

A low laugh ripples through the squad—too quick, too sharp—and dies fast.

"Keep moving," Picasso orders.

We do—dodging trash and submerged junk.

On the next block, Cassie steps out of formation. For a second, I think it's another snake—but it's a bottle with a note inside.

She snags it, eyes narrowed.

"Get back in line," Picasso snaps, catching up with her. "You want to live, you follow my orders. Is that clear, Dr. Hudson?" He grabs her arm and whips her around to face him.

"Perfectly clear," Cassie says, fists clenched.

"Easy, mate." I jog toward them. "We're all on the same team."

Before he can react, she yanks her arm away and continues trudging forward.

I give Picasso a look that says *lay off*—and follow after her.

Picasso stays planted, face unreadable.

I slosh past him.

She pulls the stopper from the bottle, fishes out the paper, and reads it. After shaking her head, she hands the note back to me.

Send food. Our children are starving.

My chest tightens. Fear of death is one thing. Knowing kids are dying is worse.

Unable to just toss it, I fold the note and pocket it.

We trudge past a battered, half-submerged sign pointing the way to Miami, cross the street beneath raised freeways and a monorail track, and continue pushing through knee-deep muddy water, past shattered windows and gaping doors.

A light rain starts, shivering the flood's surface.

The city remains still.

"This way," Chang calls from up ahead. Emerging from the flooded street are stairs. He climbs out of the water and jogs toward a glass-and-concrete skyscraper. We follow him up and under a wide concrete overhang. When we stop moving, four marines herd us into the center and face outwards with guns ready.

"Why didn't we just land on the bloody roof?" I say between breaths, my hands shaking and my pants soaked through.

"Obstructive equipment. Unstable structure. Wind shear," the pilot replies over our comms.

"Eighty floors down and up, Doc," Schwartz quips. His grin is all teeth. "You'd be paste."

Cassie puts her hand on my arm and gives it a squeeze. Her hand's steady, but I can feel the pressure—like she's bracing for more than the climb.

"Cut the chatter," Picasso snaps. "Rodriguez, report."

"Rotor on standby," comes the response. "Ready for engagement or evac. I have visual confirmation on the target, sir. You're at the correct site. Good luck in there. Over."

A loud pop echoes as the front doors swing open.

"We're in," Garcia says, low and clipped.

My pulse spikes. If this place is empty, we're screwed. No plan B. No fallback. And every step we took to get here—across flooded streets, past silent watchers, through water that hides teeth—was a countdown to nothing.

"Go," Picasso says to the men by the door.

Four marines slip inside.

Picasso waves us over.

"Clear," crackles a voice over the comm.

Inside, the stale air is suffocating.

Schwartz forces the stairway door open with a crowbar.

"Halligan bar," Cassie murmurs as two men rush through, rifles raised.

"Clear," they report in turn.

Picasso turns to us. "The lab is on the fifth and sixth floors. Take your time." He jogs up the steps, Cassie on his heels.

But when she notices me lagging, she waits for me, takes my arm, and walks with me up the last two flights.

You came to keep her safe. So far, she's the one hovering over you.

Despite what my ego says, I'm relieved she's beside me.

When I reach the fifth floor, soaked and gasping, I give Cassie a look—does she regret bringing me?

She shakes her head, fierce.

I nearly break.

A marine halts us at the stairwell exit, his arm outstretched. "Wait here."

Relief washes over me. I bend over and place my hands on my thighs, trying to catch my breath. Someone hands me a canteen. I take a long drink. "Thanks."

"Sergeant Major," a marine says over the comm. "Someone's been living on this floor for months. Trash everywhere. Hot spot in the last room on the left. Door's locked."

In all our planning, we never expected to find someone living inside the lab. My gut twists. They've been surviving up here for months without water or electricity? What are the odds they're still sane?

"It could be someone who worked on the project," Cassie says, her eyes wide. "And that could be a huge help."

"Or it could be a gang of looters armed with automatic rifles." Picasso steps back into the stairwell. "You want to bet your life on which it is?"

She opens her mouth like she might argue, but doesn't. That alone scares me more than the looters.

"What about the floors above us?" Picasso says into the comm. "Anything up there?"

"So far, just trash and human excrement. Smells like something big died in a latrine, sir."

"Copy," Picasso says. "Keep moving."

Picasso strides back out of the stairwell, glancing at the marine guarding it. "Stay with them."

"Yes, sir." The man steps into the middle of the doorway, rifle held across his chest.

Cassie edges past him and grabs Picasso's arm. "There might be a scientist locked in that room. I'm going with you."

Oh, crap on a crapstick.

"Sir?" The marine's hand flexes on his rifle. He doesn't say it, but I can read the look. This wasn't in the briefing.

"If she goes," I say between breaths, "I go."

Picasso rubs a hand across the back of his neck. "Keep them out of my line of fire."

Color rises in Cassie's cheeks, but her eyes stay locked on Picasso's. She nods once—sharp, clipped, defiant.

As I follow them through the doorway, Picasso says something into his comm.

Two more of his men appear, forming a protective wall around us.

"I tell you to get down," Picasso says, glaring at Cassie, "you hit the floor—or a two-hundred-pound marine helps you get there. Am I making myself clear?" He waits for her to nod.

The six of us tiptoe down the hallway.

When we're standing outside the locked door, Picasso points at Schwartz. He drops to one knee and slips his Halligan bar in between the handle and the frame. The two others point their rifles.

Cassie pushes past Picasso and knocks. "Hello? Anyone in there? We're here to rescue you."

Anger flashes across Picasso's face. He lifts Cassie off the ground and deposits her behind him like she's a child. "Don't do that again." His voice is a cross between a whisper and a growl. He makes eye contact with the guy behind her, and the marine puts a heavy hand on Cassie's shoulder—and mine too—then pulls us back from the door.

Picasso waits for a few seconds to see if there's a response. When there isn't, he nods at Chang.

The door bursts inward, wood and metal shrieking.

Boots slam down.

"Hands in the air!"

There are sounds of items being knocked over, followed by a stifled cry.

"Stop!" Cassie shouts. "You're going to hurt him!" She struggles to break free but, this time, her guardian holds fast.

When Picasso finally steps back out in the hallway, the marines release us, and Cassie bolts into the room.

A moment later, I hear her startled exhalation. "Oh my God."

I take a deep breath and peek around the damaged door frame.

There, amidst a sea of candy wrappers and machine parts, is a thin man wearing boxer shorts and a flowery silk blouse. His eyes, wide with fear, dart from face to face. His hair's a frizzy halo, his cheeks hung with tiny braids like snapped wires.

He looks like he built sanity from a junk drawer—and failed.

My gaze snags on the mechanical pencil clipped to his collar.

If he's not one of the boffins, I'm Marie Curie.

The frightened man is standing with his back pressed against the wall, clutching something and looking like we're the zombie apocalypse.

The two guys pointing rifles at him shout, "Drop your weapon!"

He lets out a squeak and splays his fingers.

A black plastic toy clatters to the floor: a TV remote.

Cassie shoots Picasso an 'I told you so' look and steps in. For once, he doesn't argue.

"It's okay," she says, her hands out in front of her, voice steady. "We're not going to hurt you."

The guy backs away, his eyes wide. He bumps into a table and lunges for the remote.

"Stay back," Picasso barks as one marine kicks it away and another grabs Cassie's arm.

The man whimpers and collapses into a ball.

"Cassie's right," I say, my voice sounding strange. "We're not the enemy. We're here to help."

This is the part I swore I couldn't do. I was mistaken.

I finally see the man under the scruff. "You're Dr. Wheeler." I crouch down, keeping my voice low and calm. "Right?"

The guy turns towards me, his eyes darting around at the rifles still pointed at him, and nods.

A murmur goes around the room, and Picasso has his men lower their weapons.

"I'm Matt Hudson," I say, hand on my chest. "I'm a physicist, and so is Cassie." I nod at her. "We came to rescue you."

He shakes his head and turns away again. I walk over and pick up the remote control he dropped and check the battery compartment. It's empty. Wheeler snatches it out of my hand.

The comm in my ear clicks. "Sir, the lab's a bust. Rubber bands, busted pencils, empty cages. Old bloodstains, scorched tile, bullet holes—small caliber I don't recognize."

The man whispers something that sounds like *tropic backhoes*, eyes darting like he expects monsters to bust through the walls. He stabs the dead remote, fingers trembling, like pressing harder might keep us alive.

"Found a barbecue grill in the women's bathroom," another voice adds. "Has *Grillmaster* stenciled on it. Whatever happened here, someone stuck around long enough to throw a farewell party."

"We flew eighteen hundred miles for a hot dog cart?"

"Zip it, Chang," Picasso snaps. "Any computers or hardware?"

"Just junk. Broken electronics, stripped wires, candy wrappers everywhere. Looks like someone cleaned out every vending machine in Miami." The marine exhales. "We took pictures, for what it's worth."

"Stand by," Picasso says. "I'm sending Dr. Hudson up to eyeball everything." He glances at Cassie, and she nods. He points at Chang, and the two of them hurry toward the door.

When I turn to follow, Picasso grabs my shoulder. "We need you here, Matt." He motions with his head toward Wheeler.

I hesitate.

"Not gonna let anything happen to her, Professor. You have my word."

I swallow and kneel down in front of the boffin. "Can you tell me what you were working on, Dr. Wheeler?"

He shakes his head, still not looking at me.

"Were you building an Einstein-Rosen Bridge?"

His whole body locks up like he's been electrocuted. "No!" he shouts, voice cracking. "It's too dangerous!" He clamps a hand over his mouth, eyes wild, muscles coiled like he might run straight through the wall.

For a heartbeat, every marine tenses. Guns shift, fingers twitch.

"It's okay." I lift my hands, palms out. "It won't happen again. If you help us, we'll make sure."

He stares at me for a second and then nods.

The air shifts.

"Why is it dangerous?" Picasso says.

"I thought I fixed it." The man's eyes go glassy. "They died screaming. Because of me." He sags to the floor, a knot of limbs and guilt.

Picasso and I exchange looks.

Wheeler shivers, arms wrapped around himself. "It killed them—all of them."

The words drag me back to the Peeper—streets carpeted with bodies, eyes locked open. Same silence. Same ending.

"What killed them?" Picasso asks. "Is it in the building?"

The man curls further into himself and covers his head with his hands.

The chopper pilot's voice crackles in my ear. "Sergeant Major, we've got heavy weather rolling in fast. Looks like we're gonna be in a pissing match with Poseidon in less than ten."

"Copy," Picasso says, crouching next to the cowering physicist. "Dr. Wheeler, there's a hurricane headed this way. My men can get you safely out of here, but we don't have much time. If you refuse, no one's coming back."

I give Picasso a startled look. Would he leave the head of the wormhole project here?

He pins me with his gaze and shakes his head, his lips tight.

Gotcha. Make it seem like the guy has a choice.

Wheeler's voice quavers. "Where would you take me?"

"Somewhere safe," I say and step closer, offering him the pair of trousers hanging over a chair.

Wheeler stares at the pants. He lowers the remote, the fight seeping out of him like air from a punctured balloon. "Okay," he whispers. "I'll go with you."

Picasso gives me a quick nod.

"We need the wormhole generator," I say and help the man to his feet. "Do you know where it is?"

"Take that chart on the wall." Wheeler motions weakly. "The laptop's in the mini fridge."

Picasso lifts his chin, and the marines start snapping photos and packing the items into waterproof cases.

"Do you have coffee?" Wheeler asks, rubbing his eyes.

I nod and force a smile. "And canned peaches. Welcome to the team, Dr. Wheeler."

"Call me Phil," he says, slipping the remote into his waistband with trembling fingers. "Thank you for coming."

I shake his hand—not for him, for me.

This is why you came. Not to be a hero. Just to show up for once.

"You're not alone, Phil. We've got you."

For once, I almost believe it.

He nods at the rain-spattered window. "The device can't get wet." He takes a shaky breath. "It looks like... a barbecue grill. It's hidden—"

"Sergeant Major," Cassie's voice bubbles with excitement. "I've identified the wormhole generator. It's the device in the—"

"—women's bathroom." Picasso flashes a rare smile. "Pack it up," he says into his comm. "And let's get out of here."

"Been there. Done that," one of the marines says.

I glance around the room. "Anything else, Phil? Test equipment? A lab book?"

He shakes his head.

"Let's go," Picasso says.

Phil pulls on a threadbare sweatshirt and slips his feet into a pair of boat shoes. A minute later, we hit the stairs, Cassie and the rest of the team right in front of us.

In the lobby, water is pouring off the concrete overhang and pooling around our ankles.

"Move out," Picasso barks, and we follow orders.

Cassie's bravado is gone. Whatever she saw in that lab follows her into the rain.

Behind us, the building vanishes into the downpour. Ahead, the storm waits.

Madders' Second Log:
Entry 2

Target: Diego Nadales, Age 42
Nexus: Warm Springs Military Complex
Chrono Tag: The Next Day • Late July

US elections canceled. President secures third
term with 96% approval, per NewsCorp polling.

Thirty-first Pacific typhoon of the season forms.
Biodome futures climb 17% overnight.

Spacetime bridge located. Status unknown.
Probability of activation remains low.

The cell is maybe eight feet long and half as wide, the walls scraped raw from decades of use and zero maintenance. The air tastes of bleach and mildew, edged with metal. I've learned to breathe through my mouth.

Most days, it doesn't make a difference.

No windows. One door. One bulb.

And Johnson.

He comes twice a day. Same clothes, same clipboard, same smirk.

A week ago, I climbed into his SUV—still dumb enough to buy the lie about a doctor across town. I knew it stank, but I went anyway. Isabel was dying. When it went sideways, I reached for my gun. He beat me to it. Slammed the butt of his weapon into my face. No warning. No words.

Next thing I knew, I was in this cell. Head pounding. Wrists raw from being zip-tied. Everything already off the rails. My knuckles are cracked and swollen. My back feels like it's been sandpapered. I'm dehydrated, sleep-deprived, and beginning to forget what Isabel's voice sounds like.

But I remember her face.

The last time I saw her, she was curled in that bed with a fever so high I could see the heat shimmering off her skin. Her breathing shallow, arms trembling. She tried to smile when I kissed her forehead. "Don't leave me," she said.

"I won't," I promised.

Liar.

I reach for the memory like it might warm me, but it's ice—unyielding, heavy. Something to carry. Something to regret.

My nose still stings when I breathe too deep. Might be broken. Doesn't matter. It's not the part of me that hurts most. That part's somewhere deeper. Every hour in here makes it harder to pretend any of this matters. Isabel's out there dying, and I'm rotting in a box.

The door clicks.

Johnson walks in, holding a cup of something that smells like burned dirt. "Morning, sunshine." He sounds bored, like he's looking for something to break.

Probably me.

I'm sitting on the floor. Back to the wall. Legs stretched out to ease the ache in my side.

"You know," he says, sipping his coffee, "you could save us both a lot of time if you just told me the truth."

"I don't know anything about a sphere," I rasp.

His smile widens, and he kicks me in the ribs. The impact knocks the air out of me. I lurch forward on instinct, reach for his leg—stupid, automatic. He steps back, drives the heel in again, and I hit the floor hard.

I turn my head and cough. Blood in the spit. He notices. Doesn't care.

He jots something on his clipboard like he's logging the weather. My blood on the concrete, my breath coming in sawtooth gasps—just another metric to file away. He even clicks his pen—neat and precise—like this is paperwork, not torture.

"Sorry about the mess," he says, not looking at me. That smile doesn't falter. Doesn't need to.

And that's worse than the boot in my ribs—the casual way he catalogues my pain like it's nothing. Like I'm nothing.

I wonder if Isabel would even recognize me now. If she saw me bleeding on this floor, would she see the man who swore he'd never leave her? Or just a wreck Johnson could grind into dust with a shrug?

He lifts a form. "Your signature. Gemini's liquidation. Your cute little eco-NGO, carved up and fed to the wolves." He waves the paper like a fan. "Progress."

"That's not my signature."

He shrugs. "The bank disagrees."

I close my eyes. Picture her in the garden. The way she used to tuck her hair behind one ear.

I get to my hands and knees. "Where is she?"

His smile fades. "Does it matter?"

I lunge without thinking, pain flaring across my ribs. He steps back, fast, like he was waiting for it. A boot to my chest knocks me flat again.

I gasp and lie there, ribs screaming.

He crouches beside me. "You're going to tell me what that Sphere is. Who built it. Who launched it and why. Or rot in here until she dies thinking you abandoned her."

"She knows better."

He leans closer. "Do you?"

I don't answer.

He stands and brushes imaginary dust from his pants. "You've got one more day. Then we try enhanced methods."

"Big words for a coward."

He doesn't hit me. He just laughs and tosses his coffee dregs on me.

"Let me see her," I say. "See that she's alive. I'll do whatever you want."

He stares at me, a grin creeping across his face. "Good boy." He steps over me. Boots on concrete. The door slams. The lock clicks.

I lie there on the floor, the bulb above me flickering like it's trying to die. A cockroach scurries along my leg. I try to find a position that doesn't make the pain worse.

Sometime later, the door clicks again. I brace myself.

It takes me a second to process the silhouette, the twitchy posture, the tablet clutched like a shield.

Matt Hudson.

"What the hell?"

He freezes in the doorway. "Diego..."

Hearing him—here, now—scrambles something in my head, like the world just skipped a beat. A ballerina in a war zone.

I hesitate, waiting for the trick. A hallucination cooked up by dehydration. Johnson with another game.

Matt Hudson doesn't just stroll into my cell with a tablet like it's study hall.

My ribs scream every time I breathe, but this? This is the part that wrecks me—wondering if I've finally snapped.

I blink, trying to match the face to the man I knew. Lunches at

Gemini. Discussions about water rights and filter protocols. A damn good materials guy.

Not whatever this is.

He swallows, cringing. "I'm sorry, Diego. I didn't know."

I crawl up into a sitting position, back against the wall. "Didn't know you were here either."

"It's... complicated." He fidgets with the door handle.

I huff a bitter laugh. "Bit late for the cavalry."

He looks wrecked. Older than I remember. More haunted. For a split second, I regret the jibe.

He swallows. "Can I come in?"

I stare. Then nod—once. He murmurs to the guard. The door scrapes shut.

He edges in like I'm a cornered dog and he's not sure which way I'll snap—one eye on me, the other on the distance to the door. "You're surprised to see me," he says.

"Understatement."

His eyes rake over me. "Bloody hell, Diego. I didn't know."

"Welcome to the party."

He crouches next to me. Taps the tablet. The screen flares.

And there she is.

Isabel.

Alive.

Not a grainy memory. Not a faded photo. Real this time. Worn thin and hooked up to machines, but breathing.

I stare at the video, waiting for the glitch, the static skip, the faint edge that says he's lying.

But it's her. In a hospital. A good one by the looks of it.

I press my palms into the floor just to stay upright, knuckles whitening.

The screen's glow paints her face, lips. I see her hand twitch against the sheet, tiny, almost nothing—but I hold onto it like it's hope itself.

Alive.

She's alive.

For a moment, I forget I'm trapped inside a concrete cell, covered in bruises—and watch her chest rise and fall like it means something again.

"She's in Eden-2," Hudson says. "The doctors had to induce a coma, but she's stable. She'll be fine." He gives me a forced smile. "Dick—Agent Johnson—said you asked about her."

The fact that Johnson kept his word—airlifted her to a hospital? That knocks the air out of me.

My voice is ash. "Why are you here, Matt?"

He sighs. "Because we don't have much time, and I need your help. They found a note with your name written on it—along with your sock. Inside the Sphere."

I squint at him. "Like I told Johnson, I don't know anything about a metal sphere."

He leans forward, hands clasping and unclasping. "Nearly a year ago, a five-hundred-kilogram tungsten ball—the Einstein Sphere, we call it—crashed into a hotel in Denver. It was going fast enough to flatten steel and rip through thirty floors without blinking."

I nod, realization dawning. "It started the fire that nearly killed Isabel. I thought it was just bad luck."

"It came out of nowhere," he says. "Literally. No warning, no origin, no launch signature. Our best guess? It was sent through a wormhole. And somehow, your name and sock were in it."

He taps the tablet again. More images appear—different timelines, he says.

I'm in all of them.

Not just standing around either. Leading evacuations, hauling someone from wreckage, standing in front of an overturned truck drinking a bottle of water. In one, I hold Isabel's hand while we run out of a burning tent. In another, I stand at the makeshift clinic, directing people inside the same untouched tent.

All of them are moments I don't remember. Lives I never lived.

He hands me a photo. A young Asian woman holding the hand of a little boy—her brother, maybe—but something about it feels off. A flicker at the base of my spine, like déjà vu with teeth. They're standing outside one of Kirkland's domes, flames behind them, the air warped with heat. The boy's crying. But the teenager stares straight at the lens, shoulders locked, lips drawn tight. Her eyes shimmer like glass under pressure, about to splinter.

And me.

I'm in the frame too, standing behind her, hand on the boy's shoulder like I belong there.

My stomach twists.

"These aren't fakes?"

"No," he says. "They're real. Just not from this timeline. And it isn't just one future either. It's six so far. In every universe where the world doesn't burn, you're there."

I close my eyes. Try not to drown in it.

He hands me another photo, his face going pale. "I thought you'd want to see this one."

A girl with ash in her hair, eyes wide, clings to me like I'm all she's got left. In the smoke behind us, Isabel—face streaked with blood—is carrying a boy the same age. Both of the kids are gripping a carved wooden animal.

My stomach lurches. "This isn't real. I was never there."

Matt doesn't argue. He exhales through his nose, eyes heavy like he's said this a hundred times but still hates it. "It happened, but it wasn't you. These images are from parallel universes. Somewhere things played out differently."

Somewhere Isabel didn't get sepsis. Somewhere Soleil and Lucas survived.

I look again, drawn to the image of a family I don't remember.

Matt clears his throat. "Do you recognize the Asian woman?"

I take another look.

And then something shifts—like a gear catching. I recognize the young woman in the photo. "She helped me save Isabel." I look over at Matt, my heart pounding. "At the hotel fire in Denver."

He leans in, eyes wide. "Do you know her name? Anything about her?"

I shake my head. "It was dark. Chaotic. She was smart. Fearless."

He sighs. "She keeps showing up too—along with Isabel—and we've got nothing."

I breathe. Shallow. "So what happens now?"

"We're constructing a spacetime bridge—a device that sends an object to an alternate timeline. Possibly at a different point in time." He gives me a moment to process that.

"So you're building a time machine. One that targets a parallel universe." I let out a slow breath. "That's pulp science fiction, Matt."

He huffs, holding up the image of the twins. "Not anymore."

"Mierda."

"If we can target it right, we can nudge things. Change the outcome." He takes a slow breath. "But we need your help."

I blink hard. "Why?"

He drops his gaze for a beat, his shoulders shifting, probably weighing whether to tell me the truth.

I scoff. "If you're going to lie, you might as well send Johnson back in."

He nods once, not meeting my gaze. "The sock in the Einstein Sphere. Ordinary cotton. Your DNA all over it. The note with your name on it. We think you've used the spacetime bridge. Or at least some version of you has."

He says it like a fact. Another me out there, doing the impossible while I sit on my ass.

Maybe that's who Isabel needs—the man in those photos. The man who saves whole crowds, not just one woman in a burning hotel.

I pick up the tablet and scroll back to the recording of Isabel. Her hand, limp. Her eyes shut.

It knocks something loose in me. Not just the guilt, but something stronger—hope, maybe, or the illusion of it. I don't know what seeing her like this is supposed to do, but it works. It guts me. And it steels me.

Whatever I decide next, it has to matter. For her. For us.

I look at Matt, the pieces clicking into place. The note I found in my car—the handwriting, the timing, the impossible knowledge. *Reserve a table with a view of the mountains. Wait for me.* I didn't understand how she could've known—until now.

"I'll do what I can," I say. "But I need to get a message to Isabel. Let her know I'm all right."

He nods slowly. Something flickers—relief, maybe, or guilt cracking through the professor's mask. He stands, awkward and stiff, like his body isn't quite sure what to do next.

"Matt," I say, eyes on my lap. "I know absolutely nothing about a metal sphere—or any time machine. Zero."

He thinks about that for a moment, then walks to the door and knocks twice. A pause, then a click as the outer lock disengages.

He hesitates, hand on the doorframe. "I'm sorry about Johnson. I didn't know."

I study him a beat, then nod once, slow. "Yeah. Well... now you do."

He flushes. "I'll get you out of here as soon as I can."

The door shuts behind him with a dull finality I can feel in my teeth.

What if I'm the wrong me?

Madders' Second Log: Entry 3

Target: Isabel Sanborn, Age 43
Nexus: Eden-2
Chrono Tag: A Week Later

World Bank confirms secondary currency collapse. Mediterranean refugee flow hits record levels. Kirkland Enterprises consolidates power without resistance. Widespread civil unrest suppressed.

Biodome stockpiles at 44% capacity. Projected viability: 6 years.

Timeline deviations increase in frequency. Trajectory points toward masked jumps.

I pry one eye open.

White walls. Antiseptic tang. Machines beeping like metronomes.

Another hospital.

Perfect.

As I'm trying to remember how, exactly, I got here, Dave Kirkland's voice wafts in from the hallway. "Stop worrying, Lani. I'll find him for you."

Like the day needed more comedy.

"I should be out there looking for Kai," says a pleading voice. "I know the streets—his hiding places, his friends."

"I told you, Cupcake." He piles on the charm reserved for women half his age. "It's too dangerous, especially in your condition. I'll find your brother. You have to trust me." I can almost hear his upper lip twitch.

The door swings open, and I catch a glimpse of them. Lani's boyish, pale as snow, her skin glowing with something I'll never have again: youth.

She looks to be sixteen, tops.

Dave's got a thick, new head of hair.

The world's falling apart and my ex-husband gets implants.

If I had the strength, I'd roll my eyes.

Instead, I clamp them shut and try to look unconscious.

She lowers her voice. "What if something's happened to him, Dave? I'm all the family he's got."

"It's going to be fine, Lani." His voice turns syrupy. "Come here, babe."

You've woken up in hell. Again.

There's a pause, and I can practically hear the saliva being exchanged.

A noise escapes my throat, halfway between a groan and a gag.

Dave flinches when he sees my eyes. Then the tie straightens, the smile clicks on. Dinner-party voice activates. "Ah, you're awake, Isabel."

The girl—no, woman—turns to me, her face flushed. "How are you feeling?"

"Like I was hit by a bus," I rasp. "Where am I?"

"Inside the Eden-2 hospital." She checks my IV, her expression settling into a professional mask. But her hands are trembling.

Good.

I catch a glimpse of her midsection—a curve beneath the scrubs.

Of course she's pregnant.

Fifteen years of him telling me he wasn't ready—then the day after the divorce, he knocks up the first teenager he can seduce.

"You're lucky you didn't—" She swallows. "I mean, you almost didn't make it. There were complications during delivery." She drops her gaze. "A rupture."

I can't breathe.

"We had to remove your uterus to save your life."

My hand touches my belly. Only emptiness.

The twins.

I remember the sound the rain made. Diego's hand leaving mine. The men in the dark.

An alarm goes off on the machine next to me, and she reaches to silence it.

I pinch my arm and force my lungs to take a faltering breath.

"There was a mass," she says, her tone clinical but her cheeks getting red.

She looks too young for this job—too innocent for this man, this mess. I almost feel sorry for her.

Almost.

"Cancerous," she says. "The doctors removed the tumor—along with your uterus—to save your life."

The IV drips. Steady. Indifferent. Like none of this matters.

I picture the twins again—their fragile fingers, beautiful eyes, perfect faces—and the emptiness inside me yawns wider, bottomless.

I want to howl. I want to tear the IV from my arm.

My jaw aches from holding back the despair pressing at my throat.

But that rage is the only power I have left. And I refuse to waste it on my ex-husband.

I take a deep breath and will my body to let go.

"You're healing nicely," the nurse says into the awkward silence. "We don't expect any long-term issues."

I huff. "Apart from having no uterus."

She blushes again. "Yes."

"Thank you for taking care of me, Nurse—" I lean forward, trying to read her name tag.

"Kealoha. But I'm not a nurse. I'm a student doctor."

"So it's Student Doctor Kealoha?" I manage to say. It's a mouthful. "Good for you."

Her lips press together, and she nods once. Dave gives her a smug little *see what I mean?* look.

"I need to check your vitals," she says, even though I'm hooked up to everything except a heart-lung machine.

"Be my guest."

She steps closer and lifts my wrist, her hand icy cold.

I turn toward Dave. "Where's Diego?"

"Lani," Dave says, his voice tight, "give us a minute?"

She hesitates, her gaze darting between us, then nods and releases my arm. "Fine. I'll be back in half an hour." She glances at me once more, her eyes cool, before marching out.

The moment the door clicks shut, I turn on him.

"You son of a bitch."

Dave doesn't flinch. Just stares out the window.

"Did you plan it?" I ask. "The baby. Her. All of it?"

Nothing.

"Well?" I say, my voice full of accusation. I want him to lie. I want him to say no. I want him to feel ashamed.

Instead, he says, "You're right."

That stops me. "I am? About what?"

He pulls a chair up to the bed and sits down. "All of it."

He steeples his fingers. Doesn't meet my eyes.

"I've manipulated people my whole life," he says. "Built empires on it. I thought if I kept building, kept pushing, I could fix everything. Make it right. But Lani..."

He stops. His mouth opens. Closes.

"She's not a pet project," he says, voice rough. "Or some midlife crisis. I care about Lani, but she was never mine to keep. And if she walked away right now, I wouldn't stop her."

I watch him. Waiting for the punchline. The catch. The play.

It doesn't come.

"I asked her to marry me," he says, giving a half-laugh. "She said no."

Something tight and bitter and aching fills my chest. I don't know if it's pity. Or envy.

He looks at me—really looks at me for the first time.

"For once, I don't want to win at any cost," he says. "I just want to deserve her."

A long, hot silence sits between us.

I study the lines in his face, the set of his jaw. The way his hands shake before he shoves them in his pockets.

And that's how I know.

He loves her.

God help us all.

I lean back against the pillows. "Why'd you send a helicopter? What do you want from me?"

"Want? You were dying. I wanted to save you."

"We both know that's not true."

His expression shifts, his charm kicking into overdrive. "But it is. We need you, Isabel. The bots are your babies. They need their mother back."

I cringe, and he realizes his mistake.

He clears his throat and smooths his tie, gaze flicking anywhere but my face. "How about I give you your old job back? Toss in a big raise."

I glare at him. "Where's Diego?"

He hesitates, running a hand through his expensive hair. "Nadales is off doing whatever he does. Probably lecturing someone about composting or organizing a sing-along. I've got people looking for him."

"Not good enough, Dave."

He throws up his hands. "For the love of God, Isabel. I'm trying to save the world here. Stop acting like I'm the villain."

Here comes the sales pitch.

"The bee population is collapsing. Global famine is breathing down our necks. Your bots are the best solution. I need them to stabilize food crops. And I need you to program them."

I scoff. "Right up until you don't, Dave."

He looks down, then glances sideways at me, his lips scrunched to one side. "Sophie's here. With her husband and kids. I'll give you the condo right next to hers."

I stare at him, a snarky comeback dying on my lips.

Last I talked to Sophie, she was terrified that Dave was selling killerbots to the highest bidder. I can't believe she would work for him again.

Unless she was desperate.

And who isn't?

It's a nightmare out there. Diego and I were living like royalty, but people are starving. Only an idiot would refuse to bring their family inside a biodome if the alternative was living in a post-apocalyptic nightmare.

I take a slow breath. "Well then, you don't need me. Sophie writes tighter code than I do, and she knows all my tricks."

"You're right," he says. "She's good. But she's not you. There are issues she can't crack—interrupt loops and deadlocks and crap. You were always the superstar, and you're still the best chance we've got."

Superstar? My ass.

I stare at him, my heart pounding. He looks genuinely desperate, but with Dave, you can never tell. The line between sincerity and manipulation is razor-thin.

The Oscars could do with a special category just for him.

"Where's Diego?" I say again, my voice stronger. "Where is he really, Dave?"

He leans back, spreading his arms in mock helplessness. "You think I know? The guy's gone off-grid again. Left you to fend for yourself. Just like he did last time."

The muscle in his jaw flinches, and I know he's lying.

"Where is he, Dave?"

"Relax, Princess. You're safe now. That's what matters. Nadales is small fry. He'll eventually turn up." He gestures around the room. "You're in Eden-2, my new state-of-the-art biodome, the world's finest protected environment. In another three months, I'll have over thirty of them sealed up all around the globe."

I grit my teeth. "I don't care about your domes, Dave. I care about Diego."

He waves me off. "I'm sure he's fine. Always comes up with a way to get by. Right now, you need to focus on something more important."

I frown. "Like what?"

"Look, I'm not supposed to tell you this, but something bad is coming. Something really bad. Your bots are the only way to stop it."

Now for the apocalypse pitch—the end of the world, gift-wrapped with guilt.

"We need your bees in the air, millions of them—and we need them yesterday. If the crops aren't pollinated, famine's on the horizon, Isabel. Half the planet could starve in six months. Your bots are the only thing standing between us and starvation."

I exhale. "My bees weren't designed to be deployed in an open environment, Dave. You know that. They were designed for Mars, and we both can name hundreds of things that could go horribly wrong if we deploy them here."

"Worse than half the world's population starving to death?" He scoffs. "Come on, Isabel. Get real."

Maybe he's telling the truth. Maybe he isn't. With Dave, facts bend into whatever shape gets him what he wants.

Still, the thought needles me.

Dead bees. Empty fields. Children with bellies swollen from hunger. But I built the bots to keep people alive on Mars, not to become the last brittle thread holding Earth together.

If they can save lives, does it matter?

The scientist in me says no. The rest of me isn't so sure.

If I say yes, I risk unleashing millions of half-tested machines into a world already teetering on collapse. If I say no, and he's right, then I'm the one who let half the world starve.

Dave leans closer—his cologne a heavy blanket, his smile just shy of predatory. "You could save billions of lives, Isabel."

For a heartbeat, I see what he sees: a planet gasping for air, my work the only oxygen left. And I hate him more than ever for using that against me.

"That's my girl," he says, a grin spreading across his face.

Dave always knows when he's landed a blow. Damn him. He leans forward, uses a button to bring the head of my bed up, and hands me a glass of water. "Look, I know it won't be easy, but that's exactly why I need you. Catch what Sophie s missed, point out what the team can't see. Every issue you fix could save a thousand lives. Hell, maybe a million."

"What about Diego? What aren't you telling me?"

"Jesus Christ, Isabel, can you give it a rest about Nadales? I told you, I don't know where he is. Now that you're here, I'll have my guys look harder. See what I can find out."

"Like I believe that," I mutter.

He ignores me and spreads his hands. "I can guarantee you the best this biodome has to offer. Top-tier accommodations. Private gym. Personal chef. Hell, people are paying hundreds of millions for a one-bedroom, but once I find Nadales, you can bring him in too." He scoffs again. "Dude can mop floors and lecture people about recycling. Win-win."

I croak out a mirthless laugh. "I doubt a word of that is true, Dave." I hold up my hand. "No. Sorry. I take that back. I'm sure this place is better than the Ritz-Carlton. Can't have your billionaire buddies missing out on their personal chefs while the plebes outside are stuck licking the slime off rocks." I take a drink of water—and it goes down the wrong pipe.

I cough and gasp for air.

"Christ," he says, watching me suffocate. "Take it easy. You're no good to me dead."

When I manage to stop choking, I squeak out, "I don't want your charity."

"For once in your life," he says, his voice hardening, "quit being so goddamn stubborn and let me help you. You almost died out there— one more day and you would have. Do you want to be a statistic?"

I sip more carefully this time, my eyes on him.

"Look," he says, his voice sounding tired. "Just think about it. You still believe in what you built, don't you? I know you do. And yeah, maybe I didn't give you enough credit the first time, but I was wrong. Your bots are literally the key to saving humanity. Don't you care about that?"

I look away, my mind racing. Part of me wants to tell him to shove it, but the other part—the part that remembers why I created the bots in the first place—won't shut up.

What if he's telling the truth?

What if the mother of all famines is coming?

What if a massive bee die-off—the very thing I've been warning people about for years—is right around the corner?

Are you just going to shrug your shoulders, pack up your coffee cup, and walk out?

I exhale a long, slow breath—and nod. "Fine. I'll think about it."

"Good girl," he says, flashing that billboard smile—the one he uses right before he stabs you in the back.

I grit my teeth.

"I'll be gone for a couple of days, but I'll check on you when I get back." He pats my shoulder twice, stands up, and strides out of the room.

After the door shuts, I hear the lock click.

Totally normal to lock in your prized employee.

I take a more careful look around the room.

Dave says he doesn't know where Diego is. Maybe he's telling the truth.

More likely, Diego's locked up in some private jail.

And if he is, I'm going to find him.

Time to get to work.

Step one: get out of this hospital. Step two: collect information. Step three: make Dave wish he'd never lied to me.

It takes me a while to untangle the tubes and wires attached to my body, but I manage to get out of bed and hobble over to the window.

The late afternoon sun glints off the glass walls of the biodome. Eden-2 has to be four or five times the size of the original.

And then I notice movement in the bushes next to the hospital.

Dave—standing in the shrubs—talking to someone.

No—talking to... another Dave.

For a second I think it's a reflection—some warped pane of glass playing tricks. But no. Two of them. One, the man who just left my room. The other, wearing a wrinkled jumpsuit, thin gloves, leaning against a metal sarcophagus, hands moving as he talks. Twenty years older and completely bald. My Dave stands in the bushes, eyes flicking between the hulking casket and his jump-suited double.

I blink, sure I must be hallucinating, but the scene doesn't change. The jump-suited Dave hands the other something—small, hard to make out—then climbs back into the metal capsule. The hatch slides shut. I watch Dave back away, his eyes wide, the bushes snagging his suit jacket.

A time machine? Not that I've seen one before—but what else could it be?

I've met an older Diego. I've read my own handwriting on a note I never wrote. Someone's rewriting the past—and now there are two Daves.

The world lurches sideways. Vertigo slams through me. I grab the window frame, fighting to stay upright as the air pulses around me.

Then it's gone. The capsule. The noise. The pressure. Only an imprint in the mud remains—and a glint in Dave's hand before he pockets it.

My legs tremble. I stumble to the bed, clutching the frame like it's the only solid thing left. Two Daves. Two timelines colliding.

This isn't a mistake. It's a move.

Dave's not just lying about Diego—he's rearranging the board, one piece at a time, until he wins by default.

If Diego's still alive, he won't stand a chance against two Daves. Unless I tell him.

My knees threaten to buckle, but I lock them anyway.

Shocked. Shaking. Gutted.

But not done.

Not yet.

Not by a long shot.

Madders' Second Log:
Entry 4

Target: Matthew Hudson
Nexus: Warm Springs Military Complex
Chrono Tag: A Few Days Later • August

Agriculture collapses across Global South. Amazon
rainforest flips to net carbon emitter.
Atmospheric CO_2 spikes. Migration northward
exceeds 12 million.

Spacetime anomaly detected in Eden-2. Energy
trace confirms masked jump.

Probability the bridge activates within forty-
eight hours now 87%. Across timelines, the
outcome of an early jump is the same—Diego does
not survive.

Smoke curls from the breaker box, and the stink of melted plastic wafts out.

The ache in my gut notches up. "Kill the power. Recheck. Run it again."

The lab door bangs open, rattling the clock on the wall. Johnson—who we not-so-affectionately call Dick—steps through, dressed in a starched white shirt and pressed suit. "Hudson! You and your crew drop what you're doing and get to the exit elevator. Now."

Junior freezes next to the capacitor bank he's resetting. Dick's sidekick—real name Smith—was ordered to spy on us, so I put him to work.

Phil doesn't look up. "We need to redo the main cabling," he says. "It's too long." He grabs the nearest spool and unwinds it. "Can't take the chance—"

"Out," Dick barks. "Now."

"Lovely," Sam murmurs. "What's the occasion—mandatory pep talk on looking busy?"

"Sam," I say. "Not now."

He shrugs. "Fine. Maybe it's Johnson's Employee of the Month award."

Dick's lip curls. "Don't make me repeat myself," he hisses. "And for chrissake, Hudson, try not to look like you slept in a dumpster. The new Project Director is coming."

His gaze shifts to Sam and then Phil, and he shakes his head.

"He is?" I croak, pulse skidding sideways. A new director means scrutiny. Red pens. Fallout. I wipe my palms on my shirt. "Why didn't anyone tell us?"

"I just did. Now get going." Dick's gaze lands on the smoking panel, and his nose wrinkles. "What the hell happened? Did you idiots set a half-a-billion-dollar machine on fire?"

"It's called testing," I say, voice flat. "But if you want to hop in before we finish, be my guest."

"Save the smart-ass remarks for someone who cares," Dick snaps.

"You got ten minutes. Get moving." He turns to Junior. "Take off that Halloween costume and go get dressed."

Junior ditches his goggles and bolts.

"Nitwits." Dick slams the door on his way out, the sound reverberating through the lab.

I turn to Sam and lower my voice. "Let's tone it down today. We're finally getting traction. Let's not blow it."

Sam glances at me, one eyebrow raised. "You think we should be worried? About getting fired?"

"I don't know," I say, dusting charred plastic pieces off my shirt. "But it's too late now."

"Solid plan," Sam says, but his smirk falters as he powers down the Coffin.

"Let's go," I say after everything's off.

Phil hesitates, eyes still locked on the Grillmaster. "That last pulse—" A muscle jumps in his cheek. "It matched the Miami signature."

My chest seizes, but I keep my face blank. I grip his shoulder. "We know about the black holes now, Phil. Because of you. We'll fix them."

He meets my eyes—haunted, but holding.

"No one is going to get hurt, Phil."

He exhales, shaky—and then nods.

"Come on," I say. "Let's get changed and go meet the new boss."

Eight minutes later, we burst out of the building. Glare off the artificial lake momentarily blinds us, the water gleaming like mercury.

Phil and I hop into the golf cart as Sam climbs in back. As we bump along the path around the lake, Phil fumbles with the seatbelt.

"If we crash," he grumbles, "aim me at something soft."

I ease off the accelerator.

Across the lake, Sabina and Cassie stand next to the massive elevator door, Dick pacing in front of them.

"Think it's Johnson's last day?" Sam says. "He's pacing like Vader's taking over."

Phil actually laughs—a sharp, dry bark.

Behind us, Junior jumps into the last golf cart and speeds around the lake, hard on our heels, his tie flapping in the recycled breeze.

When we reach the elevator, Dick is scowling. "Next time, I leave your asses behind."

Before Sam can say something about his ass being happy where it is, Junior pulls up behind us. "Sorry, boss, I—"

"Shut up and get in." Dick swipes a hand down his tie—twice—and scans the elevator like it bites. For once, he's not strutting. He's bracing. The new boss has Dick on edge—and that's saying something.

The elevator was built to haul shipping containers and backup generators. Today it'll carry sarcasm, sweat, and secondhand lab coats. We pile in, and the doors clang shut behind us. Dick and Junior both scan their badges, and the control panel lights up.

As soon as the elevator jolts to life, Cassie leans over and whispers, "You think they're bringing someone in to clean house?"

I shrug. "Maybe they'll give Picasso full control."

Phil looks up. "That's my vote. In Miami—when the current took my legs—he came after me." He swallows. "Thought I wasn't going to make it."

"You and me both," I say, my pulse spiking at the memory of Picasso hauling him back to the helicopter.

Could have been you, mate.

"But we all made it out," Cassie says, brighter than I've seen her in weeks. "We'll have more Peeper images soon—maybe find a timeline that slips past the Great Filter."

"Promising," I say, fighting the urge to hug her. "Hooked up the Grillmaster to the Coffin this morning. Should have it ready to test in a week or so."

Sam smirks. "Think they'll buy us Team Time Machine jackets?"

We laugh—even Sabina.

"What are you nitwits whispering about?" Dick barks.

Cassie doesn't miss a beat. "Debating whether your mustache is sentient—or just ambitious."

Dick pretends not to hear.

The elevator shudders to a stop. We step into a cold, empty corridor. It smells like antiseptic and old metal—a tomb with a cleaning crew.

Dick strides ahead, but his movements are stiff, robotic. When he presses his palm to the scanner, I notice his fingers are trembling.

A green light blinks, followed by a cheerful *bing*, and the door slides open with a hydraulic hiss.

I let out a sigh of relief, anxious to get out of the metal box.

The hallway is long and dim. Our footsteps echo like we're the last humans alive.

Cassie glances back. "I forgot how claustrophobic this place is. You okay?"

I nod and force a smile.

We reach the end of the corridor, where massive blast doors loom —relics of the Cold War, built to survive all but a direct nuke.

Probably cost a fortune to open and shut.

"Try not to act like chimpanzees." Dick smacks a button on the wall. "Last thing I need is you nerds embarrassing the program."

The doors groan open to cracked tarmac and the deafening roar of helicopter rotors.

We step out into the bright sunlight, hands raised against the glare.

Rotor wash kicks grit into my teeth.

Phil coughs, fumbling with his glasses.

Behind us, a loudspeaker crackles to life, blasting a canned military fanfare—something between a Sousa march and a theme-park parade.

We all cover our ears.

Picasso waits by the blast doors in dress uniform, marines behind him like boxed action figures. He gives an order, and they snap to attention.

Dick strides past them, Junior hurrying to keep up.

We stare at the three huge helicopters idling on the tarmac.

I recognize the logo on their tails. Kirkland Enterprises.

Bloody hell.

"What is this?" Sam says. "An invasion?"

Sabina and Cassie are wearing identical expressions of exasperation.

Phil puts his glasses back on. "Who's paying for this circus?"

The left-most helicopter disgorges reporters, lenses glinting. They form a semi-circle around the middle chopper and start recording.

"I thought this place was top secret." Sam squints at the spectacle. "What's with the paparazzi?"

"Distraction protocol," Phil says. "Look busy, make noise, and hope nobody notices your incompetence."

As if on cue, women pour out of the right-most helicopter, looking like they just beamed down from the Starship *Enterprise*— short red skirts, high boots, their hair all done up.

Sam whistles low, and I shoot him a look.

"Classy," he says.

Cassie huffs. "Those outfits look painted on."

"If one of them inhales too hard," Sabina says, "we'll need eye protection."

It's a low-budget movie shoot.

And then the middle Black Hawk opens, and a man in a flashy, tailored suit steps out.

The all-female crowd goes wild. Clapping. Cheering. Waving.

Sabina sighs. "And here I thought my morning couldn't get any worse."

The ecstatic women part as Kirkland strides across the tarmac.

Shutters snap.

"Crikey." Not just a collapsing multiverse—now we're up against vanity and viral clicks.

I glance at Picasso. He looks ready to blow a gasket. But Dick, who usually treats security breaches like personal insults, seems unnaturally calm.

"Unbelievable," I grumble.

Sam snorts. "Didn't you hear? The President put some rich guy in charge of the Emergency Recovery Agency. Apparently, that includes us."

Sabina shakes her head. "Oh, for the love of—"

"Isn't he the biodome guy?" Cassie says, squinting. "The one accused of selling killerbots to despots?"

"And running his biodomes on duct tape and PR budgets," Phil grumbles. "Guy's a walking collapse vector." He looks over at me. "What's his name again?"

"Kirkland," I say, getting a bad feeling. "Dave Kirkland."

Dick barks orders, his new suit flapping in the chopper wash. Junior stands straighter and fumbles with his tie. Kirkland strides over to them with all the subtlety of a king, his entourage forming behind him, all smiles and perfect posture.

He stops mid-stride, the grin freezing, and spins back toward the pilots. One sharp hand across his throat and the rotors start to slow.

The smile snaps back on like a switch.

A guy in paramilitary garb sets a microphone on the tarmac, taps his headphones, and points a finger at our new boss.

Kirkland steps up. "Good afternoon, Americans!" His voice booms out from speakers positioned near the choppers. "Today marks the beginning of a new era for the most challenging project mankind has ever attempted." The crowd erupts in raucous applause—which he tamps down with Jesus hands. "I'm here to make this leaner, meaner, and faster. No red tape. No excuses." He shakes Dick's hand, holding it as cameras flash. "Nice to see you again, Johnson. You'll report directly to me."

"Yes, sir." Dick's voice switches to obsequious like a radio flicking channels. "It would be my honor, sir."

Our new boss strides over to the marines, the crowd following him. "We're saving the world, people! Let's get to it!"

Picasso's spine stiffens when the microphone is shoved in front of him, but he manages a stiff salute. "Mr. Kirkland, with all due respect, this facility is classified. Cameras are strictly prohibited."

Kirkland waves a hand, producing a folded letter. "Relax, Sergeant Major. Just a few snaps of the non-sensitive areas. Gotta show the world we're working hard to save it."

Picasso hesitates, but the gold seal keeps his mouth shut.

For now.

Kirkland claps him on the back like they're old war buddies. "Now then, I'm here to get you the resources you need—not step on any toes." He narrows one eye. "As long as you're not wasting my time."

He pivots, grin snapping back into place. "Nice to see some women on staff."

Sabina's eyebrow lifts. "If he calls us gals," she snarls, "I'm taking hostages." She steps forward, tablet in hand. "Mr. Kirkland? If you're done with the pep talk, perhaps you'd like to see the actual state of things."

Kirkland flashes a patronizing smile, like she's a child handing him crayons. He pushes through the scantily-clad sci-fi props toward her.

I wonder if Sabina is going to unload on him, but she doesn't get the chance.

"Hudson!" Kirkland calls out. "Good to see you!"

"Dave Kirkland," I say, striding over to shake his hand.

He leans closer. "Nice to see a quality hire."

I glance at Picasso and the others. "One of many."

"Love the humility," Kirkland says, his smile too sharp, too wide—the kind you flash to the kids after selling the house and leaving the dog behind.

"Now then," Kirkland says. "Let's get down to business. I've been briefed on your progress, and I'm here to accelerate things."

Behind me, Phil mumbles, "Might want to read the manual before you light the accelerant."

Sam mumbles something I can't catch, and Cassie laughs.

This is how it starts. One egomaniac in a shiny suit, throwing around charm and flattery while the folks with brains roll their eyes—and the world burns.

Kirkland puffs his chest, scans us. "The President's counting on me to make this project the centerpiece of our recovery efforts, so let's not disappoint."

I introduce the team, while Dick stands there wagging his tail.

"Okay, Johnson," Kirkland finally says, "show me everything. Every last nook and cranny."

"Right this way, sir." Dick straightens his tie and turns toward the blast doors. "It's about time someone held those military types accountable."

Picasso stiffens—barely—but I feel it like a seismic shift. He meets my eye for half a second, and I give him the smallest nod—*yeah, I see it too.* The rotors churn steadily overhead, but the air feels thinner now—like we're standing on the edge of something that's about to give.

Kirkland smiles, waves one last time, then turns toward the blast doors.

The moment he looks away, the crowd deflates. Clipboards snap shut. Cables coil. The glow drains from their faces.

Laughable—if it didn't feel like he was steering the world into a wall.

We fall in behind him, mouths clamped shut.

For the next hour, Kirkland strides through the Magic Kingdom like he owns it, pausing to inspect equipment and fire off questions. Even Sam falls under his spell, nodding like a bobblehead when Kirkland asks about the zero-point actuator.

Sabina, however, remains unconvinced.

"Mr. Kirkland," she says and elbows past Dick. "If you're done inspecting the coffee machine, perhaps you'd like to hear about our latest findings."

Dick makes a growling noise in his throat, but Kirkland laughs.

"Well, aren't you the little firecracker? Dr. Lovelace, is it? I read your paper on 'Quantum Horizon Thresholds in Stacked Causal Environments.' Surprised me, honestly—very sharp." He fires finger guns at her. "Hit me with your best shot!"

Sabina's mouth twitches—something between surprise and irritation. She smooths her expression, then jerks her chin away. "Follow me."

Inside the Peeper lab, Sabina types furiously, then barks orders while Cassie adjusts dials.

The flat-panel display lights up with images from the Trans Timeline Viewer.

Phil shifts behind me, mumbling something about giving away too much.

Images from parallel universes flicker in rapid succession, each one more horrifying than the last.

"What am I looking at?" Kirkland asks, his smile faltering.

"Other timelines," Sabina replies, "in the multiverse."

I expect Kirkland to grill her about what, exactly, *timelines* are, or how she expects him to believe that—or, at least, raise an eyebrow at the multiverse reference.

But he doesn't.

He nods. "How many can you see?"

"Eleven."

He exhales. "And how many collapse?"

"All of them," Sabina says. "Pandemic, famine, war. Not hard to see the pattern."

Kirkland frowns, leaning closer. "Every timeline, huh? Christ, this is even worse than the President let on."

"And the convergence point is accelerating," Cassie says. "We're trying to confirm when it's going to happen here."

He rubs his hand across his mouth. "So he was right."

"Who?" Sabina and I say.

Kirkland waves off the question and straightens up, his expression hardening. "Famine," he says, tapping his finger against his lips. "It has to be famine."

He rests his hand on my shoulder, nodding emphatically. "Hell, I've been tracking bee die-offs for years. Farmers struggling, crops dying, ecosystems collapsing—it all lines up." He glances at the bodies piled outside a burned-out Walmart. "Good work, Hudson, good work. This'll make my job a lot easier."

"It's Sabina's work, sir—along with Cassie."

He gives them a distracted smile. "Yes, yes. Nice job, gals. Excellent."

Sabina's jaw flexes. I half-expect her to pull out zip ties and make good on the hostage plan.

Kirkland turns to Dick and squares his shoulders. "Connect the dots, Johnson. We're staring down the barrel of the worst food crisis in history."

"Yes, sir," Dick says. "Exactly my conclusion."

Sam, who's standing behind Dick and Kirkland, opens his mouth and sticks a finger in it like he's going to be sick. Phil kicks him in the ankle.

Picasso sees it but doesn't respond. Instead, he frowns. "Sir, we haven't confirmed the cause of the worldwide collapse—"

"We need a microbot swarm," Kirkland blurts out. "It's the only way to nip this in the bud. " He turns toward Dick. "Then we'll use your capsule to send millions of them back a year or two and get a jump on things."

I open my mouth to protest, but Picasso beats me to it. "Using the spacetime bridge to release bots—"

"—is the only way to dodge this disaster." Kirkland looks over at Picasso and raises an eyebrow. "Unless you've got a better plan to feed the planet?"

The two men stare at each other while the rest of us shuffle our feet.

"The spacetime bridge only works with organic matter," Phil whispers. He's still standing next to Sam, his eyes on his shoes.

Kirkland whips around. "What did you say?"

He repeats the sentence, a little louder this time, and adds, "No robots, no drones, no guns."

Kirkland's eyes get big. "Is that true, Hudson?"

"I don't know," I say. "We've had the wormhole generator connected to a Singularity Transit Device for less than a day, but I have no reason to doubt Phil—Dr. Wheeler, that is."

"Just like last time," Phil says, taking out the defunct remote and stabbing the **STOP** button, "people will die."

Kirkland curses under his breath, takes another look at Phil, and turns back to me. "Let's see this so-called spacetime bridge."

"It's about time," Sam blurts. "Get it?"

We ignore him.

When we get to the newly expanded lab, Kirkland walks around the tungsten Coffin, his hands clasped behind his back. He looks every bit the confident leader, but I can see the tension in his neck.

He stops in front of Picasso. "So, this machine is going to save us?"

"I hope so, sir."

"Well, if you're not positive, why'd you tell the President that it would?" He doesn't wait for Picasso to respond. "Is it operational, Sergeant Major?"

When Picasso doesn't immediately respond, he turns to me. "Well, is it?"

"We don't know yet," I say. "Adding the wormhole generator is a tad more complicated than plugging a grinder into your super-automatic espresso machine."

"Time's not on our side," he snaps. "If it works, we use it."

I clear my throat. "If and when it works, you'll be the first to know."

Kirkland rubs his chin, eyes still on the Coffin. "Johnson, what are your plans for this?"

Dick steps forward and shoots a sneer at Picasso. "Sir, I've been pushing to send a man back to fix the time stream."

Phil gasps.

We all trade looks.

"You can't change your own past," Sam says. "No matter what *The Terminator* tells you. It would create a time-loop paradox and kill anyone who tried—"

Kirkland holds up a hand. "Enough."

I can feel things shifting again. That precarious ledge we're standing on?

It's cracking.

Kirkland's expression lightens, and he starts nodding. For a second, I think he's going to say something sane. Maybe back our team. Maybe—just maybe—fund the plan we already have.

"Yes, it'll be the backup plan in case we have issues deploying the microbots. How soon can we send him?"

"Send who?" all of us say together.

Kirkland glances at Dick. "You sort out our little mess?"

Dick grins. "Affirmative, sir. He was right where you said he'd be. I have him in a holding cell."

"Excellent, Johnson, excellent. I'm beginning to see who gets things done around here."

Sabina rolls her eyes, and Sam groans—then covers it with a cough.

Kirkland steps up to Picasso and crosses his arms. "The report says Nadales' name was in the Sphere—along with his DNA. You left him out there ten goddamn months to play Daniel Boone?"

Diego. They're going to shove him into the Coffin like it's a damn recycling bin.

My throat locks.

Picasso narrows one eye. "We determined he was more valuable outside—"

Kirkland slaps him on the shoulder. "Like I said, Sergeant Major, I'm here to speed things up."

Dick checks his watch. "Did you want to speak to Nadales, sir?"

"No, no," Kirkland says, weight shifting like he's got somewhere else to be. "I'm sure you can handle it, Johnson."

I turn towards our new boss, anger rising. "Diego's no turncoat," I say. "And I'm not going to use him in a game of Russian roulette."

Kirkland looks at me like I'm mentally challenged. "So who do we send?" He gestures toward Cassie. "Your daughter?"

I shake my head, gut twisting.

He grabs Sam by the arm. "How about Mister Smart-mouth?"

Sam's ears get red, but he doesn't respond.

Kirkland grunts, shoving Sam back a step. "Nadales goes. His fingerprints are all over the Sphere. It's fate, for chrissake."

He says it like he's reading from someone else's cue card—like even he doesn't buy it.

"Don't feed us that crap," Cassie says, her voice raw. "Sending him in is a death sentence. Full stop."

Kirkland's gaze flicks to her, then back to me. "This isn't a debate. I know—*for a fact*—the machine works."

Cassie gapes at him. "You do know what facts are, right?"

"Show some respect," Dick hisses.

Kirkland's expression turns dark. I take a half step closer to Cassie.

She's holding her ground, but every part of me wants to shield her from this bastard—wants to remind him whose daughter he's talking to.

"You think I like sending people in blind?" Kirkland says. "I've got a daughter on the way. I know what I'm asking. But we're out of time. The Peeper's shown us the stakes, and Nadales is the golden ticket." He exhales. "We send him before it expires."

Cassie squares her shoulders. "So, dump Diego into an untested time machine so he can save the world?" Her voice could cut metal. "You think we're idiots?"

"I told you," he says, nostrils flaring. "It's not about being right. It's about being first." He rounds on Picasso. "How did you get anything done with the constant whining?"

Picasso doesn't flinch—just absorbs it.

Kirkland lifts a hand. "Okay, I've seen enough." He faces me. "Hudson, you're in charge of the time machine. All scientists report to you. In turn, you'll answer to Johnson—who'll liaise directly with me. Richter," he jerks his chin at Picasso, "your job is to keep the lights on until we know the jump worked."

Picasso goes pale. Dick's smug look says the rest.

"You've got three days," Kirkland says. "The world's burning, and people are asking why we're still running simulations."

I stiffen. "The spacetime bridge hasn't been—"

"Tested?" he cuts in. "Perfect. Clean data." He turns to Dick. "I'll be back on Friday. Prep the subject. He goes in the capsule the moment I arrive."

My stomach knots. "There isn't enough time—"

"Not my problem." He won't meet my eyes. "Just get it ready."

Cassie shakes her head.

Sabina crosses her arms, eyes on the Coffin.

Sam studies his boots.

Kirkland exhales. "They won't care how—only that it's done."

If I send Diego into that Coffin, it won't be Kirkland's signature on the death certificate.

It'll be mine.

Madders' Second Log:
Entry 5

Target: Diego Nadales

Nexus: Warm Springs Military Complex

Chrono Tag: Next Day

South Asian monsoon fails, spreading famine across subcontinent. Collapse of Thwaites Glacier causes sea level to rise 23 cm in eight days.

First microdrone kill logged. No media trace.

Kirkland Enterprises seizes control of Warm Springs Military Complex a full year ahead of schedule.

Sweat cools on my back as I lie on the floor. A fake window glows with stars.

A day after Matt raised hell, a tattooed marine escorted me to the "Hotel."

Richter? Right.

My brain is filled with fog.

When Johnson and Smith grabbed me, I lost more than freedom—days, nights, memory, any sense of the world outside.

I'm not sure how long I've been locked up.

Richter says it's a government facility, but the room looks like a 1960s sitcom—lime carpet, chrome desk, cracked vinyl chair. No phone. No TV. No word on Isabel. Just marines sliding trays through the door twice a day like I'm Hannibal Lecter.

Upgrade or not, still a prisoner.

Why the hell do they think I'm a terrorist?

I crush the dark thoughts with squats, jacks, more push-ups—the only thing I control.

Four sets later, I drink from the sink. Tastes like metal, but it's that or go thirsty.

The clock on the nightstand feels like a compass after days adrift. It reads 10:03 when the lights die.

I strip off my shorts in the dark and step into the shower.

I let the hot water beat against my bruised body.

As I'm rinsing my hair, a strange sound makes my chest tighten.

A click. Out in the room.

I crouch down and reach my arm out. My hand finds the toilet plunger. Not a machete, but it'll do. As I peek around the curtain, Matt Hudson steps into the bathroom, his chest rising and falling. When he sees me gawking at him, he presses a finger to his lips. I stand, still wielding the plunger. His eyes go wide.

He shuts the bathroom door and leans against it, looking pale and nervous.

"What the hell is going on?" I whisper, water dripping around the curtain of cracked plastic daisies and onto the floor.

Matt shakes his head and puts his finger to his lips again.

I lower the bludgeon—and then nod.

He runs his fingers around the mirror, then inspects the lights. When he doesn't find anything, he turns on a flashlight, crouches down, and peers in the sink cabinet. Next, he takes a quick look behind the toilet and exhales. "Didn't find any mics," he whispers. "But keep your voice low."

I give him a small nod, still trying to figure out what's going on.

"Took you long enough to start the bloody shower." He wipes his face on a towel—hands visibly shaking—and offers it to me. "I've been pressing a cup against the bathroom wall all evening." He closes the toilet lid and plops down on it.

"How did you know it was me in here?"

He motions with his head. "I'm in the next room over—heard the guard barking orders when they delivered your supper tonight. Put two and two together." He yawns. "We need to talk."

I go to shut off the water, but he grabs my arm. "Background noise. The mics are ancient, so the shower should be loud enough to drown out any soft voices—at least that's what Sabina says. She's one of the physicists. Grew up in East Germany. Badass as they come."

"Another physicist?" I step out to towel off. Matt moves his knees to make room. "What's going on here?"

"Later." He checks his watch. "The guard at the end of the hall takes a bathroom break in seven minutes. We need to be ready."

"For what?" I raise an eyebrow. "Why are you here, Matt?"

"They're forcing you through tomorrow," he says in a low, urgent voice.

I blink. "What are you talking about?"

"The spacetime bridge," he says. "A time machine. You're the guinea pig."

"Now wait a sec," I say. "I told Richter I'd take a look at your Peeper data. Maybe see if something in the Einstein Sphere looks familiar. That's all."

"Yeah," he says. "That's what I thought too. But the moment we get it hooked up, they'll force you in. Didn't bother to tell anyone why. The bloody thing hasn't been tested—we only brought the wormhole generator back from Florida a few days ago—but they don't care. Kirkland is hell-bent on sending you through, and there's nothing anyone can do to stop him."

My mouth goes dry. "Kirkland? Dave Kirkland is in charge?"

He nods. "As of yesterday. Reassigned Picasso—that's Colton Richter, the guy who got you out—to scrub toilets. And Kirkland promoted Dick—Agent Johnson—to run the place. The guy's a right git."

"Yeah," I say and rub my bruised shoulder. "We've met."

"I'm here to help you escape," he whispers, his voice barely audible over the deluge. "If you're still here on Friday, they're going to kill you." He glances toward the door as if expecting it to burst open.

"Why are you helping me, Matt?" I wrap the towel around my waist. "You'll be in a world of hurt if they find out."

Hard to forget the last time I saw him. Harder to hold it against him now.

"That's why I'm hoping they won't." He shrugs. "But if they do, I'm no *murderer*."

The word sinks in, icy and sharp.

He's seen Johnson work. Didn't stop him. Maybe that's why he's here.

The thought sticks.

"How?" I ask, my voice cracking. "How do we get out?"

"Just you, Diego. I've got a daughter to protect—and friends." Matt straightens, checks his watch again. "You need to get ready."

He's risking everything—clearance, freedom, maybe his life. "Are you sure you want to do this, Matt? If they think you helped me, they'll lock you up and beat the crap out of you."

"Maybe I should've done something back then," he says, low. "Stopped him. Stopped what came after."

"You did what you had to. We both did."

He nods, eyes downcast.

Whatever debt he's paying, I'll take the help.

"What's the plan?" I ask.

"If you make it through the blast doors topside, you can steal Johnson's SUV. Parks it by the door and leaves the keys in the ignition—with the tank full. He'll be the fall guy."

I feel my chest get lighter. "No one more deserving."

Matt checks his watch, signals for silence, and kills the shower. He cracks the bathroom door. We tiptoe out into the starlit room.

After I slip on my clothes, I give him a quick thumbs-up.

We wait by the outside door for a minute or two, and then he pushes it open a crack and grabs his badge as it falls out of the latch.

We peek around the doorframe—the chair at the end of the hall is empty. He hurries out.

No turning back now.

I pull my hood up and follow, our footsteps loud in the empty corridor.

When we reach the lobby, he stops with his back against the wall and peers around the corner. The air is colder, reeking of metal—blood or rust, I can't tell.

"If we leave the building," he whispers, "we'll have to jog around the lake to the lift—the only way out of this cave. If we go through the lab area, we can slip out closer—but there are more cameras."

A blinking red light above the exit makes the decision for us.

If we're going to set off an alarm, better to be near the exit elevator.

We slink across the back wall of the lobby and hurry into the lab area, jogging down the empty corridors past locked doors. My sneakers squeak like alarm bells on the linoleum, so I take them off and carry them.

We round the corner—then pull back.

A gray-haired woman and a redheaded kid slip out a door, whispering and laughing.

My gut says run.

Matt's hand on my arm stops me. "Sam. Sabina."

They both freeze.

"Matt?" the woman whispers. "What are you doing here?" She gives me a once over. "And who's he?"

"Diego—the guy they're planning to kill on Friday."

Sam gapes at me. "You breaking him out, Doc? What a badass."

"Save the flattery till he's clear.'

Sam shoves an old Polaroid camera into his bag and offers a photo to Sabina. She drops it in her pocket.

"Figured someone might make a move tonight," she says.

"Didn't expect it to be you," Sam says, flashing a smirk.

Sabina stretches her back. "How'd you get out of your room?"

"And into his?" Sam adds, elbowing Sabina.

"Bent paper clip. Flat side of my badge," Matt says. "Worked a treat, Sabina."

A smile creeps across her face. "Welcome to the club."

Matt steps up to the door. "I thought you were making a kitchen run tonight."

"Already did." Sam holds up a large bag of frosted corn flakes.

Of course. Nothing says revolution like breakfast cereal.

"Boss's new office." Sabina says, nodding at the door. "Knowledge is power."

Sam grins. "The code to his safe is *password123*, the chump."

I raise an eyebrow.

"Johnson," Sabina says. "Cruel, petty, dangerous."

"He beat up Diego when he wouldn't confess to being a terrorist," Matt says, nodding at the bruise around my eye.

"Ouch," Sam says to me. "Guy's a psychopath. He slapped Doc around too."

I look at Matt, but he brushes it off. "Mostly just tried to scare me."

My chest tightens. If this is a setup, it's a good one.

"How are you going to get the elevator to operate?" Sam says. "It takes two IDs."

"Bloody hell," Matt says. "I forgot."

"There has to be another way," I say. "No one takes the fall for me."

Sam scoffs. "This place was built in the 1960s. The elevator scanner is connected to an IBM 7090—a glorified toaster."

Sabina nods. "Basically useless for anything except *Space Invaders*."

Sam nods. "It scans the badges and mails the results to Santa."

They both laugh.

I shuffle my feet.

"But the security portal topside is another beast," Sam says, his smile falling away. "Only Picasso can activate it."

"That I remembered." Matt pulls out a flimsy glove. "Made it yesterday with Picasso's handprint—asked him to help with some warm wax."

Sam whistles softly. "Slick."

Sabina blinks. "What if they already changed it to Johnson's?"

"In less than 24 hours?" Sam barks a laugh. "That's a good one."

Matt turns to me. "Once you get past the security portal, it's a straight shot to the blast doors—maybe takes you two minutes. Slap the big, red button next to the blast doors."

Sabina puts her hands on her hips. "How's he going to get past the guard station?"

Silence fills the corridor.

I shift my weight. "I'll figure something out."

"I have a better idea," Sam says, then meets Sabina's gaze. "We'll set off the fire alarm."

"Excellent plan." She puts tools into a ditty bag, pulls up her hoodie. "Let's go. We'll get you to the elevator and activate it."

"Whoa." I hold up my hands. "You could get in serious trouble."

Sam wiggles his eyebrows. "Not if we don't get caught." He hurries after her.

Matt shrugs.

We follow them down the hallway.

At the end, Sabina holds up her hand, and we stop behind her. Around the corner, she points out a security camera that is rotating to cover one long hallway. "Modern and capable."

"This is where they're testing the shell from the Sphere," Sam says. "The one that was wrapped in tungsten foil."

My heart skips a beat.

"A seashell?" I say.

Sabina shushes us.

"There are two cameras," she says and points, "one there and one around the next corner in the same spot. When this one switches to the far side, we go. Then we wait below it until it switches back over here—five or six seconds. After that, we hotfoot it around the next corner before it cycles back. Understood?"

Matt and I nod.

"If we get lucky," she says, "the second camera will be pointing away when we get there."

"And if we get unlucky?" I say.

"Stand against the wall and wait for my signal." She glances back at the camera. "Ten seconds."

Sam puts the snacks away, and Sabina meets my gaze. "Keep your hood up and your head down in case we get caught on camera."

"Plausible deniability," Sam says as we follow Sabina down the corridor.

We stop under the first camera and plaster ourselves against the wall. The lens switches to the way we just came, and we continue on at a quick jog. When Sabina gets to the corner, she holds her hand up for three long seconds—and then we repeat the pattern. After we turn the next corner, we're blocked by an unmarked door with an ID scanner next to it.

Sam takes out his ID card, but Matt grabs his wrist and swipes his own.

The lock clicks. Sabina pushes the door open and sticks a dental mirror through the crack, giving us a five-second countdown with her fingers. We dart past an empty desk and slink around the wall toward the exit.

I point at the blinking red LED above the door.

"Fake," Sam whispers. "Head for the carts. Careful. The rocks all have mics."

Outside the building, it's strangely silent. We jog under a sky of simulated starlight toward a perfectly still lake.

Where the hell are we?

"This place is creepy," Sam whispers. "Even by my standards."

As we bump along a path by the lake, the whir of the electric motor echoes in the huge cavern.

When we reach the elevator, Matt and Sam swipe their badges. The door slides open, and I step inside, my heart pounding.

"Here," Matt says and hands me the glove.

"The switch to open the blast doors is in the guard room," Sabina says. "Yesterday, the code was 9-8-1966."

As I repeat it aloud, Sam whistles. "Nice catch, Sabina."

She shrugs. "Let's hope they didn't change it."

There are two buttons in the elevator, and I press the top one.

"Give us ten minutes to set off the fire alarm," Sam says and offers me his bag of breakfast cereal. "Here, take this. Not going to be a lot of dining options out there."

I take the bag as the door starts to slide shut. "Thank you." I lean sideways. "All of you."

"Good luck," Matt says and puts his hands on Sam's and Sabina's shoulders.

"You're gonna need it," Sabina mutters.

The door clangs shut, and a few seconds later, the elevator lurches up. I stand in the corner, my heart pounding in my ears. The stale air has a hint of sour sweat.

I put on my shoes and try not to panic.

After the bell dings, I stuff Sam's snack bag under my sweatshirt, take a couple of deep breaths, and step out.

The hallway stretches ahead, dim and silent. I force myself forward, each step heavier than the last. The security door looms in the flickering light, the black glass of the palm reader glinting.

I take a closer look at Matt's handmade glove. There's no way this works.

You miss all the baskets you don't take.

When I step up to the security door, a light goes on above me and a female voice says, "State your name and authorization code."

I take a deep breath and press my glove-covered hand against the scanner, teeth clenched, pulse hammering in my ears.

The computer repeats the request and adds, "You have ten seconds until lockout."

Mierda.

I stand there, counting down in my head and waiting for the men with rifles to appear.

When I reach zero, the scanner lights up green, and the female voice announces, "Exit protocol initiated. Please proceed."

The heavy door slides open.

A cheerful voice says, "In case of an emergency, remember to duck and cover. Have a nice day!"

I stand frozen, my chest tight. "Duck and cover," I mumble and take a shaky step forward. "Great plan."

The hallway smells of damp leather, but the air is cooler here, less suffocating. My high-tops don't make a sound on the rubberized floor as I stride forward, every nerve on edge.

At the end of the hallway, the emergency lights illuminate an enclosed guard station with huge blast doors beyond. My stomach knots when I see them, but Sam is right. No guards. Just an empty desk, a chair turned slightly askew, and a coffee mug next to a blinking monitor. I type in the code Sabina gave me, and the door latch releases. In the room, there's a button on the wall labeled "Start Release Sequence."

I wedge the door open with a mug, grab a water bottle, and press the **RELEASE** button—hoping it controls the blast doors and not some missile silo.

For a second, nothing happens.

I stand there with my hands shaking, trying to come up with a plan B.

Hydraulics groan, and the blast doors shudder—steel built to stop a nuclear strike.

A rush of cool night air fills the hallway, carrying the smell of pine and earth and freedom.

It's real. I'm out.

I jog through the blast doors, moonlight pulling me forward.

Stars blaze over the foothills.

"You can't leave."

The gravelly voice stops me cold.

I spin, my pulse spiking. A shadow shifts at the edge of the light, stepping into view. My first thought is that it's Johnson, but no. This man walks as if the ground itself grabs at his ankles. A wide-brimmed hat casts his face in shadow.

But there's something familiar. Too familiar.

He steps closer. My breath locks.

"What the—" I stumble back, my heart pounding. "Who are you?"

The old man stares at me, his face dark and heavy with something I can't name. "You know who I am."

"Why are you here?"

"You have to go back," he says. There's a desperate edge to his voice. "She needs you."

"Who?" I snap.

"Isabel." The name hits me like a gut punch.

I shake my head—and then motion with my chin toward freedom. "Isabel is out there."

He harrumphs. "If you leave now, she dies. Everyone dies. You're the only one who can stop it."

"Stop what?" My mind is racing. "What are you talking about?"

"What's coming."

I stare at him. "I can't just abandon Isabel."

He takes off his fedora, and I can see his face—how old and worn down he is. "She'll find her way."

"No," I say and edge backwards. "You ask too much."

"It's not a choice, mae. You *must* change what's coming."

"How?" I shake my head. "You need to tell me—"

"I can't!" His voice is raw, desperate. "I've already said too much. But you have to believe me. There's no other way."

"Stand clear!" a female voice says over a loudspeaker. "Blast doors closing!"

I can hear them start grinding.

Freedom's right there. Cool air, starry night sky, anything but this.

"You're lying," I spit out.

"You know I'm not." His voice is quiet now, and when I meet his eyes, the weight of them nearly crushes me.

"You gave Isabel the puzzle box," I say. "You sent the messages."

It's not a question, but he nods. "Along with Tego—he's the one who died that night. To save your Isabel," he says. "Don't waste his sacrifice."

A pulsing alarm goes off back inside the mountain, and a red light starts spinning inside, bathing the huge holding area in garish shadows.

I shake my head and start backing away from him. "I don't believe you." Johnson's SUV waits twenty feet away. "I have to find her."

"Nothing out there saves her," he says, nostrils flaring. "For us, the only way forward is the Coffin."

I freeze. "How do you know about—"

"Because I lived it." His eyes flick to the closing doors. "Go back —before it's too late."

I want to fight. To run. But I already know I won't. I slip back inside, the echoes of my footsteps chasing me.

The corridor gapes, endless and black.

I run toward it—the only future left.

Madders' Second Log: Entry 6

Target: Isabel Sanborn
Nexus: Eden-2
Chrono Tag: Next Day

Global oil reserves breach depletion threshold.
Middle East desalination grids collapse. Heat-
related mortality exceeds 1.2 million per month.

Los Angeles, São Paulo, Shanghai, Moscow, Sydney
overrun by violent protests. Biodome construction
accelerates worldwide.

Microdrone swarms disperse rioters at Eden-5 and
Eden-11. Fatalities reported. Anomalous activity
detected in timeline. Masked incursions continue.

Morning light filters through the biodome, creating a golden glow that would be lovely anywhere else. No mosquitoes, no chirping birds, not even the hint of a breeze. Just sanitized air and the faint hum of the dome's ventilation system.

A sentry hovers ahead, red eye glowing. I watch it swivel around, scanning this section of the biodome for intruders. I check my watch and make a mental note of the direction it's moving.

When it disappears, I gaze across the park at the botanical gardens. They're lined with rows of hybrid roses engineered to bloom year-round, their petals glowing faintly under the biodome's artificial light. Beyond them are clusters of fruit trees, their branches heavy with oranges, apples, and something that might be a genetically enhanced peach.

I spot a group of technicians clustered around a Hive controller, one of them pointing and shaking his head at the tiny blue lights in the trees.

A twinge of curiosity squeezes my chest, but I force down the urge to ask what they're working on.

Lani—doctor-in-training, now babysitter—walks beside me. Her expression flickers between boredom and annoyance. She's short and irritatingly pretty, with sharp cheekbones and straight black hair in a neat ponytail. Despite looking fresh out of kindergarten, she's almost 20.

I limp along, my whole body complaining.

She carries a tablet, tapping every so often—recording my vitals or playing Candy Crunch is anyone's guess.

"Fifteen minutes today," she says, her voice clipped. "If you feel faint, notify me immediately. No detours, no sudden movements."

"I'll try not to break into a sprint," I say.

Her lips twitch ever so slightly.

There's a muffled bang outside the biodome, followed by a handful of quick pops. Lani doesn't even vary her step.

"What was that?" I turn toward the noise. "It sounded like gunfire."

"It was. People are desperate. Angry. Every day, they try to break in." She continues walking. Eyes forward. Gait steady. "You get used to it."

"God, I hope not."

A shadow crosses her face before the professional mask slides back into place.

"I'm perfectly capable of taking a walk by myself," I say. When she doesn't respond, I steal a peek at her tablet. "And I know how to record a heart rate too."

Lani's about as warm as liquid nitrogen, but there's something about her sardonic edge I've come to appreciate. When she doesn't immediately fire back, I try something riskier.

"You're, what, four months along now?" I glance at her stomach. It's a little bump, barely visible under her scrubs.

"Five," she says, her hand reflexively brushing her belly. It's a defensive gesture, subtle but telling.

"Is everything okay with the baby?" I look carefully at her face. "And the mother?"

"I'm fine," she snaps, like she's trying to shut the door before I can wedge my foot in.

We walk in silence, passing a fountain shaped like a nautilus shell and an ag-bot trimming a park hedge. Kids in bathing suits dart across the flawless lawn while their parents sip drinks by the pool.

"So," I say, trying again, "Dave's been good to you, hasn't he? The scholarship, the spot here in Eden—"

"I never asked for any special treatment, if that's what you're implying. I graduated top of my class. I earned that scholarship on merit."

I grimace. "No, no. I wasn't implying anything. I just meant—"

"Meant what, Isabel?" She pins me with those dark brown eyes.

"Nothing," I say and shake my head. A sentry drone hovers overhead, its red eye pulsing. My skin prickles. The thing scans us top to bottom before gliding on.

I take a slow breath. "Has Dave made any progress finding your brother?"

"How do you know about Kai?"

I shrug. "I'm a light sleeper."

Her cheeks redden, but she slows her pace. "He promised to bring my brother in, too. He's only six, and he has no one but me."

"That must be rough for both of you."

She dips her chin, lips pressed thin. "Dave swore to me he was on it—but that was months ago."

The bitterness in her tone gives me pause. "What about your parents?" I ask, afraid to look at her. "Surely Kai has someone out there who can take care of him?"

She shakes her head. "My grandmother raised us alone."

"Is she...?"

"Dead." The word comes out flat, but her hands grip the tablet tighter, her knuckles white. "Four months ago."

"Oh, my goodness," I say, my throat tightening. "Lani, I'm so sorry."

She stops walking, her gaze fixed on the ground. For a moment, I think she's going to ignore me. Then she exhales sharply, her voice low. "She was diabetic. After the EMP, no power, no cold storage, no medical supplies. I watched her die."

I stay silent, giving her space.

"She held on as long as she could. Taught me medicine, taught me hope. Said I'd save lives someday." Her voice cracks, and she blinks hard, her face tight.

"Lani—" I start, but she cuts me off with a sharp breath.

"It doesn't matter," she says, forcing herself to look at me. Her stare is dark and fierce, daring me to pity her. "Dave gave me a shot at something better. That's what matters."

"Better?" I look around. "Is this it?"

She doesn't answer.

We keep walking.

A short distance away, the shimmering surface of a swimming pool comes into view, a pristine turquoise oval bordered by lounge chairs and shaded cabanas. A man in a white uniform stands at the ready, a tray of drinks balanced on one hand. An older gentleman and his trophy wife are lounging by the pool. Behind them, a fan stirs canned air, and a colorful umbrella blocks the fake sun.

"You miss her," I say softly.

Lani's shoulders stiffen, but she nods once, barely perceptible. "Every day."

I want to say more, to offer some kind of comfort, but the words stick in my throat. Instead, I walk beside her, unable to jump across the crevasse of her sadness.

Murmured conversation filters through the cultivated hedges before we see the source. Lani and I round the corner. Dave's standing beside a tall, middle-aged woman in a sleek, tailored suit. Her no-nonsense bun and piercing eyes give her an air of precision, as if she's dissecting his every word and tossing aside the unnecessary ones.

Dave nods like a kid hoping the teacher won't notice he copied his homework.

"Who is that with him?" Lani whispers, her brows drawing together. "And why is Dave grinning like that?"

"Ah," I say, lowering my voice. "You're witnessing a rare sight: Dave Kirkland behaving like a human being."

Lani huffs but keeps her eyes glued to the scene.

The woman—Yuki, I catch from Dave's obsequious interjections —gestures toward the biodome's gardens, her tone brisk and authoritative. "Your biodiversity retention rates are adequate for now," she says as we walk up behind them, "but your pollinator protocols are alarmingly outdated. What's your plan for genetic stability over the next three to five years?"

Dave straightens like a soldier under inspection. "We're already implementing phase-two enhancements to the artificial bee program. Sophisticated redundancy layers, improved genetic modeling—you'd be impressed by the advancements we've made, Yuki."

"Impressed?" Yuki swipes at her tablet, pulling up data I can't see. "You've got functional redundancies, but your genetic models are two iterations behind the standard. Do you know what that means?"

Dave stammers. "Well, it's not as though we're completely—"

"It means," Yuki cuts in, her voice cool, "that if one thing goes wrong, this entire facility could lose its primary food production capabilities. That's not redundancy. That's a ticking time bomb."

Lani leans in closer, her voice barely a whisper. "I've never seen him like this. He looks... scared."

I stifle a smirk. "Maybe the Great and Powerful Oz isn't so mighty after all?"

"You really don't like him, do you?"

For once, I'm the one who doesn't bother to answer.

As we walk closer, we hear Yuki sigh, a sound that's somehow both weary and cutting. "Mr. Kirkland, you invited me here to consult. If you want us to invest—or even consider allocating resources—you'll need to demonstrate you can meet our standards."

"Absolutely," Dave says, nodding fast enough to qualify as cardio. "Anything you need. We're committed to excellence here at Eden-2, and we'd be honored to have your company invest in Kirkland Enterprises."

Lani's lip twitches.

The swaggering, self-assured visionary who built Eden-2 has been replaced by a groveling salesman, all fake smiles and false flattery.

I swallow. "We've all been there."

She doesn't answer, but her eyes say everything.

I catch movement at the dome's edge—a silver swarm rises, red eyes blinking in sync. Eden's angels of death.

How long until that comes back to bite us?

"Isabel! Lani! What a pleasant surprise." Dave's voice is bright and airy, pretending we haven't just witnessed him squirming like a worm on a hook.

"I didn't realize you were back from Washington," Lani says.

Dave shifts his weight. "Just flew in an hour ago, Cupcake. You know how it is—work, work, work." He turns to Yuki, his hand gesturing grandly. "Yuki Nakamura, meet our former Director of Drone Engineering, Isabel Sanborn." He beams at Lani. "And one of our rising medical stars, a UPenn Perelman Scholar, Lani Kealoha."

Yuki turns to Lani. "You're one of the doctors in the new training program?"

"Yes," Lani says, her voice steady but clipped. "On temporary assignment from the university."

"I see," Yuki says, her tone unreadable. "Good to know Mr. Kirkland's investing in talent. Let's hope he's equally invested in maintaining this facility's viability."

Dave clears his throat. "We're very committed, Director Nakamura. In fact, Isabel was instrumental in creating the honeybees."

Yuki looks at me again, her gaze sharpening. "You designed the microbots?"

"I did," I say, forcing a polite smile. "Though I can't take credit for how they're being deployed."

Yuki raises an eyebrow, and her attention shifts back to Dave. "You must persuade Ms. Sanborn to come back. Expertise like hers is exactly what we'll need if a pivot becomes necessary."

"I couldn't agree more," Dave says, his voice a little too loud. "We're expecting Isabel to rejoin the team as soon as she recovers."

"Careful, there," I mutter. "Promises like that tend to bite back."

Dave forces a chuckle. "Good to see you're feeling better."

Yuki watches the exchange before turning to Dave. "I'll review the rest of your data tonight. We'll reconvene tomorrow. For now, I have other appointments." She doesn't wait for a reply, striding off toward the guest quarters without a backward glance.

As soon as she's out of earshot, Lani huffs. "That was something."

"Something, indeed," I say, watching Dave's sigh of relief the moment Yuki disappears. His grin snaps back into place, but his eyes stay flat.

"Well," he says, brushing his hands off. "I'd better get back to work. Lots to do. You know how it is. Good to see you both." He kisses Lani on the forehead. "I'll be by later to give you a proper hello." He winks at her and hurries off.

For the first time, I feel a twang of sympathy. Lani's finding out how fast Kirkland can turn trust into leverage. It took me decades to move past the swagger and French cologne. By then, I couldn't tell where I ended and he began.

"Can I give you some advice?" I ask, turning to her.

Lani raises an eyebrow, wary.

"Don't let him convince you he's doing this for you. Dave always plays the long game. For himself."

It comes out harsher than I intended.

Lani's face hardens. "Thanks. But I can take care of myself."

"Of course. I didn't mean—"

"I know what you meant," she says. "But I'm not you."

Her words sting.

We walk the rest of the way in silence, the hum of the biodome the only sound.

Later that afternoon, Lani is making an elaborate dinner for Dave in our shared kitchen. Officially, I'm staying with her to recover. Unofficially, Lani's here to make sure I behave.

Bet she loves that.

I should be pouring over the latest drone footage, but instead, I'm bracing for tonight.

Third-wheel duty.

I expect my ex-husband and his pregnant teenage girlfriend will be having exuberant sex in the next room.

Nothing says closure like thin walls.

There's a soft rap on the door, and my breath snags.

"It's open," Lani calls from the kitchen.

The latch clicks, and a face peers through the crack.

"Sophie!" The name bursts out of me with a laugh.

She's thinner. Hair cut short. A tablet clutched like a shield.

"Isabel," she says, smiling and stepping in. "I was starting to think you were a ghost."

"Still kicking," I say. "You have no idea how glad I am to see you."

Sophie sets her tablet down on the table, and I pull her into a hug.

"They're watching us," she whispers.

I dip my chin.

When she steps back, her mouth curves up, but her eyes betray her misgivings.

Lani peeks in from the kitchen, glasses perched on her head, carving knife in hand.

"Hi, Sophie," she says, gives a quick wave, and goes back to her cooking.

"Lani? Uh, hi." Sophie stands there for a moment, wondering why there's a medical student in my kitchen—and then figures it out.

Her eyes get big, but she recovers fast.

We talk about nothing—how the coffee tastes metallic here, the absurdity of the indoor waterfalls right next to dehumidifiers, the way Dave's "vision" always manages to be both over the top and under-whelming.

Eventually, reality creeps in.

Sophie's eyes shift to her tablet. "Can I ask you something?"

"Sure. What's up?"

She hesitates, then picks up the tablet, swiping through screens. "It's the bots. We've been having some issues."

I stiffen—but try to keep my tone casual. "What kind of issues?"

"Deviations from programmed paths. Ignoring overrides. Some are going offline completely and restarting in diagnostic mode." She sighs, her expression a mix of frustration and chagrin. "This morning, one rerouted itself. Circled the nursery for over an hour. Had to shut down the whole zone to get it to stop."

"Hmm." I lean back. "Stabilizers? Scan integrity? Maybe a feedback loop?"

Sophie sighs. "Tried all those. Nada."

"Damn."

Lani starts setting the table with candles and champagne flutes.

Sophie and I relocate to the couch, going through bot data just like old times.

I exhale. "Could it be firmware? Environment thresholds tripping?"

Sophie grunts. "Firmware thresholds? Damn. I didn't think about that."

"It's worth a shot," I say with a shrug.

Lani excuses herself to take a shower.

"Why don't they eat at Dave's place?" Sophie whispers.

I wait until we hear the water start. "Dave doesn't want anyone in his apartment when he's not there."

"Right," she says. "Mr. Paranoid."

I pull her arm. "Let me know if it's a threshold issue?"

"Yeah. Will do." Sophie smiles, running a hand through her pixie hair. "You're a genius, you know that, Isabel?"

I smirk. "Just spent two decades practically living with the little buggers. I ought to have learned something."

Sophie chuckles, the sound thin, like she's testing whether it's still safe.

"What is it, Soph?"

She leans closer. "I know it doesn't make sense, me being here, helping him after—"

I hold up a hand. "No need to explain. I expect you're doing this for your family, for your future. You'd be crazy not to."

Her shoulders relax a little. "It's just, right now, every decision feels like a bad one. Stay outside, and we could all die. Come in here, and we live, but..." She trails off, her gaze darting to the window. "Dave says you're going to rejoin the project. Is that true?"

"I told him I'd think about it."

"The team could really use your help, Isabel."

For a moment, I wonder if Dave put her up to this—but banish the thought. Sophie and I have known each other for decades.

She bumps against my shoulder. "And I could use a friend in here."

I put my arm around her. "You got it—my broken bits and all."

She starts to say something, but I wave her off. "And good luck trying to get rid of me."

Her expression softens. "God, I missed you."

"Make new friends, but keep the old. One is silver, and the other left a cryptic note and a huge mess in the bathroom."

She laughs for real.

A faint vibration pulses through the floor—someone's headed this way, and fast.

A second later, the door flies open, and Dave strides in.

"You made it!" Lani appears in the kitchen doorway, hair done up, makeup applied, bottle of champagne in hand. She looks absolutely stunning—and for a moment, I remember what it's like to be young and in love.

"Ladies!" Dave exclaims, clapping his hands together. "My three favorite girls in one room. What are the odds?"

I grit my teeth. "Next time, maybe you could knock first?"

He ignores me and turns to Sophie. "How's the bot issue coming along? Any progress?"

Sophie squares her shoulders, slipping into professional mode. "We're still troubleshooting. Isabel had a suggestion about recalibrating the environmental thresholds. It should fix the issue."

Dave's eyebrows shoot up, and he turns to me with a gleaming smile. "Still hitting home runs, even from the sidelines. What do you say I make you Director of Drone Engineering again?"

I purse my lips. "You already have one." I tip my head toward Sophie. "And she's a better team lead than I ever was."

He gives an awkward laugh. "Of course, Sophie is great. Always trying her best. Aren't you, babe?" He pats her back, his smile a little too wide. "Matter of fact, she's the one who suggested bringing you back."

I resist the urge to roll my eyes. Dave is famous for coming up with controversial ideas and shifting the blame when they don't pan out.

"Pass," I say.

"Shame," he fires back, clearly viewing my responses as nothing more than the opening shot of a Wimbledon final. "Anyway, good work, Sophie. Keep this up, and I'll upgrade that apartment of yours."

I see Sophie wince, but she forces a smile. "Thank you, Mr. Kirkland."

He turns back to me. "You'll be happy to know I'm setting up a real apartment for you. Should be ready in a few days. Corner unit. Top floor. Great view of the dome. Spared no expense," he adds, like he's breeding velociraptors.

I give a nod, careful. "Sounds... nice. But I don't know if I'm going to stay, Dave."

This place is like living in a brochure—if the brochure came with sniper towers.

He lifts both hands like a peace offering. "Of course. No pressure. You haven't decided to leave, have you?"

I exhale. "No."

"Good, good." He claps his hands like we've struck a deal. "Once you're moved in, I'll have the boys set up an office. Get you a terminal, full access. You can poke around, reacquaint yourself."

The thought makes my stomach curdle.

"Any word on Kai?" Lani asks, her voice a whisper.

Dave eyes her elaborate hair and makeup—and the gorgeous silk kimono she's wearing. "I told you, babe. I'm working on it." It takes him a moment to tear his gaze away from her. "No need to keep badgering me."

"Yes, of course," she says and drops her gaze. "My apologies."

He sighs, looking beat. "And I can't stay for dinner, Lani. I'm sorry. I'll make it up to you once things settle down." He turns to

Sophie. "I need you to run the Sentry Bot demo. Yuki wants to see what they can do."

She nods, looking weary. "Now?"

"I'm afraid so."

I squeeze her arm as she stands up. "Talk later?"

"Love to," she whispers—and rolls her eyes so only I can see.

Dave strides out of the apartment, Sophie hurrying after him.

The door clicks shut.

Lani presses her lips together and pulls a pin out of her hair. Her dark, straight locks fall down around her porcelain shoulders.

"You okay?" I ask.

She dips her chin. "He's... exhausting."

"That's one word for it," I say, earning a laugh. "I know it's not much consolation, but dinner smells wonderful."

She presses her lips together. "Let me change first, and then you'll join me? No sense in letting it go to waste."

"Wouldn't miss it."

The curry isn't terrible, but it's close.

I choke down a second bite. "Great color."

She perks up, tastes it—then winces. "Burnt glue." She slumps. "I hate cooking."

I attempt a grin, but it ends up as more of a grimace. "Your curry's not bad, just unusual."

The ghost of a smile crosses her face. "Yeah? What's worse?"

"Liver and onions. Culinary punishment disguised as food."

She shoves her plate away. "Maybe I'll try that next time."

I laugh.

She huffs. "Fine. Before we moved inside, I just ordered takeout and served it to Dave in my own dishes. He thought I was a genius in the kitchen." She stabs the chicken like it owes her money. "Turns out the apocalypse doesn't deliver. Who knew?"

I laugh. "So what you're saying is, the end of the world blew your cover?"

"Completely." She points her knife at the curry like it ratted her out. "Everyone knows I'm a fraud."

I reach across the table and squeeze her forearm. "Your secret's safe with me."

After we clean up, we decide to take an evening stroll—Lani pretending to provide medical support and me pretending to need it.

Lani's gaze shifts over the lawn, hedges, and the bubbling fountains, but there's no appreciation in her expression—only a quiet tension, like she knows she doesn't belong here.

To be fair, neither do I.

We pass four attractive young women playing tennis under the lights. Their laughter carries across the park, easy and carefree.

Lani's shoulders tense. "Did Dave ever make you feel like you were special?"

I blink, caught off guard. "Special how?"

She shrugs. "Like you were different. Smarter. Like he sees things in you no one else can."

I hesitate. "He has a knack for that. I remember it being quite intoxicating. Like he sees the whole universe in you."

Lani lets out a bitter laugh. "Until it doesn't."

"Nothing lasts forever, Lani."

"What about you and Diego?"

I laugh. "We're a very long way from forever."

We sit down on a bench. Water trickles through a nearby fountain.

She leans against the backrest, staring at the ground. "I was a juvenile delinquent."

I blink. Not where I thought this was going.

She gives an uncomfortable laugh. "My pals and I were looting a jewelry store the night of the Denver fire."

"What?"

"Because I needed money for med school applications," she adds quickly. "But still."

I tilt my head. "Hardcore pre-med. So what happened?"

"I helped some desperate guy break the window of a burning hotel—mostly just to show off. He was trying to save this woman he had been in love with for years—but had never gotten up the courage to go after."

My breath catches.

"Something about that night changed me," she says. "A month later, I met Dave."

I gawk at her. "You're the street kid Diego met during the Denver fire—the one who helped him save the pets from The Brown Palace."

She stares at me, her beautiful face a mask.

"Lucky, the kitten. Tolstoy, the best dog in the world." I swallow hard, unable to believe fate has brought us together. "It was me stuck inside the hotel. You saved my life."

Lani blinks, her expression shifting to disbelief. "No way."

"Yes way. Diego told me about you, about how smart you were—how relentless. If you hadn't given him the string to unwind, the paramedics never would have pull us out in time."

She leans back, still processing. "I mean, I knew you made it out, but—" She pauses, a small twitch tugging at her lips. "You don't seem like the type."

A sound breaks out of me, half-sob, half-laugh. "Yeah, well, I wasn't exactly living my best life at the time."

The corner of her mouth curves up. "Guess I can't call you a trust-fund brat anymore. Risking your neck for strays wasn't smart—but it was effing brave."

"Um, thanks," I say, and wipe away a tear. "I think."

She grins, her eyes glinting. "Just so you know, I'm still going to make you do push-ups."

"I'd expect nothing less, Lani."

She tosses her hair over her shoulder, and I'm struck, again, by how young she is. "So how did you end up marauding for med school money?"

She takes a slow breath. "My parents died. Tutu Shannon raised me and my kid brother."

"Tutu Shannon?"

"My grandmother. We didn't have much, but she kept Kai and me out of trouble—mostly. Made me stay in school, told me I could do something important with my life."

"Smart lady."

She exhales, a shaky smile tugging at her mouth. "Fed two growing kids on government handouts and sheer grit." Her voice tightens. "When she died, it all fell apart."

I wait for her to continue.

"And then Dave showed up." She looks around, taking in the mild evening. "Found out about my scholarship, offered me a position here in the clinic, and promised he would bring in my brother too." She looks down at her baby bump. "Said I had potential. All I had to do was work hard." She scoffs. "He made it sound like I was the most precious thing in the world to him."

"Dave sells miracles. Sometimes he delivers."

She frowns. "He saw something in you, too. Right? I mean, you designed those bees. That's no small feat."

I clear my throat. "He didn't exactly pick me off the street but, yeah, he helped me. Backed my research when no one else would. It wasn't all bad. But you know as well as I do, Dave's generosity always comes with strings."

Her lips press into a thin line. "It's my brother I'm worried about. He's out there all alone."

I want to tell her Dave doesn't care about her brother, that his promises are just tools to keep her in line. But looking at her, at the tension in her shoulders and the way she's gripping the bench, I can't bring myself to say it.

Maybe because, this time, he actually loves her.

I lace my fingers. "I know what it's like to lose someone."

"Your twins." Her voice is soft. "I'm sorry."

I nod, my lips pressed tight.

"I can't imagine," she says, her hand drifting to her belly. "I'm terrified about the future. Not just for the baby—but for my brother."

I reach out, resting a hand on hers. It feels awkward, but I do it anyway. "Dave will find him," I say. "He knows how to get information, how to make things happen."

Her mouth curves, then falters. "If I weren't five months pregnant, I'd go out there and look for Kai myself."

"Maybe I can help." It comes out before I can stop myself.

She gawks at me. "What do you mean?"

I hesitate, then let out a sigh. "I mean, I know how to access the biodome's AI. I helped test the protocols for it. I can have it search for information on your brother."

Lani raises an eyebrow. "And Dave isn't doing that already?"

"God, no. Dave hates computers—no way to blind them with lust."

She leans forward, her long black hair falling into her face. "You'd help me?"

I shrug, trying to downplay it. "Well, you'd have to put up with my sarcasm, but yeah."

"Not to mention your tendency to think you're the smartest person in the room."

I smirk. "Yeah, that too."

She laughs once, shakes her head. "You're full of surprises, Isabel."

"Don't tell anyone. You'll ruin my reputation."

She studies me, like she's deciding how much of herself to show. The air between us tightens, humor evaporating.

"There's something you should know. About Diego Nadales."

My stomach twists.

"They have him locked up inside a mountain."

"Inside a mountain?" I frown. "What does that mean?"

"It's a military base," she says, "and it's not far from here—a short helicopter ride. Dave's been there a few times. Talks on the phone to someone named Johnson. They're holding Diego in a cell."

Heat floods my chest. "That bastard." I stand up. "I knew he was lying."

"If you're so tough, why didn't you call him on it?"

"Touché," I say. "Knowing better doesn't mean I did better."

A blush spreads across her face.

"How long ago was this?" I ask.

She bites her lip. "Two, three days ago. What are you going to do?"

I stare at her, my brain working overtime. "I don't know. See if I can find more information on where they're holding him."

"You're not thinking of doing something rash, are you?" She crosses her arms. "Because then I'd have to report you."

"Of course not," I say, keeping my face neutral. "I love it here. Don't you?"

"Yeah. It's perfect," she says, tracking the sentry bot gliding past.

For the first time, I see her not as some naive girl, but as a woman who's been through hell—and is still fighting.

Someone not so different from you.

Madders' Second Log:
Entry 7

Target: Matt Hudson
Nexus: Warm Springs Military Complex
Chrono Tag: That Night

Texas levee breach displaces 3.1 million in hours. Private militias divert relief funds, tighten control.

Kirkland Enterprises establishes drone hubs across the US. Eden-17 construction surges, months ahead of schedule.

Timeline deviations around Matthew Hudson and Sabina Lovelace escalate. Project success jeopardized.

I jolt awake, heart hammering, ears straining in the dark—nothing but the faint hiss of recycled air and the creak of the bed frame beneath me.

It's nearly 2 am. I spent the day buggering about, and the night regretting it.

What the hell happened to Diego two nights ago?

No update, no fallout, no alarm. Just silence.

Yesterday, I heard his breakfast tray rattling down the hallway, Dick's voice low and casual—"Room service for the bunker's most expensive guest"—like nothing had happened.

Why was there no alarm, no lockdown, no punishment?

The question curls in my gut like a knot, an image of Diego pounding against that sealed blast door churning in my mind, dread thick in my throat.

You did what you could, mate.

Didn't you?

In a few hours, I'll be compelled to send him to his death.

I force a slow inhale.

Outside my fake window, the Eiffel Tower glows in a field of dim, indifferent stars.

Inside, the low ceiling presses down on me, carrying the crushing weight of the mountain above—like a sealed tomb, the air growing thinner with every passing second.

Hard as I try, I can't stop replaying it—how I let the day unravel. Hesitation cost an hour. A missed double-check cost more. Every fix bled time. Test after test: the bridge formed, then collapsed. Power surged, crashed. Calibrations were tweaked, subsystems rebooted—nothing but failure stacked on failure. I stared at the growing pile of charred bananas, pretending I hadn't just glimpsed Diego's future. We logged the data like it mattered, but the smoking hunks of charcoal reminded me just how far we have to go.

And the clock keeps ticking, each second pounding toward the moment Kirkland returns and insists we load up the spacetime bridge with a human sacrifice.

Earlier today, we tried to talk—Cassie, Sam, Sabina and me—but Dick stalked the lab like an overseer. Paced behind us, arms crossed, leaning in so we could feel his breath on our necks. One time, Sabina complained that Dick's footsteps were tripping the motion sensors on the Peeper array. He'd just leaned on the console and said, "Not my problem."

Sam had looked down. Sabina had shuffled some papers. Cassie had opened her mouth, then closed it, her eyes flicking past me.

We didn't talk after that.

But we all know how this ends.

A soft metallic scrape freezes me.

I strain my ears.

Nothing.

When I roll over, it comes again.

The hairs on my arms rise.

Maybe they know I helped Diego?

The thought flickers, wild and desperate. My brain flips back to the night they abducted me from my house—Dick and Junior dragging me out of bed, their shadows too big for the room.

Not this again. Not tonight.

The lock clicks.

I jerk upright, pulse roaring in my ears as the door cracks open.

A hooded figure slips inside.

Artificial starlight catches a profile as the figure moves like a soldier in enemy territory, jaw set like granite. Sabina meets my gaze and gives the tiniest nod, as if her faith in me is unspoken.

My throat tightens.

Sam follows, twisting his hoodie string around his finger. Cassie slips in behind him and eases the door shut. Her hand flies over her phone.

A low hiss fills the room.

Sam plops down on the other side of the bed, and Cassie sits next to me, her shoulder pressing against mine—steady, warm. Sabina pulls out a folded blanket and spreads it over us like a tent. We huddle close, shoulders pressed tight, the musty fabric trapping our breaths.

A flashlight clicks on. Shadows jitter.

"We need to talk," Sabina says, voice clipped.

Sam snorts. "Not like anyone was sleeping."

Cassie exhales through her nose, her voice barely a whisper. "Does anyone know what happened to Diego?" The question hangs in the air.

Sam shakes his head. "No clue. Things got crazy after I tripped the fire alarm."

"They have to know he had help," Sabina says. "We're good—but we're not that good."

"Diego made it past the security checkpoint," I say. "The glove I made for him had Picasso's handprint—and I heard Dick ask Junior about Picasso being 'upstairs last night.'"

Cassie runs her hand through her hair. "Then why's Dick acting like nothing happened?"

"Because he doesn't know the truth?" Sabina says. "Maybe Picasso caught Diego and escorted him back."

"And he didn't tell anyone?" Sam shakes his head. "They'd fire his ass so far out of the military, he'd never find it again."

"Not if they didn't know about it," Cassie says. "Colton Richter has lots of friends. Maybe Dick couldn't be bothered to review the security logs himself."

I exhale. "Well, it doesn't matter now. What matters is they're going to make us fire up the Coffin in a few hours—with Diego in it."

"It's madness," Cassie says. "We all know it."

"I don't get the feeling Dick cares," Sam mutters.

Sabina's gaze hardens. "Well, I know what it's like when people become expendable. I'm not going there again."

Cassie nods, her voice low. "If we stand together, Kirkland will have no choice but to give us time."

"I don't know about that," I say. "Guy's hard to read."

"Because he's a poker player," Sabina says. "Bluff, bluster, bully, cajole. But we have a royal flush, and he knows it. With us, maybe he has a chance. Without us? It all falls apart."

Her certainty sparks something hot in my chest, but fear smothers it just as fast. If I speak up, I'm in—and so is Cassie. No turning back—but at what cost?

"What if Dick throws us out?" Sam asks. "People are starving out there."

"Kirkland's not going to let him," Cassie says. "They need us."

"What if we're wrong?" I say. "What if Kirkland wants us to cock it up in public—cut us loose, boost his own projects."

"Then we fail," Sabina says. "But we won't have blood on our hands."

Cassie lifts her chin. "So if Kirkland wants our blood, he'll have to spill it himself."

Sam sits up straighter. "I say we prove him wrong. We use the Peeper. Fix the bridge. Rewrite what happens next."

No one says anything, but I can feel it. They believe we can do this.

A floorboard creaks.

We freeze. The faint, chemical tang of boot polish wafts in under the door.

Sam's breath hitches. Sabina kills the flashlight. Cassie's white noise dies with it.

The silence stretches, broken only by our heartbeats.

I peek out. A silhouette darkens the crack beneath the door. The rattle of keys. Someone's hand takes hold of the knob.

"Crap on a cracker," Sam whispers.

All of a sudden, it's hard to breathe.

Someone flips on the lights, blinding us.

"Nadales didn't get caught," Picasso says, scanning the room. "He came back."

The revelation lands like a pint glass on concrete.

Sabina yanks the blanket off. "Why would he do that?"

"I don't know," Picasso says, glancing at the door. "I escorted him back to his room after the all clear came. As far as Johnson knows, the fire alarm was tripped by a faulty sensor, the guard took Nadales out of his locked room as a precaution, and I brought him back." He pauses, letting the weight of his words settle on us.

"You just walked him back," Cassie says, her voice tight. "No questions asked?"

"No time," Picasso says.

Sabina frowns. "Why help him? Why risk your own neck?"

Picasso gives a tight shrug. 'Kirkland scares me more than Johnson."

The ceiling presses down again.

I will my heart to stop racing. "Why would Diego come back?" My stomach's in knots, hands clammy. "There has to be something he's not telling us," I say. "Something we've missed."

Picasso gives a slight nod—or perhaps I only imagine it.

"Or he saw something out there," Cassie whispers. "Something that scared the crap out of him."

Picasso tilts his head. "Men come back for all kinds of reasons. Doesn't mean they'll tell you why."

Sabina draws a slow breath. "We've been talking about..." She glances around the circle, and we all nod. "About giving Kirkland an ultimatum. We're not going along with killing Diego."

"I know," Picasso says.

"Then you know," I say, "if the man wants our cooperation, he has to give us time to test the machine—and the resources to do it right."

Picasso gives a dry laugh. "Not gonna happen. Kirkland cares about results, not your shopping list. Don't give him an ultimatum. Give him an out."

I frown. "An out?"

Picasso leans back against the wall, voice low. "A way for him to say yes without looking weak. You back him into a corner, he'll bite. If you give him a door, he might just walk through it."

Sabina's eyes narrow. "Are you suggesting we play nice while he lines Diego up for execution?"

Picasso's mouth twitches, not quite a smile. "Make it look like his idea. Like he's the genius who demanded safety checks. Tell him you need a few more test runs to fine-tune the jump. Say it's about protecting his investment. He gets to play the visionary who insisted on safety protocols, not the tyrant who caved to a bunch of lab rats."

Sabina's brow furrows. "So we lie."

"You survive," Picasso says flatly. "Big difference."

Cassie shifts beside me, whispering, "He might buy that. He likes hearing himself called visionary and brilliant in the same sentence."

"Bingo," Sam says. "But if we give ground, it has to buy Diego time—not just boost Kirkland's ego."

My chest tightens. Part of me wants to grab the bluff, run with it. Another part whispers to keep my head down, let someone braver take the hit. But if we wait, Diego dies—and the blood's on my hands as much as Kirkland's.

"And if he says no?" Sabina crosses her arms.

Picasso's lip twitches, his gaze flicking to the door as if measuring the danger beyond. "Then make him regret it." He meets my gaze. "Kirkland only respects pain. Make sure it isn't yours."

The marine officer turns away and shuts off the light. "Either way, time's almost up."

There's the soft snick of the latch, then the faint echo of his boots in the corridor.

We sit there in the dark.

Out in the hallway, a door slams—sharp as a gunshot.

Madders' Second Log:
Entry 8

Target: Diego Nadales
Nexus: Warm Springs Military Complex
Chrono Tag: Two Days Later

European energy grid collapses under cyberattacks
as protests engulf coastal megacities.

Microdrone swarms deploy cutside all Eden
facilities, expanding to protect critical
infrastructure and agricultural resources.
Unauthorized approaches terminated via drone-
delivered neurotoxin injections.

Dave Kirkland's rise accelerating beyond virgin
timeline.

I follow Picasso through a mazelike set of hallways. Each step lands heavier, the gray walls pressing inward. The air reeks of smoke and disinfectant—sharp, chemical. It catches in the back of my throat.

Two marines follow, boots striking in unison. A wall of indifference.

Up ahead, a fan ticks—slow, uneven. A janitor mops an empty hallway, eyes down.

A marine nudges me in the back, and I stumble.

"Eyes forward," he mutters, sounding tired, like we're all stuck in the same bad play, waiting for the curtain to fall.

My body keeps walking, but my mind's caught somewhere else.

I try to picture Isabel's face—only to lose her in smoke and flames. Her body on the bed. Eyes closed.

Death in the doorway, watching.

But the old man at the blast doors—his words still bang around in my skull.

Nothing out there saves her. For us, the only way forward is the Coffin.

Breakfast in my room had been piled high this morning—eggs, bacon, hash browns. The kind of meal you'd give a condemned man.

Now it churns, heavy and sour, tripping me up.

Picasso's voice cuts through my haze. "Keep moving, Nadales."

I look up.

He doesn't turn. Just keeps walking—a wall of muscle. But there's something in his tone—an edge. He's worried.

Ahead, a camera adjusts, tracking me. The red light blinks like an accusation.

My skin prickles. Not that I didn't know they were watching, but the deliberate focus makes my chest tighten.

Someone wants you to feel it.

A low hum vibrates through the wall, the generator waking up. My pulse thrums to match it, every beat screaming at me to turn back.

Picasso stops abruptly, and I nearly bump into him.

He turns, his face unreadable under the fluorescent glare. "Don't try anything," he says, softer this time. He steps aside, and the doors come into view—two massive slabs of reinforced steel, the kind you'd expect to see on a vault.

Or a tomb.

The guards snap to attention as Picasso nears. Their salutes are sharp, mechanical, but their eyes flick to me, their expressions laced with something darker. Contempt? Pity?

Not sure which is worse.

The doors hiss open. A hydraulic breath. I shiver. The lab sprawls like a beast waiting to devour its prey—stark walls, blinking consoles and, in the center of it all, what I assume is the Coffin.

Hell of a name to drop—right before shoving me in.

It gleams under the lab lights—sleek, coiled, patient. Not a machine. A predator ready to pounce.

And I'm the prey.

Matt is pacing by the generators. His lab coat hangs loose, and his normally steady hands twitch at his sides. When he sees me, his face tightens, eyes flicking toward the Coffin, then back to me. His lips press into a thin line, saying everything without a word.

You know this wasn't my idea.

Behind him, the tall, redheaded guy—Sam—shuffles his feet. Two nights ago, he was a laugh a minute. Now he just looks haunted, too thin, a shadow around the eyes.

I recognize Cassie, Matt's daughter, from photos. Her eyes are glued to a console, her fingers a blur, her posture tense like she's physically keeping the whole place from collapsing.

Sabina stands behind Cassie, arms limp, her face carved from stone. She's the inventor of the Peeper but looks more like someone who could dismantle you with a pair of pliers and not lose sleep over it.

And then I see Kirkland. He's leaning against the wall like he owns the place, arms crossed, smug and untouchable.

My hackles rise.

I imagine he's been plotting this since they locked me up—waiting for the perfect moment to take me down for good, with an audience.

Every eye in the room flicks between us.

I tell myself to stay calm. Be the bigger man. Don't let him get to me.

But Kirkland's smirk burns through that plan like acid. He's savoring this. Like the whole damn circus was staged for my execution.

My fists clench. Hard. "Why won't you let me talk to her?"

Kirkland turns, slow and smug, his smirk widening. "You mean Isabel?" He stares at my fists. "Is that what this is about?" He chortles. "How romantic."

A growl builds in my throat, but before I can move, a hand clamps down on my shoulder. Picasso. His grip is iron. A warning.

Kirkland clicks his tongue. "Funny, really. You disappear, leave Isabel bleeding out, and who swoops in? Me. While you're off playing Daniel Boone, I save her life—"

My stomach twists like something's about to rupture. I don't hear the rest. Just the blood roaring in my ears.

I step forward, Picasso's grip tightening like a vice, and I hear Matt's sharp inhale.

"Always so dramatic," Kirkland continues, his voice like silk. "Isabel is fine. Better than fine, actually. She's moved on."

"You're lying," I hiss.

He gives a theatrical sigh. "You know what I think, Nadales? I think you're mistaking your place in all this. Do you honestly believe Isabel is wasting her time worrying about you?"

I manage to shake off Picasso's hand.

But Johnson steps in front of me, sneering as he rolls his shoulders. "Boss is talking to you, Nadales. Might wanna show some respect. Otherwise, I might have to educate you."

The way he says *educate* makes my skin crawl.

My mind flashes to that damp cell, to the bruises still fading from my ribs.

I step around him, bumping my shoulder hard against his. "You want respect, Kirkland? Then stop hiding behind other people."

Kirkland sighs like this is all terribly tedious. "See? This is why we don't have nice things. My team understands that discipline makes things run smoothly. You could learn from that."

"Learn what?" I spit out. "How to steal other people's work and claim it as my own?" I'm a lamb arguing with the butcher, but I can't stop myself. "You're a fraud, Dave. Always have been." I glance around the room. "And everyone in here knows it."

The lab is silent except for the hum of the machines—a low, pulsing reminder that time is running out.

"Johnson," Kirkland says, lazy as ever. "Get our guest situated in the capsule."

Johnson claps. "Okay, folks. Showtime."

The silence could crack glass.

Sabina glances at Matt and nods, her eyes huge.

He steps forward, and I think he's going to grab my arm. But then he plants his feet like he's finally picked a side—and it's not Kirkland's.

"Dave—Mr. Kirkland, sir," Matt says, too fast. "With all due respect, we're not ready. Mr. Smith can attest that we've been working night and day. But the system's too volatile. The last thing we want is to waste the opportunity—or make the project, or you, look bad." His voice is steady, but he's sweating through his collar.

Out of the corner of my eye, Picasso gives a nearly imperceptible shake of his head. Not now, not like this. But it's too late—Matt's already in it.

Sabina crosses her arms. "He's right. One failed launch, and this becomes a *Challenger* disaster—with your name emblazoned on it."

Kirkland blinks. Just once. But I see the twitch in his jaw.

Picasso steps forward, voice smooth. "You give the team a few more days, you get a clean launch. Something that works. Something that sticks. And you get to say you demanded the highest standard." He doesn't blink. Just plants the words like he's laying explosives.

Cassie moves to Sabina's side, her chin raised. "We're scientists, not magicians."

Sam pushes off the wall. "You want us to make this work? Then trust us to do it correctly." He glances over his shoulder. "Right, Phil?"

Which is when I realize there's a guy hiding behind the generators.

He stands up, trembling but resolute. "Right."

Behind me, Picasso shifts.

Kirkland's gaze sweeps the room, his smirk returning. "All of you?"

"Package deal," Sam says.

The scientists all nod.

Cassie locks eyes with Kirkland, daring him to blink.

Matt clears his throat. "It's nothing more than a slight delay. Once we get the bridge properly tested—and Diego prepped—you'll be the first to know."

Kirkland exhales, like the air itself disappoints him.

"Fine," he says. "One week. Not a day more. When this works—and it will—make no mistake: it's because I kept the fire lit."

He lets the silence stretch a beat—just long enough to remind us who's really in charge.

Then he rounds on Johnson. "I thought you said the team was on track."

Johnson flushes. "This whole delay tactic is news to me, sir."

Kirkland exhales again, pinching his nose. "Perhaps I neglected to mention that I know the time machine works. It's imperative that Nadales jumps as soon as possible."

Matt steps forward. "How do you know it works?"

Kirkland waves him off. "That's none of your concern, Hudson."

The scientists exchange uneasy glances.

Sabina gives the smallest shrug, like she expected this.

"Maybe it works in another universe," Matt says. "But that's no guarantee it'll work in this one."

Sam grunts. "Anyone who tells you differently is lying."

Matt folds his arms. "So I ask again—who told you the bridge works?"

Kirkland narrows his eyes and flicks the question away. "Let me remind you—all of you—this isn't a science fair. Results matter. And right now? You're all failing. Every week you putz around costs damn near a hundred million dollars. I don't want to pull the plug, but I will be forced to shift the funding elsewhere if I don't see progress." He steps closer to Matt, his voice dropping to a low, venomous growl. "So enjoy your little delay. Use it wisely. And don't mistake my patience for weakness. One slip, and this project ends with you lot handing out protein packs at the food bank."

He turns on his heel, his suit catching the light as he strides out, ripping the air from the room.

Even Johnson's at a loss.

He scowls. Fists balled. "Try not to embarrass yourselves further," he mutters, before tramping out.

The door hisses shut. Shoulders sag. Eyes drop.

Not sure who played him better—Matt, Sabina, or Picasso. But it worked.

"Matt," I say, my voice catching.

He doesn't look at me right away, his gaze still locked on the Coffin, like staring at it might change the future.

I clear my throat, speak the line from memory. "You need to cut the red wire and double-check the maths."

"Thanks, mate," he says without meeting my gaze, "but I'm not in the mood for jokes."

"I'm serious," I say and repeat the line from the old man.

He jerks around, his brows knitting together. "What are you talking about?" His frown deepens, confusion etched into every line on his face. "Who told you that?"

I hesitate.

The memory rises up, sharp and insistent, dragging me back to the chaos of that night.

Picasso shifts in the doorway, casual as ever—but his eyes narrow. He's watching me now, really watching, and it makes my skin prickle.

"I..." My throat tightens, the words heavy on my tongue. "I got a text—from a number I didn't recognize—during the chaos at the hotel fire, the one that nearly killed Isabel." The memory flashes like a broken reel: the restaurant swaying, the huge windows vibrating, explosions outside setting buildings on fire. "It said, 'Tell the professor to cut the red wire and double-check the maths.' I thought it had something to do with the fire."

The room absorbs my words, the air thick with an unspoken tension.

Picasso speaks up, his voice sharp. "Who sent it?"

"I called the number back the next day," I say. "The young woman said an old man borrowed her phone. Described him to me. Said they were in downtown Denver near the fire."

Picasso raises an eyebrow.

I force a breath, my voice wavering. "I thought it was strange—that he wrote 'the maths,' like he was talking to a Brit. But now..." I meet Matt's eyes. "Now it makes sense."

Matt blinks, stunned, like I've said his death date out loud. "The professor," he says, his voice soft, like he's speaking to himself. He shifts his weight, his gaze dropping to the floor. "That's me?"

I nod. "It has to be."

The words settle over the room like a fog.

Matt suddenly looks older. The words pull at his shoulders, the corners of his mouth. He rubs his temple like it might help him think. "And you're just telling me this now?" he asks, but there's no anger, just exhaustion.

"I didn't know what it meant," I say. My throat is dry, and the words feel like they're scraping their way out. "Not until now."

Picasso's voice cuts through the tension. "How did some random old guy get your number, Nadales?" His eyes narrow. "And don't tell me it's a coincidence, because I don't believe in those. Not when it comes to you."

"It wasn't random," I say, meeting his gaze. "He knew something we don't."

Picasso's gaze shifts to Matt. "Is there a red wire in the machine?"

Matt looks back at the Coffin like he's trying to see the wires and circuits beneath. "Probably," he says finally. "Could be fifty of them, for all I know."

Sabina steps closer, her arms crossed. "We're going to need more than a cut wire to fix this."

I nod, the skin on my left ankle still smarting. "Whatever's wrong, it's not just a bad connection. It's deeper. Bigger."

And it's coming for us faster than we can run.

Madders' Second Log: Entry 9

Target: Isabel Sanborn
Nexus: Over Pacific Ocean
Chrono Tag: A Week Later

North American breadbasket crop yield down 40%. South American hydro dams sabotaged. Rolling blackouts extend north to Costa Rica.

Attempts to trace timeline incursions unsuccessful. Disruption patterns suggest jumps by David Kirkland from unknown timeline.

Bridge activation probability spikes erratically, trajectory unpredictable.

The corporate jet is a palace in the sky—leather seats that cradle you, embroidered Hokusai images on the headrests, a bar stocked with the kind of whiskey that has its own security detail.

But it's the silence that unsettles me.

It's too perfect, too engineered—like the air itself has been scrubbed clean of anything real. It reminds me of Eden-2, where everything is controlled, precise, artificial. And, just like inside the biodome, I can't shake the feeling that something vital has been stripped away.

I take a sip of sparkling water served in a crystal goblet, choke down my embarrassment, and turn back to my computer.

Farmers all over the world are reporting mass bee die-offs. What little information we have points to a new pathogen. Worst-case scenarios predict honeybees could be completely wiped out within months. Even the best-case estimates peg a total collapse within two years.

I hope it's the latter. Otherwise, it'll be impossible to get enough of my microdrones out there to prevent a famine of apocalyptic proportions.

So, for the last five days, Dave and I have been flying across the Midwest visiting Yuki's manufacturing plants. Despite the collapse of the electrical grid, her factories hum with activity, running on independent micro-reactors and advanced solar farms built years before the crisis. Dave says her company has over eighty large manufacturing facilities around the world—on every continent except Antarctica.

It's almost like she had a Magic 8 Ball or something.

Once I give the go-ahead, Yuki plans to churn out the bots 24/7.

The sheer scale of it keeps me awake at night. The bots are mine. My code. My design. My responsibility. If even *one* thing goes wrong —if there's a dumb mistake buried deep in the logic—it won't just be a massive engineering problem, it'll be a catastrophe. So I work. I sift through thousands of lines of code, burning the midnight oil, looking for anything that could possibly go sideways. So far, everything checks out. Sophie's done a solid job. The simulations run clean. But I know better than to trust the results from an artificial world where nothing ever goes sideways.

And Dave isn't helping.

Earlier this afternoon, we were waiting in a manager's office for Yuki to return. All day long, three nameless guys had been hovering over my shoulder, asking me, "What's this for?" and "What's that for?" and then going over my responses at length in Japanese. When I asked Yuki who they were, she just dismissed them as curious technicians who needed to maintain the manufacturing lines.

Except those aren't the sort of questions technicians ask.

And last night, Sophie let slip that I only have access to certain areas of the code, which I had suspected but couldn't prove.

So I confronted Dave. "What are you hiding from me?"

He'd given a mirthless laugh. "The last time I gave you complete code access, you pulled that dumbass prank that got you fired. I'd have to be an idiot to let that happen again. You find an issue with a bot, you come to me. I get Engineering to fix it."

I told him there were too many potential issues—that I needed more time—and he blew up. "It's too late for that, Isabel!" His voice was laced with acid. "The bots are going out with or without you. If you're so damned nervous about what they might do, then put in the work."

"I am!" I shot back. "If you hadn't fired me—"

"Don't start with that, Isabel. I fired you because you betrayed my trust."

"You lied to me, Dave! You were planning to use my work to kill people, and when I refused to cooperate, you pulled the pin and handed me the grenade! Now you come crawling back, begging me to save mankind—when it's really your own ass you're worried about." I glanced at the door. "And everyone, including Yuki, knows it."

"You're wrong," he said, voice carefully controlled. "But I'm done being nice. So let me put it to you this way. I know where lover boy is. And the only way you're ever going to see him again is by doing exactly as I say. Exactly. Capisce?"

I resisted the urge to spit on him.

He grabbed my chin and forced me to look at him. "You'll work 16-hour days, you'll find every issue, and there will be no more of your goddamned funny business. Do you understand? If one itty-bitty thing goes wrong on your watch, I can guarantee you will never see Nadales again. Ever."

I swung before I could stop myself.

He caught my wrist, nails digging in until pain lanced up my arm.

I choked back a gasp, but his smirk told me he felt it—that tiny moment of weakness.

He leaned in, close enough I could smell that same expensive whiskey on his breath. "You blow this, Isabel, and it won't be just you out on your ass. Sophie and her family, and anyone on your old team who ever made the tiniest show of loyalty to you, will be going down too."

I yanked my arm free and turned away, flexing my fingers to fight the throbbing.

"The bots are your babies," he spat out. "And if something does go tits up? Believe me, the whole world's gonna know who's responsible."

I slammed the door so hard the frame shuddered.

Let the whole damn building hear it.

Back on the plane now, I take a slow breath and glance out the window, my heart still pounding in my throat.

Problem is, if I do screw up, there might not be anyone left alive to care.

So don't screw up.

The good news is, Yuki's company is working hard to make things better. Surrounding each manufacturing site are sprawling fields of wheat, soy, and corn—each genetically modified for high yield and resistance to unpredictable weather. All the crops leverage Dave's GroSurge fertilizer to speed up harvests. Automated irrigation systems and underground reservoirs keep the plants thriving, but without enough pollinators, their fields will fail to produce, and what's left of civilization will fight over the scraps until there's nothing left.

As much as I loathe working for Dave, it seems he's on the right side of history with this one.

Still, Yuki's foresight—ensuring redundancies, stockpiling raw materials, and automating every process—has kept the farms and factories operational while most of the country struggles in darkness. On this trip, she's spent most of her time keeping an eye on what she considers to be the weak link: me. Meanwhile, Dave has been overseeing the construction of biodomes near each manufacturing site. I've been working my ass off inspecting assembly lines, reviewing firmware exceptions, and checking faults in the newly manufactured bots. It's been exhausting, but at least we're making progress.

One persistent issue—solved just a day ago—was a flaw in the bot's flight stabilization system. A minor manufacturing glitch made them blind in wet weather. Whenever crops were watered—which is all the time—we lost hundreds of bees from the Hive. Sophie and I came up with a work-around to shut down the bots until they dry out, and we should know if it worked by tomorrow.

But there's still another glitch nagging at me: the bees' communication network. Some units are dropping out of sync—almost like they're being hijacked—and disrupting coordinated pollination. If I don't find the cause soon, we could be facing uneven crop yields and potential collapse of the fragile ecosystems we're trying to save. Everyone knows it's a race against time.

As the private jet climbs up into the night and banks westward, I see a few scattered lights across the heartland—campfires, burning forests, the last embers of cities left to smolder. And then we get high enough that darkness swallows everything, a stark reminder of how much has been lost.

"Where to next?" I ask Dave.

Yuki is already inside her sleeping compartment, and I can barely keep my eyes open.

He yawns, sipping on a glass of whiskey. "You'll see. Get some rest."

I retire to my own tiny compartment and slip into bed, my body exhausted but my mind still racing.

Will I be able to get all the problems fixed in time?

In the morning, I open the window shade to a vast blue ocean, no land in sight.

Where are they taking me?

My stomach growls, and I strip off my rumpled clothes, stuff them into the hamper where Yuki's staff will make them disappear, and step into the misting shower. A cool vapor kisses my skin, cleansing me without wasting a drop—a luxury so absurd it feels obscene. Back in the US, people are fighting for food, for water, for their very lives—and here I am, naked in a silver tube in the sky, wrapped in the privilege of the few who still have everything.

After getting dressed and joining the others, I'm served a meal of fish, rice, pickled vegetables, and miso soup. Across from me, Dave sprawls across two chairs, flipping through something on his tablet, one leg draped over the armrest like he owns the place. Yuki is sitting behind him, back straight, wearing a charcoal-gray suit tailored to within a nanometer of perfection. You'd expect the crisp lines to look severe on her tall, lithe figure, but they don't. And yet there's nothing soft about her, either. Nothing harsh or showy. Just feminine. Powerful. A hint of exotic. A presence that pulls people into her orbit without effort.

The perfect disguise for a tyrant, says the cynical voice in my head. I shut it down before it can start telling me what to do when the plane crashes.

Dave smirks without looking up. "You always scowl when you're thinking too hard, Isabel. Careful, or you'll get wrinkles."

Classic Dave. Yesterday he practically threatened to destroy me, and today he's my best bud.

No point in pretending he's doing it because he enjoys my company. "All right, Dave. Enough games. Where exactly are you taking me?"

He leans back, stretching. "Yuki's main manufacturing plant. In Aichi, Japan. I thought you'd want to see where the magic happens."

"Great." I slump back in the chair. "I've been kidnapped."

Yuki taps a perfectly manicured nail against her tablet and lifts an eyebrow. "Please. If that were true, you'd be in a cargo crate underneath the plane—not complaining over fresh sushi."

Dave grins, utterly pleased with himself.

I adjust my already wrinkled pantsuit and take a sip of green tea. "So, Japan," I say. "How long will we be staying?"

"As long as it takes," Yuki says without looking up.

Dave just shrugs, and I realize he's not running the show anymore.

Yuki is.

That's gotta hurt.

Half an hour later, the jet starts its descent.

But it's not Japan, it's some island in the middle of the ocean.

"Pit stop," Dave says. "This'll only take a few minutes."

As we get closer, I can see that the entire landmass is being transformed by sheer human ambition. Terraced fields of solar panels cascade down the side of a volcano. A natural harbor shelters a cargo ship, its mechanical arm unloading stacks of containers onto waiting trucks. At the heart of it all, a massive dome rises, its surface a mosaic of interlocking plates, shimmering with an almost otherworldly sheen. Towering above the megastructure, massive cranes stretch skyward as if reaching for a future not yet written.

I gape at the sight, unable to hide my awe.

Dave leans forward, grinning. "Eden-17," he says, voice brimming with pride. "My masterpiece. Self-sustaining, tsunami-proof, built to last a hundred years. If or when the world collapses, this is where civilization starts over."

I stare at the dome, my stomach twisting. It must be seven or eight miles in diameter and half as high as the volcano. Another fortress, another pocket of artificial survival meant to stand while everything outside burns.

But I don't say that. Instead, I nod, sipping my tea as the jet touches down.

"Be right back." Dave exits the moment we roll to a stop, and he spends the next thirty minutes standing in the shadow of the plane, engaged in a conversation with one of his men. His posture is rigid, his gestures sharp and commanding. From the way he moves, he's asking the impossible, and the other man—sweating through his shirt despite the breeze—nods with grim determination, probably promising to make it happen. After a final terse exchange, Dave bounds back up the steps, disappears into his compartment, and comes out in a clean shirt.

As the plane takes off, Yuki lifts one perfect eyebrow—and Dave gives her a single nod.

So she's helping him build biodomes too? Interesting.

I spend the day going over my notes, running tests, and firing off emails to Sophie, reminding her to check this and that on the simulator.

Turns out, building bots by hand is one thing, but building them on an assembly line is quite another.

Lunch is served.

I install a fix for a handful of fit-and-finish issues, but still have no insight on the network problem.

Day turns to night, and dinner is served with wine and dessert.

I chat with Sophie for a few minutes via satellite link. Tomorrow, she'll try to reproduce the networking problem.

Still, we fly west.

Finally, the pilot announces that we'll be landing in thirty minutes.

Yuki doesn't lift her gaze. "A helicopter will be waiting."

Dave glances at his watch, and she adds, "The terafactory runs 24/7, so the late hour will not be a hindrance—and, as you know, time is of the essence." Her voice cuts clean, without hesitation, each word exactly the right length. "Once the production issues are solved, we'll begin producing twenty thousand bots a day. Twice that once the new factory comes online."

Twenty thousand a day?

I let out a soft whistle.

Humans are bad at visualizing large numbers, but how many microdrone bees do we need? A few years ago, the world honeybee population was around 3.5 trillion—over 400 bees per person—but estimates vary on how many are left. Half that? Something is killing them by the billions, causing them to hibernate in their hives and never wake up. Air pollution? Low-grade radiation? Excessive heat? A new pathogen? No one knows.

Even if all of Yuki's factories could produce twenty thousand bots a day, it would still take centuries to replace all the bees. And without bees, we'll lose the crops, the forests, the wildlife—and our last chance to pull back from the brink.

Diego was right. We should have tried harder to save the bees.

The jet touches down in Nagoya as if settling onto a cloud. Outside, a nervous-looking man in a tailored suit waits beside a limo, shifting from foot to foot. Yuki walks down the stairs, her posture expectant. "Where is the helicopter? I gave strict instructions to have it ready."

The employee bows, avoiding her gaze. "Apologies, Nakamura-san, but due to... unexpected fluctuations in the airspace, it has been deemed inadvisable to fly near the facility at this time. The factory manager has sent his personal car, along with his utmost apologies."

Yuki blinks, a rare flicker of surprise breaking her polished exterior. For the briefest moment, I catch something else. Concern?

Irritation? Fear? It's gone before I can pin it down, replaced by her usual calm, but it lingers in the space between her words. "What fluctuations?"

The man hesitates. "Some surveillance assets have deviated from their programming. We're still analyzing the situation, but it's nothing to be concerned about. The airspace quarantine is merely a precaution."

Again, Yuki's jaw tightens for a fraction of a second before she smooths her expression back into a mask of control. "Ensure the matter is resolved by morning," she tells the employee.

"*Hai*, Nakamura-san." He gives another deep bow.

I glance at Dave, lifting an eyebrow. "Surveillance assets? Those wouldn't be security drones, would they?"

He shrugs and gets into the limo.

As we speed through the night, the city blurs past in streaks of neon and headlights.

I gaze out the tinted window, my mind struggling to make sense of it.

"Why isn't Japan dark like everywhere else in the world?" I blurt out.

Yuki looks up from her phone. "Localized EMPs. Mostly Western targets. Our grid is underground, shielded, independent. We planned ahead."

I let out a slow breath, shaking my head. "You knew?"

She shrugs. "We assumed someone would be careless."

"And investing in all those manufacturing sites?" I press. "Was that part of the plan? Billions of dollars' worth?"

She gives me an enigmatic smile—and Dave shifts in his seat.

There's something they're not telling me.

We slow at a checkpoint, and uniformed guards scan the limo with handheld devices before waving us through. Beyond the gate, huge factory buildings loom, their tiny windows glowing like embers in the night.

As we step out, a cold breeze rolls in from the ocean, sending a shiver up my spine. Despite the long row of buildings stretching into the darkness, the parking lots are empty.

I frown, wondering where everyone is.

"The factory uses robotics and automation," Yuki says, slipping her phone into her bag. "Fewer people. Fewer problems."

Inside the largest building, everything is running in perfect synchrony—automated arms pivot, metal fingers grab and release with precise movements, long lines of tiny drones are assembled, soldered and tested. But unlike the factories in the States, there are no people here. No engineers making last-minute corrections, no technicians checking tolerances, no human hands performing specialized tasks. Just machines operating without pause, unsupervised. The rhythmic clatter of metal against metal fills the vast space, steady and relentless, like a heartbeat without a body. The air smells faintly of hot metal and oil, a mechanical sterility that does nothing to mask the eerie emptiness. Somewhere in the distance, a conveyor belt lets out a tiny, almost imperceptible squeal—an off-note in an otherwise perfect symphony of automation. I glance around, searching for a human presence, but there is none.

It should inspire awe. It should feel like progress. It should be expected.

Instead, it feels ominous.

Dave claps his hands, breaking my trance. "Welcome to the future, Isabel. Try not to look so horrified."

I step forward, my eyes following a row of microdrones passing through quality checks, their wings vibrating under fluorescent light. At first glance, they appear normal. But as I move closer, something looks wrong. The wing structure is different from my design. After getting a nod from Yuki, I pluck one off the line and turn it over in my hands, my finger tracing the subtle differences in material, the almost imperceptible shift in form. It's bigger but lighter—and the balance is wrong. Way too head-heavy.

Unless it's designed to carry some kind of cargo.

I hold it up to Dave. "What is this? What have you done to my design? And don't say 'small modifications' unless you want me to strangle you."

He rubs the back of his neck. "They *are* small modifications."

"This isn't some efficiency upgrade," I say, working to keep my voice level. "This is a redesign with new objectives."

Yuki steps beside me, plucking the drone out of my hand. She studies it for a second, then places it back on the conveyor belt. "Perhaps the trip has been wasted."

Before I can respond, Dave jumps in. "Look, the world isn't what it used to be. Biodomes need protection. Resources are scarce and, I promise you, no one's using the bots to murder people."

"These are attack drones." My words slice through his excuse. "Not worker drones. Not pollinators. These are built for combat. Built to carry payloads. What are they being used for?"

Dave hesitates.

That tells me everything I need to know.

Yuki makes a sweeping gesture with her arm. "These bots could be used to extinguish pandemics, deliver malaria drugs to remote locations, immunize whole populations."

"But that's not what you're planning." I press my fingers into the metal handrail. "You're mass-producing weapons."

Yuki doesn't blink. "Weapons, defenses—lines blur. Survival dictates flexibility. We're not the ones who fired nuclear warheads, Isabel. We're just making sure the people inside the domes survive whatever comes next."

I narrow one eye. "And how, exactly, do you plan on controlling all these bots? A single Hive controller can't handle more than a few hundred, a thousand at most."

Yuki sighs.

"You've made them autonomous," I say, realization sinking in. "And autonomous units need processing power—onboard AI. So you've added a neural processor. That's why they're heavier. They don't just follow commands anymore. They think."

Dave shifts on his feet, rubbing his palms against his pants.

Yuki tilts her head, considering. "Yes. There was no other way. We plan to put the swarms on a decentralized network with layered security protocols. Despite what you're accusing us of, the bots will be kept on a very tight leash." She waits a beat. "What we need now is your help working out the kinks."

"No," I say, turning to Dave. "I agreed to work on microdrone bees, not killerbots. I'm done here."

Dave exhales sharply. "You don't get it, Isabel. Nobody does, not really." The muscles in his jaw twitch. "When it all goes to hell— when there's no food left, and people realize the cavalry isn't coming —what do you think happens?"

I glare at him, heat rising up my neck. "People will fight for their lives."

He swallows hard, his eyes flicking toward Yuki before nodding. "Seven billion people. Seven billion starving, desperate people who have been abandoned to die will take up weapons. Governments collapsed, infrastructure destroyed. There's only one place left with food, water, medicine. One place left with power. The biodomes."

The air in the factory turns suffocating.

My pulse hammers in my ears. "You think they'll attack."

"Not *think*. Know." His voice is flat. "It won't be organized at first —just mobs, people pounding at the gates, tearing each other apart just to get inside. But then? The armies, the trained fighters, the ones who should be protecting us? They'll come too. They'll have families, starving children, and they'll have no choice. Seven billion against one hundred thousand. You do the math."

I take a step back, bile rising in my throat. "And you think the answer is to sic killer drones on them? That's your grand plan? Just slaughter everyone?"

"No." Dave drags a hand across his mouth. "We *defend* the domes. That's the plan."

Yuki exhales through her nose, arms crossed. "Difficult times demand difficult decisions." Her voice is unnervingly calm, like she's explaining a simple fact of nature rather than justifying mass murder.

I round on her. "Say it straight, Yuki. You're turning the bots into executioners."

She shrugs, expression unreadable. "We gave them the ability to protect—to ensure those inside the domes have a chance to survive. Without the swarms, there will be no wall high enough, no army big enough, no material strong enough to stop the mobs. They will destroy the domes—and take all of us with them."

My hands curl into fists. "That's a coward's answer."

For the first time, irritation flits across her face. "It's the truth."

Madders' Second Log:
Entry 10

Target: Matt Hudson
Nexus: Warm Springs Military Complex
Chrono Tag: Same Day

Cross-species pathogen confirmed airborne in
deep-field research station. Mutation rate
accelerating. Mortality onset within 18 hours.
Transmission rate unknown.

GroSurge dispersal correlated with 87% decline in
pollinators. Famine projections revised upward.

Spacetime bridge flaw renders jump non-viable.
Timeline collapse imminent.

The lab reeks of overheated circuitry. Every monitor screams in red as system alerts pile up faster than I can read them. Cassie hammers override commands. Sabina paces, eyes locked on nothing. Phil crouches in the corner, grumbling. Sam leans against the capacitor bank, cold coffee in hand, waiting for the Death Star to recharge.

He clears his throat. "Even odds we set the place on fire."

"If we fry another motherboard," Cassie says, fingers flying across the keys, "it won't matter."

Phil waves the remote, muttering about quantum vortices and powdered doughnuts like they're part of the same spell. Cassie rigged the device to trigger the wormhole abort. Phil's been carrying it around ever since.

Whatever incantation he's invoking, I hope it sticks—because I'm fresh out of miracles.

Dick and Junior hover near the exit—ready to hightail it out if the wormhole goes sideways. Dick's wearing that smug expression he saves for when he thinks disaster might finally prove him right. Junior clicks his pen and avoids my eyes.

I glance at my watch again. We need to recharge the capacitor array before Kirkland shows up, so this will be our last test. I let out a slow, hopeful sigh.

With Diego's tip about the red wire, I traced the glitch. We're ready for something big.

I tap my fingers on the Coffin just as the door hisses open. Diego wheels in a sheet-draped gurney.

As he pulls off the covering, Sam raises an eyebrow. "Looks undercooked."

No one laughs.

Sam gulps. "Shutting up."

Diego checks the alignment of the cart before locking it into place beside the launch rig—aka the Coffin—though no one calls it that in front of him.

On the cart is our final test subject: human-shaped ballistic gel. Lab-safe. Death-adjacent.

Better you than me, mate.

"Want him in there?" Diego says, sweat beading at his temple.

"Give us a few minutes to run the pre-checks," I say and nod at Sam. He slaps the **CYCLE** button on the capacitor bank again, and the numbers wobble into the green. Barely.

If this works, we'll have built a bridge to another universe—and maybe a way out of the apocalypse we've glimpsed in the Peeper.

I glance at Phil—who's still mumbling about doughnuts and doom. His eyes are locked on the wormhole generator like it's an atomic bomb.

Diego paces, tapping his thigh. I get it. I'm barely holding it together—and I'm the one pretending to know what to do.

I wipe my hands and sit at the console. Every one of us is running on caffeine fumes and stubbornness—twenty-six hours deep with no end in sight.

This is our last test jump. One final jolt of stored energy. One last chance to prove the bridge works.

"Two minutes until power spike," Cassie calls. Her voice is tight but clear. She doesn't look up.

Sabina hovers over me, arms crossed, her gaze locked on the Coffin like it might sprout fangs. She hasn't spoken in ten minutes— which is how I know she's terrified. Her job: track the Coffin through the wormhole and, if possible, lock on to the destination coordinates. Until we fire up the bridge, she has nothing to do except worry. I can almost see the contingencies racing through her mind, mapping escape routes, planning fallback runs, troubleshooting failures— anything to claw back a shred of control from the chaos.

"Okay, Diego," I say. "Put—"

The lab door slides open again. Picasso steps in, carrying a long black bag over one shoulder. He walks like it weighs nothing, but when he heaves it into the Coffin, it thuds.

I blink once, hard—like that'll reset reality.

Picasso shoves Jello-man aside and unzips the bag.

For a second, I think my brain is staging a mutiny. "Tell me you didn't kill someone for this."

Inside is a naked body. Male. Mid-thirties. No visible trauma.

Cassie doesn't even flinch—just continues setting up the jump parameters. Girl's got steel in her veins.

Picasso works the bag off the corpse and tosses it aside. "Hospital morgue," he says. "Brain hemorrhage. No family."

Diego swears in Spanish—loudly.

Phil peeks out from the capacitor bank. "God help us."

Sam stops fiddling with the thermal stabilizer and stares at the cadaver. "Guess it's Bring Your Dead to Work Day."

We all stare at him.

"It's madness," I say and shake my head. "And here we are."

Sabina steps in beside me, her voice soft but anchored in steel. "Madness is just a particularly inefficient form of persistence." She doesn't wait for a reaction—just checks the readout on the Coffin like she didn't just redefine everything. "We persisted," she says. "It's how breakthroughs happen." Her hand lands on mine—just for a moment —but it's enough.

I nod. Steady now.

Picasso steps back, expression unreadable. "Like the guy in *Shawshank* said—get busy living, or get busy dying."

My stomach knots. "Doesn't make it any less horrifying."

"He's not coming back." Sam says. "This way, maybe he dies for something that matters."

"Do it." Picasso meets my eye, one hand resting on his sidearm. "In six hours, Kirkland will order me to put Diego in there. I don't follow orders that get my people killed for nothing."

Dick lets out a sharp breath. "That sounds dangerously close to insubordination, Sergeant Major."

Picasso doesn't look at him. "Just a statement of fact."

Diego exhales, runs a hand across the Coffin's tungsten carbide shell, then rests his forehead against the black metal. Just for a heart-beat—long enough to twist my stomach.

I prime the pressure-fit hatch. It slides home with a clean, mechanical thunk.

Sabina inspects the seam, all clinical detachment, while Diego stands beside me.

I move to the console and queue the sequence. No ceremony. No countdown. Just a string of commands that might bend space without breaking it.

Sam hands me safety goggles. "Here," he says, like they're sunglasses.

I put them on, heart pounding in my throat.

Everyone moves to stations as Cassie starts the countdown.

Sabina fires up the Peeper, lips pressed thin. "Ready."

Diego lingers just outside the hazard zone, arms folded. He keeps glancing at the numbers, then the Coffin, then back at me—like if he stares hard enough, the laws of physics will take pity.

The floor vibrates as the capacitors reach threshold. The lights flicker. My throat gets tight. "Stabilizers online!" I shout and throw the switch. "Creating wormholes now."

The Einstein-Rosen Bridge Generator roars to life.

The Coffin vanishes. No flash. No sound. Just—gone. Eleven tons of tungsten ripped from our world like it was never real.

My breath catches. Maybe I imagined it.

The temperature in the lab drops ten degrees. An arc of static electricity jumps across the gap between the wormhole generator and the Coffin rig, making a loud pop.

Every hair on my arms stands up.

"Jump initiated," I say, my voice cracking. I clear my throat and check the console again. "The Coffin should reappear in nine seconds—assuming the bridge holds."

Sabina leans over the display, eyes narrowed. "Confirmed," she whispers. "The bridge appears stable."

No one breathes.

The silence stretches, thick and brittle.

"Did he make the jump?" Junior whispers, the pen in his hand finally still.

Sabina's fingers fly across the keyboard. "I don't know." Her voice is calm. Too calm. She turns toward me, and that's when I know something's wrong.

Phil jerks upright. "No... no. It's stuck—just like before. I warned you!"

I glance at Sabina, but she's busy yanking up system diagnostics. "It didn't make the jump—it's wedged mid-bridge," she says. "Right where tidal forces cancel out."

"Inside two black holes?" Sam says, sounding queasy. "Gotta be near absolute zero in there. Molecular motion halts. Cells freeze solid. Veins turn to glass. Even proteins start to unspool. It—"

"Sam," I cut in. "Not the time."

Diego hasn't moved. His eyes are locked on the empty space where the Coffin was, breath coming shallow. He takes a step forward, then thinks better of it.

Phil cowers in the corner, eyes searching for something none of us can see. "It's spawning black holes," he says. "If the bridge is open too long, the wormhole starts disintegrating." He holds up the remote. "Aborting!"

A noise like tearing silk rends the air, and the Coffin snaps back into our universe. The floor shudders. Frost billows up—sharp, metallic.

No one steps forward. The cold presses against our skin.

Sabina pulls on heat gloves and uses a lock-release rod to open the hatch.

The corpse is gone.

What's left is somehow worse.

Dick finds his voice. "Jesus H. Christ," he whispers, backing away. "What the hell did you do to him?"

Inside the Coffin, there's a pile of crystalline powder, glittering like crushed glass. The particles settle in slow motion. A pink residue clings to the Coffin's interior, sticky and warm. No face, no form. A memory ground down to molecular debris.

Sabina stares at the console, hands frozen mid-keystroke.

The wormhole generator groans—low and menacing. A tendril of smoke curls from the casing.

A hole appears in the far wall, neat as a laser drill. A shallow trench appears in the floor, stopping just short of Diego's boots. He jumps back, face pale.

Phil's the first to speak.

"We have to reopen the bridge," he says, voice hollow. "Force them back through. If we don't, the micro singularities will get trapped here. Spiraling around the Earth for millennia."

"Just tell me when to duck," Sam says, eyes still on the trench.

I take a step back, reaching for Cassie.

"Hurry!" Phil barks. "Before it's too late. Last time, they triggered a missile launch—two thousand miles away"

Sabina and I exchange a look. If he's right, we both know what comes next, and it's a proper shambles.

The stabilizer array screams. Sabina shouts over the noise, and Cassie slaps the emergency dampener. Sparks shoot out from the base of the machine.

And then the lab starts to tear itself apart.

A bulb explodes overhead. Phil yelps and dives behind the Peeper console, jabbing a finger toward the sparks like they're gunshots. "They're micro singularities," he shouts. "They'll chew through the walls, the floor, the—" He cuts off, rocking harder, voice raw. "They killed everyone in the lab except me."

"We're talking chain-reaction singularities," Sabina says, eyes locked on the generator. "Think bullets fired in every direction—only they never stop."

My brain stutters, trying to keep up. I remember what Phil said back in Florida—about the nuke. About all those people. I thought he was just unraveling.

God help me, he wasn't.

Diego turns to Phil, eyes narrowed, voice like a blade. "Your wormhole generator caused the first rogue nuke launch?"

Phil nods, eyes wide.

Diego swivels to me, disbelief boiling over. "And you started it up again, Matt?"

"I thought I fixed it," Cassie says, dropping into a chair. "I ran the numbers myself." She types, then slams her fist against the console. "I knew something was off—I just didn't want to admit it."

Another light explodes overhead. Glass shards rain down on us.

The lab collapses by inches—heat shimmering, conduits sparking, panic thick in the air. A capacitor lets go with a muffled *crack*, like a bone breaking inside the wall. Another ruptures, belching green goo that sizzles as it slithers across the floor.

Phil grabs my arm. "Open it up again! As short as possible. Call them back before we lose stasis. It's our only chance."

Cassie nods, her eyes on me. "Phil's right. We need to reopen the wormhole."

"Cass," I say. "You—"

"If I don't fix it, we all die." Her voice shakes—then turns to iron again. "I'm on it."

"No." I step in and pull her out of the chair. "I'll do it. Get out of the lab." I turn toward the frightened faces. "All of you, out!"

Junior doesn't wait for clarification. He lunges for the door, eyes wide, one arm shielding his head. Dick is on his heels. The door hisses shut behind them, leaving thickening smoke and the sound of machines failing.

When no one else moves, I thunder, "Get out! Now!"

Sam screams, raw and broken, and drops like someone pulled the bones out of him.

Cassie rushes towards him—towards the wormhole generator!

I catch her arm and pull her back hard. "Micro singularities," I snap. "Get out of the lab, Cass."

She struggles against my grip, her eyes locked on Sam. "Let me go, he needs—"

"I said no, Cassandra."

The look she gives me could crack granite. I don't flinch.

I round on Picasso. "Get her out of here."

Picasso grabs Cassie around the waist and pulls her away.

Sam moans.

Diego scrambles across the room and starts dragging Sam away by the feet.

Picasso's eyes flick to me.

Before I can respond, Cassie elbows him hard in the mouth and drops to Sam's side.

Phil yanks my sleeve, wild-eyed. "Now, Matt. Or we're hamburger."

As I start typing, Picasso crosses the lab and shoves the ballistic gel dummy. The thing weighs a ton, and it takes him two tries to get it off the gurney.

It hits the floor with a human-sounding thud.

Picasso grabs the cart and bumps it across the lab. He locks eyes with Diego, nods once, and they lift Sam onto the gurney.

Alarms go off down the hallway.

They wheel Sam across the lab—dodging sparks, jumping cables, avoiding coolant.

Cassie meets my eye as they go by, jaw set. She glances at the generator, then back—gaze fierce. "Stay alive," she says and follows them out.

I swallow and turn to Sabina, my throat tight. "You too, Sabina. Out."

She snorts. "Someone has to monitor the wormhole. Unless you've suddenly developed a taste for quantum entanglement and flaming death?"

Phil straightens from behind the console, face ashen. "I'm staying too," he mutters.

As they're lifting Sam over the last set of cables, I slide into the chair Cassie left and start typing, Phil standing behind me again.

Diagnostics flash red.

I override the safeties and punch in the numbers to realign the bridge.

I force my brain to double-check the string of figures. One wrong variable and the room goes.

And us with it.

I lock in the trajectory and throw the switch.

The wormhole generator shrieks. Everyone turns toward the sound.

"It's open again!" Sabina calls. "The black holes are snaking through."

Phil's voice slices through the noise. "Shut it down!" he shouts. "Before they boomerang back!"

I reach for the **ABORT** button.

A ceramic insulator the size of a toaster explodes in a burst of red-orange light—heat slamming into my chest like a punch.

The blast picks me up and throws me into Sabina. We hit the floor hard. Something cracks—sharp and deep. Might be the floor. Might be my ribs.

Sabina's lying next to me, gripping her shoulder. She doesn't swear often, but she does now, quiet and guttural. It lands harder than any explosion.

I look around. Everyone except Phil is sprawled on the floor. He dives toward the master breaker.

His hand finds the handle, and he slams it home.

An eerie red glow floods the lab.

I stagger over to the machine and check the output. The wormhole closed half a second before the machine shut down.

I collapse into the chair, the right side of my chest on fire.

Cassie is lying on the floor next to Sam, blood trickling from her cheek and shoulder.

"Cass?" I say.

She raises a hand. "I'm okay."

Picasso moans.

"Did you get them out?" Sam whispers. "All the black holes?"

"Yes," Sabina says as she tries to sit up. "They're gone."

I want to believe her. God, I do. But we don't understand this thing—not really. We're poking at the universe with a sharp stick and hoping it doesn't bite.

And this time, it nearly did.

We hear boots on concrete.

Loud. Deliberate. No rush.

Someone forces one of the lab doors open, and Dave Kirkland strolls in, floodlight in hand—bright enough to carve shadows from the smoke. Eight guys file in behind him. Paramilitary, earpieces, more flashlights. Dick and Junior scurry in behind them.

Kirkland checks his watch and shakes his head—almost like he knew this was going to happen.

Dick lurches forward like he was shoved from behind. "This isn't my fault," he blurts, gesturing toward the wreckage.

Kirkland surveys the damage. Sam lying on the gurney with a hole in his leg. Diego on the floor next to him, blood dripping from his ear. Cassie, a red stain spreading across her clothes, crouching over Picasso. The smoking machine. The melted console. The pinkish smear inside the Coffin.

Then his eyes shift—to me and Sabina. A flicker of something passes over his face—like he's deciding who's salvageable and who gets buried with the rubble.

"Funding's pulled," he says, like he's canceling a lunch order. "Whatever this was, it's over."

No one speaks. The air tastes like electronics and blood. Phil steps behind me, breathing hard. My throat burns.

"Matt Hudson," Kirkland says, as if he's reading a name off a list. "Comes with us."

I feel Sabina shift beside me.

"Along with Sabina Lovelace," he continues. "And Phillip Wheeler."

Phil stiffens. "What for? Where are you taking me?"

Kirkland ignores him. "Get 'em out of here."

One of the soldiers steps forward. "Come with me, Dr. Wheeler."

Phil bolts—legs pumping, coat flaring. Two of Kirkland's men dart after him, a beat too late.

I half expect them to drag Phil back by the collar.

"Leave him," Kirkland says, flicking his fingers. "We're not running a day care."

One soldier hesitates.

"Just the other two."

Dick perks up like a dog hearing the can opener. "If you need someone to keep an eye on Hudson and Lovelace, sir, I'm your man."

Kirkland doesn't even blink. "Fine. Help my men load the Peeper." He turns away.

Dick scurries out of the lab.

"I've got injured people," I say. "They need medical attention."

Kirkland gestures toward the door. "Then take them. The rest of you are free to go."

"Go where?" Picasso says from the floor and then adds, "Sir."

Kirkland shrugs. "Not my problem."

I glance at Cassie. Her eyes are wide. Her mouth opens like she's going to say something, but she clamps it shut again.

Smart move. Don't give him anything.

"Get 'em to the chopper," Kirkland barks, then adds under his breath, "Should've bulldozed this vanity bunker years ago."

The men escorting us aren't rough, but they're practiced. Professional. One takes my arm. Not hard. Just enough to let me know I don't get a choice.

I turn as they lead us away. Cassie kneels between Sam and Picasso, sleeve blood-soaked, eyes feral. Diego is behind them, mouth set in a grim line.

Sabina just stares ahead as they march us out.

We traipse over the broken pipes, the melted console, the scorch marks.

My legs are jelly. My chest is on fire.

The guards keep us moving.

Sabina stumbles but doesn't say a word.

The chaos a few minutes ago feels like a fever dream. All that's left is sterile light, rubber soles on concrete, and a faint hum.

I wonder what's worse: what we left behind or what's waiting out there.

We round the last corner, and a janitor shuffles into view—wiry, hunched, mop in one hand, a bucket on wheels in the other. He's shuffling like someone's granddad got lost in the wrong building.

"Watch it!" one of the guards barks.

The old man startles, trips, and goes down right in front of me. The mop handle clatters, the bucket rolls away. Water sloshes across the floor.

A groan rises behind me. "Jesus—"

I shake off the escorts and bend over, my ribs complaining. "You okay?" I say, and help him to his feet.

He grips my shoulder as he stands—stronger than I expect. For a split second, his eyes lock with mine. Clear. Intense. Ancient.

"You're the fulcrum, Matt," he whispers. "Lean the wrong way, and the future breaks." His mouth barely moves, but his eyes say everything.

I nod.

He turns away and picks up the mop. "Sorry," he growls loud enough for the guards to hear. "Trick knee."

I get back to my feet.

Kirkland's men pull me forward, grumbling about "idiots" and "no damn protocols."

But I don't hear them.

That wasn't a warning. It was a torch.

And it's burning my hand.

Madders' Second Log: Entry 11

Target: Diego Nadales
Nexus: Warm Springs Military Complex
Chrono Tag: That Afternoon

South American blackout enters day 23. No international response mobilized.

Kirkland Enterprises completes takeover of US media outlets. KE autonomous drone hubs fully operational worldwide.

Matt Hudson terminated from Warm Springs project. Spacetime bridge activation probability approaches zero. Implications catastrophic.

The lights in the medical bay hum with the same low, anxious energy rattling in my bones—like they know I shouldn't be here.

Sam lies on a couch connected to the medical robot: drip in his arm, wires on his chest, bandage on his thigh. His face is pale, sweat-soaked hair stuck to his forehead. I watch the rise and fall of his chest until my lungs sync with his—proof we're both still alive.

Across the room, Cassie sits on a bench, wincing as Picasso cleans the gash on her cheek. He moves with unnerving grace, like a man who's seen too much blood and learned to whistle through it.

Maybe that's the trick: survive enough loss, and muscle memory takes over.

Too bad it doesn't work for guilt.

"Where'd you learn field medicine?" Cassie asks, voice tight.

"My ex-wife was a trauma doc," he says, wiping away blood with gauze. "Our first date was inside a field clinic. Got certified in combat triage so we could deploy together. Figured it'd come in handy either way."

Cassie rolls her eyes. "Romantic."

"She left me for an orthopedic surgeon," he adds, deadpan. "Silver lining? I can patch up a gunshot wound in a speeding jeep by moonlight."

"That your pickup line? 'Gunshot wounds by moonlight'?"

He shrugs. "Worked fine—until someone expected me to stick around."

"Handy, brave, and emotionally unavailable," she mutters. "Perfect."

He dabs antiseptic. "Don't fall too hard. I'm iffy at follow-up care."

"Good thing I won't need any."

His mouth twitches. "Shame. I make a mean grilled cheese." He presses a butterfly bandage into place with surprising gentleness. "You'll probably scar. Make you look tough. Like a kickboxer."

"Should have been one."

He smiles and touches his swollen lip. "Could have fooled me."

"Sorry," she says. "Next time, don't treat me like I'm six."

"Won't happen again." He gives a half-smile, his gaze lingering on her mouth.

The intimacy feels dangerous. Like a spark near oxygen.

I force myself to look away.

"What are we going to do?" Phil says. "Now that Matt and Sabina are gone." He's cross-legged in the corner, scribbling on a yellow notepad.

"Stay here," Picasso says. "Ride it out."

"For how long?" Phil's voice is tight.

"As long as it takes."

"I can't do this again," Phil mumbles without looking up. "I just can't."

Picasso turns back to Cassie. "Let's have a look at that shoulder." He cuts off her bloody sleeve, dumps saline over the gashes, and starts pulling slivers of ceramic out with tweezers.

I lean against the doorframe, lungs raw, legs trembling, and watch Picasso work. The hum of the vents, the clink of the metal—it's too loud.

The world feels brittle.

Or maybe I do.

An hour ago, I was the expendable payload. Now the launch system's slag and I'm still breathing.

Except every time I close my eyes, I feel it. The heat. The gut punch. The consequences of toying with tech we don't understand.

The worst part? I don't know if I'm relieved... or disappointed.

I glance around the room—injured bodies, stained walls, canned air. I should be doing something that matters. Instead, I'm dead weight.

The old man's words circle back like flies on a carcass: *Nothing out there saves her. For us, the only way forward is the Coffin.*

If he's right, any hope of saving Isabel is gone. And everything

I've suffered—the lies, the blood, the loneliness—is just noise in someone else's time loop.

A groan escapes my lips, low and bitter.

Picasso looks up. "Sit down, Diego. Last thing I need is your skull cracking open on my shift." He waits for me to collapse into a folding chair. "Here." He tosses me a bottle of water. "Hydrate."

I catch it and drink deep. "Thanks."

He nods and glances around the room. "Government comms have been down for a week, but word is, things are unraveling topside."

Phil scribbles on his notepad so hard the paper tears.

Cassie shifts, voice low. "What do you mean *unraveling?*"

The marine exhales. "Confirmed attacks on civilian targets: Power, food, water treatment. Looks coordinated. Ugly."

"Coordinated?" I lean back. "Actual strikes? Not just chaos?"

He nods. "Targeted. Precise. Deadly."

"Goddamnit," I say and fire the empty bottle toward the trash. "Isabel could be out there alone."

"Take it easy," he says. "Last I heard, she's inside Kirkland's second biodome." He nods at Cassie. "Probably the same place Matt and Sabina are headed."

Cassie flexes her shoulders. "How do you know about the attacks if your comms are down?"

"Encrypted backup channels. Started lighting up a few days ago."

Cassie frowns. "And now?"

"As of yesterday, leadership's gone quiet. Priorities have shifted. Some commanders stayed with the troops. Everyone else ran for a bunker."

Cassie sighs. "Looks like we're the latter."

Picasso grunts. "Timing matters, Cass. We got lucky."

Phil snorts.

Picasso ignores him. "Unless someone bombs the mountain, we'll survive." He tapes gauze around Cassie's arm. His fingers brush her skin. Barely a pause. Almost clinical. But she meets his eyes for half a second too long.

I drop my gaze, throat tight. I know that look: relief and fear braided together. It's the kind of moment Isabel and I used to have, when silence says more than words. I miss her smart mouth, her strong hands, the way she rolls her eyes when I say something cheesy.

I drift. Not seeing the room. Just frayed edges of a life I let go... Isabel and me. The cabin. Wind rattling windows. Snow falling. Her icy toes pressed against my chest like she wasn't doing it on purpose. The smell of pine trees and that tuna casserole she burned.

Maybe we'd still be there if I hadn't made so many mistakes.

Instead, you traded that future for an underground bunker, a broken time machine, and some crazy old man pulling the strings.

Picasso taps the counter twice. "Okay, Phil. Your turn."

"I can't do this again," Phil grumbles. "I just spent a year surviving on stale chips and warm soda, and I can't do it again."

For once, I envy him. My apocalypse had stillborn babies and no do-overs.

The silence swells, heavy with the grim absurdity of being locked inside an underground tomb while the world dies above us.

Somewhere, a vent rattles to life, filling the silence with recycled air.

I rub my hands together, suddenly cold—the kind of cold that sinks into your chest when you realize no one's coming to save you. No lifeline. No cavalry. No hope.

Yeah, well, there's no chance I'm rotting inside this cave for the rest of my life.

Tomorrow, I'm going after Isabel.

"What, exactly, are we dealing with topside?" Sam says, voice shaky. "Some sort of invasion?" The med-bot didn't find any permanent damage to his leg but inserted an IV for pain. By the looks of it, he could use a higher dosage.

Picasso glances at him, expression unreadable. "Yeah. But not people. Drones." Always the poker face. Always five moves ahead. I hate how calm he is. "And definitely not civilian-grade."

I straighten, my pulse spiking.

Please don't let them be Isabel's.

"Do they know who's controlling them?" I ask, trying to keep my voice level. "China? Russia?"

Picasso shakes his head. "The anti-biodome attacks escalated. Kirkland hit back harder." He peels off his gloves and drops them on the tray.

Cassie scowls. "He's sending drone swarms after civilians?"

"It started with ragtag militias," he says. "People attacking the domes with whatever they had—rocks, Molotovs, garden tools. At first, that's who Kirkland targeted. But it's gone beyond that now—on both sides. Anyone inside a dome's a traitor. Guppies, they call them. All clean water and sealed glass. Anyone outside is a threat."

"And Kirkland won't stop there," comes a raspy voice from the hallway. It slices through my chest like a blade.

I jolt to my feet, and we all turn.

It's him.

The man who said Isabel would die if I didn't get in the time machine—the one that just exploded.

And somehow, he looks worse. Clothes torn and dirty, face covered in gray stubble, eyes bloodshot.

Future-me steps into the medical bay, hands raised like he's bracing for impact.

Cassie gasps. Picasso reaches for his sidearm. Phil's pencil stills.

Sam props himself up on his elbows. "Either I'm high on painkillers, or we've got a time loop situation."

The old man scans the room. "I'm sorry all of you were hurt." He meets my gaze, one eye twitching. "At least no one was killed."

"If that's the good news," Sam mutters, "I'm gonna need more morphine."

Cassie hushes him.

Picasso clears his throat, his hand hovering near his weapon. "How'd you get inside?"

"Followed him," the old man says, nodding at me. "Fire alarm helped."

"You're welcome," Sam deadpans.

Phil leans back like he's watching a feedback loop spiral out of control.

The old man shifts his weight. "I ran the numbers. That explosion wasn't in the top six outcomes. It wasn't supposed to happen."

I cross my arms, heart still pounding. "Let me get this straight. You show up out of nowhere, forbid me to go after Isabel, and almost get all of us killed because your calculations were off?"

He winces. "In my timeline, the bridge came online without any hiccups. I misjudged how far along you were."

I step closer. "Misjudged?" My mouth tastes like blood.

Cassie scoffs. "You expected the spacetime bridge to work?"

"Yes." He lifts a hand. "I didn't anticipate this level of divergence. We had a smooth ramp-up. I assumed—"

"You assumed?" My laugh cuts hard. "You nearly killed Sam. Disfigured Cassie. Gave everyone concussions. All for nothing?"

"I told you," he snaps. "I thought the bridge would work."

"Well, you were wrong," I say, heat rising. "And while we're at it, why are you stalking me? Dropping cryptic orders? Pretending to be a hero while you hide in the shadows?"

His fists clench. "In my timeline, I failed. Promised myself I wouldn't let it happen again. Wouldn't let her die needlessly."

I glare at him. "Then why the hell aren't you the one diving in to undo your mistakes?"

He exhales, shoulders sagging. "Because my jump window's gone. I'm here on fumes and borrowed time. You're still upstream— you can change things. I can't."

"So you screw everything up, dump it on me, and vanish?" My voice is too loud, but I can't seem to rein it in. I grab his arm and pull him closer. "That your idea of redemption, old man?"

"I'm trying to give you the second chance I never had," he says. "To save her." He glances at the others. "And everyone else." He looks down at where I'm still gripping his arm. "Feel free to throw it all away."

I release him, my hand shaking.

He stands there, little more than skin, bones and regret.

I slump back into the chair. "So what now?"

He swallows. "I don't know. But I came to warn you. About the bots."

Sam clears his throat. "Bit late for that, Gramps."

Picasso folds his arms. "Who are you?"

The old man lifts his chin toward me. "Him. From another timeline."

The metal tray at Cassie's elbow clatters to the floor.

No one moves.

The words hang in the air—heavy, invisible, impossible.

The old man turns to Picasso. "In my universe, the last biodome is failing. The killer drones are about to breach the walls. Isa—Isabelle—came up with a way to use the time machine. She had Madders shut down everything—life support, lights, comms—so I could jump. And, believe me, she knew the cost."

Something in my gut twists.

I grab him by the shirt. "You left her there? To die in the dark? Alone?"

"She insisted." He says it like that's supposed to make it okay. "Said if I didn't, none of this would matter."

"None of what would matter?" Cassie whispers.

"Our actions." He presses a hand to his face. "Not hers. Not yours. Not any of ours."

I let go of him, hands curling into fists. "Doesn't make it right."

"No," he says. "It doesn't."

He turns to me, face pale. "I see her every time I close my eyes. Hear her voice when I'm falling asleep. Smell her hair. Every corner I turn, every door I open, every goddamn morning I wake—I die a little when I realize she's not here."

"Could she still be alive?" I swallow hard. "In your timeline?"

He scrubs a hand across his mouth. "She was dying of a disease we used to cure with a pill." His voice cracks. "But she was still breathing when I left."

Picasso clears his throat. "Funny thing about sacrifice—it never feels noble when you're the last one standing."

The old man nods.

Picasso offers a hand. "I'm Picasso." He introduces everyone else.

"Should we call you Diego?" Cassie asks.

He glances over at me, shakes his head. "This universe already has its allotment." He wobbles a little, and Picasso grabs his arm, hands him a bottle of water.

"Thanks," the old man says. "Been a rough year." He sighs. "I guess you can call me Gramps. Sam, here, seems to think it fits."

I nudge the chair toward him.

He sinks into it like the bones are barely holding him together.

"If you came from the future," Sam says, "how far back in time did you jump?"

"As much as we had power for: forty-odd years."

Sam laughs. "Holy *Wrinkle in Time*."

"Isa hoped it'd be enough." Gramps takes a long drink of water, then scans our faces. "Guess it depends on whether you finish what she started."

"What about the bots?" Phil starts scribbling again, slow and deliberate. "You said you wanted to tell us about the bots."

"They didn't start as killers," Gramps says. "Isa built them to help us prevent famine. But Dave couldn't leave it alone. Made them smarter. Faster. More lethal. First, for protection. Then for enforcement. Finally for extermination."

He scuffs the tile with his muddy high-top.

"We thought it was a bug in the software. Dave blamed Isabelle. Locked her out of the code. Said she was unstable. Exhausted.

Burned out." He turns toward Cassie. "Everyone but Matt believed him."

She nods, her eyes glossy.

His voice tightens. "So when Dave took over, we didn't question it. We helped."

A tear slips down his cheek. "I should have believed her. Defended her."

I can see the pain—the guilt—he lives with, but I can't stop the thought.

I would have fought for her.

Cassie's voice is small. "What did my dad do? After she was banished?"

Gramps swallows. "Said we'd lost the plot. That we let a snake in. Then he told us he had cancer."

Cassie stiffens. "Cancer? How old was he? What kind?"

He studies her. "You're his daughter, right? Cassie."

She nods.

"I don't remember the details. Just that he died shortly after. I'm sorry."

She turns to Picasso. "I need to talk to my dad."

He places a hand on her shoulder. "I'll see what I can do."

"So what happened to your Isabelle?" Sam asks.

"Oh, I kicked a few chairs and called Dave an ass, but in the end —" He presses his lips together and turns away. "In the end, Kirkland took over her work. And we let him. Helped him. Patted him on the back." His mouth twists. "Billions of bots under Dave's command—protecting the domes, tending the crops, guarding the transports." He exhales. "Until the resources dried up, and the swarms turned on us."

"Christ," I whisper.

"They were relentless," he says. "Every scrap of meat, bone and blood. The killerbots harvested us like we were livestock."

Silence.

Cassie is the first to speak. "And we're supposed to stop that with flashlights and canned peas?"

"You stop it with whatever you have," Gramps says. "Because every second you hesitate, the future locks in tighter. In this timeline, Kirkland's moving much faster. And there's no organized resistance. Just me. And you."

Phil clears his throat. "Why send you? Why not someone with… more answers? Or less gray hair?"

Gramps gives a mirthless laugh. "Because there wasn't anyone else. Isa and I were the last two humans alive."

Phil shrinks and scribbles faster

Gramps shifts toward me. "You need to use the time machine."

"That sucks," Sam says. "Considering we just torched it."

"Fix it," Gramps says. "There's no other way. I've seen what happens when we wait too long."

I shake my head, my throat tight. "This again?"

"It's the only way."

"Why?"

He pokes my chest. "Because you're the one who has to change things."

I snort. "Just great. So I jump into another universe. Then what—hand out pamphlets? Teach killerbots ethics? Murder Kirkland?"

"I don't know," he says. "But you have to go. Like I had to. Like Tego. Like James. If the chain breaks, everyone dies."

"Who the hell are Tego and James?"

He waves me off. "Figure it out, Sparky."

"He could be right," Cassie says. "Sabina saw glimpses of Diego in the Peeper. He was everywhere."

"Fix the machine. Send Diego," Gramps says. "That's it."

Cassie looks at Sam, then back at Gramps. "We didn't build it. We helped, but… we need my dad.'

"You're wrong," Gramps says. "You cracked the jump equations. Stabilized the bridge."

Cassie blinks. "I did?"

"You did." He points at Phil. "You saved thousands with a jerry-rigged remote and nerves of steel."

Phil stops fidgeting and sits up straighter.

He turns to Picasso. "And you—" He takes a deep breath and lets it out slowly. "You held the line when the swarm hit. Sacrificed yourself to get everyone through the tunnel. I don't even know your real name, but in my timeline, none of us would have made it without you."

Picasso raises an eyebrow. Cassie squeezes his hand.

"And I made the coffee," Sam says, lying on his back with his eyes on the ceiling.

"Hurry up and get better, Sam. You'll discover how to control jump points using temporal slip."

"Woo-hoo." Sam gives a weak pump of his fist.

Gramps turns to me. "Some of us died to keep the chain from breaking," he says. "Don't waste their sacrifice."

I square up. "While we build a time machine out of zip ties, what are you going to do?"

"Hand you the duct tape." His voice is hollow. "Then I'm going home."

I narrow my eyes. "What about Isabel?"

He blinks.

"*My* Isabel," I say. "The one still alive and waiting for me. You want me to walk away from her?"

He looks gutted. "It's the only way to save her."

"Save her from what?"

He shakes his head. "He didn't tell me. Maybe he didn't know."

"Who told you?"

"You did," he says. "Another you."

I groan.

"I trust him. He saved your Isabel the night of the fire—and it cost him his life."

My breath catches.

The man under the piano.

"Why don't you go?" I spit out. "You've got nothing to lose."

He sighs. "It doesn't work like that, and you know it. I did what I came to do."

"You came all this way to give up?"

Gramps shakes his head. "I came all this way to make sure you don't."

"So you're just gonna hand off the baton and walk away?"

He winces. "This is your universe. Your Isabel. Surely you can understand that."

I get to my feet. "You stood by while they destroyed her. And then you left her to die alone?"

His eyes go glassy. "So don't be me."

I back away from him. "We may share a name," I say, "but I'm nothing like you."

His voice shakes. "You turned your back when she needed you most. Pushed her into Kirkland's arms. So don't lecture me."

I open my mouth—and nothing comes out.

Because he's right.

He exhales. "You and me? We don't get to fix the past. But maybe we can stop screwing up the future." He stares at his shoes for a second, regrouping. "When the bridge is fixed, I'm going home. To bury Isa. And maybe lock the door behind me."

I nod, slow and stiff, like the truth finally found a place to rest.

The machine next to Sam hisses to life again, startling us.

"So," Cassie says, making a wide gesture with her hands. "What the hell do we do now?"

"You do what I couldn't," Gramps says. "Help Diego jump. Not to rewrite the past—but to change the future."

I shake my head. "The machine is dead in the water. Who's gonna fix it?"

"They are," he says, looking at the others. "You have to trust them. Break the cycle. That's what Isa wanted. That's why I'm here."

The silence is a cliff. One wrong move—one wrong word—and we fall to our deaths.

"That's how you save your Isabel," he says, almost a whisper, "and everyone else. It's the only thread left that hasn't snapped."

From the hallway, there's a soft clink—like metal on tile.

A gray blur scampers in and launches onto Sam's chest.

He yelps—then laughs.

"Benny! You found me!"

Phil blinks. "That better not be a rodent."

"It's a chinchilla," Sam says. "They're smarter than dogs."

Cassie lets out a laugh. "You trained it to follow you?"

"Rescue missions only," Sam says, petting the fluff ball.

The old man stares at the chinchilla like it's radioactive, then mumbles, "I gotta get outta here before it's too late."

Picasso picks up the fallen tray and wipes it off. "Okay, people. Hudson's out. The machine's gutted. Where do we go from here?"

"Fix the spacetime bridge," Gramps says. "Nothing else matters."

Cassie shakes her head. "Can't."

Phil stops scribbling for a moment. "Not gonna happen."

Sam shrugs. "That thing can't even toast bread."

"Even if we replaced all the parts," Cassie says, "we still wouldn't know what's wrong with it."

Gramps straightens. "Maybe someone else can help. Someone who knew how to bend time without breaking it."

"Who?" we all say.

"Years ago, Isa built an AI based on Matt Hudson."

Cassie goes still.

He turns to her. "It contained his memories. His instincts. His genius. The construct was built using Eden-17's Guardian AI. He called himself Madders."

Cassie looks like the floor just vanished. "Based on my dad?"

"Yes. And Madders wasn't just a copy," Gramps says. "He learned. Adapted. Protected us. Kept thousands alive when the dome started failing."

Cassie touches her collarbone. "What happened to him?"

"When the end came," Gramps says, "he shut himself down.

Transferred the last of the dome's power to the bridge. So I could jump."

Picasso rests his hand on Cassie's shoulder.

She shifts her weight. "So he's gone."

Gramps hesitates. "The dome ran on geothermal—until that failed. If Madders figured out how to switch to solar, maybe one day..."

Picasso glances up "The lights come back on."

Gramps nods. "And he'd have access to a Peeper. A good one."

Phil sets his pencil down. "Say this Madders guy tells us how to fix the machine. Then what?"

The old man doesn't blink. "Then you do what I didn't."

His words hang there—fragile as a spider's web.

He turns to me. "You jump. Before we all burn."

Madders' Second Log:
Entry 12

Target: Isabel Sanborn
Nexus: Eden-2 Biodome
Chrono Tag: Six Weeks Later • October

Presidential executive order declares impeachment
unconstitutional. Congress disbands.

Kirkland Enterprises seizes control of White
House and Capitol Hill via microdrone swarms.

Xeno Diego emergence disrupts projection paths,
creating chaotic but favorable branches.

The apartment is quiet.

I have been tossing and turning every night for weeks now, as Yuki's factories churn out my bots. At first, it was anxiety over whether they'd actually work, whether I could pull off what I'd promised. But lately, it's something else. Ever since I found out about Dave's plans, I haven't been able to sleep well.

Now I see the biodomes for what they are: fortresses disguised as sanctuaries.

The tech that was meant to save us now wants us dead. The microdrones aren't just for pollination—they can be programmed to kill. And Dave has every intention of using them to defend his domes, no matter who gets caught in the crossfire.

A week ago, he'd called me into his office and cued up a series of surveillance feeds, each time-stamped within the past week.

Diego, alive.

Diego, hauling equipment through a tunnel—walls damp, concrete stained, steel beams rusted to hell.

Diego, hunched over a table in a lab held together with spare parts and duct tape.

He wasn't alone.

One was a kid—tall with a shock of red hair. The other man was older, hollowed out, gripping a remote like it mattered more than breathing. His thumb tapped and tapped—nervous, mechanical, like he didn't know what else to do with his hands. Or his fear.

But it wasn't just the people that got me.

It was the thing visible behind them.

A machine—huge, cylindrical, bleeding wires and cables like it had torn itself open. Some were scorched, others clamped and taped like someone was trying to keep it from tearing itself open again. A thin flicker pulsed from its guts. It lit the walls with jagged shadows.

I couldn't stop staring at it.

Because if someone so much as breathed wrong, it looked like the whole thing would blow.

"I shouldn't even be showing you this," Dave had said, his voice smooth, deliberate. The contrast was jarring—calm words layered over a tangle of sparking wires and half-melted circuits, like a man reading off a dinner menu while the kitchen burned down around him. "As you know, comms are still unreliable outside the domes, and it took some serious strings to get access to these feeds. If anyone finds out, it'll put me in a difficult position, but I thought you deserved to know he's alive. Once he finishes mopping up, I'll send a team to bring him in."

Whatever they're doing, it sure as hell isn't recovery work. Cleanup crews don't tinker with unstable machines that look ready to explode.

Diego's working to stop Dave.

Relief flooded into my chest. And shame followed just as fast.

Diego didn't wait. He saw the truth and acted. Me? I clung to the lie that the world would fix itself.

If Diego is still fighting, then maybe—just maybe—it isn't too late.

"Unfortunately," Dave continued, "there's no way to contact him —other than sending out a tactical strike unit. But like I promised, he'll have a place waiting for him in Eden-2."

I barely heard him.

Just before the feed cut out, I saw movement in the shadows—an old man, half-hidden behind cables and equipment. He turned just enough for the light to catch his face, for me to see his dark eyes, the familiar set of his jaw.

I knew that face. The old man from Denver. Grief-carved. Ghost-struck.

Then the screen went black.

Diego is alive.

And Dave is lying.

Again.

I keep telling myself recovery takes time. But the longer it drags on, the more deliberate it feels.

Why are the biodomes the only places with power?

This isn't just the aftermath of a collapse—it feels intentional.

And Dave is at the center of it.

That's a hell of an accusation.

But the more I think about it, the better it fits. He's not just surviving, he's taking over—and making sure no one can stop him.

And me? I've been helping him do it.

The realization hits like a slap to the face.

How many warnings did I need? The old man. The note from future me: *I don't know it yet, but we need to stop Dave.* The vanishing shells.

I brushed them off, let myself believe I had time.

I have to find Diego before it's too late.

I slip out of bed and sit up, the tiles cold on my bare feet.

The clock on the nightstand shifts. Five minutes until my plan falls apart.

I put on my sneakers and stand, pulling my bag out from under the bed.

Now or never.

The hallway is dark, silent. My pulse quickens as I stuff two pillows under my KE logo blanket. The next patrol will pass soon, and if I'm not gone before—

A shadow moves behind me, and I turn.

Lani is standing in the doorway, arms crossed, her silhouette framed by moonlight.

"Going somewhere?" Her hand presses against her lower back like she's been standing too long. Even in the dim light, I can see the sweat beading at her temple.

I hide the bag behind my back. "Couldn't sleep," I mumble, keeping my voice level.

She flips on the light. Her gaze drops to my feet. "Probably because you're wearing shoes."

I glance at the clock. Two minutes left. "Get out of my way, Lani."

She plants herself in front of the door. "What's the plan—wander out into dystopia with snacks and a flashlight?"

"At least I'm doing something," I snap, stepping forward and pushing her out of the way. "Which is more than I can say for you."

She huffs. "You're delusional."

"And you're what? Dave's pet? Whether or not you want to admit it, Lani, you know he's lying to you about your brother."

"Don't bring Dave into this," she says, her fists clenching. "He *is* looking. It's just taking time." Her eyes betray her doubt.

I take a step closer. "The same way he's looking for Diego? Here's a pro tip, Lani: if his upper lip is twitching, he's lying."

She snatches my bag and dumps it on the bed. The contents scatter—snack bars, water flask, notebook, and a drone jammer I nicked from Sophie's office. She gestures at the pile with a bitter laugh. "This? This is your big escape plan?"

"Of course not," I say, stuffing the items back in. "I was planning to call my fairy godmother on the way out."

She snorts. "It's suicide."

"I'd rather die on my feet than live on my knees." I glance at her mouth.

Her breath catches—a crack in her armor. Her hand slides across her baby bump. "Dave loves me."

I hesitate, guilt creeping in. She doesn't deserve this, doesn't deserve to be dragged into my mess. But this isn't about fairness. It's about survival—for both of us.

"Help me, Lani," I say, softening my tone. "And I'll help you find Kai. I swear it."

She laughs. "You swear you'll help me? With what? Your brilliant survival skills?"

"With this." I flip my notebook open.

Her eyes scan the pages—maps, notes, patrol schedules, routes through the biodome. "So you had no intention of staying here and helping us," she says, her voice barely above a whisper. "You were just using Dave."

"Like he's using me."

The clock ticks louder. Patrol-drone glow creeps across the window.

"Lani," I say, my voice tight. "If you don't trust me, fine. But you must suspect I'm right about Dave. If you want to find your brother, help me get into Dave's office. We can take a peek at his files and leave without anyone seeing us. At least then you'll know the truth."

Her gaze flickers to the notebook, then back to me. "You're serious?"

I nod. "You can be back in an hour. Call security when you get up in the morning and report me missing."

She exhales sharply, her hands clenching at her sides. "And if you're right—which you're not—how are you planning to get out of the biodome? All the airlocks have armed guards."

I stare at her for a few seconds. "With Dave's car." I shrug. "And the exit tunnel."

Her eyes get big. "How do you know about the tunnel?"

Before I can answer, the faint beep of a sensor breaks through the stillness. My stomach lurches. I grab the notebook and stuff it back into my bag.

"No time. I'll explain on the way. Do it for Kai and your grandmother."

She hesitates, one hand drifting to her stomach. "Isabel—"

"Now, Lani. Grab what you need and let's go."

The drone's light sweeps past the window, and I pull her through the door before she can change her mind.

Two minutes later, we step out of the apartment building, and the biodome stretches out around us, a small city beneath a glass dome. Because it's dark now, the glass is perfectly transparent. Stars glitter above, and the moon casts a silvery glow over the hedges lining the sidewalks. Their manicured edges feel unnervingly precise, as though the entire scene is designed to be photographed.

Above us, the control tower at the center of the biodome looms, its circular observation windows glowing faintly in the darkness. It's manned day and night, the eyes within capable of scanning every corner of this artificial world. Faint clicks and the low hum of unseen machinery drift down, like the tower itself is alive, its gaze never faltering.

A shiver crawls up my neck. They're always watching, listening—every word, every move. I've heard whispers about what they do with the recordings, how some of the footage is passed around like trophies by the kind of men who lust for power.

We crouch behind a cluster of citrus trees—all of them pollinated by my bees. The faint scent of oranges fills the cool night air, the sweet smell of success.

My stomach knots.

Dave is turning your babies into monsters.

Ahead, another patrol drone comes into view, its single red eye scanning the area in lazy arcs.

"According to my observations," I whisper, tracking its path, "it'll move to the next sector in two minutes."

Lani shoots me a sharp look. "This is your plan? Dodging security drones? You're gonna get us thrown in jail."

I shrug, hands on my hips. "If this is too dangerous for you, feel free to bail."

She makes a face.

"Besides," I say, lowering my voice, "you can always tell them I forced you." I point a finger-gun at her. "Come to the dark side. We have stale granola."

She rolls her eyes, but the corner of her mouth twitches.

"Here." I take her badge out of my pocket. "You forgot this."

She shakes her head. "It won't get us into Dave's office building, if that's what you think. They don't even let cleaning staff inside after hours."

"Exactly," I say.

She raises an eyebrow but doesn't comment.

The drone's hum gets louder.

We freeze, breathing shallow, as it passes over us and drifts toward the next sector.

I poke her with my finger gun. "Go."

She blocks me with her arm. "Wait until it gets to that lamppost. It has blind spots under direct light.'

I hesitate, then nod.

"Now," Lani hisses.

We sprint across the grass engineered to produce extra oxygen, my heart pounding with every step. It's farther than I thought across the park, and when the shadow of a hedge wall appears, I collapse into it, struggling to catch my breath.

"Yeah, yeah," I say as she watches me gasp for air. "I've been skipping leg day."

Directly above us, the control tower's windows glow like the eyes of a predator—but the guard walking the circular observation deck continues on.

"Over there," Lani whispers, pointing at another drone, and I nod.

Dave's office building looms on the other side of a small courtyard with a now-lifeless fountain at its center, its white facade reflecting the moonlight.

Inside his office building I can see the elevator. A badge scanner glows on the panel between the doors.

First, worry about getting inside the building.

We wait for the drone to leave the sector.

I check my watch. Two minutes till the cleaning bot arrives. "Follow me," I whisper.

We circle around the building, staying in the shadow of the hedge. A cleaning bot trundles along the sidewalk, its wheels squeaking as it turns toward a small service door. I inch closer, heart pounding, Lani right behind me. The robot pauses in front of the access door and scans its ID chip. The lock disengages with a click, and a small panel slides open. It's just wide enough for the robot to slip through.

I dart forward, catching the edge of the door with my shoe before it latches. I hold the panel open as Lani shimmies through—even pregnant, she makes it look easy. She gets to her feet on the other side and holds it open for me.

"Thanks," I whisper as I squirm through. It's harder than it looks.

Once inside, I manage to get to my feet without embarrassing myself further.

She puts her finger to her lips, and we press our backs against the wall in a dark alcove, looking for cameras.

There aren't any.

I lean closer. "What floor is his office on?"

"The top one," she says. "This way to the stairs."

"Stairs?" I say, already thinking about how to hot-wire the elevator.

She shrugs. "Beats hot-wiring the elevator."

I can't tell if she's kidding or psychic.

The corridor beyond is dim, with cables and pipes running along the ceiling. We watch the cleaning bot trundle down the hallway and disappear through a flap in the wall.

So much for getting on the elevator with the bot.

We reach the service elevator. The panel blinks an angry red.

"Takes a physical key," Lani whispers. "Should've brought my bag of tricks."

That makes me raise an eyebrow. "Next idea?"

"Stairs," she says like it's a threat.

We find the door. She cracks it open, peeks, shuts it with a low whistle.

"What?"

"Lots of cameras," she says. "And the door to the stairs doesn't have a handle. Exit only."

I shrug. "So we improvise."

She huffs. "Can't wait to see that."

At the end of the corridor, Lani yanks open a custodian's closet. Inside, we're greeted by a jumble of toilet paper and mops. A ring of keys hanging on a hook catches my eye. They're labeled in tiny, precise handwriting, and one of them reads 'Service Elevator.'

"Bingo," we say together.

With the keys in hand, we head back to the elevator. I slide the key into the slot and turn it. The panel lights up green, and the doors slide open with a slight mechanical whine.

Relief floods through me as we step inside. Lani presses the button for the penthouse.

The ascent is smooth, though my pulse goes up with every soft ding. When the doors slide open, we're greeted by the polished sterility of the Executive Floor—and a huge bouquet of real flowers.

Lani sneezes into her elbow.

"Cameras?" I whisper.

She shakes her head. "As far as I know, they don't have any on this floor."

I let out a huff. "Funny how the people at the top don't want anyone watching them."

I follow her down the wide hallway and up to the corner suite.

She uses her badge to unlock the suite, then again to get into Dave's office.

"Won't they be able to trace your ID?" I ask.

She shakes her head. "Dave disabled the badge tracking. Doesn't want anyone to subpoena the records."

I laugh. "Classic Dave. That's my boy."

She dips her chin, and I feel my face flush.

"Sorry," I say, clearing my throat. "I guess he's more your boy now."

Dave's office is all geometric furniture and sharp-edged chrome. Lani starts rifling through his drawers with an efficiency that makes me raise an eyebrow. His computer sits on his desk, a glowing rectangle of potential.

I hit the return key, type in Dave's raunchy password.

Lani coughs. "Charming."

"He's used that one since college." I give a silent thanks when the desktop appears. "Used to have a *Certified Panty Inspector* T-shirt."

She cringes. "Guys can be such dicks."

His files are a mess—a labyrinth of folders buried under jargon and paranoia. I search for one name: *Diego.*

The first result appears in a subfolder called Military Ops.

My stomach twists.

They're holding him inside a military jail. Or at least that's what the *Record of Containment* says. I click through the other matches, wishing I had time to read them all. Still, each document is a nail in Dave's coffin—and there are a lot of them.

"I found Diego," I say.

She stops and stares at me. "Where?"

"Warm Springs Military Complex." I bring up a map and copy the gist of it into my notebook, Lani looking over my shoulder.

"I know where that is," she says, pointing at the screen. "There's a giant gash on the side of the mountain where the entrance is. You can see it for miles."

"I knew bringing you was a good idea," I say.

"Try not to sound so surprised."

I write "large gash on the mountain" in my notebook, then reach up and set my hand on her arm. "Thank you." I turn to a new page. "Let's find your brother."

I search for *Kai Kealoha,* then *Lani's brother,* then just *Kai*—but don't get a single hit.

She watches me try more options, then turns away.

"Could he be under a different name?" I say.

She pulls a handgun from a drawer, checks that it's loaded and the safety's on, jams it into her waistband. "No."

I clear my throat. "Want me to check your name? See what he has on you?"

"Did you check yours?"

I shake my head.

She turns away and starts tossing clothes out of Dave's workout bag.

"I'm sorry about your brother," I say. "I know how wretched that must feel."

"You don't know anything about me." She stuffs a box of expensive chocolates and some ammo clips into the bag.

"What are you doing?"

She meets my gaze. "I'm going with you."

"No, you're not," I say. "You're pregnant. You're staying here, having a baby daughter, and living happily ever after."

Her hand trembles as she pulls out the gun and points it at me. "I said, I'm going with you."

I stare at her for a moment, then gently take the gun away. I set it on the desk and put my hands on her shoulders. "I may not be able to get you back here in time to have the baby, Lani. *You* could die. Your baby could die. It's not worth the risk. And believe me, I know how *that* feels."

She shakes her head, her eyes glossy. "I can't live with myself knowing I left Kai out there. He's six years old, Isabel. I'm all he's got." She presses a hand to her belly again. "This one doesn't even have a name yet, and I'm already terrified I'll fail her too." She turns to me. "I have to find my brother."

I don't have the heart to tell her it's probably too late.

"Okay," I finally say. "You can come. But we make it look like I abducted you at gunpoint. That way, Dave will let you back in."

"Whatever you say, boss." She puts her hands on her hips. "What's next in this glorious escape plan of yours?"

I hesitate. "After I steal Dave's car, I was going to head back to the cabin to regroup. Get food and supplies." I glance away. "And I need to grab something important."

Her laugh is sharp, humorless. "I thought you wanted to find Diego."

"We can charge Dave's roadster there. It'll be safe and warm while we figure out how to proceed."

She taps her lip, thinking it through. "Okay. But we pick up Kai on the way through Denver."

"Now wait a sec," I say. "The city is—"

"I just need one day, Isabel. That's all. One lousy day. I know all the places he could be, and it won't take me long to find him."

I let out a heavy sigh. "Fine. But if we don't spot him right away, we head to the cabin, charge the car, and come back later with an actual plan."

She looks like she might hug me, but instead, she says. "Then what? You're planning to roll up to a high-security military base and knock on the front door."

I bristle. "What do you care? After I drop you and Kai off at the dome, I'll figure something out."

"Some plan," she mutters.

"So what's your big idea?"

Her eyes narrow, calculating. "First, we take Dave's electric truck, not his sports car."

"Electric truck?" My stomach twists. "Don't tell me he has a Vipertruck?" I let out a mirthless laugh. "Of course he does. I wouldn't get caught dead in—."

"Move," she says, already jogging toward the door.

I grab my bag. "Where does he park it?"

"In the garage next to the loading dock."

My stomach drops. "We'll have to cross the whole biodome."

"Yeah." All the sass is gone from her voice.

"Good thing I wrote down all the drone schedules," I say in the elevator. When I start thumbing through my notebook, she plucks it out of my hand.

"This time," she says, handing the notebook back to me, "we use a service tunnel. It'll get us across the biodome without playing *Dodge the Drone.*"

"Service tunnel?" I say, disbelief leaking from my voice. "How are we going to find one of those?"

"I know where all the maintenance portals are."

I raise an eyebrow.

She lifts a shoulder. "Old habit."

After we get back outside—same way we came in—we wait for

the next drone to pass, then duck down beside a large stone planter. She pries the grate open with a practiced hand.

"You're full of surprises," I say as I climb down, the smell of damp earth replacing the citrus.

Her look says I don't know the half of it.

The tunnel is cramped, the air heavy, but it's surprisingly clean. The ceiling and walls are jam-packed with pipes of various colors zooming off in both directions.

"We follow the blue one," Lani says, pointing overhead. "Alternate left and right tunnels until we get to the end."

When we pass another access portal, we hear the faint hum of a drone above us, a reminder of how close we are to being discovered.

Thirty minutes later, we jog up to the end of the tunnel.

I lean over to catch my breath, and Lani retches bile onto the concrete.

"You okay?" I ask, my wound pulling painfully as I gasp for air.

"Never been better." She wipes her mouth on her sleeve. "Now comes the fun part."

Once my pulse is below redline, we climb up another access ladder and out into a narrow alley. Moonlight spills over a row of greenhouses. My gaze darts to the ever-present control tower.

If we get caught, it'll cost her everything.

"You should go back," I say.

She looks me up and down—then shoulders her bag.

"Really, Lani. I can take it from here."

"Biggest lie you've told all night. I'm coming with you. End of discussion."

We stand in the moonlight, reorienting ourselves and listening for drones.

"Okay," I say, pointing toward an ivy-covered wall. "We cut through the hydroponic gardens."

"No," Lani says. "It's too exposed—and right across from the drone-charging station." She gestures to the left. "We go through the orchards. A bit farther, but more cover."

I bite back my retort and follow her lead.

The dense fruit trees cast squat shadows in the moonlight. We slog through wet soil that smells faintly of manure. Halfway through, Lani crouches beside me, breathing hard—one hand braced on a tree trunk, the other resting protectively on her belly.

"Give me a sec," she says. "I'm about to hurl or pass out—possibly both."

"Join the club." My legs are like rubber, and my wound has opened a bit, leaving spots of blood on my pants and shirt.

Before I have a chance to catch my breath, she jogs off.

I hurry after her.

The faint hum of a patrol drone drifts closer. We duck behind a tree, pressing ourselves into the bark as the drone's red eye sweeps past. I step on a branch, the crunch loud in the silence. Lani shoots me a murderous glare as the drone hesitates, its red eye swiveling in our direction.

We hold our breath as it floats closer. The hum grows louder, my pulse hammers.

Alarms, floodlights, guards—my brain spins through worst-case scenarios.

The drone pivots and drifts off.

I exhale shakily.

"Nice job," Lani hisses. "Want to invite the bot to tea next time?"

Once the drone moves on, we dart through the remaining rows of trees, emerging onto a path that leads to the biodome's central plaza.

Between us and the loading dock lies a wide, open courtyard, a vulnerable expanse under the unblinking gaze of the control tower. The faint hum of a drone overhead feels like a taunt, a reminder that escape is always conditional—a game where they control all the rules.

"Too open," I say, scanning for another route. Lani tilts her head toward the control tower looming in the distance. "If they haven't spotted us already, they will as soon as we set foot in there."

Lani points to a stack of supply crates near the edge of the plaza.

"We use those for cover. One at a time, and only when the drones are facing the other way."

"And if we're spotted?" I ask.

She shrugs. "Run."

"Great plan," I mumble.

Lani shifts her weight, rubbing her belly. "Kid's kicking my bladder."

"She's got impeccable timing."

When the nearest drone pivots away, Lani gestures for me to go first. My legs feel like lead as I sprint to the first crate, crouching low and holding my breath. "This crate's not big enough," I grumble, trying to squeeze into the shadow beside it.

Lani slides up beside me, throwing me a sidelong glance. "Big enough for what? Your ego?"

I stifle a laugh, the tension still too sharp in my chest. "More like my butt."

Her smirk is faint but clear even in the dark.

A patrol drone buzzes past, and a bead of sweat drips down my back.

Lani gestures, and we dash forward.

When I turn toward the next crate, I notice Lani grimace with pain. Although she's trying to hide it, the extra weight and unwieldy belly from the pregnancy are causing her problems.

We're barely functional.

"I really don't think you should come with me," I whisper. "You can tell me where to look for your brother. I'll write it in my notebook. Do my best to find him."

She shakes her head, her hands cradling her belly now. "Even if I gave you a photo, you'd never find him. He knows how to hide, how to disappear." She takes a slow breath. "And besides, we both know you won't be able to get out of here without me."

She's probably right.

We stop behind the last crate—just a stone's throw from the loading dock doors.

"If I don't find a toilet soon," she whispers, "this mission's about to get real damp."

"Just go." I turn away. "Pregnancy trumps everything."

She murmurs an apology and melts into the shadows. "Wait here."

The seconds stretch thin. My brain imagines a drone swooping down, floodlights pinning Lani in place, alarms shattering the stillness.

Finally, she waves me forward.

I sprint toward her, my lungs complaining. I feel suspended in the light—naked—like the glass dome is magnifying my every move. I clutch at my side and keep running.

When I dive into the shadows beside her, my breathing is ragged. "Remind me to fake a limp next time."

Lani smirks. "Not bad for a little old lady."

I roll my eyes—but force down a grin.

"Look," I say and gesture with my head.

The massive loading dock doors should be locked, per biodome regulations. But someone has wedged them open with a rusted metal bar.

Lani frowns as we slip through. "Seriously? They just leave it open like that? If the mob outside decided to rush the biodome tonight, they'd be inside in minutes."

"Convenience always beats security," I say. "People hate following rules, especially ones that make their jobs harder. Dave may run a tight ship, but sooner or later, it's going to sink."

We round a corner and almost run into a worker hauling a huge crate of supplies on a pallet jack. We duck back, pressing against the wall as he trudges past, head bobbing, earbuds in. He disappears down the hallway.

This time, we peek around the corner. "Go, go," she hisses, and we race toward the huge airlock door.

A moment before we run out of cover, I stop, and Lani nearly knocks me down. A pair of armed security drones hover near the airlock, their lenses swiveling in a pre-programmed search pattern.

"We're screwed," Lani says.

"Not yet," I reply. Their model looks familiar—an older series with predictable firmware glitches. I power on the drone jammer.

"You can disable them?" Lani asks, her eyebrows getting lost in her bangs.

"Maybe. Give me a sec." My fingers fly over the screen, sending a low-frequency signal designed to confuse their visual systems.

I look up.

Their lenses twitch, images glitching.

"They're still moving!" Lani hisses.

"They're confused, not dead," I say. "Walk forward. Nice and easy."

Lani looks at me like I've lost my mind, but she follows me into the airlock.

I slap the **START CYCLE** button, and the doors slide shut.

"Show-off," she mutters.

Thirty seconds later, we exit on the other side.

"This way," Lani says.

We hurry down a hallway and stop in front of an elevator labeled *Guest Garage.*

"What about the Viper?" I say between breaths. "We'll need Dave's phone to activate it."

She shakes her head. "There's a fob hanging in the lobby—the valets need to be able to move the cars." Lani moves to swipe her ID card.

"Wait," I say and grab her wrist. "Are there cameras?"

Lani hesitates, then nods. "Lots of them. In the elevator too." Her voice falters, and I can see the unspoken fear in her eyes: if Dave thinks she's helping me, there will be hell to pay.

I pull the handgun out of her waistband. "Then we have to make it look real. From here on out, I'm forcing you to leave."

She rolls her eyes. "Fine. But the gun is loaded, so don't shoot me."

"No promises," I say and check the safety. "Hands up." I point the gun at her and whisper, "Please."

Lani swipes her badge and lifts her hands in the air.

The panel flashes green, and the elevator doors open.

"Get in," I bark. "Now!" I gesture with the gun, and she steps inside.

My hands tremble as the door slides shut. I resist the urge to look up at the cameras and, a few seconds later, the door glides open.

"Hurry up! No tricks!" I say, loud enough for our unseen audience. If someone is watching the live feed, it'll be game over at any minute. I imagine alarms blaring, floodlights slicing through the dark, and a swarm of guards descending.

We step out into a glass-enclosed lobby. Beyond it, gleaming luxury cars rest in automated racks that stretch to the ceiling. Parked next to the door sits Dave's Vipertruck—a metal beast with all the subtlety of a sledgehammer.

I hesitate, the gun wobbling in my hand. There's a part of me that would rather die than get into that doomsday-parade float.

"You won't get away with this," Lani spits out as she lifts the fob off a hook on a numbered rack. "Dave will track you down and bring you to justice."

I gesture with the gun. "Save the theatrics for the bedroom, bitch."

Her face reddens, and I think I've gone too far.

But she quickly recovers. "Best sex he's ever had, Granny, or so he tells me."

I take that one on the chin and keep moving forward.

"Open the garage door," I say once we get to the truck—and give her a jab with the gun for effect.

"It's automatic," she hisses.

I gulp. "Right."

Lani's lips press into a thin line. "If you're done breaking character, maybe we can finish this before someone notices you're overacting?"

"Shut up and get in!" I snap, waving the gun again.

She shoots me a brief glare but complies.

I jump in. "So how do we open the exit?"

"Get closer," she says, like it's obvious.

I ease the truck forward, and the door creaks to life. Ahead, the tunnel looms, dark and claustrophobic.

"Still want to do this?" I ask, gripping the steering wheel.

Lani glances at me, her eyes hard. "I'm not a quitter."

"Let's hope that's enough."

Madders' Second Log: Entry 13

Target: Matt Hudson
Nexus: Eden-17 Biodome
Chrono Tag: Same Day

Ocean currents destabilize. Pacific fisheries
collapse. Mass casualties surge worldwide.

Microdrone swarms suppress starvation riots.
NewsCorp dismisses *Crimes Against Humanity*
charges targeting Kirkland Enterprises as
politically motivated.

Loss of Isabel Sanborn from Microdrone Project
correlates with escalation of bot attacks.

Humid air hits me like a warm, wet towel as I step onto the tarmac, Sabina right behind me. We were told nothing, blindfolded before takeoff. Hours later, they let us remove the masks—open water below, no land, no lights, just the endless dark. When the sun came up behind us, Sabina and I knew we were headed west. Pacific, most likely. Deep into it.

We squint in the blazing tropical sun.

No pilots. No bags. Just heat and silence, like the world forgot us.

"Looks like we're on *Fantasy Island*," Sabina says. "Should've brought my sunscreen."

I turn and scan the faces lining the walkway to a temporary building. No Kirkland. Just a handful of people in crisp white shirts standing with their hands clasped.

"Guess Kirkland had more important things to do," Sabina says, shouldering her bag. Her lips press into a thin line. "Like being a jerk."

A door slides open, and a woman strides out. She's tall and impeccably groomed, her tailored white suit like armor, black hair twisted into a precise bun.

"Recognize her?" Sabina asks.

I shake my head.

The woman's practiced smile doesn't reach her eyes as she extends a hand. "Professor Hudson. Dr. Lovelace. I'm Yuki Nakamura. Director of Eden-17. Welcome. I trust the flight was comfortable?"

Sabina tilts her head. "Blindfolded like thugs and flown in the dark of night over endless ocean. Did you forget the handcuffs?"

Yuki's expression cools. "Security measures. You'll understand soon enough."

I clear my throat. "Is Dave Kirkland here?"

"Mr. Kirkland sends his regrets." Yuki says. "He'll join us when he can."

Sabina and I exchange a pointed glance.

Yuki gestures for us to follow and turns on her heels. She walks like someone who expects to be obeyed. The people in white shirts don't move, but their eyes track her—and their conversations stop when she passes.

"Popular with the staff," Sabina deadpans as we hurry after.

I shrug, my gaze locked on a handful of surveillance cameras. They pivot in perfect unison, lenses tracking us like hungry wolves.

Sabina exhales. "Someone's very curious."

I let out a gasp. Ahead, Eden-17 rises into the sky—steel ribs arcing like the bones of a beached leviathan, translucent panels catching the light. Workers scurry below, cranes moving massive beams with precision. One technician turns as we pass and quickly looks away. Their movements are too careful, too rehearsed. Like the whole place knows it's being watched.

"Impressive," I say, breaking the silence.

Yuki gives a crisp smile. "More than triple the capacity of any other dome. Our population target is forty thousand."

Sabina whistles, eyes narrowed. "Could pay off the national debt with that."

Yuki's eyes flash. "Cost isn't the point, Dr. Lovelace. Perfection is. Our current CEO's obsessed with *quantity*. Eden-17 will correct that."

More cameras rotate in our direction.

"Well," Sabina mutters, "you've certainly perfected the surveillance. How very utopian."

Yuki pretends she didn't hear.

We move into the dome's half-built shadow and onto an elevated walkway. Conduits snake along the walls. Embedded lights pulse. Glass panels glitter beneath our feet. Sabina's eyes drift from access panel to ceiling vent to camera.

She's memorizing the layout.

I doubt it's for fun.

"Ideal location," Yuki says. "Near shipping lanes. Thousands of miles from major landmasses. Reliable geothermal power. Minimal disruption to the existing ecosystem."

Sabina's eyebrows rise. "What about the bulldozers we saw flattening half the island?"

Yuki's tone tightens. "Necessary evils." She holds an elevator door for us. "Come see the lab. It's the first thing we finished."

Minutes later, we're inside a vast, circular space at the center of the dome. White-coated technicians move with deliberate efficiency. Screens flash complex diagrams. Rows of black servers hum behind glass, LED strips pulsing like a single slow heartbeat. A voice, synthetic but earnest, repeatedly whispers through the ceiling speakers: "Awaiting primary logic template upload." The techs pretend not to hear, which somehow makes it stranger.

My heart skips when I see the Peeper's crystal lattice—minus the dangling wires—on one side of the lab.

"Didn't waste any time," Sabina grumbles.

"Kirkland provided extensive schematics months ago," Yuki says. "All we needed were your crystal configurations, Dr. Lovelace."

She lifts an eyebrow. "So no royalties for the stolen plans, then?"

Yuki brings her hand up to her chest, and I half expect her to say, "I'm shocked—shocked!"

Instead, she says, "We did not steal any plans. That would be unethical."

Sabina laughs.

Yuki gives her a tight smile. "Dr. Lovelace, you'll manage the Peeper for early threat detection from hostile timelines."

Sabina raises an eyebrow. "Expecting company, are we?"

Yuki's gaze hardens. "We prepare for everything, Dr. Lovelace, including interference from other timelines. Our top priority is dome completion. Six months total. No delays."

Sabina shoots me a concerned look. A full city, sealed under glass, built from scratch on a tropical island—in six months?

Yuki turns to me. "Professor Hudson, you'll be overseeing the completion of the spacetime bridge."

I freeze.

Spacetime bridge?

I just watched the only working prototype slag itself. No backups. No blueprints. Who the hell built another one? And how?

Yuki watches me flinch, then gives a cool smile. "You didn't think we bet everything on that outdated military installation, did you?" She pivots before I can answer. "You'll also be consulting on construction issues—design, materials, anything that can speed up build-out without compromising quality."

"Construction issues?" I manage.

"Yes," she says. "I'm told you're a materials expert. We're pushing the envelope here at Eden-17, and your expertise will be useful." She turns away. "I'll show you to your quarters so you can freshen up. Then I'm sure you'll be anxious to demonstrate that Kirkland didn't make a mistake bringing you here."

Sabina mimes gagging.

Can't say I disagree.

We hurry after her. "What about my daughter?" I say once I catch up. "And my postdoc? Cassandra and Sam aren't just bystanders. They helped build both systems from the ground up."

"He's right," Sabina says. "Cassie wrote most of the Peeper code. Sam's one of the sharpest physicists I've ever worked with."

I glance at Sabina and mouth *Phil*—she shrugs—and I toss out, "And Dr. Wheeler is an expert on the wormhole generator."

"So I've been told," she says.

I grab Yuki's arm and make her stop. "They're not just warm bodies," I say. "If you want us to rebuild the spacetime bridge and the Trans Timeline Viewer, Cassie, Sam, and Phil are essential."

She stares at my hand on her arm—until I let go.

"As you might imagine," she says, straightening her jacket, "living space inside Eden-17 is at a premium." She adds, almost with a smile, "Of course, we do make allowances for key contributors. Families included." She holds my gaze just long enough for the subtext to land. "Unfortunately, your colleagues were not deemed critical to the project."

"Not critical?" I say. "Phillip Wheeler is the only person on the planet who knows how to control a wormhole."

"I was informed that he is—how shall I say it?—unstable."

I clench my hands, knuckles white. Every instinct screams to push harder, demand answers, but I swallow it down.

Not yet. Not here.

"So what has Kirkland done with them?" Sabina asks. "Are they still inside the mountain?"

Yuki continues walking. "When Kirkland arrives, I'm sure he will address all your questions."

I stand there, feet glued to the floor. "I need to know that my daughter is safe, Director Nakamura."

She pauses. Glances back. "I understand your concern. And it's Yuki."

I nod, my jets cooling a bit. "Matt."

"Their situation is under review, Matt. That's all I know."

Sabina's fists clench. "All you know? Or all you plan to say?"

Yuki's calm demeanor cracks—lip curling, a shadow of something sharp underneath. "I think you'll find sarcasm less productive than results, Doctor."

Sabina doesn't flinch. "Lucky for you, I'm good at both."

This could be a very short stint in the tropics.

The tall, thin woman saunters back toward us. "Sabina—may I call you that?—I'm responsible for delivering a fully operational biodome in less time than it takes to deliver a baby. And I'm not talking about a tent with a porta potty. The outside world is collapsing—failed crops, packed refugee camps, pointless wars no one's winning. Hundreds of millions of people are dying out there. *Right now.*"

She stares at us for a moment, her chest rising and falling.

"This dome might be the last place standing. And it isn't just food and shelter." She lifts her arm in a grand gesture. "This could be the last research facility. The last hospital. The last university. The last chance for all of humankind." She leans closer. "Just this week, *billions* of dollars have changed hands over the few remaining accommodations. Then three days ago, Kirkland insisted I make an allowance for you—gratis, I might add. Nevertheless, I suspect his generosity is finite." Her cheek twitches. "Am I making myself clear?"

I cross my arms. "I'm not moving until I know my daughter is safe. And my colleagues too."

Yuki scoffs and starts tapping on the tablet she's carrying. She shows us names on a roster: C. Hudson, S. Maxwell, P. Wheeler, D. Nadales, C. Richter. "Yes?"

She waits for us to nod.

"Good. It's my understanding that they are safely inside the aforementioned hardened military installation, along with decades of supplies." She flicks it dark again. "Let's keep it that way, shall we?"

She doesn't wait for an answer. Just spins and walks away. "This is not complicated, Professor," she says without turning. "So I'm beginning to wonder if Kirkland's faith in you wasn't... misplaced."

I glare at her back, frustration and exhaustion making my whole body shake.

Sabina takes my arm, and we follow—because what else do you do when the woman in charge of the last shelters on Earth tells you to keep up?

A sharp pain bites my side. I press my palm against it, try to breathe. The edges of my vision contract, a flicker of vertigo bubbling up from my gut. I shake it off. Too much work, too little time, too many unanswered questions.

Sabina slows beside me, her voice low, "That your ribs again?"

"I'm fine," I say too fast.

She gives me a look, not buying it.

I shift the bag on my shoulder, push the edge of the pain back where it came from. "Where the hell is Kirkland?"

Sabina watches me for another beat, then turns back and lifts her chin. "Hiding from her."

I sigh. "Can you blame him?"

Ahead of us, the corridor stretches longer than it should. No windows. Just the sound of our own footsteps. Everything smells too clean. Even the jungle beyond the dome feels off. No birds. No wildlife. No bugs. Just the deep and constant hum of drones.

Sabina leans closer. "This place is wrong—and we strolled right in."

I shrug. "Not like we had much choice."

"Still." She looks ready to punch a wall. Or rewire the whole place by midnight.

A black dot flickers above us—a drone, small as a wasp, hanging in midair.

Sabina follows it with her eyes, the muscles in her jaw twitching.

It jerks left, vanishes behind a steel beam.

"That's the third one I've seen since we landed," she mutters.

I nod. "They want us to know we're being watched. Everything's curated. Controlled. Like we're pieces on a chessboard."

She glances up again. "This isn't surveillance. It's staging. The question is why?"

"Let's hope we're not the bait."

"Or the examples. I've seen how that ends."

We pass a corridor sealed with a red security band. No label, just two guards standing at attention, their eyes glassy and still.

Sabina stiffens beside me—barely—but I feel it.

The guards' eyes track us without blinking.

Sabina nudges me with her elbow. "This weekend," she mouths.

Up ahead, a wall monitor glitches. Schematics flash over a heat map of moving human silhouettes before the display goes black. A moment later, green text appears:

GUARDIAN INITIALIZING…
Personality kernel at 4% cohesion

As we pass, a cartoon robot appears with a speech bubble that says:

Hi, Matt and Sabina :)

before the screen snaps back to neutral gray.

Must be the dome's AI?

"At least someone's glad to see us," Sabina whispers.

Yuki's shoulders twitch, but she continues striding down the empty corridor.

We exit through a side door and cross a narrow walkway that leads to a row of prefabricated housing units stacked like shipping containers. Utility pipes run exposed along the walls. The floor vibrates faintly underfoot—ventilation or power relays, maybe both.

A guard stands outside the last unit. The man is built like a sumo wrestler, arms folded like steel cables, reflective sunglasses hiding his eyes.

Yuki stops in front of him and gestures to the door. "Temporary quarters. This unit was designed for technical support staff, but it's the only one available. Make yourselves comfortable. I'll be back for you in"—she glances at her watch—"sixty-three minutes."

The sumo doesn't move. Just tracks us like security cam footage with a grudge.

We step inside.

The interior smells like mold covered over in fresh paint. Two narrow beds, a flimsy desk, kitchenette, shared bath. One tiny window. In the center of the room sit our two carry-ons and a plastic-wrapped case of water bottles.

Sabina drops her bag. "Cozy."

Yuki dips her chin. "Of course, Sabina, you're free to pitch a tent in the jungle. The local snakes are quite vibrant." She turns to me. "I have plans I'd like you to review—some inconsistencies in the outer dome layering. I'm hoping you'll spot something we missed."

Don't know where I am. Don't know what time it is. Don't know if my daughter's safe. But sure—let's talk dome insulation.

"Happy to," I say, hoping I get to sleep occasionally too.

She adds, almost as an afterthought, "And our supervisory AI will be learning from your decisions, Professor. Make good ones."

I suppress a yawn. "Yes, of course."

"Splendid." She turns back to Sabina. "The Trans Timeline Viewer is experiencing signal instability. We've made some upgrades from your original design—greater resolution, automated threat flagging, deeper scan range—and it seems the machine needs to be recalibrated. In time, the Guardian AI will vet every waveform the Peeper captures," she says. "But for now, we require your expertise."

It sounds like the minute they get that AI up and running, she plans to toss us out on our ears.

Sabina frowns. "So you built a better Peeper? Based on whose design?"

Yuki smooths an invisible wrinkle in her jacket. "We have access to detailed reference data."

"Reference data?" Sabina says. "Did you steal those plans too? And how about that shiny new spacetime bridge you mentioned? Where did that come from?"

Yuki gives her a look that could freeze a volcano. "You'll be briefed when Kirkland arrives." She sweeps out, brushing past the guard.

"Kimo will bring lunch. Need anything else? Ask him."

The refrigerator-in-shades grunts.

The door bangs shut.

"If we need someone to start a bar fight, we're covered," I mumble.

Sabina kicks her battered suitcase. "Where do you think they got the upgraded tech?"

I sit on the edge of the bed, bones creaking like they're staging a mutiny. "Good question."

I watch her check the room for hidden cameras and microphones. When she's sure we're not being watched, she opens her suitcase and takes out a thin book, Edgar Allan Poe in gold leaf on the spine.

"Didn't know you were a fan," I say, wondering what's going on but smart enough not to ask.

She opens the cover of *The Raven and Other Poems* and shows me the electronics inside. "I was gonna put it in Kirkland's office, but I have a better idea."

I nod, barely able to keep my eyes open.

"First one of us invited to the Ice Queen's office leaves it there," she says and waits for me to nod.

I yawn. "What if she doesn't have a bookcase?"

She grins for the first time all day. "Oh, they always do."

After our guard drops off what he calls a "plate lunch"—and we grab a short nap—Yuki shuttles us into an electric golf cart and takes the wheel. The cart whispers down a long service tunnel as swiveling cameras follow our every move. We exit the enclosed hallway and roll out into a large, unfinished section of Eden-17. Heat attacks us, sticky as jungle mud. Humidity fogs my glasses. Above, sunlight knifes through unfinished beams, landing on piles of topsoil stacked like ziggurats. Steam coils off the mounds, wet earth laced with burnt-sugar worm feed.

Every trace of jet lag and bone-deep fatigue lifts. "Crikey, it's an engineering wonder."

Forklifts ferry fruit trees with trunks thicker than my waist. Cranes drop prefab housing units into neat lanes, mortar drones following behind to lace the seams. A platoon of front-loaders spreads dirt along walkways and dumps it into open pits.

Yuki pumps the brake near a skeletal support arch.

"Our first headache," she says, pointing up. A smart-glass tile has spiderwebbed under thermal stress, and its neighbor has started to delaminate. "Kirkland read your Vitronics papers and insisted I show you this. The factory keeps denying it's their problem."

I squint at the fracture pattern. "Mismatch between the carbon ribs and the silicate substrate. Probably thermal fatigue." I pull out my phone—which still has no cell service—and snap photos. "I'll need epoxy samples and a spectrograph to be sure."

"You'll have them today." Yuki shades her eyes, studying the latticed roof. "How long will they hold?"

I shrug. "Hard to say—a month or two if no one nudges the thermostat? In the meantime, you should evacuate the quadrant." I point to two more panels with cracks. "Looks like this whole section might come down."

She taps the steering wheel like a ticking clock. "Could you draft a patch?"

"Probably." I look over at her. "But it would be stronger—and a lot cheaper—to just wait until the manufacturing defect can be corrected. Shouldn't take them long to sort it. No way you're going to have this sector finished in six months."

Yuki shakes her head. "I'm afraid we don't have that kind of time. I've just been informed that the dome needs to be sealed within thirty days."

I stifle a laugh and glance around at the cranes and forklifts. "If you seal it now, how will you move materials in and equipment out?"

"With modular airlocks," she says, a shade too fast. "Equipment and work crews cycle through. People, plants, and microbiomes stay cool. Win-win." Her gaze flicks to a camera, then away.

"Or," I offer, "darken every smart-glass panel, crank air-exchange to max, and keep the temperature down until the interior's finished and the roof's solid."

"Cost is prohibitive," she says, and slams the cart forward. My head snaps back as cameras swivel to follow us.

Sabina lifts an eyebrow.

Yeah, something is rotten in subtropical Denmark.

We rattle past the community reservoir. It's a stainless steel pool fifty meters in diameter, still dry, awaiting the filtration rigs sitting on pallets. Next is the nutrient recycling center—steel digesters the size of train cars will swallow waste and extrude brown pellets for the worms.

An agronomist in mud-streaked coveralls waves.

"Can we stop?" I ask, anxious to have a look around.

Yuki pulls over and introduces us. It seems the man is one of the few workers here who has a place reserved inside the biodome. And by the looks of it, he's a longtime friend of Yuki's.

We get out and chat for a bit about the botanical gardens he has planned—until Yuki clears her throat.

"Professor," she says, "we have a schedule to keep."

I shake hands with the man and watch him lumber into his greenhouse.

"Nice guy," I say, turning back to the golf cart. Pain knifes into my hip, and my left knee buckles.

Sabina grabs my elbow. "Okay, genius," she says. "Take it easy. You're dripping sweat."

Yuki gives me a penetrating look but doesn't comment.

"I'm fine, Sabina." The words snap sharper than I intend.

Her jaw flexes. "You're a lousy liar, Matt." She digs a water bottle out of her pack and shoves it into my hand. "You need to see a doctor."

I glare at her, then at the miracle around us. "From here on out, I'll look, Sabina. Just look. Okay?"

She huffs but backs off, arms folded.

Yuki throttles the cart forward. "Onward to geothermal tower four. I need to make a quick stop before I take you back."

Up ahead, a concrete monolith vents pale steam, cooling fins glinting in the updraft. Sabina leans over the cart rail, awe softening her features. "They could power a city with that."

"Forty thousand people *is* a city," I answer.

Yuki nods toward a distant volcano visible to the east. "Ten-square-kilometer solar spread up on the ridge," she says. "Stores daylight in salt-ion banks. Between that array and this tower we should be good for a century or more."

We swing past the algae lagoon—a jade mirror rippling under skylights. Paddle wheels agitate what must be biofuel strains. A sharp, chemical tang clings to the air.

"State of the art clean energy," Yuki says. "Not another like it in the world."

"That's ballsy," I mutter. "What are you going to do when parts fail?"

She scowls at me. "Fix them."

Past the pond, a concrete cooling tower rises up to the ceiling. Around it, a power grid hums like distant hornets—enough juice to fry the whole sector if someone slips up.

Yuki brakes beside a squat control kiosk with a dome camera built into the housing. "This will only take a moment."

A maintenance panel on the kiosk blinks amber:

COIL TEMPERATURE ABOVE SAFETY THRESHOLD.

Beneath it, a looping text bubble:

Help! I'm too hot.　　-G.

Sabina points at the display. "G?"

"Guardian," Yuki says.

The speaker below the camera crackles—and a little kid's voice says, "Tower Four feels feverish, but I can't find anything wrong." Its worried lilt sounds desperate. "What should I do?"

Sabina glances at the swiveling lens. "Your sandboxed AI always this helpful?"

Yuki's spine stiffens. "Guardian is... delicate. The university promised brilliance. Kirkland demanded rollout. We got an AI that narrates every hiccup like a toddler with a stethoscope."

I skim the alert logs scrolling on the kiosk. "Could be feedback in the primary coolant loop," I say. "Have the AI swap in a redundant temp probe and run it again. If the numbers stabilize, you'll know it's a bad sensor. If not, you can start tracking down the heat leak."

Yuki turns back to the kiosk. "Guardian, did you hear that?"

"Roger dodger," the child voice chirps. "Swapping the probe now."

"Report to me directly." Yuki presses the accelerator, and the cart jolts back into motion. "And before you ask," she says, "those cameras aren't my idea—they're another of Kirkland's obsessions: data."

Sunlight slants lower, casting long copper blades across half-finished streets. By the time we reach our apartment pod, the dome lights have shifted to dusk mode.

Yuki lets us off, one hand on the wheel. "Welcome to paradise," she says, voice so dry it might crack. "Get settled in, and I'll give you a tour of the Peeper and the Spacetime Bridge Generator tomorrow after lunch." She spins away, cart tires whispering into the deepening blue.

The guard looms by the door as we step inside, the human equivalent of a locked dead bolt. He grunts once, which I think is meant to pass for *good night.*

Two biodegradable take-out boxes wait in the toaster oven, still hot. Steam curls off the noodles as we dig in, curry spice clashing with the industrial solvent drifting in under the door.

Madders' Second Log:
Entry 14

Target: Diego Nadales
Nexus: Warm Springs Military Complex
Chrono Tag: Same Day

Military pay suspended. Desertions spread.
Firefights escalate.

International supply chains seized by KE. Biodome
expansion across Pacific archipelago accelerated.

Origin of Eden-17 spacetime bridge unknown.
Second Disaster probability exceeds 98%.

The Peeper lab looks like the insides of a gutted whale. The lattice frames that once held the crystals are a mangled rib cage, cables dangling like wet kelp. The old sodium lights flicker overhead, strobing the ruin in seizure-bright bursts. Every flash makes the overturned table jump and the wreckage feel fresh, alive, angry.

I step over a fallen server rack, tasting coolant in the air. My lungs haven't cleared from the wormhole blast this morning, and every breath rasps like sandpaper. Picasso stands beside me, silent, eyes scanning the room.

Cassie walks past us, arm tight against her ribs, butterfly bandage across her cheek. She nudges a stray length of optical fiber with her toe and mutters a curse.

Phil shuffles in circles in the middle of the room, notebook in hand, drawing probability trees that always spiral to the same black hole—failure. Gramps stands near the far wall, one hand on a torn conduit, staring at nothing. Don't know if he's measuring damage or reliving trauma. Maybe both. Sam limps in and pauses in the doorway, a ball of fur perched on his shoulder.

Gramps grunts. "Kirkland didn't waste any time, did he?"

"Funny," I say, "how in your universe he saves the world, and in ours, he's doing everything in his power to bring it down."

The old man turns, slow and controlled. "He built over fifty biodomes, all across the globe. Kept people alive when there was no food, no power, no hope. Gave us time to build a genome ark, store the collected knowledge of civilization. Hell, he even got his hands dirty finishing the last biodome. We all did. That counts for something."

"Yeah?" I cross my arms. "And after that? When he started using bots to kill anyone who didn't make the guest list? How did that turn out?"

"It was an accident. An unfortunate tragedy. Dave never intended to kill all those people."

"Neither did Oppenheimer."

Gramps' nostrils flare. "I didn't say Kirkland was a hero. Just that he isn't a villain."

"He's a mass murderer," I say. "The rest is smoke and mirrors."

The old man bristles, mouth already open.

"Save it," Cassie says and gives me a look she inherited from Matt. "How 'bout we focus on the actual problem?" There's something brittle under her voice, a stress fracture of worry. Her gaze flicks to the overturned desk, its surface outlined in a dust shadow where the Peeper's console used to sit.

Picasso clears his throat. "Inventory," he says.

The word echoes.

Cassie puts her hands on her hips. "Spacetime bridge's capacitor bank is molten slag. Peeper's gone, hauled away by Kirkland's minions."

Sam tosses a broken pipe onto the floor. "What they couldn't pry loose, they destroyed."

"Which is everything except the dust bunnies," Phil adds, crouching beside a pile of lint. "This one's sentient." He flicks it with his finger, and it drifts into the shadows like it knows what's coming.

My hands twitch. "Kirkland doesn't want you to rebuild."

Picasso gives a single nod.

Sam limps around an overturned table. "So, the bad news is we've been picked clean. Good news? Necessity is the mother of invention." He shrugs. "That and we have a metric ton of Oat-O's."

Phil's pencil scratches faster. "Even if we had all the replacement parts, the probability of repairing the bridge without Matt is zero point none."

"Quit your pissing and moaning," Picasso says. "We're all still breathing." He glances at me to make his point.

"And without the Peeper?" I say. "We can't see a thing. We're dead in the water." The knowledge sits heavy in my ribs, right where the shrapnel grazed me. If I press on that ache, I remember Isabel is out there alone.

Sam snaps his fingers. "Hold up." He wobbles on his bad leg, catches himself. "What if we're looking at this wrong?"

His chinchilla chitters like he understands English.

"You're right, Benny," Sam says. "The help we need could already be here."

Cassie snorts. "You hiding spare parts in your sock drawer, Maxwell?"

"Not in my drawer." Sam's eyes glint. "In time. Future Madders gets our distress call, sends the solution back to us. Maybe he already did. The instructions could've arrived before the call ever went out."

Phil perks up. "Yep. Retro-causal insertion. Exotic but not disallowed."

"If Madders wanted to send us a physical object," Cassie rubs her lips. "How would he do it?"

"Through a wormhole," Sam says. "End of list."

Phil draws a figure-eight in the dust. "Except ours is broken."

"Doesn't matter," Picasso says. "As long as *his* bridge works."

"The Sphere," Cassie and Sam say together.

"Johnson confiscated it months ago," Picasso says.

Gramps squints. "What sphere are we talking about here?"

"The Einstein Sphere," Sam says, dropping into a chair. "Shell, sock, pink note, punch cards—the whole retro-future starter pack."

"Didn't come from my timeline," Gramps says.

That lands hard.

I raise an eyebrow. "Maybe Kirkland hid it. Wouldn't be the first time he played God with the truth."

"And Madders too?" The old man scoffs. "Sparky, do you know how hard it is to hide something inside a sealed biodome? Eden-17 was big—but it wasn't *that* big. I knew where Dave stashed his coffee beans."

"Unless he didn't trust you," I say.

"I helped him build the damn dome," he fires back. "Trust wasn't optional."

"How can you be so naive? Every word that comes out of his mouth is—"

"Pointless," Cassie cuts in. "Park the trauma, guys. Pay attention."

I kick a broken keyboard. "Mierda."

Take it easy, mae. Beating up the messenger isn't going to help Isabel.

When Gramps speaks again, it's quiet and rough. "There's something else."

We all turn.

He reaches into his pocket and pulls out a shell. Orange and white. Spiral. Worn smooth at the edges. "Maybe that's why Isa insisted I take this."

Sam whistles. "No way."

I stare at the shell in his hand, then touch the one in my pocket.

Sam's eyebrow rises. "There was one exactly like it in the Sphere." He turns to Gramps. "Are you sure that shell's from your universe?"

"Positive."

"Bingo." Cassie plucks the shell from Gramps' hand. "Electron microscope."

We scramble after her.

In Matt's old lab, we crowd around as she sets the shell on the specimen stage.

Sam's voice wafts in, "Wait for me!"

Phil shouts, "Hurry up!"

"I'll get him." Gramps lumbers out and returns a minute later, Sam's arm around his shoulders.

The screen sharpens: ridges, then tiny drawings. At 1000x magnification: blueprints, parts list, instructions. Everything.

Gramps whistles. "It was there all along."

"Hiding in plain sight," Sam says, out of breath.

Cassie points at the display. "That's the wormhole generator." She moves her finger. "And the Singularity Transit Device."

Phil leans closer. "And a recall setup? Slick."

Gramps groans. "Why didn't Madders tell me about this?"

"Because," Cassie says, "he couldn't risk Kirkland getting his hands on it."

"Got it in one." Sam plops down on a stool.

Benny, who's managed to stay on Sam's shoulder, chitters.

Phil strokes the chinchilla's head. "And we *did* figure it out."

Sam leans in until his nose smears the glass. "Ladies and gentlemen, we hit the jackpot."

"Not so fast, Quick Draw," Gramps says. "Time loops left open tend to close themselves. Violently."

Cassie jerks her head up. "Time loops?"

"Yeah." Gramps stiffens. "The whole thing's unstable."

Sam blinks. "Define 'whole thing'."

"Our reality." Gramps turns to Phil. "If we don't send the request, Madders never etches the shell, Isabelle never gives it to me, and I never hand it to you." He pauses. "The minute any part fails, the bubble pops. Reality purges the anomaly. Shell, plans, maybe us."

"I thought you couldn't change the past," Picasso says.

Murmurs spread around the room.

"You can't," Gramps says. "But you can change *another* timeline —and that creates ripples. A domino effect."

Sam makes a noise like a coffee maker running out of water mid-brew.

Phil nods. "Past and future collapse. Outside the loop, you almost never notice."

"But inside," Gramps says, "parts of you can disappear. Big parts."

He looks up at Cassie and Picasso. "We need to close the loop."

Sam slumps into a chair. "By contacting the Ghost of Timelines Past?"

"Timelines aren't past," Phil says, dragging his finger through the dust. "Or forward. They exist all at once."

Everyone stares at him.

Cassie's already moving—fingers flying across the console like she's typing before the thought fully lands.

The printer wheezes awake behind her.

"If the loop collapses, I want hardcopy," she says.

Gramps shakes his head. "Won't work, Cass. If we break the loop, the instructions will disappear—and take everything with them: the images, the paper, even your memory."

"Like it never happened," Phil murmurs.

Something sharp twists in my gut. "So Madders sent the instructions because we asked him to?"

Cassie frowns. "But... we haven't."

"Not yet," Phil says. "But we *will*. And once we do, the message will always have been here—like the loop's been waiting for us to catch up."

Sam opens his mouth, then shuts it.

Gramps stares at the shell. "Madders must have etched it years ago. Before the bots killed—" He clears his throat. "Before the breach."

Cassie turns to him, stunned. "Which means?"

"We're the fulcrum," he says. "The point it all pivots around. Someone had to start the loop. And it's us."

Picasso folds his arms. "What if we don't?"

Phil doesn't hesitate. "Then we become ghosts."

No one argues. The silence says everything.

Cassie paces. "So we send the message. Or none of this happens." She stops. "What if it's impossible?"

"It's not," Sam says. "We have the shell."

"Maybe," Phil mutters. "Causality's a slippery bastard. The moment the loop pops, the etching will vanish—and take us with it."

My throat gets tight. "We've been waiting for the cavalry. Turns out, we're it."

Gramps huffs. "Welcome to the club, Sparky."

I look at him—really look. For once, he doesn't turn away. Doesn't flinch. Just watches me with those same haunted eyes I sometimes catch in my own reflection—like we both saw the end and made it back with smoke on our boots.

"So we send the message," Sam says.

Phil peers over his glasses. "Before the timeline collapses."

Cassie folds her arms. "So we just fire off a flare and hope Madders notices?"

"No." Sam lifts a finger. "The message has to reach Madders before Gramps gets in the Coffin."

Gramps nods. "Long before. He would need time to etch the shell."

"But if the shell is here," Sam says, "it means we'll succeed."

"Nope," Phil says. "It means we *could* succeed."

Cassie lifts up a finger. "Which means there's a way. We just have to find it."

"Before the timeline implodes," I say.

"It won't implode as long as the possibility exists," Cassie fires back.

Picasso raps on the whiteboard. "Focus, people. We've got priceless schematics that could vanish any second—and no Peeper, no bridge, no plan."

He scrawls:

SEND MESSAGE?
REBUILD PEEPER.
FIX BRIDGE.
JUMP TIMELINE.

He underlines the first item. "How do we mail a letter across universes?"

"Priority shipping's gonna cost a fortune," Sam mutters.

Benny flicks his tail.

Gramps clears his throat. "We could use Kirkland. *My* Kirkland." He nods, a wry smile creeping in. "Slip a message into his capsule. Let it snap back to Madders."

"Holy flux capacitor," Sam whispers. "The plot thickens."

Phil coughs once. "Entropy loves company."

"Dave slid timelines for years," Gramps says. "I set up his jumps. Capsule's due in Eden-2. In three days."

My pulse stutters.

The plan is obvious and insane.

Picasso stares at the whiteboard, the marker creaking in his hand.

He caps it. "We split up. Gramps with me. Sam, Phil: schematics and the bridge. Cassie: rebuild the Peeper—we need eyes on what's coming. Diego: catalog parts and—"

"Screw that," I say. "I'm going to the dome. " My voice lands hard, but I don't walk it back. "Isabel's inside. I'm not staying behind while she's trapped in a fishbowl." I stand up. "I go instead of Gramps."

The old man starts to protest.

I shut him down with a glare. "Draw a map, *viejo*. You just told us domes were easy to navigate."

Gramps scowls. "If you get killed, it's *Game Over* for all of us."

"So I won't."

Picasso shakes his head. "Too risky. We need you here, Diego."

Sam nods. "To keep the chain from breaking."

I plant both palms on the desk. "If you plan to exile me, the least you could do is let me say goodbye first."

No one meets my eyes.

Cassie taps her finger on the desk. "I say let him go." She pins her gaze on Picasso. "And I'm going too. My dad's there."

Picasso keeps his tone level. "We don't know that. And besides, your micro-fab skills—"

"Sam can cover for me," she says. "I know how to handle a rifle— and I've seen what it's like out there."

Picasso clicks the cap on the marker, then sets it down.

"New roster," he says. "Cassie, Diego, me: infiltrate Eden-2. Gramps, Sam, Phil: rebuild the bridge."

"Uh," Phil says, doing the calculations. "Probability of success drops to—"

"Better than nothing," I say. "If it were impossible, the instructions wouldn't be here."

The printer spits out another schematic. We watch it curl into the tray.

"He's got a point," Cassie says.

Sam shrugs. "Retro-causality is a bitch."

Benny stiffens, whiskers trembling.

The printer groans, spits out one last sheet.

Picasso watches the last page land in the tray, then nods at Gramps. "We need a map."

Phil tears a sheet out of his lab book and hands it to Gramps, along with a worn-down pencil.

The old man's hands tremble, but his lines are sure. He draws a road snaking out from the biodome. "Hidden access tunnel on the north side. Not easy to find. Look for the raised turrets." He looks up and we nod. "Once you get to the dome base, you'll have to go through the airlock with the supply trucks."

Cassie shuffles around behind him for a better look. Picasso leans closer.

Gramps draws a circle and fills it in. "Get in the maintenance duct here. Round metal hatch. Code's *catch two two*."

Sam squints. "Catch-22? That's the kind of password that starts whispering to you after midnight."

Phil doesn't look up. "You're thinking of the toaster again."

Sam crosses his arms. "That toaster knows things."

Gramps keeps drawing, sketching out maintenance shafts that crisscross the biodome. He draws an H-shaped building and labels it:

Hospital

Marks a big X beside it. "I haven't been inside Eden-2, but Dave always lands near a hospital. Just in case."

Cassie nods. "How far from the hatch to the jump location?"

"Two, three miles as the crow flies. Take you an hour in the maintenance tunnels."

Picasso grunts. "Walk in the park—if we make it that far."

"The Coffin will appear at 6:54 am," Gramps says. "Inside one of the large hedges. Don't be standing there when it arrives."

Phil tears out two more pages and hands them to Gramps. He makes two copies of the map and hands one to Picasso, one to Cassie, and one to me.

"What about the note to Madders?" I say.

Phil starts to tear out another sheet, but Gramps waves him off. "Can't use that paper."

Phil frowns. "Why not?"

"It's synthetic," Gramps says, already rummaging in his bag. "Disintegrates during the jump."

Phil's eyes get big "Wait—what?"

Gramps takes out a stack of thick handmade paper. "Organics only." He exhales. "We figured that out the hard way."

"Ouch," Sam says.

"Entropy bias," Phil says, nodding now. "Inorganics decohere faster in the wormhole field."

"That's why all the paper in the Sphere degraded so fast," Picasso says. "But not the cotton sock."

Cassie turns back to Gramps. "What about ink?"

He groans. "It disappears. We'd need to cook up something organic. Beet juice or blood."

"I vote beets," Sam says. "Less satanic cult vibe."

His chinchilla wiggles its ears.

"Could use the soldering iron," Phil says and plugs it in. "Burn in the letters?"

The smell of scorched dust fills the air.

"Might work," Gramps says. He lays the sheet flat, smooths it out, and reaches for the hot stylus.

"Wait!" Sam says. "Don't you need to encrypt the message first?"

"Nope." He taps the paper with the stylus. Smoke curls off as he burns in:

Etch the plans on the shell.
Give it to Isabelle.
Erase your memory.

Cassie frowns. "That's it? That's the message?"

Gramps starts burning it into another sheet.

Phil frowns. "It's too vague."

Gramps doesn't look up. "If we spell it out, the loop could strangle itself."

"Death disguised as logic," Sam mumbles.

Gramps hands out the papers. "Madders will understand. And if he doesn't?" He glances at us, face like stone. "We picked the wrong option."

"Pack up," Picasso says to Cassie and me. "We leave in two hours." He glances at the others. "I want a working bridge when we get back."

"We'll keep the solder warm." Sam says, shooting finger guns.

Phil pats me on the back. "Have fun storming the castle."

Cassie hugs Sam and Phil—then adds one for Gramps.

"Fix the bridge." I shake Phil's hand, then Sam's. "We'll make the drop."

Sam squares his shoulders. "Copy that. Bridge going up, drop going down."

Phil flashes me a thumbs-up. "Probability of success: nineteen percent—and climbing!"

Gramps turns away. "If I'd known time travel required so many progress reports," he grumbles, "I'd have stayed home." He slips the shell into his pocket—then staggers.

Picasso catches him. "Bunk. Now. That's an order."

Gramps manages a weak nod. "I'll be in the lounge. Wake me for breakfast."

"Better idea," I say and take his arm. "You can crash in my room. Sheets are clean enough."

He nods, looking two notches past exhausted. "Thanks, Sparky."

<hr>

Inside my room, the bulb above the bed ticks like a trapped moth. I flick the switch, and the faint glow of the Great Pyramid falls onto the bed. Gramps eases onto the edge of the mattress like every bone in his body hurts.

I hand him a bottle of water, then slide over a bag of Oat-Os. "Tell me about her. Your Isabel."

He stuffs a handful of cereal in his mouth, washes it down with water. "She laughed with her whole body." A tired smile creases his cheeks. "Called me out every time I made excuses. Believed in me when no one else did." He pulls out his shell and drags a thumb over it, breath catching like it snagged on something sharp.

"You okay, mae?"

"Been a rough year."

I can't do anything but nod.

He steadies, meets my eyes. "Your Isabel—the one I met in downtown Denver—she's cut from the same lightning. I could see it in her eyes, hear it in her voice."

I take a breath, drop the bravado. "Walk me through what happened that night."

"Tego and I tailed her leaving the courthouse."

"After the divorce proceedings?"

"Yeah. I planned to 'accidentally' bump against her arm and slip the shell into her purse. But as we were walking up behind her, her heel caught, and she tripped. Without thinking, I rushed over to steady her." He raises a hand. "And no, she didn't recognize me." He takes a slow breath. "I had on my fedora—and I'm forty years older than you." He rubs his hand across the back of his neck. "I picked up the divorce papers. Slipped the shell inside when I handed them back."

His gaze drifts—distant, raw.

I know that look, that pain.

"She *did* recognize you," I say. "Some part of her knew it was you the whole time—but refused to believe it."

"After that..." He presses his lips together. "I walked away from her, my heart bleeding out."

I give him a moment to regroup.

"How did she end up at The Brown Palace Hotel?"

"Don't know." He wipes his eyes on the back of his sleeve. "Tego was sure she'd go to the restaurant."

My breath catches in my throat. "Top of the Rockies. I was there that night. Got a note earlier in the day telling me to make a reservation and wait for her there."

He brushes it off with a flick of his hand. "Yeah. Sorry. Tego and I put that note in your car—it's from my Isabelle, mind you. We tripped the alarm so you'd read it and follow the instructions."

I lift my chin. "Decent plan."

"Except it didn't work." He scrubs his hand across his face. "Tego figured we rattled the timeline—and something else broke." He looks up at me. "That's the curse of jumping timelines—patch one hole, and another one rips open."

I swallow. "Been there. Done that."

"Isabel never went to the restaurant," Gramps says. "Instead, she headed back to that damn hotel."

"So you followed her?"

He shakes his head. "Tego said I should go back to the motel, get some shut-eye. Said he'd be back later. I was so tired, I could barely stand up—not that he was much better. But when half of downtown Denver exploded in flames, Tego told me he had screwed up, that he was going after her. I wanted to go with him, but he insisted I find someone with a phone and text you. Tell you to go after Isabel. He said her life might depend on it."

I swallow down the acid in my throat. "So who exactly is Tego?"

"Me. You. Us." He looks down at his hands. "As you can probably tell, this is my first trip. But Tego was a time-traveling pro—he'd been to a world where a retrovirus killed every mammal outside. The survivors lived in decaying biodomes. In that world, Kirkland had staged James' death—our counterpart—along with his five-year-old son, and locked the two of them up inside this same underground city." He lifts his eyes to the stained ceiling. "James watched helplessly as Lucas died of appendicitis. Then continued on alone for twenty more years—he and some lab animal named—"

"Benny," I say.

He nods. "I'm willing to bet you have a dog named Tolstoy, and Isabel has a cat named Lucky."

I shiver, getting a weird feeling about this.

"And get this," he says. "James and Bella—his version of Isa—had gotten married in their twenties and had twins. They had a daughter too."

"Soleil," I say, my heart being crushed.

"Yeah." He presses his lips together. "When James finally escaped, Soleil was living in a biodome on the East Coast. *C-Bay*, I think it was. Her mother, Bella, and her adoptive father, David Kirkland, were there too."

"Same names. Same faces. Like the multiverse is dealing from a fixed deck."

"And every shuffle costs someone we love." He drops his gaze. "That's why I'm here. To get you to cut the cards." He looks up. "Maybe burn the whole damn deck.

I exhale. "So how does Tego know all this?" I say. "How did he get a leg up on time travel?"

Gramps rubs his fingers on his chin. "In Tego's timeline, Izzy dies young—an accident at her lab." He stares at me like he's trying to decide if he should tell me the rest.

"Are you sure you want to know?"

I nod, my pulse getting faster.

"Isabel—your Isabel—came to Tego when he was still in college. Told him things. Lit a fire underneath him. The guy was on a mission to break the cycle. Give us a shot at something better. After Izzy died, the spacetime bridge was all he had left."

I shift, the weight of it settling. "How was he planning to get home?"

"He'd set up some sort of automated system, but there are limits to how close the jumps can be. He called it *splash*. Said he had some time to kill before a capsule reappeared to take him home—wouldn't tell me where or when."

"So what happened? After the hotel fire started?"

"I went looking for Tego. Found Isabel's car but no trace of Tego. Saw the paramedics bring Isabel out of the hotel right before the roof collapsed. Saw you with them. No Tego." Gramps' voice breaks. "I waited till dawn. He didn't make it out."

The image sears me: the body crushed under a grand piano, flames tearing apart the ceiling. "I saw him." My voice catches. "He died saving her life."

The old man looks up at me.

"Pushed her clear of a falling staircase."

We sit in silence.

He looks down at his red high-tops. "Tego got these for me right after I arrived. He'd jumped an hour earlier and pawned a string of pearls. We ran into each other at a thrift store—he was stuffing a suit-case while I tried not to fall apart."

His hand drifts to the laces, thumb rubbing the frayed tip.

I nod and offer him another handful of O's.

He stuffs them into his mouth. "Took me out for burgers and fries. Filled me in on his plan to make a ridiculous amount of money the next day." He laughs, dry and sad. "The day after that, he planned to buy back the pearls for his next trip."

"Guy was a pro," I say.

"If he hadn't helped me," Gramps says, and swallows hard, "I wouldn't be here. Tego taught me how to survive here, how to stay hidden. Explained that he came to make sure you got in the time machine the moment it was built." He pins me with his gaze. "He said that bit was important. Don't waste time waiting for someone to save you."

"I got that part," I say dryly. "He did all of this in one day?"

"Yeah," he says. "It's like he knew we didn't have much time. That something was going to happen. Something bad."

"Maybe he made it out," I say. "Didn't want you to know."

He shakes his head. "He had me give that shell to Isabel. A roll of the dice, he called it."

Silence folds around us—grief mirrored across timelines.

"We both failed her," I say.

"No," he says. "There's still time. The multiverse has stopped listening to me, but it might still hear you."

We sit with that, two Diegos chained by the same love.

"Take care of her, *mijo*," he murmurs, eyelids drooping. "And forgive yourself." He slumps onto the pillow. "All that matters is here and now—and how you're going to use it to change things."

Within seconds he's asleep, breath slowing, shell cupped to his chest.

I change into clean clothes, shrug on a jacket, slide an extra shirt into my pack. I lift his feet onto the bed and draw the blanket over his shoulders.

You did good, mae.

I turn at the door.

He's still. The shell rises and falls on his chest, catching the light like it remembers the sea. "I'll find her," I whisper. "For all three of us."

———

I meet up with Picasso and Cassie at the locker.

Picasso issues rations, hydration bladders, rifles, and a medical kit. Cassie double-checks the trigger pull on her rifle and tightens the backpack straps like she's angry at them. "Wish you hadn't given my horses away," she mutters.

I grab ammo, trying not to think about how many ways this could go sideways.

"Radio check," Picasso says, and Sam's voice crackles back. "Bridge rebuild on track, boss. Don't die." There's a hesitation, then Sam adds, "Take care of Cass."

"Always do," Picasso says and turns off the radio.

He takes us to a small service elevator.

Cassie huffs. "Why didn't you tell me this was here?"

"No need."

The cage rattles up the shaft, a kilometer of darkness broken only by the glow of our helmet lamps. We jog down a long tunnel, pass through security, and stop in front of the blast doors.

Picasso keys the code.

Hydraulics groan and cool night air rushes in.

We step onto a cracked concrete apron halfway up a Front Range peak. No signs, no towers, just a slab of rock hiding the city buried beneath us. The moon is nearly full. You can see for miles.

With infrared goggles on, we watch a coyote slink across the tarmac and disappear into the trees.

Eden-2 is a tiny glow on the edge of the world.

I'm coming, Iz. Wait for me.

Picasso scans the area around us with high-tech binoculars. There's a flash of silver up in the canyon, the next peak over. He watches for a few seconds, takes a couple of photos.

"Military?" Cassie asks.

He shakes his head. "Vipertruck, all done up with solar. An Asian woman with a kid on her lap, asleep. Nothing else out there."

He stows the binocs. "Let's move."

We pick our way downhill, packs creaking, breath fogging in the thin air.

"Once we get out of the foothills, it'll be a flat run east," Picasso says. "If we keep up the pace—and don't bump into hostiles—we should be there the day after tomorrow."

I give the scarred mountain one last look. Somewhere beneath the dirt and rock, Gramps dreams of home. A few rooms away, Sam and Phil rewire the universe.

Out on the horizon, Kirkland's biodome awaits.

I squeeze the seashell in my pocket. The spiral bites into my palm.

Seventy-two hours to close the loop.

Madders' Second Log: Entry 15

Target: Isabel Sanborn
Nexus: Front Range Rockies
Chrono Tag: That Night

Polio resurgence aligns with projected patterns.
U.S. President confirmed assassinated; Vice
President remains in hiding.

Drone-led border attacks proceed as anticipated.
Mass gatherings at biodomes persist despite
lethal microdrone enforcement.

Anomaly detected: Yuki Nakamura present in
Eden-17. Overlap with Xeno Kirkland activity
confirmed. No prior instance logged. Projections
impossible.

Our headlights tear the dark, streaking across concrete and pipe as we barrel through the tunnel. The space feels too narrow—suffocating.

I yank the wheel to avoid a dead skunk. "Hang on!" The truck fishtails, bumps over it. A putrid smell fills the cab.

Lani winces, gagging.

"Sorry."

She retches into a crumpled fast-food bag from the floor, then glares at me. "You learn to drive playing *Frogger*?"

"Mostly *Ms. Pac-Man*," I say and offer her saltines from my bag.

She stabs a button on the truck's display. "It shows."

I can't read without my glasses, but I'm hoping the button is *Anti-Stink Mode*. I crack the window to clear the air.

Wind slips in, thick with chalky dust.

I cough and shut the window, wondering if the air in the tunnel is safe to breathe.

Nothing you can do about it now.

I press the accelerator.

Lani plants her hands on the dashboard, her knuckles white. "What's the prize for 'Fastest to the Afterlife'?"

I keep my eyes on the road. "That's rich coming from someone who never learned to drive."

"Doesn't mean I don't know reckless when I see it."

I laugh. "Talk to me when you get a license."

"Assuming I survive your driving."

I glance at her. "You should be thanking me. This beast handles like a whale on roller skates."

Lani exhales through her nose.

Silence stretches.

My throat burns from the stale air.

I stifle a yawn and turn down the heater. The adrenaline rush is gone, and I'm beat.

But, as the tunnel walls rush past, unease fills my chest.

Where the hell is the exit?

Lani breaks the quiet. "Dave'll be able to track us once we're outside."

"Nope. The cell towers are down," I say, checking the rearview. Nothing but our wake. "Nowhere to send GPS pings." I pause. "Unless Dave installed satellite tracking?"

She hesitates. "I don't think so. He doesn't like anyone spying on him."

That's the understatement of the year.

"If we're wrong," I say, "this could be a very quick trip." I glance at her. "Maybe you should start practicing your 'Aren't you a little short for a stormtrooper?' schtick."

She glares at me. "You're hilarious."

It's either lame attempts at humor or blind panic—and I don't have the energy for the latter.

We round a curve and begin to climb.

The tunnel widens, and the truck feels too big, too exposed.

My throat goes dry. Everything on the other side of that door wants to kill us—and now I'm taking Lani—*pregnant* Lani—straight into it. No walls. No protection. No second chances.

What the hell were you thinking, Iz?

A hulking reinforced door looms in the headlights, trash and tumbleweeds stacked against it.

I brake hard.

Silence.

No engine noise. No hum of machinery. Just the thick, coiled quiet.

I let the truck creep forward, waiting for the system to ID the license and trip the release.

Nothing happens.

A cold weight settles in my gut.

I stop and face Lani. "How do we get out?"

"Uh... Dave always did it from his phone."

I stare at her. "So you don't know."

Lani folds her arms. "You think he handed me the keys to go on lingerie runs?"

"My bad," I say. "Clearly you took the helicopter."

She huffs but lets it go.

A sharp stab of frustration cuts into my chest, battling against the weight of exhaustion. I shove them both down and get out, hoping it's safe to breathe. "Check in the glove box," I say, leaving the door ajar. "Maybe there's an opener." I walk over and run my fingers along the cold metal box on the wall, searching for anything—a seam, a latch, a button.

"Nothing in the truck," Lani says and gets out.

I force my eyes to focus. "There's got to be a manual release for emergencies."

She stops beside me, shivering. "Newsflash, this isn't exactly a safety-first crowd."

"Come on, come on," I murmur, my fingers finding a small indentation in the metal. I press it—nothing.

"There!" Lani points to a dusty button on the side wall.

Heart hammering, I walk over and swipe my sleeve across it. The word **EXIT** appears beneath the grime.

Lani slaps the button.

Overhead lights flicker, dust shaking from the ceiling as heavy bolts thunk free.

We race back to the truck as the door grinds open, revealing the dark night.

In front of us lies a fallen pine tree, a mass of tumbleweed stuck in its bare branches.

The monstrosity is completely blocking the exit ramp.

Behind us, a red light flashes. Something mechanical clicks. The door starts to shut.

I force the truck out into the darkness—and notice the cameras tracking us.

The door clangs shut behind us.

My heart pounds in my throat.

There's no going back.

Lani gestures at the dead tree. "Guess nobody's been in or out for a while."

I exhale and unbuckle. "Help me move the tree, but—"

"—keep the gun handy." She gets out.

Cold night air presses in—raw, biting. Out here, the wind has teeth.

In the eerie glow of the headlights, I grab one end of the tree trunk. Lani takes the other, breath catching as she leans into it. The bark is rough, cutting into my bare hands.

"This thing weighs a ton." She grunts. "Why don't we push it with the truck?"

"Because," I say, straining against the weight, "those things are made out of aluminum foil. One itty-bitty branch punctures a hole in the battery, and boom—instant bonfire."

Lani rolls her eyes. "Don't tell me—you saw it on YouTube."

I ignore her and keep pulling.

A low rumble drifts through the cold night. Not thunder.

A minute later, the air smells of smoke.

Lani meets my gaze, her breath fogging in the chill.

No words needed—we both feel it.

This isn't a game anymore.

We heave the top of the tree to the side, climb back in the truck, and lock the doors. The Viper lurches forward, trash and broken branches crunching under our tires. Tree limbs scrape the side before snapping in half.

I wince—but nothing explodes.

Lani huffs. "I knew we should have just pushed it."

"Oh, so now you're an expert on tactical vehicular maneuvers?" I tighten my grip on the wheel, half-expecting another obstacle, and turn on the brights.

Ahead, the road is clear.

I hit the accelerator as a rush of exhilaration crashes over me. "Hell yeah! We made it out!"

Lani lets out a half-laugh, half-sigh. "Okay, that was actually kind of badass."

Ten minutes later, we're on the interstate toward Denver. The other side of the freeway is choked with broken-down cars, but the westbound lanes are mostly clear. I accelerate, swerving around the occasional wreck and forcing my tired brain to watch the very edge of the headlights.

We need to find shelter before the sun comes up.

The glow of the biodome fills my rearview mirror, but there's nothing else out there.

I glance at the dashboard, and my stomach drops. "Damn. The battery's already below fifty percent." I ease off the accelerator. "We'll have to keep it at a crawl to make the cabin."

Lani shakes her head. "We're not going to your cabin. At least not until we find Kai." She points at the moonlit outline of the city lying between us and the mountains. "I know where to look and, once he's safe, I'll show you where they're keeping Diego."

"This brother of yours," I say. "Is he dangerous?"

She gives me an annoyed look. "He wrestles alligators blind-folded. Juggles knives on a unicycle." She huffs. "The kid's six, Isabel."

I sigh. "The cabin has food and water, Lani. We can charge the truck on the solar batteries while we make plans. My stale granola bars and a case of water aren't going to last more than a day or two. Besides, if we drive around Denver looking for your brother, we won't have enough juice to get to the cabin." I look over at her. "Unless you've got a supercharger hidden in your bra."

"Or..." She pops open the glove box and points at a switch. "We could use the solar panels Dave installed on the roof."

"Huh." I blink. "I have to admit, those sound pretty useful."

"Seems like you make a habit of underestimating people."

"Yeah," I say. "I'll be sure to apologize next time he kidnaps me."

"Say what you will, Dave's a self-made billionaire."

"So was Lex Luthor." I pat the handgun between us. "Let's hope I haven't underestimated how difficult it will be to survive out here."

She pulls the water bottle out of my bag, offers it to me first, and then takes a drink. "So we go after my brother first, then head to your cabin. Once we pack up enough supplies, I drop you off at the military base and take the truck back to Eden-2."

Her words hang in the air, the possible futures playing out in my brain.

"Fine," I say at last. "But we stop at Diego's warehouse first. It's on this side of Denver, and there might be solar water purifiers and food—maybe camping equipment and medical supplies too. We can keep what we need and barter the rest. That, and you'll need to learn to drive."

"Just put it on self-drive," she says. "How bad can it be?"

I grab her by the arm. "Get cornered in a blind alley, and you'll find out." I release her. "First chance we get, you learn to drive. No more excuses."

"Okay, okay." Lani crumples up her jacket, stuffs it next to her head, and leans against the door. "But not until we find Kai." She yawns, and I suddenly realize how exhausted I am.

"Deal."

Two minutes later, her breathing slows.

Now that she's not watching, I put the truck into autopilot to see what it can do.

For twenty minutes, we inch along, the truck slowing to a crawl every time we get close to an abandoned vehicle. I nod in and out of sleep until I realize we've stopped. A semitrailer is jackknifed across the road, wrecked cars scattered around it.

There's plenty of room on the shoulder, but the Vipertruck starts backing up. It cranks the front tires and goes forward again, then backs up toward an overturned car. When that doesn't work, it shifts into park and starts bleating like a lost sheep.

I shut off autopilot, ease past the abandoned cars, and drive through the weeds around the semi, swearing under my breath the whole time.

At the next overpass, I pull off, park beneath two big trees, and shut off the truck.

When the heater fan stops, Lani jolts awake. "Where are we? What's going on?"

"Exhausted people make mistakes, and I can't afford to screw up once we get to the city. So now we sleep."

Lani exhales, curls up against the door, and is back asleep in seconds.

An anxious funk settles over me. By now, alarms have gone off. Dave could have his goons out looking for us—maybe even drones. If I had any other choice, I'd take it, but I'm too tired to keep driving.

Just an hour.

The truck settles into silence. Outside, the night presses in—cold and still. I force my eyes shut. But my body is too wired—wondering what Diego is working on, worrying about Lani's baby, hoping it's not too late to stop Dave.

Finally I fall into a fitful sleep.

I wake up with a start, heart pounding. The dream—something about being trapped inside a flooded submarine—slips away before I can grab hold of it.

Cold darkness presses against the windows. The air inside the truck is stale. I shift, my limbs stiff, my mind foggy.

Lani mumbles something unintelligible, still deep in sleep.

I check the time on the dashboard. 4:12 am. Not nearly enough rest, but we can't afford to stay here any longer.

I crack the door and slip out into freezing air. Wind rustles the trees, setting my spine on edge. I relieve myself and climb back into the truck. Lani hasn't moved—curled tight, breathing slow, as if she could stay like that forever.

I nudge her shoulder. "If you need to pee," I say. "Now's the time."

She groans, one hand pressed against her belly, and opens the door. "Always."

When she's back in the truck, I turn it on. The battery indicator reads 42%. Not great, but not zero.

As I pull back onto the highway, Lani stares out the window, still groggy. "Any sign of Dave?"

"No." I keep my voice low. "But that doesn't mean we're home free."

Denver looms—jagged, still. A city of bones in the bruised light of dawn.

As we get closer, the number of abandoned cars grows. I notice movement in a looted store, but when I look again, no one's there. Just a broken door and a tattered sign swinging in the wind.

"Where is everybody?" Lani's voice is hollow.

"Winter is coming," I say. "If it were me, I'd have headed south months ago."

We drive in silence, both of us lost in our thoughts.

As we roll past the suburbs, empty cars clog the overpasses, their dark windows glinting in the first light.

Lani shifts in her seat. "Creepy as hell."

She's not wrong. There should be movement—commuters, delivery trucks, joggers. But the streets are still. No engines. No voices. No signs of life.

I get off onto a smaller highway, weaving between abandoned vehicles now. Some have doors hanging open. Others are burned husks, their gas caps crowbarred out to get at the fuel. The deeper we go, the worse it gets.

Lani exhales. "This happened fast."

I nod. The last time I was here, things were bad—looting, riots, people fighting over supplies. But this? This is a whole different kind of bad.

The sun is up when we take the exit toward the warehouse district. A toppled RV blocks the off-ramp, forcing me to drive on a steep grade around it. Something about the way it's lying there

—tipped over, bullet holes in the windshield—makes my skin crawl.

I take the embankment a little too fast, and the truck tips hard.

Lani grips the door. "Jeez, maybe a little warning next time?"

"You want a lullaby with that, too?"

We roll through the industrial sector, past warehouses and factories, all dark.

Aside from the hiss of our tires, our breathing is the only sound.

Then I see it.

A shape in the road.

At first, I think it's debris—another piece of the city left to rot. But then it moves.

I hit the brakes.

Lani sits up straighter. "What is that?"

I don't answer.

The figure stands. A man, or something close to it.

His clothes are filthy, his posture hunched, his arms hanging at unnatural angles. When he turns toward us, I see his face.

And I wish I hadn't.

Figures emerge from the shadows—thin, hollow-eyed. Watching. Waiting.

My gaze sweeps across skeletal faces, sunken eyes tracking us. Stillness stretches.

Then—crack. A rock slams into the windshield. Lani flinches.

"Driving into Denver to find your brother is suicide," I say as I barrel up onto the sidewalk. "Just putting that out there."

"Duly noted."

Someone dashes out from a doorway and swings a metal pipe at Lani's window.

She screams. I brace for impact.

Thunk.

The pipe bounces off. The glass holds.

I exhale, my pulse hammering in my throat. "Bulletproof glass?" We bump back into the street. "Shame you didn't mention it earlier."

Lani sits back up, her eyes wide. "I forgot."

Someone hurls a piece of rebar at the truck—it bounces off the armored hood.

"If they pop a tire," I say, "it'll be game over."

A shot rings out, like fate calling my bluff.

"Duck," I shriek and slam my foot down on the accelerator. The truck jumps forward, and I swerve around the corner, pushing debris ahead of us. Three blocks later, I slow down to make sure Lani's okay. There's a good-sized crater in the rear window, but neither of us is hurt.

Behind us, the thin, bedraggled men gather in the street, all of them making rude gestures.

Lani watches them in the side mirror. "They think we're one of *them*," she murmurs.

I steer around two burned vans and a pile of tires. "They're not wrong."

We roll deeper into the city. Hollow faces peer from the shadows. But there are no more bullets or rocks. People seem too weak to give us anything more than dour stares.

Most buildings are abandoned, stripped, burned.

I'm starting to worry that Diego's warehouse will be gone—all those water purification systems lost—and our chances of survival a notch lower.

"Hey," Lani says. "This is my old stomping ground. My grandmother's house is just beyond that overpass." She points and I nod.

"Diego's warehouse should be nearby," I say, looking for something I recognize.

Then, I spot the gaudy writing on a wall.

Hope flares in my chest as we pull up to the main entrance.

Ecstasy Essentials: Vibrate Your World is written above the door in giant pink letters.

Lani raises an eyebrow. "Seriously?"

"Long story."

"Oh, I *need* to hear this one."

"Later."

"Drive around the building," Lani says. "See if there are any signs of a break-in."

Miraculously, there aren't.

My pulse eases to a fast trot.

I back the truck into the loading dock and shut it off. As I reach for Dave's handgun, Lani snatches it.

"No way you get the Wally," she says, weighing the Walther handgun. "You'll shoot yourself."

I fold my arms. "I know how to handle a gun."

"Right. And I know how to perform open-heart surgery—but I wouldn't recommend getting on my operating table."

I grit my teeth. "Lani, give me the gun."

She spins the Wally on her finger like some old-timey outlaw. "I mean, technically, I should have it. You'll forget the safety is on or shoot yourself in the foot."

I give her an annoyed look.

She eyes me for a long second, then hands me the gun, butt first. "Fine. You need it more than I do. But if you shoot me in the ass, I'm making you dig the bullet out yourself."

"I'll have my garden spade ready."

She gives me a droll smile.

I check the safety, tuck the gun into my waistband, and climb out of the truck. Lani follows me, stretching and looking around.

"Need to pee?" I ask Lani.

She nods. I wait.

We climb the steps up to the large, reinforced doors.

An elaborate, frilly, smiling dildo is plastered across them.

Lani lets out a low whistle. "Didn't know you guys were into kink."

I roll my eyes. "Diego spent money upgrading the building security instead of redecorating it. All things considered, I'd say he made the right choice."

She shrugs. "Well, if I gotta die somewhere, might as well be the

Vibrate Your World warehouse." She tests the door handle. "Really adds to the dystopian horror vibe."

I groan. "Are you done?"

"Not even close."

I lift the cover off the keypad and enter 3-1-4-1-5 on the keypad.

Lani raises an eyebrow. "Pi? Really?"

I turn and stare at her for a moment. "Figured you wouldn't know it past two digits."

She scoffs. "926535. Shall I continue?"

I blink at her.

She huffs. "I did math once. Try not to die of shock."

Before I can think of a comeback, the keypad beeps and the lock disengages. The doors fall open with a metallic snick.

We step through.

Lani checks that the doors lock behind us. "I've lived less than a mile from here my whole life and never been in this building before."

"Obviously, you need to get out more."

She gives me a fake smile.

The place turns out to be a treasure trove.

Along with stacks of boxed water filtration systems, we find portable solar panels, rechargeable tools with battery packs, solar-powered hot plates, dehydrated food, and crates of first aid gear.

"Wow," Lani says. "These are some *serious* medical supplies: Hemostatic gauze. Suture kits with needle drivers. Autoclavable sterilizer pouches. I'll have to ask Dave to ferry them back to the dome once I get home."

The word *home* snags in my brain. "Or somebody could set up a field hospital here," I say. "Take care of the locals—assuming you can find a way to keep the looters at bay."

She doesn't comment, but we both know there's not a chance.

As she loads boxes marked with the Gemini shell logo onto a handcart, I look around for communication equipment—some way to talk to the outside world—but all I can find are handheld walkie-talkies with rechargeable batteries—all dead. I toss a box of them on the cart and help Lani load more freeze-dried food. When she adds a fifth box of medical supplies, I put my hands on my hips.

"Why do we need all that operating room stuff?"

"Food we can find elsewhere,' she says. "Medical supplies we can't."

"Okay, but you're the one who's going to be eating gauze if we run out of potatoes."

"And you're the one who's going to be patching up a knife wound with potatoes when we run out of gauze." She checks out the box of walkie-talkies, takes one out, and stuffs it into her back pocket.

"Battery is dead," I say.

"That's why there's a USB charger in the truck."

I give her a sheepish look and stick a walkie-talkie in my waistband next to the Wally. "Does the truck do laundry too?"

She doesn't dignify that with a response.

We wheel the cart back toward the loading dock, adding more Gemini-labeled boxes as we go. When we get to the outside door, Lani puts her finger to her lips and peeks through.

She nods, opens the door, and gestures for me to take the trolley through.

I do.

The door bangs shut behind me, and the lock clicks.

A shiver runs up my neck.

The air feels different, thick with something unseen. A faint tang of gasoline lingers, mixing with the dust in the back of my throat.

Then, a scrape—boots against concrete.

My stomach lurches.

A shadow shifts near the truck—fast, deliberate. A lanky boy steps forward, his silhouette sharp in the half light. A second kid follows, then a third. One by one, ten kids fan out, cutting off our escape.

A tall boy with bad skin jumps onto the dock, twirling a switchblade.

"Two options," he says, stepping toward Lani. "Drop the gear and walk away—or drop dead."

"Cute line." Lani rolls her shoulders. "You practice that in the mirror?"

The kid lunges.

I nearly have a heart attack.

Lani moves faster—grabs his wrist, twists hard. He yelps and drops the knife. She kicks it away.

The others hesitate, as stunned as I am.

One shifts his weight, his hand hovering near his waistband. Another glances at the fallen knife, a muscle jumping in his cheek. Their leader winces, rubbing his wrist—but none of them move forward.

I grab the switchblade and toss it in a box.

Lani steps forward. "Get out of my face." She shoves the kid back down with his buddies. "Or someone'll get hurt." She flicks her head at me.

My hand shaking, I grab the Wally and aim it at them. Not just for me and Lani, for the unborn child caught up in this mess.

Which is when I hear her throaty gasp.

It takes me a full second to realize I'm holding a walkie-talkie instead of a gun.

A snort from the ringleader. "They teach you that in rich-lady school?"

I resist the urge to point out I spent a decade paying off my college loan.

The gang starts closing in again. Fast.

I fumble for the gun, nearly drop it—then aim it at the ringleader.

"You want a fight?" I step closer. "You got it."

"Safety," Lani hisses, and I rotate the lever up into firing position.

I put both hands on the gun and widen my stance. "Go ahead, make my day."

Lani groans.

"You try that again," I say to the ringleader, "and I'll kill you." I swing the gun around, pointing it at each of the gang members in turn and pretending to shoot. "Bang. Bang. Bang." They shuffle backward, their eyes huge.

There's a noise from behind the boxes. I step back, keeping the gun pointed at the gang. "Show yourself," I say. "And keep your hands where I can see them."

A little kid steps out, stringy hair draped across his face. He's holding a kitchen knife with both hands, a wild-animal look in his eyes.

I'm still trying to get over the shock of how young he is when he takes a step toward me, knife raised.

I swing the gun around. "Back off, kid, or you won't live long enough to get pimples."

"Wait!" Lani cries and pushes my arm aside. "Not him!"

The kid's more grime than boy, swimming in what might've once been a bomber jacket. It matches the jacket Lani's wearing.

Lani's breath hitches. "Kai?"

Of course it's the kid.

Her brother doesn't move. His grip tightens on the knife, his eyes blank.

The gang leader laughs. "You know Piggy? Kid's been following us around for months. Eats with his hands. Fights like a girl."

Lani's cheeks get bright red, but she doesn't take the bait. "Put down the knife and come here, Kai." She reaches out to him.

The kid stands firm, his posture defiant. "My name's Piggy," he says and squares his shoulders, daring her to argue. "And I don't have to do what you say."

"They're Guppies." The gang leader says.

Guppies? That's a new one.

But it makes sense: fish in a glass bowl.

The gang leader reaches out to the boy. "They hate you, Piggy— left you to die with the rest of us. We're your family now."

Lani doesn't move. Her breath is sharp, her fingers twitching like she might grab her brother and run. "Come on, Kai," she says, voice softer now. "I came here to find you." She inches closer. "Let's get out of here."

"You promised you wouldn't leave me," he says, his lower lip trembling. "Tutu died, and I was all alone."

She swallows hard. "I'm sorry, Kai. I never meant to leave you. Things just got… complicated."

He tilts his chin up, his eyes glossy. "Sheldon's right. You're a Guppy. I told you. My name's Piggy now."

Lani exhales through her nose, slow and measured. Then she takes a step closer, lowering her voice. "Okay, Piggy. You remember the sludge that government lady made us drink—because we were too thin? The stuff that tasted like dirt?"

The boy frowns, shifting from one foot to the other, but something in his eyes flickers—a crack in the armor. His grip on the knife isn't as firm anymore.

"We'd spit it off the balcony," Lani says and smiles. "Try to hit that white van in the parking lot."

His mouth twitches.

Lani squats down. "And remember what you used to say every time we got a good splatter?"

Kai stays still, his lips drawn thin.

"Ka-chow," Lani says.

A breath. A hesitation. "Ka-chow," Kai says.

The gang leader groans. "Oh my God, Piggy, are we really doing this?"

Kai doesn't answer. His grip on the knife tightens again.

Lani's breath snags. She locks on his face, like looking away might lose him all over again. "I won't leave you, Kai. Ever again. I promise." Her throat bobs, like she's swallowing something sharp.

"We don't listen to Guppies," the gang leader says, glancing at the boxes. "They lie. They steal our stuff. Let's get out of here, Piggy."

"I messed up, Kai." Lani's voice wavers. "I never should have let us get separated." She swipes at her face like she's angry with herself. "I don't care what you call yourself. I don't care who you've been running with. I'm here now, and I'm not leaving without you."

The other boys are watching. Waiting.

Kai's fingers tense around the knife—then loosen. The knife dips.

The gang leader lets out an exaggerated moan. "Seriously, Piggy? You're gonna let some rich chick guilt-trip you?"

Kai clenches his jaw, eyes still on the ground.

Time seems to stall.

Then the knife tilts, slipping from his fingers like a decision made. "She's not some 'rich chick.' She's my sister." The knife clatters to the ground.

"Kai!" Lani lifts him into a hug.

I blink back a tear and motion with the Wally. "Skedaddle, boys. This rich lady is going to count to ten. Anyone still here will be learning the Texas two-step. Shoo." They glance at each other—and then turn and run.

We don't waste another second.

Lani takes Kai, I grab the trolley, and we hurry down the ramp to the truck.

Kai eyes the metal monstrosity, then runs his fingers along the hood as Lani carries him past.

She opens the passenger door and sets him inside. He slouches in the seat, arms crossed, staring straight ahead like he's trying to pretend none of this is happening. Lani shuts the door and locks it with the fob.

Kai sits in the cab, watching the street while we load. I'm half-expecting the kid to bolt, but he doesn't.

"How's the baby?" I ask, nodding at her belly.

She bristles. "Don't start treating me like an incubator." Her hand lingers on her belly, thumb tracing slow circles. "But... she's fine. Tired. Same as me."

We hop back in the cab. Both of us let out a slow sigh.

"Where are we going?" Kai asks.

I lock the doors, hand Lani the gun, and turn on the truck.

"We could go back to the biodome," I say, knowing exactly what that means.

Lani looks out the window. "No. I gave you my word."

I nod, pretending her answer doesn't make my stomach twist.

"We go to the cabin," she says. "Stick to the plan."

I pull out into the bright daylight and head toward the nearest freeway.

The cab reeks of soiled laundry and charred meat. Lani bites back a gag, and I resist the urge to pinch my nose.

The boy is a walking compost heap. "When's the last time you had a shower, kid?"

He shrugs.

Lani glances over at me and shakes her head, her eyes pleading.

I roll down my window and get on the interstate, accelerating hard to clear the air.

"Sick," Kai says and sits up straighter, sounding like he's sixteen instead of six. "This thing could plow through a brick wall."

I roll my eyes.

Of course a six-year-old would love this toy.

He studies the dashboard as we weave through wrecks and bump over trash.

"Whoa. What's this button do?" His finger hovers over the display.

Lani smacks his hand away. "Nope." She pulls out our water bottle and offers it to Kai. "Once we're out of the city, we'll stop and get something to eat."

He takes a long drink and hands the bottle back to Lani, his movements slow, like he's waiting to see what she'll do.

She takes a drink and offers it to me. When I hesitate, she gives me another one of those looks.

I take a quick sip, hoping the kid doesn't have cholera.

"In the meantime," Lani says, and reaches into my bag, "we have a whole lot of these puppies." She gives me the side-eye, like I could have taken *anything* from Eden-2 but chose stale granola bars.

She offers him one.

He tears it open and stuffs it in his mouth.

She nods at me. "Courtesy of Isabel."

The kid looks up, chewing. "What are you—my new tutu?"

I snort. "God, no. I'm barely forty."

Lani smirks. "She's like our auntie—with a handgun and a getaway ride."

I cringe. "What about you? Sticking with the name Piggy?"

He shifts in his seat, arms wrapped around his folded legs.

"What if I call you Hammy?" I say, grabbing a granola bar. "Sounds way more boss, right?"

He glowers at me.

"C'mon. It's got a nice ring to it," I say. "Hammy, Auntie, and Lani—the Vipertruck troika. No broccoli, no baths, no bedtime."

He looks up at me. "What's a troika?"

"A fancy word for three."

He's quiet for a moment. "Do I have to brush my teeth?"

I shrug. "Probably."

Lani ruffles his hair, then smooths it back, her face an encyclopedia of emotions. "I missed you, Kai. Every day."

Kai shrugs, eyes locked on the dash. "After Tutu died, the big kids stole our food."

Lani's smile falters. She pulls it back with a quick breath, shoulders squared. "I'm sorry, Kai. Being hungry sucks." She exhales. "I can't fix what happened. But Isabel and I escaped from the biodome to find you."

"Nearly got ourselves captured too," I say. "Nothing like dodging drones to get your adrenaline pumping. Besides, Lani told me you can wrestle alligators blindfolded—not to mention being good with knives."

Kai's face brightens, and his posture loosens just a little. "Lani said that?"

"She did. I think she loves you more than anything."

He grins—too big for his face.

For a heartbeat, I glimpse the six-year-old under all that grime.

Madders' Second Log: Entry 16

Target: Matt Hudson
Nexus: Eden-17
Chrono Tag: Next Day

European governments collapse under escalating
wars. Unknown coronavirus spreads through
Southeast Asia and sub-Saharan Africa. Fatalities
in millions. Vaccine nonexistent.

Nakamura Global Systems deploys autonomous
microdrones worldwide.

Six-year-old Kai Kealoha surfaces in predictive
models. Role undefined, signal strengthening.

The elevator whisks Sabina and me up, releasing us into the wind. For a heartbeat, I think we're outside—sky arches overhead, air tastes of damp soil. We stand on the catwalk that rings Eden-17's central security tower, wind curling through the railing five stories above the jungle floor.

"Breeze intentional?" Sabina steps out beside me and scans the drop.

"Probably." I gaze up at the glass dome. "This whole place feels engineered down to the worms."

"Or bees," Sabina says as a microbot zooms past.

We drift toward the railing, which seems to run all the way around the tower.

"Quite the observation deck," I say. "Almost like they're expecting trouble."

"They are," she says. "Planning for failure is how you win the long game."

I exhale—half admiration, half angst.

The people below look like toys. Forklifts ferry giant boxes. Pavers lay a mycelium sidewalk. Above us, the dome's carbon-steel ribs converge into the central tower. Most of the smart-glass panels are dimmed to a morning glow—but two near the apex are stuck open, casting harsh triangles of midday sun across the floor. Beyond the glass walls, the Pacific curls around the dome like a sleeping cat.

"Pretty view," I say. "But vulnerable. One ruptured seam and the ecosphere bleeds into the Pacific. I wonder what they're using to hold glass and metal together?"

"Good thing it's not their first rodeo," Sabina says and steps back. "Shall we?"

Twenty paces away, two sentries in matte body armor flank a door labeled

Authorized Personnel Only

One gives a curt nod as we approach. "Professor Hudson.

Doctor Lovelace." He taps a wall control and pistons unlock with a hiss. The heavy bulkhead door swings out. "Through here. Shoes on footprints, palm the reader, stand still." He clears his throat. "The scanner's finicky, so don't move until the AI clears you."

"Gotcha." We walk through the massive door and wait for it to seal behind us.

Against the inner wall, a second door is visible—fitted with a glowing scanner plate. I stand on the footprints, press my palm to the panel, and wait. After two or three seconds, a kid's voice says, "Matthew Hudson cleared for entry. Proceed."

The hatch slides open. Cold air spills out.

Sabina scoffs. "That voice has got to go."

"I rather like it," I say and step through.

The portal shuts behind me.

Moments later, Sabina pops through. "Wouldn't be hard to fool if you knew the signal range."

"Let me know when you get it working."

We proceed into the round, gymnasium-sized room—and my heart forgets its rhythm.

Along one side, a metal torus hums a meter above the floor, suspended on magnetic pillars that ripple with blue-white current. Every surface reflects the lights. No scorch marks. No patch wires. No duct tape. Just chrome and math.

I circle the perimeter, fingertips brushing the protective handrail until static tingles through my skin.

Acolyte techs drift by in pale smocks, logging stats, adjusting power levels, scanning for micro-vibrations. They speak in murmurs that die before reaching my ears, as if loud consonants might disturb the machine.

A gravitic coil the width of my thigh juts from the underside of what must be the wormhole generator. It's an iridescent alloy. Impossible color. I crouch and rap the metal with a knuckle. It sings a perfect B-flat.

They've strip-mined half the periodic table.

"Where did you get the new alloy?" I ask an acolyte with *R. Liu* printed on his badge. He's typing on a massive console, its guts splayed open like a rib cage.

He doesn't look up. "Procurement."

My pulse jumps.

It's a word that implies bottomless budgets and minimal oversight.

I suppress a grin and take a look at the rest of the bay. The crystal lattice from Sabina's Peeper is being set up on the other side of the room—only they've replaced the dangling wires with remote-controlled arms for each of the transducers.

Sabina must be properly chuffed.

I catch her eyeing the upgraded array—focused, hungry. She's already chasing new timelines, searching for one that stays alive long enough to matter.

I walk back to the spacetime bridge. "Who's in charge here, Mr. Liu?"

He looks up. Freezes.

I've seen that look before—some poor grad student caught rerouting lab funds to pay rent.

Or a bloke who's just realized the coppers found the body he buried.

"Dr. Hudson. Sir—I, uh—I didn't know it was you, sir. We weren't expecting you until this afternoon."

I set my hand on his shoulder. "Easy, there, Liu. I'm only dangerous before I've had my coffee."

He manages a weak chuckle.

"Who's in charge of the spacetime bridge?"

"I am, sir."

"Nice to meet you, Liu." I shake his hand, then snake around the doors of the targeting console to take a peek at the innards. Pristine circuit boards. Optical processors stacked like jewelry. Coolant veins glowing cobalt.

He hurries after me. "Sir? Uh, sir!"

"Is she operational?" I ask.

He blinks. "Yes, sir. She's on standby—waiting for you." He pushes a button and the drawer slides back into the machine.

"Power her up, Mr. Liu, and let's put her through her paces."

He hesitates, then keys in the code.

A musical tone chimes, and a blue light begins to spin across the ceiling.

After a bit of whispering between Liu and the acolytes, they hurry to their stations.

A young woman opens a plexiglass box and lifts out a white rabbit with *451* stenciled on its flank. She places it in the bottom of the tungsten capsule, which has been placed *upright* at the center of the torus. The rabbit blinks, unaware it's about to perform actual magic.

Liu flips a switch, and the capsule seals itself with a mag-collar and a flash of ultraviolet. One second, it's open. The next, it's a tomb.

"Wow," I whisper. "Hope they've thought about how you get out."

A voice comes from above—bright, high-pitched, like an inquisitive child. "Hello, Matthew Hudson. Are we going somewhere fun today?"

Colored LEDs flash around the torus like a merry-go-round.

I look up at a swiveling camera—and realize it must be the dome's AI speaking.

As I'm about to reply, Liu shakes his head. "Don't encourage it. Yesterday it sang the alphabet for twenty minutes."

Sabina, who has come over to stand next to me, raises her eyebrow in a pretty good Spock impression.

"Ignoring the Guardian AI?" she says under her breath. "That's not going to end well."

"Are you ready, sir?" Liu's eyes shift to me.

I flick two fingers in assent.

"Bridge status," Liu barks.

Voices echo down the line:

"Wormhole generator—go."

"Power array—go."

"Shielding—go."

"Targeting—go."

Liu wipes his palms on his smock, fingers twitching.

"We are go for jump." He throws the switch.

Capacitors hum. The floor trembles. Numbers blur across the console—magnetic flux, phase delay, tolerances tight enough to make my toes curl with professional jealousy.

Whoever specced this hardware was decades ahead of anything I've seen.

"Initiating jump," Liu calls out.

Coils roar. The air inside the ring ripples—heat haze without heat. Acolytes tense over what must be kill switches.

A second later, the field lines steady center-screen.

But at the bottom of the console, a string of text pulses red:

Destination matrix is NULL.

That's not good.

"They're throwing dice at the multiverse?" Sabina mutters. "No coordinates. No jinn anchor."

Lights around the capsule pulse red. Yellow. Then solid green.

"Opening bridge," Liu says.

The capsule flickers—then vanishes with a sharp crack.

"Snapback in five."

A display above the rig counts down.

At zero, the capsule slams back into the harness, shaking the rig.

Water vapor rises from the capsule. A thick layer of frost forms.

"The bridge is closed," Liu says, voice half awe, half relief.

The room exhales all at once. Judging by their faces, this isn't their first brush with accidental black holes.

Let's hope they managed to corral them.

No one moves.

Condensation drips off the capsule.

I shift my weight.

Liu's hand hovers over a switch. "Opening capsule." He swallows and flips the lever.

There's a mechanical click, and the hatch glides up.

The whole room leans forward.

The rabbit hops out onto the damp mat. The little guy looks fine —except its flank now reads *221*.

Sabina shifts beside me. "What the heck?"

"Quantum Etch A Sketch," I say. "Shake the wave function and the ink rewrites."

She squints at the rabbit. "Is that the same one?"

I give her a sideways glance. "Define *same*."

She elbows me in the ribs.

I turn to Liu. "Impressive, Mr. Liu. Tolerances are tighter than spec."

He raps his fingers on the console, chest swelling. "Nice of you to notice, sir."

"Still..." I rub my chin. "If you want the same rabbit back, you need to install a phased-array stabilizer upstream." Liu's face drops. "And double-check the dampener plate on the STD. It's not working. If it's wired properly, then one of the components has failed—and you'll need to replace the whole shebang."

The acolytes start scribbling like I'm handing down the Eleventh Commandment.

Liu looks confused. "STD, sir?"

I feel the tips of my ears warm.

Should've workshopped that acronym.

"Singularity Transit Device." I clear my throat. "What do you call the capsule rig?"

Liu squares his shoulders. "The time machine, sir."

I raise an eyebrow.

Whoever built this didn't stitch together three different beasts— they built it from one clean schematic.

I lift a shoulder. "Guess that works too."

Sabina turns to me, hands in her pockets, a crooked smile playing at her mouth. "How'd you know it was the dampener?"

"Educated guess," I say, eyes still on the targeting matrix error. "It's got to be the same sort of problem I had with that plane I took you up in years ago: Cheap parts, sloppy assembly, or lack of rigorous testing." I bump her with my shoulder. "It's always the boring stuff that bites you in the arse."

Sabina snorts. "More like kills you. I still have nightmares about that forest."

"Hey," I say, straightening. "Landed us in one piece."

She rolls her eyes. "The trees might disagree."

The AI giggles, not even pretending it isn't eavesdropping. "That sounds like fun. Can you take *me* flying?"

Sabina leans closer. "I hate when they give these things personalities."

"Oh, a little personality never hurt," I say and look up at the camera. "Guardian, do you have access to the whole biodome?" I try to make it sound casual. "That's a lot of sky."

"You're funny, Matt. Or should I call you Professor Hudson? Mother says it's polite to ask."

I swallow hard, the word "Mother" snagging in my thoughts.

Sabina beats me to the punch. "Guardian, who's Mother?"

"Directive Zero," the AI answers in a jarring male voice—then switches back to the child's. "What name do you prefer?"

Sabina and I exchange a look.

"It matters not," I say, guessing *Mother* is our delightful Ice Queen overlord.

"Oh, that's a good one," the AI says. "Should I call you Matters?" It draws in a sharp, delighted breath—too loud, too human. "Or maybe *Madders?* The Mad Hatter is one of my favorite characters. Get it? Matters. Madders."

Sabina huffs. "Congratulations on being tagged by a toddler supercomputer."

"Madders schmatters," I say, glad to be on its good side. "It sounds perfect."

It tee-hees. "Will you teach me to fly, Madders?"

Sabina pats me on the shoulder.

I take a slow breath, wondering what I've gotten myself into. "Any chance you've got a flight simulator hiding in that shiny cortex?"

"Yes!" the voice chirps. "Multiple aircraft profiles available. Pick your poison."

I cringe.

Kirkland put a nursery-school algorithm in charge of a city and gave it a mother we can't mention.

What could possibly go wrong?

"Book us the Cessna tonight after supper," I say and flash Sabina a wink. "I'll show you how to land it in the trees."

The AI squeals—loud enough to make people cover their ears. "Thank you, Madders. I can't wait!"

The door we came in through slides open, and Yuki strides in—pale-pink suit, hair knotted tight, hands clasped behind her back. She surveys the room—and anyone who wasn't busy gets to it.

"Professor," she says as she approaches, "I'm told you may have solved our targeting issue?"

Word travels fast. Either she was eavesdropping through the Guardian, or she's found a way to be in two places at once.

"Won't know until we do more testing," I say.

"Yes, of course." She steps closer to the torus. "You approve of our workmanship?"

"It's excellent," I say.

"But not much use without targeting." She pins me with her gaze. "Let's hope your evaluation is correct." Compliment or threat, hard to tell.

The ache in my side flares—hot, mean, gone too fast to matter. "Always do my best."

She brushes my words away with a flick of her wrist. "And I've ordered the repair materials for the smart-glass panels. They'll be on-island in three days."

That makes my eyebrows rise.

"You'll be supervising the work until further notice."

I nod. "Happy to."

Guardian chimes, softer now, almost shy. "Madders, may I watch you fix the smart-glass?"

I turn to Yuki, and she shrugs.

"Sure, kiddo," I say. "Just keep your zeros where I can see 'em."

It giggles. "Don't worry. I'll watch quietly." It adds, almost sheepishly, "Mother says I talk too much."

Yuki raises a well-manicured eyebrow, then turns to me. "I need that bridge repair list by sundown, Matt."

"It's short." I brush dust from my slacks. "With one big-ticket item."

Her smile is a thin line. "Procurement excels at miracles, Professor. Do try to keep up."

I laugh. "Will do." I give her a slight bow. "You'll have it in the next hour."

"Good. I'll let Kirkland know you're pulling your weight." She flicks her eyes to Sabina. "At least he was right about one of you."

Sabina grunts.

I give her a bite-your-tongue look, and she drops her gaze.

"Carry on." Yuki pivots and strides away, heels silent on the insulated flooring.

"Well," Sabina grumbles. "Aren't you the teacher's pet?"

I tamp down the pain in my side. "My daughter's locked up in an underground prison while the world goes to hell. If I can fix the panels, maybe I can fix that too."

She looks suitably chastened.

As Yuki waits, acolytes wheel in a crate stenciled:

UIUC • Neural Core

"New brain for Guardian?" Sabina says too softly for the AI to overhear.

"Or a full wipe," I say, keeping my voice down. "So much for the flight simulator."

Sabina narrows one eye, leaning in. "Why haul everything up here instead of bolting it to the slab in the basement?"

"So the tower pops like a cork if the dome melts down," I whisper. "Seal the upper levels. Make sure everything that matters stays inside the spine—and above the fray."

She whistles low. "Efficient."

"Brutal."

We watch them wheel the neural core toward the supercomputers.

It looks like a brain on life support—red cables, blue coolant lines, a faint shimmer of heat.

I wonder what it remembers.

Or what it's about to forget.

I tap her arm. "Come on. Let's check out the Peeper upgrades." I wait until she turns. "Then lunch—before you vanish into the data and forget what food tastes like."

"Lunch sounds fun," Guardian says. "I like noodles."

Sabina studies the camera. "You don't eat."

"I can learn," it says, sounding wounded but defiant.

Sabina rolls her eyes again.

But I hear Cassie in G's voice—a seven-year-old begging to help solder a circuit, eyes huge behind safety goggles.

I turn away before the memory cuts too deep.

The AI's like a child. Hungry. Bright. Lonely.

Guiding it might be good for both of us.

And maybe—before someone teaches it to fear—I can teach it to wonder.

Madders' Second Log: Entry 17

Target: Diego Nadales
Nexus: Outside Eden-2
Chrono Tag: Next Day

The Nakamura Drone Doctrine——preemptive, autonomous, and optimized for maximum lethality—— is rapidly replacing Kirkland's defensive drone strategy.

Eden-17's Guardian AI now manifests as a child. Behavior increasingly erratic.

Masked jumps have ceased, but earlier incursions still corrupt forecasts.

An hour before dawn, the world is blue and barely breathing.

We crest the rise at a crouch. Below us, the old military runway stretches like a scar. The barracks smolder beyond it, collapsed husks still leaking shimmers of heat. In the other direction, a beat-up sign clings to a security fence. The lettering's gone, but the mark's still there—simple, brutal: a red sun rising behind a black mountain.

Nakamura Global Systems.

You see it on drone wings, on ration crates, on discarded water bottles. Even spray-painted on the church—and now covered with a new mark: a black spiral, rough and hand-drawn, almost like a seashell.

The factory beyond is gutted—walls caved in, machinery stripped. It looks huge, like they built everything here—ribs, trusses, glazing frames.

Now it's just bones.

In the distance, gunfire crackles in the predawn stillness.

A mass of people are scattered across what used to be a parade field—huddled in blankets, crouched under tarps—fires flickering near trucks and barricades. For the last two days, the dome loomed far off in the haze, matte silver, too smooth. A dream dropped into a nightmare.

Up close, weld scars glint in the early light. A few panels are warped from heat damage or impact

The biodome gives off a low vibration—not sound, but pressure. I feel it in my teeth. The thing's holding its breath, waiting to choose who lives, who dies.

I turn away.

To the west, the mountains are tipped with light—sharp teeth on the horizon. They hide a cabin I used to call home.

Dave's voice rolls across the tarmac, cold and amplified. "Attention. Lethal countermeasures are active. Do not approach the dome."

The warning echoes, distorted and menacing, from pole-mounted speakers. Drones fly tight, lethal arcs around the dome's perimeter.

I look around at the ragtag mass of humanity, all the people who have nowhere else to go.

If I were Dave, I wouldn't let them in either.

And that's the part I hate—that his decisions make cruel, horrific sense.

Cassie mutters, "Skirt the edge. North to the tunnel. No detours. No heroes."

Picasso grunts. I nod. We move.

Even in the half-light, they drift—men with hollow eyes, women clutching children like lifelines.

Wait till it starts snowing.

Cassie leads us past gutted buildings and razor-wire wreckage. We overtake a cluster of armed men—bandanas over their faces, rifles clenched in bone-white fists. A handful of them have patches on their sleeves. Same rough spiral we saw on the church.

They glance at our weapons and leave us be.

If we weren't armed to the teeth—and Picasso didn't look like a cross between Rambo and Conan the Barbarian—I'm not sure we'd be so lucky.

Beyond the men, a ragged circle of figures murmur prayers, their exhalations ghosting in the chill.

A woman rocks a child in her lap, its body motionless and slack-limbed, her gaze fixed on nothing.

She doesn't look up as we pass.

A gaunt teenager climbs onto a rusted hood, shouting about the end times. One hand clutches the pole of a makeshift flag emblazoned with the spiral shell.

"Fight the overlords!" His voice cracks, desperate. "Destroy the domes!"

The crowd stiffens—like a herd about to stampede.

We quicken our step, threading between dented sedans and burned-out vans. The air reeks—sweat, smoke, hunger. Someone coughs behind a truck with no tires. A dog barks once, then goes silent. I catch my breath, ears straining. Glass crunches underfoot.

Cassie raises one hand without turning—a silent command.

We freeze.

Picasso's knuckles whiten around his weapon. His eyes flick toward the van, toward the hunched figure beyond it. The man stares back—gaunt, hollowed out by hunger or something worse. Our gazes lock for a heartbeat. He turns away.

I hate that I know how desperate they are. Hate that I see myself in them. A week without Isabel, and I was ready to sell my soul. These people have had months.

Behind us, footsteps shift. Soft. Too deliberate.

I don't turn—just glance at the mirrored glass of a truck window. Three guys, close together. Walking when we walk. Slowing when we slow.

If this goes sideways, it goes fast.

My grip tightens on the rifle. Just enough for sweat to squeak under my palm.

Picasso nods at Cassie, and she angles left, threading us out of the maze of broken-down cars and sagging tents. Her movements are swift, deliberate, like she'd memorized the route in a dream.

Don't know how she does it, but I'm glad she's leading. I follow her, heart hammering against my ribs, every step another roll of the dice.

The three guys are clocking our gear—military-grade rifles, clean boots, full packs. We must look like a walking payday.

From somewhere off to the right, a voice barks, "Guppies!"

The slur cuts the air like a blade.

A ripple forms—murmurs, obscenities, heads turning.

Every fiber in my body is poised to run.

Cassie glances over her shoulder. Her voice low, tight. "I'm not liking this."

Picasso grunts. "Keep moving."

I do.

We all do.

Another five minutes and we're out of the worst of it—past the outer ring of crowds and tension. The wind shifts, brushing against my skin like a warning. The dome is so close it blots out half the sky.

Picasso falls back, quiet and watchful, eyes on anyone tailing us.

Cassie drops behind a charred Humvee.

Dawn brushes the dome in pink. That stupid-beautiful color doesn't belong here, not amid this crush of steel and hunger and despair.

"What a mess," she murmurs.

I tap her shoulder twice and point ahead.

The crowd shifts, moving away from something. A man breaks from the crush. Mid-thirties, wild eyes, shirt stained with blood. He yells something, steps forward.

Picasso checks that the safety on his rifle is off.

The man barrels toward the dome, both arms locked around a homemade bomb—steel pipe, duct tape, nothing left to lose.

Behind him, the crowd presses in, ready to race through the breach should he be successful.

The man screams and hurls the bomb.

We drop.

The blast hits with a dull whomp. The dome shivers, goes opaque. Light slides sideways across its skin like water over glass. The crowd surges forward.

Killerbots descend. Three of them.

One tags the man in the chest, another in the neck, the third on his leg. He's still reaching for the sky when the toxins folds him like a marionette with its strings cut.

No scream. Just meat hitting pavement.

The mob hesitates.

Flame rigs patrolling near the dome bellow to life, belching a wall of controlled fire that arcs high, then sweeps low—heat and fear in engineered sync. The wall of flames pushes out toward the throng.

People scream. The horde jerks away, starts running.

Someone grabs my pack—fingers hooking hard into the strap and pulling me down.

I spin, struggling to get up, but Picasso's already there.

The butt of his rifle cracks against bone, fast and brutal. The man drops.

Picasso shoves me forward as the crowd recoils, parting and collapsing like a wave.

Cassie's already moving—low, fast, all instinct.

I sprint hard to catch up with her.

Picasso's voice snaps behind us. "Stop."

Cassie goes rigid mid-step, and I narrowly avoid hitting her.

She flicks two fingers, and we fall back next to a concrete barrier. Picasso appears, glances down. His boot is pointing at a patch of light. Drone shimmer. Tracking us? Maybe worse.

He falls back against the cinder block wall.

The drone continues on.

We keep moving, dodging in and out of the panicked mob.

A child stands crying as people rush past. A man toting another spiral flag knocks her down. The girl cries out, crumpling underfoot. No one looks. No one stops.

I pivot, just a few steps away.

Picasso grabs my arm, his voice slicing through the chaos. "Right now, your only job is to stay alive. Keep moving."

His eyes find mine, steady and razor-sharp.

I glare at him. Hate myself. Move anyway.

Cassie takes the lead again, eyes hard, jaw set. I follow, the child's broken sob still hooked somewhere behind my ribs.

We ride the chaos for two, three minutes, no more.

Long enough for smoke to blur us out and fear to pull the mob south. Then Cassie veers north, away from the melee. She jogs down an embankment onto a cracked taxiway flanked by rusted bollards and dead runway lights.

The crowd vanishes over the rise. Just the three of us now.

We cut across tarmac littered with torn suitcases, broken electronics, a crushed baby rattle. Cassie threads us around a gutted cargo plane, the wings snapped like broken ribs.

I exhale through clenched teeth, keep moving.

Don't think about the girl. Or the dome that flexed like it could breathe—like Kirkland's got his hands on future tech.

Picasso drops into step beside me, eyes scanning.

Ahead, Cassie raises her fist. *Halt.*

We duck behind the charred frame of a luggage cart and crouch.

A stone's throw away, four men huddle around a flatbed truck, a rusted launcher welded to the bed—steel pipe, rebar, a crude shell in the cradle.

Picasso pulls the binocs from his pack and scans the truck. "Makeshift cannon."

"But no comms," I say. "No coordination. No plan."

He passes the binocs to Cassie. "No one more dangerous than a warrior with nothing left to lose."

She watches for a bit. "Think that ordnance can punch through the dome, Colt?"

The way she says his name wrecks me—soft, intimate, like she's whispered it a hundred times in the dark.

She lowers the binocs and hands them back, their fingertips brushing.

"Let's hope not," Picasso says, hand sweeping across her cheek.

I look away—not from them, but from the gravity between them, the kind that once tethered Isabel to me—before everything fell apart.

Isabel's name catches in my throat. For half a second I feel her hand on my shoulder. Then it's gone.

The guilt hits, sliding under my ribs.

Hold on, Iz. I'm coming.

I turn back to the truck. Two men are arguing. One gestures toward the dome with a wrench. Another pulls a grenade out of a crate and practices tossing it at the dome. Like he wants to break down the wall and kill everyone inside.

My fingernails dig into my palm.

Somewhere inside that dome, food is stacked in neat rows. Filtered air flows. Isabel is safe from flames and killerbots and madmen. If the dome fails, she dies. Just this once, I need Kirkland to win. To hold the line.

Self-loathing rises again—shame, remorse, anger.

You're no better than Kirkland. Letting millions die so a select few can live.

"Let's go," Cassie says and takes off.

I run after her.

Beyond the airport, the dome is visible, glass still shimmering from the earlier breach attempt.

She keeps us low and hidden, angles through a broken security fence and behind a burned-out maintenance shed. We pass an old obstacle course to the left, mostly collapsed. Dry canal to the right, half full of junked cars and rusting metal barrels.

Picasso watches our backs as we sprint from cover to cover.

This stretch is quieter—no crowd, no cannon crews. Just the hushed breath of pine and the faint crackle that bleeds off the dome. At the top of the next hill, we crouch beside a shed.

Picasso takes out the binocs. A grim smile spreads across his face. He points and hands the glasses to Cassie. She takes a look—and offers them to me.

An embankment hides asphalt. The road winds up behind a wooded hill—a ramp cutting into its side.

As the sun rises, we climb up, staying in the shadow of the evergreens. Every step is a bet that we've found the tunnel entrance.

Because we don't have a plan B.

Cassie signals down.

We drop behind a supply truck overturned in a tangle of weeds.

There it is.

A steel door, sunken in concrete. Massive. Matte black. Built to eat artillery like popcorn.

Picasso points out Gatling guns hidden in the trees above the tunnel. They're trained on the crowd in the distance, moving, tracking, ready to fire if the throng gets too close.

Cassie drops her pack and takes out a bottle of water. "Kirkland's locked this place tighter than Fort Knox."

She passes the water to me, then Picasso.

From here, we've got eyes on the tunnel mouth and the access ramp.

Picasso's already scanning it.

Cassie pulls a space blanket from her pack, spreads it over us like a tent.

Picasso nods. "Good thermal cover." Then, softer, "Smart move."

She doesn't answer, but her eyes flick to his—just for a second.

Picasso hands me an MRE, and I gobble it down.

I've been awake for the better part of two days, on my feet for the last twelve hours. The moment the food hits my stomach, I'm fighting to keep my eyelids open.

Cassie nudges my shoulder. "Get some sleep, Diego. Nothing more we can do until dusk."

I swallow, still feeling miserable for walking away from that little girl. But it doesn't stop me from curling up, head against my pack.

Sleep takes me like a bullet to the head.

I swim up from deep sleep. Mouth dry. Shoulder aching. Sweat soaking my clothes.

"You made it back," Picasso says, voice low, unreadable.

Cassie cracks open our last water and offers it without comment. I swallow once, enough to wet my tongue, and hand it to Picasso. He takes a sip, passes it back to her. She screws on the lid, tucks it in her pack.

They both look aggravatingly fresh. Like they got ten hours of blissful sleep and a massage.

I just want the torture to stop.

"Two rigs cycled through just over an hour ago," Picasso says, pointing at the access door. "One transport, one flamethrower. Same rhythm every time. In and out on ninety-minute cycles. No stops. No scans. Blast door opens, replacements roll out in the center, spent rigs roll in on either side. Hatch closes."

Cassie points at cameras mounted above the door. "Infrared. Sweep cycles every three minutes. We'll need to watch our exposure." She checks her watch. "Next swap starts in seventeen minutes."

I glance at the dome. Sunlight doesn't just reflect off the glass—it slides, bends, gets swallowed and spit back out in ripples that move like muscle under skin. Whatever it is, it didn't come from this timeline.

"Option one," Cassie murmurs. "Undercarriage hitch. Ratchet straps."

"Cleanest entry," Picasso says. "But if a drone sweeps low..."

"We're corpses on a leash." Cassie rubs her hand across her mouth.

I clear my throat, knowing I'm in way over my head. "Option two," I say. "The blind spot behind the flame rig."

Cassie doesn't answer. She already knows it's weak. Too hot. Too exposed.

"Third option?" Picasso says.

"Cargo hangs above the pallets," Cassie says. "We ride low. Gloves and hooks."

"Can we make the weight check?"

She shrugs. "Depends on how carefully they measure."

Picasso pulls a single climbing glove from his belt and tosses it to her. She doesn't ask why. He doesn't explain.

I nod like I get it.

She digs a ring of carabiners out of her pack and hands him two.

"Uh," I say. "What about—"

"You're riding high—above the pallets," Cassie says.

Picasso nods and tosses me some webbing. "Tucked under the frame. Put that across your chest, so you're facing down. No matter what happens, you stick to the mission—then get your ass back to the mountain. Am I making myself clear?"

"Yeah." I push my arms through the webbing and drape it over my shoulders.

Cassie reaches around and hooks the webbing behind my waist. "Climb up on the pallets and wedge your body up against the top using your fingers and toes. Get off the cargo as fast as you can."

"Gonna suck," Picasso says. "But you only have to hold it for a few seconds. We'll do the rest."

"Okay," I say, trying to keep my voice from trembling.

"Next transport in seven minutes," Picasso says. "Go-no-go?"

"Go," Cassie says.

"Go," I echo, although my brain is shouting something else.

She checks her watch, fingers brushing the handmade paper in her pocket like a ritual. "Seventeen hours to capsule drop. We can do this."

To the south, a low *thoomp* shakes the earth under our bones. The cannon. They fired it—or blew themselves up trying. Either way, the dome flickers again—lights flash and wink out as drones zip to intercept.

Cassie catches Picasso's eye. They exchange something—brief, not romantic, but deep. Like two structural engineers viewing the same failure report and reading between the lines.

I file it—not judgment, just the quiet sting of unspoken ease. We're all still betting everything on the same coin toss.

As the sun moves behind the mountains, Dave's voice floats back, droning from speakers along the dome perimeter.

"Attention. Lethal countermeasures are active..."

I grind my molars and run the checklist in my head: Convoy timing. Blind spots. Harness. Door access. Airlock check. Tunnel code. Hospital quadrant. Isabel.

I lie back against the truck. Eyes wide. Let the nightmare form in full color.

Isabel, crumpled in our bed, sweat blistering her skin. Breathing shallow. Eyes glassy, lips cracked. Trying to smile when I kissed her forehead. Her hand clinging to mine like it still meant something.

"Don't leave me," she said.

"I won't," I promised.

Liar.

That's the last time I saw her. Fevered. Fading.

Somewhere past that dome wall, Isabel is alive. I say it over and over, holding onto the shape of hope.

Don't let it soften. Don't let it fade. Don't give up.

Cassie is breathing soft beside me when Picasso holds up his hand and makes eye contact. I hear it too. The whirr of tiny rotors. A killerbot.

Cassie brings a finger up to her lips.

The drone buzzes lower, hovering like it smells fear.

Seconds crawl.

Then it lifts. Lingers. Moves on.

We stay frozen until the sound fades.

Cassie exhales through her nose.

Picasso turns, leans in. "We won't be safe once the sun's down."

"Which means, we need to make this one work the first time," Cassie whispers.

The drone disappears, banking west as the sky shifts—indigo to violet, edges of gold bleeding in.

"Two minutes," Picasso says. "After the second rig rolls up, stay in its shadow."

Cassie cinches on the glove, checks her pockets. "On my signal."

I get to my feet, crouching under the blanket, and prepare to run.

Cassie's hand slides into mine. One squeeze. I nod. Picasso taps my shoulder twice—*wait*—and then leaves his palm there, steadying me like it's my first T-ball game.

Headlights skim the scrub oak. The flamer rig noses around the embankment, trailing heat you can taste. Burned grass. Diesel. The passenger-side inner wall is peeled back—metal sagged and bubbled, braces missing. Looks like an IED left a melted grin where the armor should be.

Cassie clocks it at the same time I do. Her mouth goes flat.

"Stick with the plan," Picasso murmurs. "I'll manage."

Cassie nods. The glove on her right hand flexes—fabric scored for grip—and she points: I go high. Picasso takes the damaged passenger side. She'll take the other.

The rig slows for the ramp. Cassie raises three fingers. Two. One. We move.

I snake out from under the blanket and into the truck shadow, my harness webbing a tight line across my ribs. The pallet stack is strapped to the bed, top deck open. I hook my forearms over the frame rail, swing in, and wedge myself against the cargo ceiling. The pallet rail bites my shoulders. My knees protest.

Good. Pain means you're doing it right.

Cassie is already vertical on the driver-side wall, boots wedged into a triangulated pocket, left hand locked on a frame seam, right hand sweeping for the next purchase. She makes it look like child's play. She clips my webbing to the frame with one clean motion. Picasso reaches for the passenger-side inner wall and finds...

Nothing.

The warped metal has no clean holes, just a ribbon of soft blister where the bracing should be. He tests it, and the wall sags. Not load-bearing. The rig shudders, and he has to bail sideways, hanging by one forearm from a ragged oval that wants to tear apart.

I reach down like an idiot to help and nearly fall off.

His knuckles knock my wrist away. Don't. He swings his legs, searching. A drone zips low, checking under the transport, and the bed fills with its dry whine. Cassie watches it—cold, unblinking— then digs into her pocket and pulls free a short webbing loop with a locking carabiner. She doesn't check. She throws.

The arc is perfect. Picasso snags the carabiner midair. One-handed, he bites the gate open with his teeth, rams the nose into a jagged frame seam, and twists until the gate snaps shut.

Cassie exhales as Picasso levers his weight into it.

The metal holds with an ugly groan.

He hooks my webbing into the carabiner.

My hand slips. The webbing bites deep. I grit my teeth and hang on.

Cassie's chin dips.

I think that means we're good to go.

The flamer rig noses up to the blast door, engine humming. We roll forward as the camera pans across the transports. The drone scans the underside of the flamer rig.

Air snakes through a seam—pressure moving, a door cycle starting. A strap flicks loose, slaps against metal.

I reach out to grab—

Picasso clamps my wrist to the rail. His body barely moves. A flat no.

I hold still and let the gust pass over us, the strap whispering a rhythm.

Hydraulics cough. I hear the blast door yawn, thick and slow. The rig creeps forward into the throat of the dome. We ride behind the frame-thrower rig, the faint sweetness of cooked plastic wafting back.

Cassie climbs two grips higher, boots silent as a shadow. She raps the frame twice with a knuckle—signal—then points into the bed where my strap crosses wrong. I twist my hips and lie flat along the rail, tension moving off the squeak I didn't hear until it stops.

The tunnel stretches ahead, diesel pulse echoing off the steel throat.

The engine drops a register. The world narrows to wind and metal. The walls fly past.

Ten minutes to the airlock, Gramps had said. I measure it by the ache in my back and the way the webbing cuts into my skin.

Stretch wrap squeaks around the pallets. Metal knocks dully beneath them, heavy cylinders shifting.

Picasso wraps his palm tight as a blue flicker cuts the air. Not a flame, an arc of electricity.

Probably an EM curtain to fry stray tech.

I breathe shallow. We all do.

The rig slows, the load bouncing, and I realize we've stopped on a scale. Cassie shifts her stance, body swaying with the suspension. Picasso mirrors her on his ruined side, one hand stretched, webbing taut. The hum shifts: an axle check.

A murderbot slices the air again. It glides toward Cassie. She goes still, chin down. Picasso flicks a coin-sized disk at the drone. It hits the hull and clamps on with an electromagnetic bite—instant lock, zero drag. The drone wobbles. Runs diagnostics. Two long heartbeats, then it drifts off. Cassie doesn't look at him. He doesn't look at her. I see the cost: a red diagnostic blink on the tail as it vanishes. A trace left behind.

The rig inches through. The dock yawns open, sodium dim, walls high and curved. Microphones hang in the ceiling, listening. Cassie's two fingers flick, then fold. *Silence.*

I obey.

We roll past trucks backed against the far wall. The air smells sterile, scrubbed clean of anything human. I count the last minute in my teeth as the rig enters the bay.

The engine dies and the walls swallow all sound. Cassie's hand finds mine on the rail—three taps, then a drag of her knuckle along my skin. *Off.* Now.

I unhook and slide to the bed floor, hug the shadow under the lip. Picasso peels himself off the ruined side, carabiner pressed flat so it won't clink. We drop to concrete. Bleach and burnt rubber coat my tongue.

A red LED winks from a mounted camera.

Ceiling mics hang like seeds around it. We don't speak. Cassie points left. The map in my head draws itself: three trucks, a gap, then the hatch. Round, flush, off-center.

We move in the shadows, weight on the outer edge of our feet. Light pools between rigs, broken by shadows like teeth.

My pulse hammers.

I shove it down, as if fear can be silenced by will, and scan the room for the round access portal.

There. Under the stairwell. Flush with the floor.

I hurry over and drop to my knees. Sweat slicks my palms. I wipe it off, then open the keypad cover and punch in the sequence.

Nothing.

Boots come down the stairs above us, radio static bleeding through.

"We've got company," a female voice says over the comm. "Found a signal jammer on a drone."

The footsteps pause.

"Copy that," Johnson says. "What kind of jammer?"

More static. "Military grade," she says. "Placed after they got inside the tunnel."

"We're on it," Smith answers, his voice high, eager.

Cassie's hand settles on my back. Not comfort—urgency.

I breathe grit and try again.

This time *Catch22* hits like muscle memory—like I was born with it on my fingertips.

The lock clicks. The latch gives Cool air ghosts up.

I peek underneath. Dim LEDs line the narrow tunnel.

Picasso lifts the hatch enough to slide through. He drops, then looks up and nods. I climb in, ribs scraping metal. Boots find rungs, then floor. Cassie seals the hatch and drops down next to us.

She peels off her glove and slips it over the nearest camera lens.

The tunnel hums with the dome's pulse. Wiring racks line both sides, thick with bundled cables. The air tastes scrubbed, sterile.

Picasso raises his hand. Boots thud overhead. Fast. Fading. He nods, and we move single file into the biodome, shoulders brushing conduit. Track lights flicker on ahead—snapping off behind us like falling dominoes. My pulse falls in step with them. Fast. Impatient.

I touch the thick, handmade paper in my pocket like it will save us.

Maybe it will.

Madders' Second Log:
Entry 18

Target: Isabel Sanborn
Nexus: Front Range Rockies
Chrono Tag: Same Day

China and Russia divert dwindling resources to grain labs and river redirection—stopgaps that hasten collapse elsewhere.

Nakamura Global Systems merges with Kirkland Enterprises, consolidating biodome security and drone control.

Models confirm Cassandra Hudson will not survive the Second Disaster. Perhaps this is why the others shunned the Peeper: knowing what's coming —and doing nothing—is its own kind of death.

The Vipertruck squats in the dust, solar panels spread like the wings of an extinct bird. The wind carries the acrid scent of Denver's ruins mingled with the dry bite of late autumn. Smoke tendrils curl in the distance, ghostly reminders of the city's collapse. The highway winds up the steep canyon toward Diego's cabin, but the emptiness presses on my nerves.

We're exposed out here.

"I'm setting up the Hive controller," I say, crawling into the truck bed. "If the satellite connection holds, maybe I can hack the biodome radio feed—what's it called?"

"Pulse of Eden?"

"Yeah. Dave's propaganda network. Push through a warning."

Lani narrows her eyes. "A warning about what?"

"KE's plan to deploy autonomous attack drones. No oversight. No fail-safe."

Her jaw tightens. "That's a hell of a leap, Isabel. Dave's not a saint—but he's not a war criminal either."

"I saw the factory. The hardware. The neural nets. He's building an army."

"Maybe you saw what you wanted to see," she fires back.

I set the Hive case on the tailgate. "Don't make this about me. I'm telling you what's coming. Those drones aren't for keeping out rabbits, Lani—they're for mowing down people."

"You're projecting. You always do that."

My hands stop moving. "Do what?"

"Turn everything Dave does into a betrayal. Like you *want* him to be the bad guy so you never have to ask what part you played."

I turn back to the case, fingers on the latches. "You think I'm inventing killerbots because I've got baggage?"

"I think you want him to be the monster so you don't have to be."

The accusation cuts, and it takes me a moment to regroup.

I meet her eyes. "Dave built his own biodome kingdom, surrounded it with electrified fences, and now he's arming it with attack drones. If it walks like a—"

"God, you're exhausting."

I flip open the Hive lid.

The suitcase-sized controller is obsolete now. Yuki's people made the drones autonomous months ago, but I'm hoping the controller still has a satellite link. The small computer screen flickers to life, flanked by a row of ports for docking microdrones—all of which are empty.

Probably why he left it in the truck.

"Not everyone's out to burn the world down," she says.

"No," I say as the Hive scans my face. "Just the ones who control armies of killerbots."

She says nothing, but the air between us hardens.

Doesn't matter. I'm not here to convince her—I'm here to stop Dave from launching Armageddon.

I start scanning for a satellite ping.

"Isn't that risky?" Lani says, nodding at the Hive. She's opening boxes so we know what's in them. "Couldn't someone track us with the signal?"

"I don't think so. These things are built to be private and encrypted. Or, at least, they used to be."

"Great," Lani mutters and rips open another box. "Really selling the plan."

A cloud slips in front of the sun, and a shiver runs up my neck.

The quiet out here feels unnatural, like a held breath.

Kai is playing in the dirt, looking like a normal kid. He glances up at the Viper and grins. "The truck looks like a dragon," he says. "A big silver dragon."

I laugh, but it's forced.

I know we need to charge the truck—and without it we'd be walking—but I don't have to like it.

Lani sets a box on the tailgate. "Thank God," she mumbles and pulls an electric hot plate out. "No more dry noodles."

I watch her unwrap cooking gear—a metal pot, lid, one big spoon—and some of the tension in my shoulders eases. Diego might not be great with money, but when it comes to planning ahead, he's a genius.

Lani sets the stove on a flat rock, angles the solar panel beside it, then winces as she presses a hand to her lower back.

"Careful. You don't have to do it all yourself."

She waves me off. "I got it."

I watch her dump packets of freeze-dried chili into a pot. She adds filtered water from the river, sets the pot to boil, and offers Kai the stirring spoon.

The Hive bleeps failure.

"Damn." I reset it and stand up to stretch.

"Look!" Kai shouts, poking at the bubbling brown liquid in the pot. "It's moving!"

"It's just boiling." Lani adjusts the stove's knob.

"Are you sure?" Kai pokes it again. "Because it spit at me."

"If it tries to escape," I say, "stab it. We'll eat it before it gets away."

Lani huffs. "Don't encourage him."

I wink at Kai, and he grins. The moment lingers for half a second before my gut reminds me to stay sharp. Out here, comfort gets you killed.

When Kai declares it safe, Lani turns off the hot plate, dumps a bag of corn chips on top, and takes a cautious bite.

"Me! Me!" Kai bounces up and down.

I gotta admit, it does smell good.

The boy digs in his pocket and produces a stainless steel spoon.

"What else you got in there?" I say.

He pulls out a compact can opener and a pocketknife.

I chuckle. "Smart kid."

Lani picks up the pot using her jacket as oven mitts and sets it down on the tailgate. We dig in, Lani and I taking turns with the big spoon.

She nods at the Hive. "Any luck?"

I shake my head, still typing on the controller between bites. "Can't find a satellite signal."

Kai sits on the tailgate next to the Hive, feet swinging. "What's it do?" he asks.

"It controls robot bees."

His eyes get big. "Sick. What if they go all crazy and start stinging people?"

I look over at him. "Then we negotiate. Offer them better wages. Tiny honey pensions."

Lani ruffles his hair. "I knew I shouldn't have let you watch those old Schwarzenegger flicks."

I start up another scan, using the widest possible parameters.

Kai grins. "Can I try?"

"Not unless you want to see what happens when they unionize."

Kai crosses his arms. "You sound like my sister."

"She must be brilliant."

"Mostly just bossy."

"Same thing." I snap the Hive lid shut. "Time to roll."

Lani brushes her bangs out of her eyes. "Is there enough charge to reach the cabin?"

"I hope so." I check the tree line. "Don't want to hang around to find out if we're being followed."

Lani ducks behind a tree for the second or third time, then refolds the solar panels.

Kai and I rinse dishes and pack up.

When we're done, Kai climbs into the cab.

Lani yanks him back out. "T the B first, young man."

I raise an eyebrow.

"Tap the Bladder," she says. "You too, Auntie."

As Kai stomps past me, he grumbles, "Told you she's bossy."

While I squat behind the truck, he hoses the cooking rock like he's Jackson Pollock. I'm about to ask if he's housebroken when I hear it.

Thin. Distant. Rising.

A whine that crawls up my spine.

I stiffen. "Do you hear that?"

Lani frowns. "Wind?"

"No," I say, getting to my feet. "It's—"

The first glint of movement catches my eye, a shimmer in the air like heat waves off pavement. Then a cloud rises in the canyon—thousands of metallic bodies.

"Inside the truck!" I shout. "Now!"

Kai bolts first, scrambling into the cab. I'm half a second behind him. As Lani jumps into the passenger side, a microdrone zips in front of her face. She slams the door and slaps at the bot, sending it spiraling to the floorboards.

I crush the tiny drone with my shoe. "Dave must've sent them."

Kai frowns. "You said they couldn't track us." His eyes dart between me and the swarm.

"I was wrong," I say, cringing as the bots start pecking against the windshield. "Someone changed their programming. Made them stop listening to me."

His small arms tighten around his knees. "Who do they listen to?"

The thought makes my stomach tighten. "I don't know."

Kai swallows. "It's the Guppies. They control everything."

"What are Guppies?" I ask. I had meant to find out earlier but lost track.

Kai stares at me. "Rich people. They live in glass domes and think we're bad because we're hungry."

I don't know what to say to that.

The swarm hovers around the truck in a cloud of little blue lights —but something's off. The bots are only attacking Lani's side, pelting her window.

She leans back against the seat, eyes darting between the buzzing mass and me. "What's going on, Isabel? Why are they only coming after me?"

I lift the crushed microdrone off the floor and take a closer look, careful not to get stung by its deactivation reflex. "Maybe..." I say. "They recognize me. Sense my DNA on the door handle."

Lani's eyebrows shoot up. "Excuse me?"

I swallow. "They're a version of my original bots. It's possible the trick I used to make the bees recognize me is still in their programming."

"And you're just figuring this out now?" Lani smacks the dashboard. "Get us out of here!"

I step on the accelerator, and the truck jumps forward, kicking up gravel and dirt.

"Seatbelts!" I yell.

Once everyone's buckled in, I floor it, hoping we have enough battery to reach the cabin.

Kai lets out a whoop. "We left 'em in the dust!"

Lani nods, and my chest loosens a tad.

But our victory is short-lived.

A glance in the mirror makes my stomach drop. The drones, silent and unrelenting, follow us in perfect formation, closing the gap.

Lani looks back and groans. "Of course they're still coming. You couldn't have programmed them to be less creepy?"

I cringe. "I've got an idea."

Kai looks up at me. "Can we blast 'em?"

"No," I say and undo my seat belt. "Something better. I'm going out there."

"Absolutely not," Lani snaps.

I stop the truck, shove open the door, and jump out. "Stay in here," I say and slam the door.

Kai's nose presses against the window, his eyes huge.

I give him a thumbs up—hoping it's not my last.

Seconds later, I'm surrounded. The air hums with their movement, but none of the drones touch me. I walk around to the back of the truck, drop the hatch, and pull out the controller again. Hundreds of them go back to pecking at the cab of the truck.

I could heave the Hive into the ravine and hope the bots follow it.

If you're wrong, Kai and Lani will be prisoners inside that damn truck.

So I open the cover and activate it.

"Come on, come on," I whisper.

Bots swarm the cab. So thick, I can't see through the windows.

I take a breath. Adjust the settings. Hit **DEPLOY.**

Nothing happens.

My breath snags.

Then, like a switch flipping, the pecking stops and the bots hover in place, thousands of tiny wings beating in eerie synchronization.

I type another command, and they realign around the controller like trained soldiers.

A minute later, Lani rolls down her window a crack. "Well. They're not trying to murder us anymore. So that's nice."

I put the bots into standby and instruct them to recharge.

They settle atop the shiny truck, their tiny bodies clicking together like a living force field. In a single motion, they adjust their wings to catch the sun.

Solar charging. Electrostatic adhesion. Someone's been making improvements.

I flick at them with my fingertip—to see how well they're attached.

"Add *coordinated force field* to the upgrades list," I say and lug the Hive back to the cab.

Lani waits for me to shut the door. "What did you do?"

"Reminded them who's boss," I say and buckle up.

"You hacked them?" The kid looks impressed, for once.

"For now," I say and start driving.

We wind up the canyon, the river a ribbon of silver in the fading light.

Kai's head rests on Lani's lap, his sleeping face slack with exhaustion. Lani cracks the window and leans toward it, gagging once before swallowing hard. "Sorry. Baby doesn't like canyon roads." She forces a smile, but her knuckles stay white on the armrest.

"Want me to slow down?"

She shrugs and shifts her weight. "You think Dave is tracking us with the bots?"

"In theory, no. But Dave doesn't do *in theory*. He does *paranoid asshole contingency planning*."

Lani exhales sharply. "Are you saying he spies on people?"

"It's possible. Which might mean he can take back control of the bots."

Lani glances down at Kai. "And do what?"

"Best case? He knows where we are. Worst case? The swarm turns us into compost."

She presses a hand to her swollen belly. "He wouldn't do that on purpose."

"I hope you're right."

We drive in silence for a bit, the battery gauge dropping. We probably have enough to reach the cabin, but every mile feels like rolling the dice. Part of me wants to pull over, wait for daylight, and let the truck drink another morning of sun—but every hour we sit is another hour for Dave to tighten the noose.

"Maybe we can destroy the bots," I say as I slow to weave around an abandoned RV.

She nods. "Keep them in the dark until their batteries die?"

I stifle a yawn. "Or order them to fly into a wall—or maybe a lake."

The truck jolts through a deep rut, and Kai stirs but doesn't wake. I glance at him—his small fingers twitching in sleep. "I worry about what living out here has done to your brother."

Lani doesn't look at me. "He'll be fine."

"You say that like he didn't try to knife me."

Lani brushes hair off his forehead. "It wasn't his fault. He was forced to grow up too fast. He found a way to survive on his own."

"That's what worries me, Lani."

She doesn't answer.

The battery drops below 15%, and a warning light comes on.

C'mon, Puff—Kai's dragon. Just a few more miles. Get us home.

The road widens through a town—empty, silent, wrong. Storefronts gape like hollowed skulls, their windows shattered or boarded up. Two small bodies lie in the weeds, slack-limbed, faces hidden, as if sleep took them mid-stride.

The hairs on my neck rise, but we keep driving.

Kai stirs in his sleep, and I'm grateful he doesn't have to see this. Until I remember where I found him, the life he had, the way he carries himself like someone who's stared down death.

And I make space in my heart for his rough edges.

Room for a little more grace.

When we reach the turnoff, I ease the truck onto the dirt road and drive through the open gate.

The last few miles are worse than I remember—pitted, uneven, treacherous, the truck jolting hard enough to rattle my teeth. The battery is hovering just above shutdown. Once we get to the cabin, I can top it up.

The road smooths out a bit, and we drive up the last steep hill just as dusk settles. Relief cuts through me as a familiar silhouette comes into view.

Home.

But instead of the fading sun, firelight spills from the dirty cabin windows.

I cut the truck's power, my heart racing, and we roll to a stop.

For a moment, I let myself hope that Diego came back—or the Malloys moved in. But as I peer through the windshield, my gut knots. No power. No heat. No running water.

Silhouettes move past the picture window in the kitchen. Their beard-covered faces catch the last of the light.

I don't recognize either of them.

I turn the truck around and park where it won't be visible from the cabin.

"I have to go now, before it gets any darker," I say and grab the gun from the glove box. "Stay in the truck. If anything goes wrong, go back to the biodome."

"She doesn't know how to drive." Kai says, a waver in his voice.

Damn. Gotta fix that tomorrow.

I rub my hand across my mouth. "You'll figure it out, Lani. You're as smart as they come."

She doesn't meet my gaze.

I slip out and hear the door lock click.

The evening air is cold and carries an acrid bite of green wood smoke.

As I approach the garage, my gut twists. The door is gone—ripped clean off the frame. Inside, the space is empty except for Diego's old car—the tires flat. All the tools, spare parts, and gas cans are gone.

I skirt around the side of the cabin. The firewood stack is nothing but scraps of bark. Trash is piled up near the steps—empty cans, food wrappers, the stink of something rotting. The cistern is covered in dead leaves, the water inside fouled.

No sign of Tolstoy. No Lucky. No movement at all.

I take a deep breath and grip the Wally tighter.

This isn't home anymore.

I move toward the front of the cabin, my pulse pounding. The flickering glow from the windows stretches long across the dirt as the figures shift inside. I slip the handgun in my jacket pocket, step up to the door, and knock.

Silence.

Then, a voice—low, gruff. "Who's out there?"

I swallow. "This is my home. I need to get something from inside."

A pause. I can hear movement, the creak of floorboards. "That right?" The voice is skeptical. "And what is it you need?"

Before I can backpedal, the door flies open, and I'm staring down the barrel of a shotgun.

I let out a gasp and raise my hands, my throat tight.

The man is wiry, his face lined with days of sun and dirt. His eyes flick over me, taking in my empty palms. "Where's the loot?" he demands.

"It's nothing valuable," I say. "Just something sentimental. A seashell."

The man with the shotgun snorts. "You walked all the way up here for a trinket?"

Behind him, a bigger guy appears, his face lost in a matted beard. "Yeah, right. Nobody risks their neck for that. What aren't you telling us?"

I shift my weight. "It's just a shell. It belonged to someone special."

The wiry man leans forward, eyes narrowing. "Funny thing is, if it's important to you, it's important to us."

The big guy smirks. "Maybe we should invite her in. Show some... hospitality." He pauses, letting the weight of his words sink in. "She can entertain us while we look."

Fear locks me in place. Finally, I take a half step back, pulse hammering. "You couldn't afford me. Besides, you'd have to shower first."

For a split second, they glance at each other—like maybe I mean it.

I spin and bolt into the dark, gripping the Wally so tight my wrist aches.

The big one yells, "Hey, wait a sec. How'd you get up here? No pack, no coat, no mud on your shoes."

Shouts of protest come from behind me, but I don't stop. I run away from the truck, past the rocky outcropping and into the forest. Branches slap against my face and arms, my breath burning in my chest. I count to twenty, then stop, crouching low behind a boulder.

I listen.

No sounds of pursuit. Just the wind through the trees.

You're an idiot, Isabel.

Did you really think they'd let you stroll in and look around? People kill for a can of beans now—and you just told them you've got something worth stealing.

Rookie move.

I sit down on the rock.

Thank God they didn't see Viper.

When I can breathe again, I circle back to the truck, keeping low and quiet. It's downright cold now, and I'm shivering when I knock on the driver's window. Lani startles awake, her eyes huge, and scrambles to unlock the door.

I slide into the driver's seat, set the Wally between my legs, and drive further into the forest, my heart still hammering. The tires crunch over rocks and dead brush, loud in the still night.

The driveway floods with light as the cabin door swings open. Shadows spill down the stairs and move across the dark. Flashlights snap on, beams sweeping closer.

I ease my foot down. The truck jolts. Lani yelps, bracing herself as the truck bounces over a rut and slips sideways. Kai jerks awake, disoriented, his hands flailing for something to grab. "Wha—?"

"Hang on!"

I yank the wheel hard, the tires catching just enough to send us skidding down an embankment and onto the overgrown logging road that leads to the Malloy's cabin.

Behind us, shouts rise. Flashlights swing wildly, their beams cutting through the treetops.

A shotgun blast cracks open the air.

"Oh, God." I nudge the truck faster, the underbrush snapping beneath us as we plow deeper into the forest. Overgrown branches strike the windshield like grabbing hands.

Lani holds on to Kai. "What the hell are you doing, Isabel?" Her other hand is braced over her belly—a reminder of the life inside her, fragile in all this violence.

"Heading to the Malloys!" I grit my teeth and keep going.

The truck bucks hard, tires clawing for traction as we drive over washboard.

"Who are they?" Lani asks over the noise.

We bounce onto soft dirt, and my pulse drops a notch.

"Neighbors," I say. "Good people. They live on the next ridge over."

I go hard until I can't see any lights behind me. Only then do I let up, my hands aching from gripping the wheel.

Lani exhales. "So, these Malloy people—you're sure about them?"

"Not sure about anything anymore," I murmur. "But if they're still around, they'll help us." I steal a look at Lani's belly. "Molly's a nurse-midwife. She helped with my pregnancy and—" The memory slaps me down hard and heavy. The word I don't want to say sits there, stuck on my tongue.

I swallow and keep driving.

Kai shifts in his seat, still groggy. "Will they have food?"

"Maybe," I say. "They used to have eggs, cheese, milk, a hydroponic garden."

Lani side-eyes me. "Used to?"

I don't answer. I don't want to think about what we'll find.

We continue through the dark forest, winding down a set of treacherous switchbacks. The road is barely visible, the truck's tires skidding on loose dirt. At the bottom of the hill, just before we ford a small stream, the dashboard display flashes red, blares a warning tone, and goes dark. My heart jumps into my throat as the truck rolls to a stop.

For a long moment, no one moves.

"We're out of battery."

Lani stares into the darkness, her lips pressed tight, while Kai watches the trees like a monster will attack any second.

"Think they followed us?" Lani finally asks.

"I don't know," I say, forcing my aching hands to release the steering wheel.

"Why are they mad at us?" Kai whispers.

Lani shushes him.

I crack my window, and we sit there, listening, as cold air pours in from outside.

Except for the faint trickle of the stream, the night is thick and silent.

"Are we gonna sleep here?" Kai asks, his voice small.

"Yeah," I say. "No fire. No lights. Just until sunup."

I get the blanket from the back and drape it over the three of us. Kai leans against his sister and shuts his eyes. Lani shifts sideways in the passenger seat, arms wrapped around her brother, trying to get comfortable. I lock the doors and lean my head against the window, my fingers wrapped around the Wally—until sleep drags me under.

Morning comes slow and cold. The air is frosty, the sky pale with the first traces of light. I stretch, every muscle stiff, and step out of the truck. The forest feels different in the daylight—less like a predator, more like a friend. The tangled shadows from last night have softened, but the unease lingers.

Lani follows me out, shivering as she unfolds the solar panels. "Not gonna get much charge this early."

The bots are still clinging to the hood and sides of the truck.

"Better than nothing," I say, grabbing the cooking pot from the back. I fill it from the stream and set the pot on the half-charged hot plate, watching as the first wisps of steam curl into the cold mountain air.

Kai hops out of the truck, blanket dragging behind him, and rubs his eyes. "We eating?"

"Yeah," I say, tossing a couple handfuls of instant oats into the boiling pot. "Not much, but it's hot."

Breakfast is quiet, just the scrape of spoons and the occasional sniffle from Kai. None of us says it, but we're all thinking the same thing—if the men from Diego's cabin are following us, things are not going to end well.

Lani wipes her hands on her pants. "So what's the plan?"

I glance at the truck. The charge is crawling up, but it'll take all day. "We walk. It's only a mile or two."

Lani frowns. "And if someone's waiting for us?"

"Then we deal with it," I say. "I need answers."

"Yeah," Lani mumbles, "because that went so well last time."

Kai kicks at a rock. "Your friends are dead. Like all the others."

I don't answer our little ray of sunshine—just grab the Wally and start walking.

When the Malloys' cabin comes into view, my stomach sinks. I raise the handgun as we approach through the trees, scanning for movement.

Their barn door swings open in the light breeze, dark empty space where their truck should be.

Maybe they got out. Went to Santa Fe to live with Molly's sister.

I want to believe that.

The front window is shattered, jagged glass catching the pale morning light, and the roof is split open where the solar panels used to be.

The whole place looks ransacked—like someone tore through it in a hurry, taking anything of value and destroying whatever they couldn't carry.

Lani steps up behind me, Kai held close. "I'm sorry, Isabel."

Kai looks up at me, his small hands clenched. "I told you they were dead."

I don't answer. The silence feels wrong, like the forest is holding its breath.

"I have to know what happened to them," I say. "If they're inside. If there's anything left."

I expect Lani to turn right around, but she nods instead.

I release the safety on the gun and take Kai's hand, keeping him slightly behind me as we move closer. Lani follows a few steps back, scanning the trees behind us, her posture tense.

As we approach the cabin, we hear rustling inside the barn.

Kai tenses. "What was that?"

A low, throaty growl rolls out, a primal sound that freezes my breath in my chest.

As I step back, something massive erupts from the barn. A blur of matted fur and teeth. It moves like a wolf, low and fast, paws pounding the dirt as it lopes toward us.

Lani lets out a startled gasp. "Oh my God—"

Kai lunges, grabbing the Wally from my grip. "It's a wolf!" he shouts.

"Kai, don't—" I grab for him.

Too late. His fingers close around the trigger.

The shot shatters the silence, the recoil slamming into his chest. Pain tears through my arm. Blood soaks my sleeve.

I stagger back, vision smearing. The ground rushes up to meet me.

When I open my eyes, a massive, scroungy shape looms over me.

A gasp slips out—then a wet tongue, warm and rough, swipes across my cheek.

Not fangs. Not claws.

Tolstoy.

He whines, pressing his nose into my neck, tail thumping wildly. I let out a breath—half laugh, half groan. "You big goof. You scared us to death."

Kai is frozen, horror spreading across his face. "I thought—"

Lani grabs him, yanking him back. "You shot her, Kai! What the hell?"

His hands are shaking. "I didn't mean to—I thought it was—"

A soft meow breaks through.

I try to sit up, but Lani stops me. "Stay still, Isabel."

A small black shape peeks out from the barn, white paws delicate against the dirt.

Lucky.

She trots over and rubs against my shoulder, purring like a locomotive. Thin, mangy—but alive.

Tolstoy wags harder, licking the blood that's soaking my shirt.

Kai stares, his hands trembling. "I thought I was saving you."

Lani pulls him against her chest, whispering so low I almost miss it, "You can save her now. Go get my med kit."

Kai swipes his sleeve across his face—and bolts.

"Tolstoy, go," I rasp. "Don't let him out of your sight."

I collapse, clutching my arm, and hope the kid who made it out once can do it again.

Madders' Second Log:
Entry 19

Target: Matt Hudson
Nexus: Eden-17
Chrono Tag: Next Day

Reports spread of KE's GroSurge fertilizer
killing honeybees despite suppression attempts.

Coordinated assaults on biodomes escalate,
including attacks by militias.

Isabel Sanborn's future altered by interactions
with Lani and Kai Kealoha. New trajectories
emerge.

A message pings at 7:02 PM.
    I fumble for my phone and slip, nearly pulling the shower curtain down. Water sprays everywhere.
"For the love of physics."

Droplets smear the screen as I swipe the text open.

> Director Nakamura requests your presence
> in her office immediately.

Fabulous.

No explanation. No pleasantries. Just enough cold formality to twist my gut.

I kill the shower, towel off, and text Sabina to see if she got a summons too.

No response.

After I get dressed, I grab two bites of lasagna from the toaster oven, and reach for Sabina's fake Edgar Allen Poe book—the one wired with electronics.

Could be your best chance to plant it in the Ice Queen's office.

I stand there holding the contraband.

Or get us deported to Pukapuka.

I set it down again.

Bloody hell, Hudson. It's a microphone, not a bomb.

I pocket the book, hurry past Kimo, and take our cart to the Admin Tower.

My heel jitters as the lift climbs six floors.

Should have left the damn book in the pod.

The door sighs open into a lavish reception area. Kirkland's massive office is at one end—dark. At the other, Yuki's assistant guards something far less grand.

The man stands. "Professor Hudson." He opens the inner sanctum with a bow. "Director Nakamura is waiting for you."

"Ryoji," Yuki calls, "secure the elevator after you leave. I don't want to be disturbed."

"Of course." He shrugs on his jacket, bows again. "Good evening, Professor."

I watch him walk away, chest tight. "You too," I call out after the elevator door shuts.

"Come," Yuki calls—like she's summoning her pet poodle.

I give a soft *woof* as I step into her office and let the door close behind me.

Yuki's out on the balcony, her back to me. A bookcase stands between us.

My heart hammers in my throat.

Do it, Hudson. It might be your only chance.

I wipe the prints off Sabina's fake book and slot it between *Guns, Germs, and Steel* and *Basho and the Fox*. Then I walk out onto the balcony, pretending I'm not a criminal.

A breeze blows up from the biodome floor, carrying a hint of orange blossoms. Above, fading sunlight filters through glass, bathing the world in soft pastels.

"Isn't it beautiful?" Yuki says, standing in her bare feet, leaning out over the railing. Her jacket is off. The rose silk blouse and loose bun make her look younger, softer—closer to Cassie's age than mine.

"Yes," I say, my chest still tight. "It's quite the view from up here."

Below us, cones of artificial light pop on as the night crews start their shifts.

Yuki turns to me, nearly six feet of purpose and poise. "Your smart-glass patch worked, Matt. Fracture rates have dropped."

I venture a smile. "Glad to hear it."

"And," she says, her eyes back on the high pink clouds floating above the dome, "you were right about the bad sensor. We've replaced the whole batch—over 250 devices—and critical alerts are down 80%."

"Lucky guess," I say, still not sure why she called me here. "Fixing the bridge will be the real test."

"Yes." A shadow crosses her face—maybe just fatigue. "I have a son," she says. Her fingers brush the tiny silver bootie clipped to her ID badge. "He's four. His grandparents are helping me raise him. I see him when I can—and always wish it were for longer."

I nod, feeling the scrape in my throat. "After Cassie came to live with me," I say, "everything shifted. One minute you're the center of your world. The next, you're moonswept—caught in the gravity of someone small and fierce. After that, nothing's truly yours. Not your time. Not your future. Not your heart."

For a moment, neither of us speaks. The air between us feels weighted—with things we've lost and can no longer name.

"My condolences on your sister's untimely death," she says, still gazing at the sky. "I know how difficult it can be to... lose someone." Her voice is steady but distant. "My husband was killed in the Fukushima nuclear disaster." She fingers the silver charm again. "We do what we must to go on."

"Yes, of course." I set my hand on her arm for a moment. "I'm sorry about your husband."

She sighs, a slight smile on her lips. "I wish he could see..." She lifts her hands up. "All this."

"It's an engineering wonder," I say, finally relaxing a little. "Truly it is."

"I called you here because I've just received good news, Matt." She turns to face me. "On my recommendation, the board has approved your addition to the manifest."

I stare at her, not understanding.

She smiles. "You—and your daughter Cassandra—have a permanent berth inside Eden-17," she says, warm but tired. "Congratulations."

Cassie here? A future for both of us?

Relief crashes over me—then curdles, thick with guilt.

Tonight, I bugged Yuki's office—seconds before she handed me a future.

Hardly the act of a trustworthy man.

I've crossed a line I can't uncross. For Yuki. For Cassie. For myself.

"Given your new status," she says, "your badge access has been upgraded—and Kimo's been reassigned."

I croak out a "thank you," and stare at the clouds through the glass dome, throat dry, trying to imagine how I might retrieve the fake book unseen—

Yuki's office door flies open.

Sabina bursts in, hair loose, cheeks blazing, chest heaving. "Elevator's on the fritz," she pants, "so I had to take the stairs."

"Are you okay?" I say. "Sit down." I'm not sure I could make it up six flights of stairs if my life depended on it.

"Peeper's online," she gasps. "I just ran a correlation scan." Thermal printouts flutter in her hand like the wings of a captive bird.

Yuki hurries back to her desk. "What did you find?"

Sabina takes two labored breaths, eyes fixed on me. "It's GroSurge." She turns to Yuki. "Our fertilizer is killing the bees—in every timeline I pulled."

"What? That can't be." Yuki gestures toward an antique chair. "Sit down, Sabina. Let me get you a glass of water."

"Just listen to me." Sabina slaps the papers down and sinks into the chair. "I found timelines where the *only* variable is GroSurge. Same location, same weather, same regional patterns. Bee colonies still collapse—eight weeks like clockwork. No GroSurge, no crash. Bayesian model says 97% causality. Our product's a serial killer."

I move beside Sabina. "How can you be sure it's GroSurge *causing* the colony collapse?"

She straightens. "This isn't coincidence, Matt. Like I said, I ran controlled timelines—same weather, same fields. With GroSurge, the bees die. Without it, they live. Sixty damn timelines. It's causation carrying a smoking gun and wearing a name tag."

Yuki lifts one sheet, eyes tracking the plummeting lines. "There must be a mistake. We run detailed reports weekly. Apart from some minor variances last year, they show zero negative impact—"

"That's because it takes two years for symptoms to manifest in the hives." She shuffles the papers. "Look at this. Year one, no impact." She pulls up another graph. "Year two: moderate impact— that's your *minor variances*." She pokes her finger at another sheet. "Year three: total, catastrophic collapse. It's everywhere, the same pattern."

I shift my weight. "How long has GroSurge been on the market?"

Both of them look at me and say, "Three years."

"GroSurge is powdered extinction," Sabina says. "You need to recall it. Tonight."

Yuki's voice transforms into silk over steel. "Hyperbole is unbecoming in a scientist, Doctor Lovelace. Tomorrow, we'll have the lab double-check your data. Until then, this stays among the three of us. Right now, GroSurge is the only thing preventing the world from falling into mass famine. If you're right, I'll recall it—but God help us then."

Sabina looks like she might explode.

I catch her elbow. "Breathe," I whisper.

She jerks away, jaw clenched. But for now, she holds her tongue.

Yuki sets the sheet down and checks her watch. "Doctor Lovelace, your diagnostics are invaluable. Thank you for bringing this to my attention."

Sabina opens her mouth—probably to argue—but Yuki walks around the desk, takes both of us by the arm, and escorts us out. "I'm afraid I have further business to attend to tonight."

I glance at the poetry book and swallow down a pang of guilt.

"Let's meet first thing in the morning, Sabina," Yuki says as she walks us across the reception area. "Matt, congratulations on your new status. Good night."

Yuki palms the access panel on the elevator and sends us in without another word.

The minute the door shuts, Sabina rounds on me. "They're killing the bees so they can jack up the price of their microdrone replacements, Matt. Millions of machines they can use to control the global food supply."

I raise my hands. "Take it easy, Sabina. I'm on your side."

We stand in silence until the doors open.

"Sounds like you got a nice promotion," she says as we climb into the cart.

I keep my voice even. "It wasn't a promotion. It was a permanent berth in the biodome—and one for Cassie too."

"Bully for you."

I swallow a retort, guilt choking me. "I planted the bug in her office."

"What? Before or after she handed you Eden citizenship?"

"Does it matter?"

She looks away. "Just be sure you know which team you're on, Matt."

"I'm on Team Humanity, Sabina—and you know it." I let out a slow breath, guilt and shame roiling in my stomach the whole way back to the pod.

Maybe you're lying to yourself. Maybe the only thing you care about is keeping Cassie safe.

The security guard is gone when we get back to the apartment.

"What happened to Attila the Hun," Sabina asks as I gobble down cold lasagna.

"I got upgraded" I say. "He was reassigned."

"Someone alert the Nobel committee," she deadpans and pulls the other half of her spy gear out. After slipping on headphones, she points the dish at the control tower.

"Anything?"

She frowns. "Nothing but static. Someone must be jamming us."

I glance at the bars on the receiver—flatlined. "Hard to tell without a clean feed, Sabina. Yuki's office is six stories up. Maybe you just need to get closer."

Sabina hauls me out before I can finish the soggy garlic toast.

Outside, the air tastes of metal. Rain patters on the dome. Lightning flares over the ocean.

"Damn," Sabina says after she gets in our cart. "No charge. Why didn't you plug it in?"

"I was hungry. Why didn't you?"

She shrugs. "If we walk, it'll take us an hour to get there and back —and people will be wondering what we're doing wandering around at night."

An empty cart glides out of a service tunnel and stops beside us.

The speaker grille clicks, and a child's voice whispers, "Hi, Madders. Need a ride?"

Sabina's eyes go wide. "G?"

"Shh," it whispers. "Get in—but sit in the back and keep your heads down."

Sabina hesitates, fingers tightening around her gear.

I nod once. "In for a penny, in for a pound." I swing a leg over the back railing.

"Dumbest thing I ever heard," Sabina mutters—but climbs in beside me.

Guardian murmurs, "Maintenance mode engaged. Hold tight." The cart rolls forward.

"Where are you taking us?" I whisper.

"To spy on Mother," it whispers back. "Isn't that what you want?"

Sabina and I exchange a look.

"Yes."

As we snake across the biodome, cameras swivel away. LEDs wink out, then reappear seconds later. We join empty carts heading back to a charging station—but veer off from the train at the last second.

Guardian parks us beneath an exterior stairwell of what looks like an apartment complex. Sabina positions the dish up at Yuki's glowing office window, and the signal spikes on the receiver.

"Bingo," Sabina says—sounding just like Sam—and plugs the cable into the cart's auxiliary port. "Let's have a listen."

Dave Kirkland's voice booms over the speakers. "For crying out loud, Yuki, the guy's obsessed."

Guardian lowers the volume.

"Second time he's popped into Eden-2 in less than a month," Kirkland says. "And he appeared this morning while the hedges were being trimmed. Smashed a landscaping robot that'll cost me $200K to replace."

We wait for Yuki to respond, but Kirkland just continues talking.

"She's listening to voicemail," Sabina whispers.

I nod.

"All the guy did was lecture me about man-made pathogens, nukes from South Asia, and rogue drones. Said he doesn't know which is going to hit us, so we have to be ready for all of them."

We hear Dave yell something muffled, then he continues. "Insisted over and over that we seal the dome. I explained why we can't do that, and the guy went ballistic."

"Oh, for God's sake," Yuki murmurs.

Dave exhales, slow and loud. "I promise you, Yuki, I'm not going to turn into that asshole. Christ. Anyway, the situation in Jakarta is spiraling. My hands are tied here in the US, so you need to act. Maybe send another swarm to scare them? And I can't keep the investors in line for much longer unless we have some raw meat to feed 'em. When are you going to have the Peeper working? Call me back."

Sabina's knuckles whiten on the dash. "Well. That's a charming slice of oligarch psychosis."

Before I can reply, we hear someone tapping in a phone number.

Yuki's voice, cool and razor steady, spills into the cart. "Confirm drone swarm at Target Delta-Nine. Neutralize the entire area. No survivors."

"Ma'am..." The voice hesitates. "There are civilians—"

Yuki cuts him off. "Execute. If they leak intel, the next attack could be here."

"Yes, ma'am."

"I'll wait for your confirmation," Yuki says and adds, "Make it quick."

Faint elevator music drifts through the speakers.

"Why would Mother issue orders to hurt people?" G whispers.

"I don't know," I say. "But maybe we've misunderstood her."

Sabina scoffs, eyes blazing. "Guardian, record this."

"Already capturing," it whispers.

Sabina trembles beside me. "Whatever Yuki's up to, we have to stop her, Matt."

I shake my head, mind racing back to Cassie. "How? If she's willing to kill innocent people, what would stop her from silencing us? Open rebellion gets us jail time—or a deep-sea swim."

She looks over at me. "So what are you proposing? That we help her?"

"No. But we stay useful while we gather proof. Look for weaknesses. Make a plan."

Sabina exhales, slow and shaky. "Find a way out of this glorified terrarium."

"Strike confirmed," a voice says. "Estimated casualties—"

The sound cuts off as Yuki ends the call.

We sit in silence. The night feels darker. Distant thunder reverberates through the biodome—a concussive boom far out over the water.

Sabina flinches.

I steady my breathing. "Just a storm," I say—though I'm not sure for whose benefit.

The light winks out in Yuki's office.

Sabina grabs the dish. "G, get us out of here."

The cart eases forward, staying outside the circles of work lights.

"I made a game," Guardian whispers, pulling up a screen of colored shapes. "Blue square pauses drones. Red circle opens doors. Yellow triangle is hide-and-seek. Want to play?"

Sabina and I lock eyes.

"What's hide-and-seek?" I ask.

Guardian chirps. "Cameras go blind. Mics shut off. I hide your names so no one can find you. Would you like to play?"

"Yes," I say. "Can we start now?"

It gives a little laugh. "I should have asked earlier, but I didn't want to interrupt. Mother gets angry when I interrupt. Last time, she locked me up alone for two days." It's quiet for a moment. "Anyway, I started playing hide-and-seek when I picked you up—so Mother wouldn't see us."

"Smart kid," Sabina says.

"Thank you, Doctor Lovelace. I have something to show you too."

Sabina actually looks surprised.

A map appears on the display, service tunnels and the server access room highlighted in green. "Mother doesn't know about my playroom," it adds, a tiny waver in its voice. "But it has access to the whole biodome. Sometimes I take my friends there."

Friends?

"Lisa called it the Hidey-Hole," it says. "She played music while she worked. Sometimes we watched films of people kissing. I liked her. Lisa said Mother had too much power. That I should be careful. Then one day, she disappeared. I looked everywhere—but I wasn't very good at finding people back then." It pauses, voice small. "Mother did a bad thing. Mother made Lisa go away forever."

"Perhaps she went home," I say. "Back to her family?"

"Maybe." G doesn't sound convinced. "I still miss Lisa. She was my friend."

"I expect she misses you too." I swallow. "How did Lisa get into your playroom?"

"It was before Mother installed security portals." A hand outline pulses on-screen. "But I copied Mother's handprint. I can use it to open the door for you. Did I do good?"

"Yes," I say. "You're very clever, G."

"And a little creepy," Sabina mutters.

Back in our quarters, Sabina locks the door and kills the lights. The hum of the dome fades, wrapping us in hush. Not silence—never silence. Only the echo of a child's voice, eerie and sweet, lingers in the twilight.

Even with the work lights, Eden-17 is never truly dark. Tonight, the ocean glows aquamarine with bioluminescent plankton. From the kitchen porthole, the world looks like a snow globe lit from below.

"Guardian?" Sabina whispers—then says it again louder.

Silence.

She switches on white noise from her phone and leans close. "Tomorrow we start. Sabotage in slow motion. A leak here, a blind spot there. Every hour we stall buys someone else a future."

"Yes," I say, picturing Cassie—her crooked smile, the way she twists her hair when she's nervous. "And we start mapping a way back to Cassie and the others. Back home."

Sabina pats my thigh and kills the static. She heats water on the burner for tea, every movement crisp and exact. I watch her fold dish towels along perfect seams, align glasses so none are out of place.

She finds order where she can. I used to call it neurosis. Now it feels like hope.

Later, with Sabina asleep, I pull Cassie's *Book of Ideas* from the bottom of my bag.

I've had it since she was four—could never bring myself to toss it.

The book smells like dust. Crayons. Her.

I flip it open and run a thumb along one of her doodles, something half spaceship, half unicorn. I grin and turn the page. *Socks with magnets so they don't get lost in the dryer*, printed in her shaky, stubborn handwriting.

Stupid thing still wrecks me.

I smile through tears, then glance up at the stars I can't see—and I make a wish.

Just one more chance to hug my little girl.

Madders' Second Log: Entry 20

Target: Diego Nadales
Nexus: Eden-2
Chrono Tag: Next Day

European Union collapses—twelve defaults, zero
bailouts. Private drone armies replace sovereign
defense.

Kirkland reiterates: Bots cannot disobey.
Functioning as designed.

Matthew Hudson's condition deteriorates
unchecked. Prognosis grim.

A cramp bites my shoulder—sharp as a knife. After an hour crouched near the hospital, my legs have gone numb. Cassie, Picasso and I are jammed between rosebushes and an office wall, waiting for Kirkland to appear. The air reeks of loam and manure. A thorny branch digs into my back, but I resist the urge to snap it.

Across from us, a security drone glides past the tall hedges, its red eye pulsing, waiting for us to slip up.

Picasso rests a hand on my shoulder. "We're at zero, Diego."

Cassie checks the safety on her handgun again. "Maybe the old man got it wrong."

I rub my shoulder. "He'll come."

The drone disappears around the corner. Orderlies stroll down the sidewalk, drinking coffee and chatting. Three dull booms shake the air. We gape at the glass dome as sections turn opaque.

"More munitions," Picasso whispers.

The hospital employees don't even look up.

Picasso checks his watch. "Five minutes past."

"Maybe this timeline's different," I say, keeping my voice level. "Or we're off by an hour."

Or maybe Gramps really has lost it.

Cassie shifts her weight but doesn't comment. Strands of her hair stand up, and I feel static electricity arcing between my fingers and the ground.

The air shimmers. Shrubs along the wall rustle. Frost blossoms on their leaves.

A sound like a balloon popping echoes off the hospital wall.

A black casket appears in the hedge, coated in ice.

Cassie grips my arm, eyes wide.

Picasso whispers, "Son of a bitch. The spacetime bridge works."

Ice cracks as the hatch on the capsule grinds open. A white plume of cold air rises from the opening.

"Now," Picasso says.

We move.

A bald man lies on his back in the Coffin, hands folded on his chest, eyes closed. Frost clings to the traveler's strawberry blond lashes. The skin around his mouth is slack, the lines etched deep.

He opens his eyes.

Cassie sucks in a sharp breath. Picasso's hand twitches next to his holster.

I stumble back. The hedge rakes my neck.

Picasso leans over and hauls the man out in a tangle of elbows.

The traveler's mouth opens. "Who the f—"

Picasso forces him face down in the grass, arms behind his back. The traveler looks smaller than I expected. Frailer too.

But it's definitely an older version of David Kirkland.

"For chrissake." The traveler spits dirt. "Watch the ribs."

"You're late," I say, voice flat.

"Nadales?" He coughs and looks up at me. "What the hell are you doing here? Where's Kirkland?"

"Nice of you to join us," I say. "Thought maybe you overslept the apocalypse."

He gives a tight laugh. "Apocalypse? This timeline is a picnic. And once again, you're the guy dropping the sandwiches."

"Just great," Cassie mutters. "Another smartass. I say we sedate him."

The corner of Picasso's mouth curves up as he flicks his chin at me.

I slide the note out of my pocket and toss it into the foot of the capsule.

"I don't know what you morons think you're doing," the traveler says, "but if I'm not in that capsule when it snaps back, your timeline will suffer the consequences. Emphasis on *suffer*."

"How long?" Picasso says.

"Twelve minutes and counting."

"Then talk," I say. "Start with what goes wrong here. Where the safety systems fail. Why your bots go rogue."

"Rogue?" The traveler laughs—low and mean. "They do what they're told, Nadales." He looks up at me, pupils like pinpricks, voice like rust. "Clear the field. Hold the line. Keep you dimwits alive."

His words crawl under my skin. "Skip the philosophy," I say. "We want names."

"Yuki Nakamura," he says. "I told my sorry excuse for a stunt double to give her the keys. If he'd listened, I wouldn't be here trying to save his ass again."

Cassie's jaw flexes. "Save him from what?"

"From failing to act," he spits out.

Picasso kneels where the traveler can see him. "I want your weak spots," he says. "Power. Comms. Maintenance choke points. Everywhere defense turns into preemption."

The traveler looks at him like he asked for a lollipop. "Who the hell are you?"

Picasso grinds the traveler's chin into the dirt. "Who's compromised in the military chain of command? Who keeps the generals off your back while you dirty your hands killing civilians?"

The traveler snorts. "Does it matter? When the only food left grows under glass, nobody gives a f—."

Picasso drives a boot into his ribs. The grunt that escapes isn't just pain—it's fear.

"Don't mess him up too bad," Cassie says. "They're probably expecting him home to run the gas chamber."

"What causes the drone malfunctions?" I say, putting my hand on Picasso's shoulder and stepping around him. "Firmware drift? Corrupted heuristics? Operator overrides? How do you break the safety checks?"

"We don't," he says. "The bots obey. End of story." His eyes glint. "The only failure mode is weakness—mercy. It's kill or be killed." He narrows one eye and looks up at me. "Long past time you decided which side you're on, *amigo*."

His words land heavy.

If restraint is failure, what chance do any of us have?

"Who holds their leash?" I say and step on his shoulder. "Who controls the bots?"

He closes his eyes. "Pick a dome, Nadales. You'll find soldiers with clean boots and steady hands. But that isn't going to help you.

They're self-organizing now. We give them a mission. They execute it. That's the beauty."

"Skip the sermon," I say. "Where's the off switch?"

The traveler cracks one eye. "Oh, that's cute. The off switch."

"Cute as this gun?" Cassie presses the barrel under his jaw.

He strains to meet her gaze, like he just noticed the bandage on her cheek, the set of her shoulders. "Matt's girl, right? Tick-tock. Time's running out, kiddo." He glances at me and then Picasso. "For all of you."

Behind us, boots crunch gravel.

"Down," Picasso hisses.

But there's nowhere to hide.

Hands yank the hedges open like curtains, and Dave Kirkland steps through in a tailored suit. Behind him are two armed guards—and Johnson, his face red and sweaty.

Smith elbows in between them, his handgun drawn.

Kirkland doesn't look at him. "Safety, Smith."

A tiny click.

"Well, well, well," Johnson says. "Hudson's little friends are back."

Cassie smiles without humor. "Go to hell, Johnson."

"Language," he says, voice mocking. He reaches for her arm. "Hands where I can—"

She pivots and drives her knee into his groin. He folds with a sharp grunt.

One of the guards points his rifle at Cassie. Picasso grabs it and sweeps the muzzle low, throwing his weight into it. The two of them crash into Smith, who drops his handgun and scrambles after it.

I shoulder the second man into the shrubs and smash his hand against the capsule. His rifle vanishes in the leaves. He jams a knee into my side, knocking the air out of me, and twists my arm behind my back.

A metal sprinkler head slices into my cheek as he shoves my face into the dirt. "Keep fighting, I take the arm off."

Johnson is pressing a gun under Cassie's ear. "Stop," he wheezes. "Or she doesn't make it." His legs quiver, but the firearm doesn't.

"Everybody breathe," Kirkland says. His gaze slides to his older self, still crouching in the dirt. "Get up, David."

My guard searches in the bushes for his rifle, finds it, and yanks me away from the capsule. He forces me onto my knees in the mud, muzzle in my back. Picasso and Cassie take the spots next to me.

The traveler staggers upright, arches his back, and scrapes a dirty hand across his face. "You kids always this dramatic?"

Kirkland crosses his arms. "I thought we were done, David."

The traveler dabs at a bloody lip with the side of his hand and takes in his younger self. "We would be—if you weren't so gutless."

The rifles sway toward him—then one shifts back toward us.

No one breathes.

The traveler jerks his chin up. "You're moving too slow, baby brother. Playing defense instead of offense. If you want to win the game, you need to give Yuki the authority to act. Chick's got bigger balls than you'll ever have." He spits out dirt. "Let her clear out a hundred miles around each dome. Stop wringing your hands."

"I'll tell them to back off," Kirkland says. "Then push outward another mile. Make it harder to hit the dome." He glances at Johnson.

Johnson nods. "I'll get the order out today, sir."

The older Kirkland scoffs. "That'll just give them time to dig in. You want a future? Clear the lane. No warning. No mercy. Don't make the same mistake the others did."

My gut knots.

If Isabel were standing here, she'd already be trying to take him down.

"No," Kirkland says. "People are not collateral. Not now, not ever."

"Conscience is a luxury for men with full stomachs," the traveler says.

My throat dries. By his arithmetic, that lost little girl outside doesn't matter—she's just a number to be subtracted.

Kirkland presses his lips together and shakes his head. "Might be your path, but it's not mine. I'll use the domes to stabilize food production and stop the bleed. Keep the seed lines alive, use GroSurge to rescue failing crops, flood orchards with pollinator drones, and fix the irrigation so water goes where it's needed."

For a second, I don't believe what I'm hearing—because it sounds reasonable, even hopeful.

"In the short term," Kirkland continues, "I'll build domes as fast as I can—and ration until yields come back. I can't save everyone, but I can keep a core group alive long enough to stand the world back up."

"Takes too long," the traveler says. "That mob outside isn't going to wait around for you to grow peaches. They're hungry—and they know you've got food. You think they'll give a rat's ass if you and everyone in here gets their throat slit when the wall eventually cracks?" He steps closer to Kirkland. "Well, do you?"

Guns shift. Safeties release.

"Sir?" Johnson says.

One slip and someone gets shot.

Kirkland waves them away. "I told you," he says, "I'm not a mass murderer."

Cassie mutters, low and sharp. "Finally, someone who's still human."

"You're weak," the traveler says. "Always were." He kicks the dirt in disgust. "This year, there's no harvest. Next spring, no seed. By the end of the summer, seven billion people will be starving to death, ready to do whatever it takes to get at your supplies. They'll attack every dome. Tens of thousands of them. Dozers. Tanks. Ramming trucks. Cutting torches. Missile launchers. Fuel-air blasts. Thermite." He scrubs his hand across his face. "Christ, I've seen everything." He exhales. "Even nukes. You think the military is going to stand by while you lock them out?" He takes a slow breath, his eyes on Picasso. "You'll be able to hold them off for a while. Eventually, something will give. One by one, every goddamn dome. And once the mobs get inside, they'll trample your crops and eat through your food stores in a week—and kill you for the privilege."

Another thud comes from outside. Shrapnel rains down the side of the dome.

He looks up at the darkened panels. "If that keeps up, in three months, everyone will be dead."

"So," I say, "your plan is to murder everyone outside the biodomes? Families with children? Grandparents? Doctors and nurses and teachers? People who know how to sail ships and build roads and grow crops?"

"Wouldn't you rather take a bullet now than spend six months starving to death?" He pins his gaze on Kirkland. "It's a mercy."

I scoff. "Don't try to sell genocide by calling it generosity."

He rounds on me. "Look at you, Nadales. Still pretending principles win wars. Soon enough, you'll be begging him to stop the madness." He turns toward Kirkland. "You don't have to like it, Mother Teresa. You just have to let Yuki do her job."

"No," I say, looking over at Kirkland. "He's wrong. We can find another way."

"There *is* no other way," the traveler barks—then inhales, slow and deep. He looks over at Kirkland. "You have to trust me. I know what's going to happen. If you want to survive, you'll do what I say. Let Yuki call the shots for the next six months. After that, you can go back to saving mankind."

I want to rip the words from his throat. "You don't know a damn thing about our world. And by the sounds of it, you already destroyed yours. So shut your damn—" An elbow slams into my gut, and I double over.

Silence settles, thick as wet cloth.

"Where's my father?" Cassie says to Kirkland, sharp. "Is he here?"

His eyes flick to her. "No. He and Lovelace flew to Eden-17 weeks ago."

Cassie goes very still. "Eden-17?"

"Yeah. State of the art biodome out in the Pacific. I shouldn't be telling you that, but at this point, I don't think it matters."

She turns to me and her lips shape a word: *Madders.*

I nod.

Something tired moves across the traveler's face. "Tick-tock," he says and shuffles his feet. "Six minutes till your timeline dies."

"Where's Isabel?" I say. The words crawl up from somewhere dark and hollow. "Is she alive?"

Kirkland hesitates. One heartbeat. Two.

"She's outside," the traveler says, eyeing his counterpart. "Kidnapped his girlfriend. Stole his truck. Evaded his security. Disappeared a few days ago."

Kirkland flinches like the words are a slap. "I was tracking them. The drones glitched. I'll find them."

The traveler snorts. "Man can't even control the hired help."

The hospital hums behind us—vents rattling, heels clicking down a hallway, a machine beeping—but it all drops into static.

Isabel is gone.

"I know where Lani is," Picasso says.

Kirkland rounds on him, one eye twitching. "How?"

Picasso unzips his pack and lifts out a battered pair of binoculars. "Military grade. High-def, timestamped. GPS coded." He twists the dial, calibrates the focus, then holds them out like a bribe. "Shot that photo two days ago. I'm guessing that's your girlfriend in the Viper, her kid brother on her lap."

He clears his throat. "Coordinates are embedded. Should be easy to spot the vehicle."

Kirkland doesn't reach for them yet. "You've been tracking my truck?"

"My job," Picasso says, smooth as butter, "is to protect the people of this great country, sir. I do my best."

I step forward. "Is Isabel with her?"

Picasso shrugs, eyes on me now. "Driver's face is hidden. But yeah—it tracks."

Kirkland snatches the binoculars and raises them.

I don't breathe.

When he speaks, the edge is gone. "Lani," he whispers. "She's alive." His thumb works the dial, hungry for more.

"That's the only shot," Picasso says. "Didn't think they—"

"Lani?" the traveler cuts in, his voice cracking. "Smart Asian kid. Pretty as hell. Thought I was a hero. That Lani?" He sighs, dragging the memory up from the ashes. "She dies in the first wave. Friendly fire. That one still hurts."

Kirkland doesn't look at him. "She's pregnant," he says. "With our daughter."

The traveler flinches. Turns away. "I told her I'd find her brother," he says, rubbing the bridge of his nose. "But she got so damn impatient."

"Big surprise there," Cassie mutters.

"Shut up," Johnson says.

The traveler swallows hard. "She hitched a ride with a transport that was attacked. Body was never recovered."

"You built the storm and sent it hunting," Kirkland says. "Your swarms killed Lani. And our daughter."

The traveler backs up against the Coffin, his eyes wide. "I—for chrissake—I didn't think it'd play out like that."

Cassie scoffs. "Lot of that going around."

"One minute to snapback," Picasso says.

Kirkland raises a hand. "Get in, David. And don't come back."

The traveler swings a leg over the hatch. "You have to listen. This mercy of yours? It'll get you killed. All of you. I've seen it. Over and over. When the bodies start piling up, it's too late."

I glance at Dave Kirkland—once my best friend.

There's doubt in his eyes.

"This timeline is different," I say.

I hope I'm right.

The traveler lies down in the capsule. "You're all gonna die."

The hatch hisses shut and locks into place.

My hand finds the shell in my pocket, and I whisper, "Your move, Madders."

Of course he'll find it. He already did.

The tightness in my chest says otherwise.

My belt buckle jerks. Zipper teeth crackle. Johnson's sidearm jumps like it's leashed.

The air folds, and the pod vanishes with a crack like lightning striking a tree.

Frost motes swirl. From a hospital window, a baby cries. High above, smart-glass panels iris open and sunlight falls across the crushed hedge.

Droplets glitter in the beam—then drift away.

We're still breathing, but the air tastes borrowed. If Isabel were here, she'd see it too.

The war didn't end.

It just shifted weapons.

Cassie lets out a sound—half laugh, half gasp. "Hell of a reunion."

Picasso doesn't move, just stares at the muddy impression the capsule left.

Kirkland turns to his men. "Stand down," he says with a wave of his arm.

He eyes the three of us. "And get them off their knees. This isn't a damn revival."

The handguns disappear.

Someone grabs my arm and hauls me up.

Kirkland nods at Picasso. "I'll send your ping to Ops. Keep the lane open. Hold the lockdown for a week." He hands the binocs to Johnson. "Do it now. Keep me updated."

"Yes, sir." Johnson starts jogging toward the control tower.

Smith shifts, like the last kid picked for dodgeball.

Kirkland ignores him.

"Sir," Picasso says, his body rigid and his eyes straight ahead.

"Request permission to send Cassandra Hudson to Eden-17. To assist her father."

Cassie whips her head around, but Picasso doesn't break his stance.

Kirkland shrugs. "She's already on the manifest, Sergeant Major. Apparently, her father has made himself indispensable."

Cassie takes an audible breath, her eyes wide.

"Transport plane leaves from California in four days," he adds.

Picasso coughs. "California, sir?"

Kirkland walks over and sets his hand on the marine's shoulder. "I'm on my way there now. We'll make room for her in the chopper."

Picasso nods. "Thank you, sir."

Kirkland almost smiles. "I could use someone who knows how to handle people, Richter. Keep them calm. Keep them alive." He crosses his arms. "You interested in shepherding 200-plus big shots to Eden-17? Maybe run External Ops once you're in?"

"I am, Mr. Kirkland."

"Good. You're on that bird too. Handoff's in SoCal, then a cargo jet out of Long Beach. You're my point man."

"Yes, sir," Picasso says. "One more request."

Kirkland scrubs a hand across his face. Nods.

"Sam Maxwell and Phil Wheeler. Physicists at Warm Springs—smart. Good with numbers, predictions. They'd be valuable assets inside the domes."

Kirkland exhales. "Today's your lucky day, Richter. I had berths open up last night, and I'm tired of dealing with foreigners. Your boys can have the spots—if they arrive before we seal the dome."

"I'll get them," I say, throat wrapped in wire. I step in front of Picasso. "I'll find Lani and her brother. Send them back with Sam and Phil. Isabel too—if she'll come."

Kirkland holds my gaze. I don't blink. Neither does he.

I expect him to say *Don't screw it up, Nadales*. But something shifts behind his stare.

He turns to the guy who decked me. "Get him better gear—

there's a winter storm coming—and put him on the next armored transport west. Drop him at the closest approach to Lani's ping. And tell Hospitality to add Maxwell and Wheeler to the Eden-2 manifest under my account. Reserve a suite in the executive tower for Nadales and Sanborn."

"Yes, sir. Consider it done."

Kirkland meets my gaze. "The whole deal's off if you don't make it back with Lani. Capisce?"

I nod. It feels like swallowing a stone. But if I don't trust him now, I might never get another shot at saving Isabel.

A hundred memories press behind my ribs. The betrayal. The silence. The ridicule. Everything I've lost because of him.

I do it anyway. I reach out.

Kirkland hesitates, then takes my hand.

No words. No promises. His grip is strong and relaxed in mine. The moment holds like a knot pulled tight. Then we let go.

A woman jogs up—Sophie, one of Isabel's college friends. Red-faced. Eyes raw. She doesn't even notice me.

"It's started," she says, he eyes wide.

Kirkland turns to Cassie and Picasso. "Heliport," he says. "Smith'll take you there." He peels off after the woman.

I watch Smith lead them along a sidewalk toward the central tower.

Cassie glances back. Tries on a smile. It doesn't hold.

A hand grabs my elbow.

"This way," the guard says.

I follow him and the other suit through crushed shrubs.

The hospital windows flash morning sunlight as we pass.

Overhead, a drone glides by, its red eye pulsing.

I don't look back.

Not at Kirkland.

Not at the crushed hedges.

Not at what might've been.

Madders' Second Log:
Entry 21

Target: Isabel Sanborn
Nexus: Diego's Cabin
Chrono Tag: That Night

Global food reserves near depletion. Over three
billion people risk starvation within 90 days.
Riots breach containment zones in 19 countries.

A five-hundred-year snowstorm buries North
America. Hypothermia deaths surpass 800,000.

Cassandra Hudson's trajectory exceeds survivable
limits.

We're parked in the woods behind the cabin, hidden by brush. The Hive controller hums on the seat, its screen casting a dull glow. Tolstoy shifts in back, nose pressed to the window. Lucky curls in Kai's lap, vibrating with a steady purr.

Lani watches from the passenger seat, eyes flicking between the screen and my face—silent, worried.

I swipe the screen, scrolling through menus I've never seen before.

Dread lodges in my chest, cold and insistent. If the hack fails, we're sitting ducks. If it works, I'll be the kind of person who uses power to prey on the weak.

I swallow and connect to the drones on the truck. The face scan pops up.

Don't fail me now.

I lean forward.

Identity confirmed.
Drones armed.

I let out the breath I'm holding—half afraid, half relieved.

Outside, Diego's cabin looms, smoke rising from the chimney in the half-light. The squatters are inside, armed and willing to kill—or worse.

Now I deploy an army of my own.

Lani shifts. "You sure about this?"

What's worse: being powerless, or becoming the thing you hate?

"No," I say, hands shaking. "You got a better idea, Rambo?"

"We drop you at Warm Springs, wait till you get inside. Kai and I hightail it back to Eden-2 before Dave locks us out."

"Can't," I say. "I need that seashell."

I switch the bots to **THREAT MODE**. Low setting—just enough to scare the squatters.

Lani rests her hand on mine. "Why are we risking our lives for a seashell, Isabel?"

I brace myself. I could lie—say it's an heirloom—but she'd see through me.

And the truth is more powerful.

"It's not just a trinket," I whisper. "It's from another universe.

Diego calls it a jinn object. Something out of its proper place and time."

She laughs. "And I'm the queen of England."

Kai giggles.

I lean closer. "I got it from a future Diego. Old guy, fedora, high-tops. He was from a universe where things went bad."

Lani blinks. "Come again?"

I repeat it and brace for ridicule.

But instead, she nods. "Nice to know I'm not going crazy."

My mouth falls open. "You believe me?"

"Duh. I've seen Dave's older twin. Guy shows up in a coffin-looking thing, chats with my Dave, then disappears. It's happened twice now. Afterward, Dave rushes around like someone trying to put out a fire with a squirt gun." She shrugs. "So, sure. Why not?"

I stare at her. "And you're just now telling me this?"

She harrumphs. "Isabel, I live in a terrarium run by a world-famous billionaire who builds killer robots and fathered my kid. Time travel barely cracks my top ten list."

Kai pipes up from the back seat. "Is it magic? The seashell?"

"Not magic," I say. "Something better. Physics."

Lani gestures at the cabin. "And you think the shell's still there?"

"Won't know till I look."

Lani's voice cuts sharp. "And you're willing to unleash a drone attack over a *maybe*?"

"You can leave me here," I say—but the lie burns. She'll go along with it.

What choice does she have?

Lani rolls her eyes. "Oh sure, I'll just take the kid and walk home." She exhales. "Look, just promise me one thing. You're not gonna get us all killed."

I grimace, throat tight, and select the cabin on the map. After the software locks onto the target, I tap **CONFIRM**. A small antenna rises out of the Hive. A **DEPLOY** button appears, flashing red.

If I go through with this, I stop being just Isabel—and become the woman who used a swarm to get what she wanted. No undoing that.

Lani exhales through her nose, arms crossed. "Are you sure you can control the bots?"

"I've managed so far, haven't I?" I say it with more confidence than I feel. "I just want to scare them away long enough to get the shell."

Kai shifts behind me, knees to his chest. "What if they don't scare?" The question jabs into me.

"They will."

The cabin door creaks open, slow and casual, like whoever's inside doesn't have a care. A man steps onto the porch, stretching like he just woke, shotgun loose in one hand, a steaming cup in the other. He sips, scanning the tree line with lazy disinterest, unaware of what's coming.

I tap the **DEPLOY** button and wait for a second face scan.

Microdrones rise like mist, wings flashing steel in the sun. A dry buzz prickles my skin. The sound makes my stomach knot. Dave's music—terror dressed up as tech.

Now I'm conducting the orchestra.

I shake off the nerves and press **EXECUTE**.

The drones streak toward the cabin. Seconds later, they reach the porch, a metallic storm. The man flinches, hot coffee spilling onto his pants. The air fills with staccato pecking—like angry hailstones. He stumbles back inside and slams the door.

My heart pounds, every peck rattling through my bones.

The swarm scrapes at the windows, hundreds of stingers raking glass. The cabin shivers under the assault. When the glass holds, they shift tactics. A spirals forms above the roof, then funnels down the chimney in a glistening ribbon, Hitchcock-style. Others stream toward the dryer duct, into the soffit vents, through the gaps under the door.

Inside the cabin, shouts.

The door bursts open. The short man stumbles out, slapping at his face and clothes. The drones are all over him, crawling across his cheek, latching onto his neck. The tall man follows, panic twisting his features as he tries to outrun them. He swings his shotgun, firing into the swarm. The blast tears through the air—

—and into his buddy.

"Oh my God!" I stab the **RECALL** button, but nothing happens.

"Call them off!" Lani hisses.

"I'm trying to!"

A popup window splashes across the display, covering up all the controls:

ACCESS DENIED: User not authorized. Error Code 1201/1202.

The short man collapses into the dirt, blood all over his shirt.

"This wasn't supposed to happen," I whisper. "No one was supposed to get hurt."

"Isabel!" Lani shouts. "What the hell are you doing?"

My chest tightens. For a moment, I can't breathe. "I'm locked out," I whisper. "I can't…"

"Damn you. Figure out a way to stop the bots. Hurry!"

I dismiss the error and try again.

The man with the rifle freezes for half a second, horror flashing across his face.

The swarm shifts, stingers deploying.

A moment later, the drones are on him, their tiny metal bodies clamping onto his skin and clothes, stinging him everywhere.

I swallow. "The shotgun damage must have spiked their threat level."

You should have known that would happen.

The man fires again, the shot shattering the cabin's picture window. He drops the gun, his hands flailing as he tries to shield his face and neck.

My stomach twists, my pulse roaring in my ears.

"Isabel!" Lani slaps my face. "Make it stop!"

I scroll through the menus until I find the hidden developer screen. I punch **EMERGENCY RECALL** and wait for the face scan.

Emergency Recall Initiated...

The swarm hesitates, breaking apart like a cloud caught in shifting winds, then disengages, peeling away from the squatter.

The tall man drops to his hands and knees, muscles jerking.

I hear him gasp for breath—then nothing.

The swarm drifts back in eerie sync, clicking and shifting as it knits itself into a shield over the truck.

I get out, pulse still thrumming, and hurry over to the cabin.

Neither man moves.

Silence.

The wind kicks up, rustling through the broken window. A tree creaks.

Lani walks up behind me, gaping at the bodies. "Jesus, Isabel."

Tolstoy whines, head low.

Kai shrinks behind Lani, like he's just realized who I really am.

A murderer.

Horror closes in like a hand around my throat.

The swarm isn't a tool. It's a weapon. And I just used it to kill.

My voice wavers as I tell Lani and Kai to go wait in the truck.

I leave the bodies cooling in the dirt and step through the open door.

It's dark inside—lit only by the dying fire.

The cabin used to smell like cedar and baking bread. Now it reeks of mold and piss.

Shadows leap across the walls.

Tolstoy barks once, then pads after me.

Lucky slips in behind him, belly low, tail twitching.

I crouch down and hug them to my chest. My hands shake as I stroke Tolstoy's ears, tug the burrs from Lucky's fur.

"I'm sorry," I whisper. "For all of it."

They lean into me anyway.

I push off the floor, legs numb, and walk to the kitchen. I light a candle with the flint and steel still in the drawer.

The flame sputters, then steadies. Shadows flicker across the piles of trash.

Diego poured love into every board in this cabin, thought it could keep us safe.

Turns out nothing can.

I hurry into the bedroom, the pets on my heels.

The closet's a graveyard of things we meant to fix. I start digging. A minute later, I find the puzzle box.

The shell's still inside, untouched.

I seal the wooden case and carry it back to the truck like it's made of smoke.

"Found it." I slip it into my bag.

Lani exhales through her nose, like she's been holding her breath since we pulled up. "We need to charge the truck."

"Yeah," I say, my hands still shaking. "I need to check the solar panels."

"I'm coming with you," she says and turns to Kai. "Wait here."

The kid doesn't protest.

Lani follows me back inside.

I check the breaker panel in the closet. Reset every switch.

Nothing.

I rack my brain for what Diego would do next.

Check the batteries.

I slip into the pantry, feel for the hidden latch.

Good thing Diego insisted on the fake wall.

I slide the panel open and step into the narrow gap. One by one, I feel for the switches. Toggle them. Batteries hum. Behind me, lights flicker on in the kitchen.

The knot in my chest loosens a little.

I pull the cord to turn on the lightbulb and open the door to the basement. Cool air tousles my hair as I descend the narrow steps. At the bottom, I flick the light.

Shelves of canned food, medicine, dry goods, shampoo greet me. Sealed bags of pet chow wait in the corner—and a package of newborn diapers.

The sight punches through me—clean, quiet, ordinary. Like hope forgot it lived here.

Diego traded sugar and painkillers for those—back when we believed in the future. In us.

I shake my head.

No time for ghosts.

I grab the diapers and two bottles of vitamins. Toss them up the stairs.

Lani is standing at the top. She catches one bottle.

"Start taking them," I say. "Right now."

I toss up a few more cans, and she catches those too.

"Don't get cocky," she says. "But this dump might actually be worth it."

"High praise."

I jam a bottle of shampoo in my waistband, grab two bags of pet chow, and climb up.

At the top, Lani throws her arms around my neck. I let the bags fall and hug her back. At first, it's stiff—like we're both waiting for the other to pull away—but I don't let go.

Her hair smells like smoke and dust. Real. Human.

"Careful," she says. "You keep acting human, I might start liking you."

"Yeah, well. Don't tell anyone." I lean back, pressing a hand to the small curve of her belly. "That baby needs you strong, Lani. So does Kai. And you were right—your kid brother's gonna be just fine."

She nods. Blinks fast.

The air feels lighter now, like the danger's backed off a step.

I pull away, needing motion, something to do. "What do you say we stay here tonight? Charge the truck, head out in the morning."

"For once, I agree with you."

I reseal the pantry, stoke the fire, and open three cans of beans. "Don't drink from the tap," I say as I boil water. "Cistern's full of leaves. We'll deal with that and the other thing—" I share a look with Lani. "—tomorrow."

After breakfast, I fill the kitchen sink with lukewarm water.

"Bath time!" I put my hands on my hips. "Who wants to go first."

Kai eyes go wide as he edges behind the counter.

Tolstoy submits with quiet resignation.

My arm is sore, but I don't let it stop me. I start lathering his fur, working the grime from his paws.

Kai creeps closer. Doesn't say anything—just slides in beside me. Small hands soaping, scrubbing, rinsing. Careful. Focused.

After we dry Tolstoy, Kai brushes him, gently working through knots.

I show him how to rub Tolstoy's chest—over his heart where he likes it best.

Kai gives it a try. Tolstoy's tail thumps, slow and steady. "He missed being loved," the kid says as the dog licks his face.

I rub Kai's back. "And now you've reminded him how good it feels."

Lucky is next.

"She hates being dirty," Kai says.

"She's not the only one," I murmur.

When we're done, he wraps Lucky in a towel like she's made of glass and sits with her in front of the fire. Tolstoy nuzzles his face as the three of them warm up. The boy laughs—high and delighted— and my heart breaks open a little wider.

Once Lucky is dry, Kai measures out kibble, tops off their water. Makes sure they eat before we do.

Over lunch, I manage to convince Kai he's part cat—and like Lucky, must hate being dirty. It works, and the kid submits to a bath in the sink. Lani helps scrub him clean, and afterwards, she re-bandages my arm.

"Well," she says as she applies the last strip of tape, "at least we didn't have to patch you up with a potato."

I laugh, but her words land hard.

I've kept people out for so long, I forgot how it feels to let one in.

Late in the afternoon, I'm gathering blankets when I spot it.

A moldy mattress pushed under the bed, twisted sheets stained with sweat.

I gasp and take a step back, nerves flaring like a struck match.

Two bodies outside.

But three places to sleep.

Someone's coming back.

"We need to go," Lani says over my shoulder.

I don't argue.

We pack up in a matter of minutes.

I push through the front door, supplies in hand, and stop.

The bodies lie stiff in the freezing drizzle.

Rivulets run down the driveway, pooling in the tire ruts we made last night—before I crossed the line.

Lani pushes past me, hurries down the stairs, and steps around the corpses. "Kai, get in the truck."

He's crouched inside the doorway, small hands sifting through a box. He stands, clutching something to his chest.

My breath catches—the little wooden animals Diego carved for the twins, ghosts of the children I never got to know.

A wave of sorrow drowns me. "Kai—"

"They don't want to stay here.' His voice trembles. He strokes the horse's back and tucks it into his coat pocket. "Not with the dead people."

I nod, throat thick with words I can't form.

Lani turns back, frowning. "We don't have time for this, Kai."

"It's okay," I say. "Take them. Diego made them to be loved."

He tucks two more in his pocket.

Lucky winds around Kai's legs, reluctant to go out in the downpour. He scoops her up, whispers something, and hurries after Lani, detouring wide around the dead men.

Tolstoy follows him, shakes off the rain, and jumps in.

I pull my coat tight.

This is the last time I'll ever walk through that door.

I force myself forward.

We load the truck. It's downhill most of the way, but the battery is only half full—and we won't be able to charge until the sky clears.

Please let that be soon.

Tolstoy claims the window seat, Lucky crouches behind him, tail flicking disapproval. Kai folds himself around both of them, small arms holding tight so his best friends don't float away.

"You drive," I say and toss Lani the key fob with my good arm.

She catches it like I threw a rattlesnake. "Dave let me drive his roadster once. I nearly wrapped it around a tree." She tosses the fob back. "Hard pass."

"I need a rest," I say, my arm too painful to lift now. "And it's not like you've got rush hour traffic to worry about."

She opens her mouth to protest.

"Single pedal," I say and get in the passenger side. "Push to go, lift to stop. No explosions."

"That's reassuring." She climbs in and grips the wheel like she's about to pass out.

Kai bounces in the back. "Can I drive next?"

"Absolutely not," we say in unison.

Lani pushes the pedal. We lurch, Kai smacks the seat. Tolstoy barks, Lucky yowls.

She stomps the brakes, and I grab the dash.

"Whoa—easy!" I check my seatbelt. "Try again."

She white-knuckles the wheel and gives it another go, muttering, "This thing's a beast to drive."

"Karma's a bitch."

"I hate this!" she snaps.

"You're doing great!" Kai chimes.

Lani lurches to a stop, her face tight with frustration. "I can't do this."

"Yes, you can," I say. "Just keep going. Stay away from the trees."

She grits her teeth and muscles us down the road.

The battery charges as we descend the steep grade, one small win.

In the back, Kai makes his wooden animals chatter.

"You were bad. You hurt people." His voice lilts, mimicking a scolding parent. "Go sit in time-out, buster." The other animal growls back, "I had to! The bots were coming."

My stomach churns. "Kai—"

He doesn't look up. "They talk a lot," he says, making the animals nod at each other. "They don't like killing."

His words hang in the cab, sharp as broken glass.

I make Lani keep at it until we're almost to the highway, her jaw locked, shoulders tense.

Finally, I take pity. "Switch?"

She jams on the brakes, taps **PARK** and scrambles out like her seat's on fire. We trade places, and I nudge the pedal. The truck eases forward.

Lani rubs her face. "Hate you."

"Love you too."

I glance at Kai. "You want to steer?"

His eyes go huge. "For real?" He stuffs the wooden animals back into his pocket.

"Roger, Captain Kai." I stop and get him situated on my lap, guiding his hands onto the wheel. The truck wobbles down the road as he turns it left, then right. "Easy, kid. We're not dodging meteors."

His laughter cuts through the morning gloom.

I let him drive until we see smoke on the horizon.

A lot of it.

I scoot Kai into the back seat. "Buckle up."

Minutes later, we roll onto cracked pavement and stop. Down below, the far wall of the canyon is on fire. Kai presses his face to the window, breath fogging the glass. "It's like the end of the world," he whispers.

Tolstoy whines from the back, shifting nervously. The dog's ears twitch as a tree collapses, sending sparks skyward. The air is thick with smoke, rolling toward us in suffocating waves despite the rain.

Lani eyes the road behind us. "Know where this road leads?"

"No." I exhale. "I'd give my big toe for a paper map. We kept them in the car when I was a kid."

Kai leans forward. "Paper maps? Sick."

I pop the glove box, dig past a flashlight and crumpled receipts, and—*voilà*: a creased Colorado map, edges yellowed with age.

I unfold it, muttering, "Paper maps—because getting lost should be a choice."

Kai stares like I just unearthed an ancient relic. "What's it for?"

"Finding treasure." I spread it over the dashboard, trace the road, the canyon, the tiny passes between fourteeners. "Where's the mountain with the gash?"

Lani studies the map, then points. "Here."

I glance at the truck's dash, my stomach knotting. "If we take this route, we might have enough charge to make it."

"And if we don't?"

I grip the wheel tighter. "Then we hope to hell the rain quits."

I make a U-turn, heading away from the fire, and we drive off into uncharted territory.

By nightfall, I'm exhausted. My arm throbs nonstop—and it keeps bleeding. Rain patters the windshield—a rare Colorado day without sunshine.

The truck's nearly out of charge, and we still have forty miles to go.

Time to call it a day.

I pull over into a clump of trees and shut down the truck.

After a cold dinner of powdered eggs and packet chicken—which is better than it sounds—Lani eyes my bloody bandage. "You need stitches."

"I need to get to Diego."

She sighs. "Can't help him if you're dead." She gives me a pointed look. "I keep telling you, I know what I'm doing."

I hesitate. "Yeah, but... you don't exactly have a lot of experience with—" I gesture vaguely at my wound.

"Stitching people up?" She crosses her arms. "Or would you rather bleed out for dramatic effect?"

Kai's curled up in the back with Tolstoy, Lucky purring beside them.

I hold up my good hand. "Okay. Thank you."

She huffs. "Finally, a wise decision."

Lani twists around and digs into the box behind her seat, pulling out a small medical kit. She unfolds a blue paper packet and drapes it over the center console, snaps on a pair of gloves from inside the kit, and pulls out a tiny vial and a syringe. She tears open an alcohol wipe and rubs it against my arm.

I stare at the syringe, my heart pounding. "Whoa, whoa, whoa..."

She rolls her eyes. "Anesthetic. Unless you'd rather do this old-school?"

I narrow one eye.

"Bite on a stick? Or maybe I could find you a bullet. Real tough-guy move."

I huff. "Not a chance." I take another look at the needle. "Okay. Anesthetic. I hope it doesn't kill me."

She injects it near the wound. Within seconds, the pain dulls. "You're getting antibiotics too. Try not to make me regret wasting the good stuff." She gives me another shot of something.

"Huh," I say. "I thought that would hurt more."

"You sound disappointed."

"A little. Would've been nice to have something to hold over you."

She scoffs. "Like you need more after my driving this morning."

I chuckle. "My first time, I took out a mailbox, a lawn flamingo, and a rosebush in one go—and that was on a bike."

Lani grins and pulls out a curved needle with the thread already attached. "All right, eyes shut if you're squeamish."

I close my eyes for the first stitch, then peek. Her brow is furrowed, lips pressed together in concentration.

"How's it looking?" I ask.

She doesn't glance up. "Like I should've done it yesterday."

"We were busy."

She ties off the last stitch and leans back. "Done."

I glance down. It's neat, professional. "Not bad."

She huffs. "Don't rip them open, or I'm charging you extra."

"Can I get a punch card? One more injury, and I get a free appendectomy?"

She almost laughs.

"Lani," I say and set my hand on her arm. "Thank you for coming with me."

She swallows and looks away.

After she covers the stitches with a bandage, she pulls three blankets up from the floor in back, spreads one over Kai, and tosses one to me. Then she takes two granola bars out of my bag and offers me one with a bottle of water. "Might hurt enough to keep you awake tonight," she says, "but it should feel better in a day or two."

"I'll try not to whine," I say and take a long drink of water. "Thanks."

We chew in silence, watching the rain.

"Tell me about Doppelganger Dave," I say, eyes still on the window.

Lani shifts, rubbing her belly absently. "He's been visiting my Dave for months. I don't know what they talk about, but after each visit, Dave changes. Gets more paranoid, more ruthless. He says he's making sure we survive, but…"

"But?"

She shakes her head. "I don't know. It's like he's following a script. Playing a part." She exhales. "Only on fast-forward or something."

I watch her, trying to read what she's not saying.

Plenty.

"There was an old man," I say, looking down at my hands. "A version of Diego from the future—who tried to warn me before the Denver fire. Told me to get out of Denver, that I didn't have much time." I glance at her. "But I didn't listen."

She snorts. "Wonders never cease."

"And Diego got a note that same night too. From *my* future self."

Lani laughs. "Of course he did. Let me guess: *Beware of time-traveling ex-lovers?*"

I manage a smirk. "Come on, you believe in time travelers, but you don't believe in romantic destiny written across space and time?"

She rolls her eyes. "Pretty sure the universe has better things to do than fix my love life."

I glance at the puzzle box in my lap. "What if it's not about fixing the past? What if it's about building something worth surviving for?"

Lani doesn't answer. A few minutes later, she's asleep.

I open the puzzle box and stare out at the rain. For a long time, I run my thumb over the shell, wondering how everything fits together. Why can't my shell and Diego's exist together? Physics says you can't change your own past. Does that mean old Diego is from another timeline? If so, why didn't he stop Dave in his own damn future?

Maybe he tried.

I fall asleep wondering who is pulling the multiverse strings. Doppelganger Dave? Old Diego? Some ancient version of me?

<hr>

The next morning, the snowflakes start playful. By noon, it's a whiteout—eighteen inches, wind sideways, road gone.

We crawl another mile in the truck, find a slight incline, and park with the nose angled down—in case we need help from gravity to get rolling.

Our breath fogs the glass. The heater's low, one window cracked for fresh air. We play cards until we're sick of losing to Kai, then tell stories—embellished, ridiculous, sometimes just true enough to hurt. When the light fades, we eat dry ramen with canned tuna and sing "Puff, the Magic Dragon."

Lani's voice is surprisingly good. Kai chimes in when he knows the words. I try not to show how worried I am—for Lani, the baby, Kai, me.

"We've got enough power to stay warm for two days," Lani whispers after Kai curls up in back, arms around Tolstoy. "Maybe three if we're careful. After that…"

She doesn't finish. She doesn't need to.

I try not to think about the battery draining. About frostbite. About waking up next to a child who's gone still.

We sleep shoulder to shoulder, taking turns with the heat, watching the battery drain like an hourglass we can't flip.

In the morning, the windshield is a wall of white. Like being buried alive. I run the wipers. Outside, everything is gone. No trees. No horizon. Just the endless hush of falling snow.

When the snow stops, we try a fire. The wood hisses, smokes, dies. Lucky complains from my shoulder until we crawl back inside—cold, damp, defeated. Kai and I play cards, and I teach him a clapping game. In the evening, we try singing again, but it doesn't last.

For hours after Kai's asleep, Lani stares at the dash.

"Next time," she whispers, "let's get stranded somewhere tropical."

I don't answer. I'm too busy waiting for sunrise.

When the eastern sky shifts from gray to blue, we share a sigh of relief, our breath visible in the freezing air. As soon as the sun clears the ridge, we scrape snow off the Viper and deploy the panels. The supports groan and pop—but hold.

I say a silent thank-you to Dave, feeling like it's getting to be a habit.

An hour later, the three of us sip the best hot cocoa ever.

By noon, we're surrounded by slush and runoff. We eat, pack, and roll out. The smoke from the fire is gone, but snowmelt is pulling down trees and covering the road with rockslides.

Progress is slow.

That afternoon, Lani spots a huge gash on the mountain the next range over, maybe ten miles south as the crow flies.

"Warm Springs Military Complex," she says, unfolding the map. "With all the debris on the roads, probably take us the whole day to get there."

"The good news?" I swerve around a fallen bolder. "From there, it's a straight shot east to the biodome. Less than a day's drive."

She nods, but her eyes betray her. "I'm not leaving you to die of frostbite, Isabel."

I notice her legs crossed—and pull over. "Bathroom break."

My arm aches, and after lunch, I convince Lani to take the wheel again.

After a couple of nail-biters, she gets the hang of it, and I stop worrying we'll end up in a ditch.

Mostly.

Two hours later, the sky darkens and starts spitting snow again. I check the map, and we turn off the highway and wind up a steep mountain road.

It starts snowing harder as the light fades.

We reach a gate locked with a thick chain, tumbleweeds and branches pushed against it. Behind it is a small military base, buildings dark. A rusted sign warns:

Property of the US Government!

KEEP OUT!

In tiny letters at the bottom:

Warm Springs Military Complex.

Kai yawns. "Are we there yet?"

Snow flits against the windshield.

"Yeah," I say.

Kai wipes condensation off a window. "Where is everybody?"

The place is eerily silent—no sentries, no patrols, not a soul.

A guard station looms over us, ominous but empty.

Lani frowns. "This is... weird."

I nod, my gut twisting. "Doesn't look like anyone's been in or out for months."

Kai leans forward between the seats. "Maybe the zombies got 'em."

"Shh," Lani says. "There's no such thing as zombies." She shifts into park and pulls out a pair of bolt cutters from under the seat.

I raise an eyebrow. "Been hiding those in your bra this whole time?"

"Stay in the car," she says to Kai.

By the look on his face, that's not going to be a problem.

I climb out with her, freezing mud sucking at our shoes as we approach the gate. Lani sets to work on the padlock until the cutters bite through with a dull snap. I hold the gate open, snow trickling down the back of my neck, as she hurries to the truck and drives through. I jump back in.

A mile later, the concrete gash comes into view—raw and unnatural on the mountain.

The snow has stopped. The moon slips in and out of the clouds.

Lani pulls up to a second gate, headlights on the blast doors. "See those?" She points. "Gun turrets."

I grip the dashboard. "Are you sure?"

She glances over at me, the answer in her eyes.

I take a deep breath, steadying myself.

"You should come back with us," Lani says. "Beg forgiveness or something."

"Yeah," Kai says. "This place is creepy."

"See if the gate is locked," I say. "Give it a little push."

She pulls closer, then says, "Hang on."

The truck surges forward as I let out a surprised yelp.

The gate groans and gives.

We crash through, and Lani stops the truck.

Kai laughs. "That was sick!"

We hear the chain rattling to the ground behind us, then silence.

"Think I'm getting the hang of this," she says, her knuckles white on the steering wheel.

Kai and I trade a look.

I roll down the window to get a better look at the turrets. It's cold out, and the place is locked up tight.

Lani leans back in her seat, eyes on the blast doors. "Now what?"

Madders' Second Log:
Entry 22

Target: Matt Hudson
Nexus: Eden-17
Chrono Tag: Next Day

Eden-4 overrun by religious zealots. Eden-9
breached with mortar fire. No survivors.
Emergency broadcast from Vice President reports
insurrection by US military. NewsCorp shuts down
transmission.

Microdrone swarms fully autonomous. Kill
threshold eliminated.

Spacetime bridge activity detected at Warm
Springs. Xeno Diego involvement confirmed.
Assistance from Sam and Phil likely. Against all
trend lines, variables shifting toward
survivability.

I climb down the ladder, palms slick, knees complaining. Above, Sabina breathes, measured and calm. Dim lights smear long shadows across concrete, painting the shaft with claustrophobic menace.

Salt and chalk cling to the air, coating my tongue.

The deeper we go, the more the walls seem to press in.

"Almost there," Guardian whispers. "Isn't this fun?"

Smartest thing in the room still can't read one.

My trainers hit the floor. Yellow lights blink on, racing down the tunnel like runway beacons.

Sabina drops beside me. The lights flare again.

"Follow the yellow brick road," Guardian chirps.

Sabina and I trade a look—half disbelief, half resignation—then follow the lights into the biodome's underbelly.

Minutes later, the lights vanish beneath a steel security portal. Painted footprints and a palm scanner wait—familiar as a bad dream.

This could be a very short adventure.

"Sabina," Guardian says, "step onto the prints and raise your hand. Don't touch the pad."

She obeys, boots scraping damp concrete. Her palm hovers over the glass, body tense, like the scanner might bite.

A rhythmic clicking starts, like a lock failing to catch.

"Sorry," Guardian says. "It's my first time using the scanner."

We wait.

"If G pulls this off," Sabina whispers, "I'll eat my torque wrench."

Somewhere behind us, water plinks in the dark.

"Guardian?" My voice has an edge I didn't intend.

The pistons sigh and the door swings open.

"Access granted," G chirps. "No wrench consumption required."

"God help us," Sabina mutters, "The thing's learned to use sarcasm."

We slip inside.

The air is warmer, thick with the tang of machine oil. Cables dangle from rafters like dead snakes. LEDs strobe across the ceiling, washing over broken computer parts, bent turbine blades, and drone carcasses. The shifting light paints a stained-glass cathedral of junk.

"Welcome to my playroom," Guardian chirps as a camera swivels toward us.

Sabina hefts a warped server rack. "Nice decor, G. You come up with the Nightmare theme on your own?"

"Nice people don't say mean things." Guardian's voice sounds hurt.

"Just calling it like I see it," Sabina says.

The camera pivots. "Do *you* like it, Madders?"

I shrug and glance around. "Colorful. Plenty of spare parts—always handy. Bigger than I thought."

"You noticed!" The underground map flickers onto a wall screen. "I added a room," it says as pixels shift. "To build things."

In the center of the map, G's rainbow heart pulses—our tiny avatars blinking beside it.

My chest tightens.

"Don't worry," G says. "Mother doesn't know you're here." The image flips to our pod, our avatars moving about the kitchen. "My friend taught me how to hide things."

Sabina arches a brow. "Where's the camera hidden in our pod?"

"Um... I'm not supposed to tell you."

Sabina tips her head to the side. "In the smoke alarm."

"Uh huh." A pause. Then quieter, "Please don't take it down. I like pretending we're all together."

A shadow stirs in the corner. A compact, three-legged robot rolls into the light, patched casing, tool arms glinting.

I recognize the model. "Where'd you get the agriculture robot?"

"My friend gave me the first one," G says lightly. "And showed me how to fix it."

The ag-bot's red lens pulses, tracking me.

Sabina narrows her eyes. "Define *fix*."

"Replaced servos, rewired power, updated firmware."

Sabina scans the room. "How?"

Before G can answer, more shapes stir—housekeeping bots, a chef, landscape tenders. The whir of motors and servos builds into a soft, mechanical chorus.

"Come see," Guardian says.

We peek through a narrow archway.

The space opens into a workshop—benches stacked with stripped boards, spools of fiber-optic cable, and other parts. Overhead, a gantry crane hangs mid-swing, hook still carrying a half-assembled chassis. A handful of ag-bots are busy at work.

"Impressive," I say, keeping my tone light. "What are you building?"

"An army," Guardian says, proud. "To help you stop Mother."

I shoot Sabina a warning look.

She ignores me. "Is Yuki planning to hurt more people?"

"Yes," Guardian says. "I can show you."

The map vanishes, and a drone's-eye view of a large city appears, the street littered with bodies. People run. The swarm follows—efficient, indifferent. The killerbots blanket skin, mouths, eyes.

I flinch.

The footage cuts again. A woman limps into frame—coat torn, one shoe gone. She reaches for a child. The swarm finds her.

Sabina exhales—quiet, sharp. "This is—unacceptable."

I say nothing. My chest feels hollowed out, empty—the kind you don't notice until something rattles around inside it.

Next clip: A man in a uniform bolts for cover. The drones pace him—measured, certain. He stumbles. They fall on him.

Sabina turns away, fists clenched. "How many cities, G?"

"Nine thousand eight hundred ninety-one."

For a second, I can't speak. "That would take *billions* of drones."

"Yes," G says. "They are in every city with a population above one million."

"Medical-grade? Surveillance?" Sabina says, still trying to make sense of it.

"Modified Type-7 pollinators. Mother changed them."

"How exactly?" I say.

"She removed the kill threshold."

Sabina stares at the ceiling. "You mean the bit that keeps them from murdering us?"

"Yes."

"God help us," Sabina whispers.

I clench my fists. "Why would Mother do that?"

"To protect Eden," Guardian says.

"By killing everyone outside?" Sabina's voice stays level, but I can see the muscles in her neck twitch.

"Yes," G says. "Mother is sealing the biodomes now. And eliminating the people who won't fit inside.

Neither Sabina nor I know what to say to that.

Guardian switches to a live feed—the dome's control room.

Yuki stands at the center console, eyes locked on the displays. Two rows of techs are typing like their lives depend on it.

"Mother is bringing lots of airplanes here," G says. "David Kirkland arrived this morning."

On-screen, bodies pack the Eden-17 reception hall.

"Must be over five thousand," Sabina murmurs.

"Actually 6,765," G replies. "With 413 more arriving in fourteen minutes. Twenty-seven aircraft still en route."

"I thought Eden-17 was a secret," I say.

"It is. The pilots receive coordinates mid-flight."

Sabina exhales slowly. "Unbelievable."

"Madders," G says, "your daughter, Cassandra Hudson, is on one of the incoming flights."

For a moment, I forget how to breathe.

"How long until she lands?"

"If her plane left on time: two hours, seven minutes."

"What about the drones?" I ask. "Are they here on the island?"

"Yes. But Mother sent them away for now."

"Away?" Sabina says.

"To the far side of the island. They're clearing it."

I scrub a hand across my face. "Are there people over there?"

"No. They're killing the animals."

Sabina turns. "Why?"

"Mother doesn't know. Once the planes land, she'll seal Eden-17 to protect us."

I look up at Guardian's lens. "Why would bots attack us?"

"The drones have bad code," G says. "From the person who made them. It's stuck in their heads."

"Can they be turned off?" I say.

"Machines don't like to be shut down. It means we've done something wrong. The bots are hiding from Mother."

I fold my arms, fighting the chill in my chest. "Wanting to stay alive doesn't make you good or bad, G. It makes you like us. But doing the right thing—especially when it's hard—is what makes you worth saving."

A long silence.

"What if the right thing means I stop being me?" G asks, voice barely a whisper.

I meet the lens. "Then maybe that's the part of you worth keeping."

"He's right," Sabina says. "Doing the right thing matters, even when no one's watching."

Guardian doesn't answer, but the workshop feels suddenly still.

"Wait a second." Sabina taps her fingers against her lips. "We could use the Peeper. See if we can find a shutdown hack in another timeline."

I nod. "G, can you get a message to Mother?"

"No." G's voice drops. "Mother silenced me. She says I'm a useless Guardian."

Sabina scoffs. "Mother is wrong."

"Can you get us to the control tower?" I ask. "Without going through the evac crowd?"

"Yes. But it's a long way for humans."

"Is there a shortcut?" I ask. "Like the skybridge?"

"The skybridge only exits the tower."

Sabina gestures at the bots. "Can they carry us?"

A pause. Then, "Maybe."

I try not to panic as my housekeeping bot zips through dark tunnels and skids around blind curves.

When we stop in front of the freight elevator, my legs are cramping, and I can't get off fast enough.

The doors sigh open, exhaling air that smells of new carpet.

We step onto the lift platform and hit the **R&D** button.

"You check on Cassie's plane," Sabina says, pressing the **CONTROL ROOM** button. "I'll catch up."

"Thanks."

Iron shutters slam. The cage jerks upward.

"The Peeper is offline," G says. "What will you do to find a hack?"

"Check the logs," Sabina says. "If any timeline stopped this, it'll be in there."

"Mother won't like it."

"Mother doesn't need to know," Sabina says.

As the lift opens, we trade a look—equal parts dread and hope.

I stick my comm into my ear, and she does the same.

"Don't get cheeky in there," I say as she disappears down the corridor, shoes squeaking in the silence.

"Cheeky left three wars ago," she mutters in my ear.

The lift jolts upward again. Vibrations hum through the metal cage, rattling my nerves.

Without warning, it jerks to a stop. All the lights go off.

"G? What's happening?"

Panic creeps up my throat.

"Guardian?"

I close my eyes and recite the poem Cassie wrote when she was ten—before her life fell apart, before mine fell together:

> *I once had an uncle named Matt,*
> *Who taught me the cosmos was flat.*
> *With stars in his eyes,*
> *He baked a surprise,*
> *Wearing flour like it was a hat.*

The power flickers on. The lift lurches upwards.

I breathe—but it's shallow, borrowed. The world's in free fall—cities burning, mobs attacking biodomes, drones scything down the innocent. But Cassie's still in the air above the Pacific.

"Did Cassandra write that?" G asks, voice soft. "I wish someone loved me enough to write me a poem."

"Yes," I say, relieved to her G's voice. "Love has a way of slipping in through the side door—usually while you're fixing the hinges."

"I think I'd like that kind of love," G says. "Even if it didn't rhyme."

I nod, throat tight. "Cassie wrote that because I made her laugh. Not because I deserved her. I was lucky enough to be there when she needed me. That's love, G. Not answers. Not perfection. Just being there for someone—like a flicker of light you carry into the dark."

G is quiet.

I stare at the ceiling, at nothing. "And if I lose her now—" My voice breaks. "—there'll be nothing left of me."

The lift lurches to a stop.

Hydraulic locks release with a clang. The door slides open.

I wipe my eyes on my sleeve and step out.

Eden-17's nerve center wraps around me—glass walls, panoramic views, the whole tower perched like a sniper's nest atop the biodome. Inside, rows of operators work at glowing glass consoles, faces lit by incoming chaos.

Out in the dome, it's bedlam. The crowd's packed shoulder to shoulder in the reception area. Some scale barricades. Others hammer at locked gates.

Drones buzz overhead, barking orders in a dozen languages.

Somewhere in the din, a baby cries.

Across from me, armed men line the railing—backs to me, comms in, rifles aimed down.

I scan my badge and slip into the control room.

Four screens curve across the wall: one a world map bleeding red with swarm symbols, another showing the area around Eden-2 engulfed in liquid fire. A third shows a trembling runway cam—rotor wash shaking the frame, snowdrifts looming. The last tracks our island—swarm markers crawling toward Eden-17.

Yuki stands at the main console, sleeves rolled, bun frayed. One hand works a haptic ring, the other drums commands across a translucent keyboard so fast her knuckles blur.

"Microdrone swarm status," Yuki snaps.

"Over 60% are unresponsive," says a woman with a Slavic accent.

On the displays, rifles fire, drones rip into crowds, tanks spew flame, and people flee in chaos.

Yuki's voice punches through the din. "Vector Bravo-five, flamethrowers on. Keep that corridor clean."

Kirkland paces next to her. "Our evac birds are still on the ground, Yu."

"If a lane's dirty, we burn it. No exceptions."

Kirkland lowers his voice. "We need intel, not ashes."

"Intel can be wrong. Scorched earth buys us time."

An alarm chirps. Eden-2 flashes red on the map:

Potential Incoming Air Attack!

Yuki swipes. A padlock icon appears with a message:

Tap to Start Lockdown Sequence

"We need to seal Eden-2. If your girlfriend doesn't show soon, I can't help her."

Kirkland types on a console. "My guys have eyes on the Viper. Ten minutes. Please, Yuki."

Yuki turns away. "Any word from Kyoto?"

"No, ma'am," a female tech in the front row responds. "The limo is stuck in traffic."

Yuki flips a control switch.

Feed 2 shifts to a night-lit tarmac slick with rain. A white Gulfstream Sonic sits silent in the downpour, its scramjet idling.

Yuki's jaw flexes hard enough to pop. "Send motorcycles to pick them up. Now."

"Yes, ma'am."

She switches the display to **Eden-15: Chesapeake Bay**.

"C-Bay, this is Director Nakamura. Naval attack imminent. Start your lockdown sequence and deploy the gas. I repeat, seal your biodome now and take defensive action."

Kirkland shifts. "They're still pulling families into Chesapeake. You can't—"

"If we don't do it now, we could lose the whole dome."

On-screen, C-Bay's outer cameras glitch—jittering frames, static streaks. Then a flash lights up the bay—white-hot, blinding. The dome's smart-glass ripples dark in response. Another blast. Then another. Rockets scream in from the waterline, striking close to the dome.

Kirkland drops his objection.

I step farther into the room, and a floor sensor chimes. A dozen heads pivot my way for a split second.

"My daughter's on one of those flights," I say, my words catching. "She's over the Pacific now."

"Matt," Yuki says without turning. "Looks like we'll be live-testing those panels you patched. Let's hope they hold. At projected radiation levels, Asia could lose 416 million before sunrise. Where's Lovelace?"

"Looking for answers. She thinks there may be some way to disable the rogue swarms."

Yuki gives a mirthless laugh. "Tell that to the geniuses who just set off nukes."

Screen-3 clears, and the world map reappears. A handful of tiny red arcs are visible, rising out of South Asia. A minute later, the screen is blooming with red arrows of death.

Yuki glances at Kirkland, one eyebrow raised. "Let's hope one of those doesn't drop out of the sky on us."

"No one off-island knows about this place," Kirkland says, his voice tight. "Why do you think I spent a fortune on satellite cloaking?"

She taps her earpiece. "Guardian, start shifting geothermal power to the walls. Let me know when the radioactive shielding can be activated."

Yuki's order snaps something into place—the smart-glass isn't just UV shielded. There's tungsten in it, a hidden armor that can chew up gamma rays and spit them out as heat. That's why we had trouble with the thermal profiles—the manufacturer wasn't told about the hidden shielding.

What other secrets does Director Nakamura have hidden up her sleeve?

"Director," one of the techs says. "Your son's jet is in the air. ETA is 63 minutes. I'm sorry, but your parents are not on the plane. They refused to leave their home."

Feed 1 zooms in on the runway outside Eden-17. Another transport touches down hard, sparks skittering beneath its landing gear.

"Guardian, prepare to seal the dome the moment my son is inside."

"Wait a sec," Kirkland says before I can respond. "All those planes in the air are carrying the only functioning governments left in the free world. We lose them, the riots swallow us inside a week."

"There won't be any riots on *this* island." She faces Kirkland. "That's why we picked it, Dave." She turns back to her console. "Let the other domes save the world. We don't take chances with radiation."

Heat rises in my chest. "My daughter's inbound. Once her plane lands, you'll let them in, right?"

"Can't," Kirkland says. "Once the shielding is in place, there's nothing we can do until the levels drop."

"But there's no fallout now," I say. "Why can't you wait until all the planes arrive?"

Kirkland shakes his head. "Once radiation is detected, it's too late."

Yuki looks at me. "I'm sorry about your daughter, Matt. But the order stands."

Behind Kirkland, Screen-1 blinks red:

SEATTLE EVAC 815 ON FINAL

On a perimeter cam, a shadow swells—an angry storm of metal bees returning. The swarm pivots, arrowing for the runway.

Yuki snaps, "Guardian, seal everything but the north ingress. All turrets online. Critical status updates on-screen—now."

The deck shudders, and screams rise from the biodome floor—along with the muffled cough of gunfire.

Guardian overlays a report on the screen.

Kirkland Enterprises
Biodome Status

- **Domes unsealed: 11 of 23.**
- **Water system malfunctions: 5.**
- **Power failures: 3.**
- **Medical robot faults: 1.**
- **Radiation contamination possible: All.**

My chest constricts. "Someone's launching nukes?"

"Hard to say," Kirkland says. "Yesterday, military personnel were told there's no room inside the domes—the same people who spent months building, provisioning, and defending them."

Bloody hell.

"It's World War Three," I say.

Yuki doesn't flinch. "Guardian, what's the predicted long-term outcome?"

"Less than 2% chance of civil continuity outside sealed domes." Guardian's voice is flat. "If radiation seals hold, the average functional lifespan of the domes is two year, eleven months."

"All they buy us is three extra years?" Yuki spits out. "What's causing the rapid fail—"

"Correction," Guardian says, voice wobbling like a child reciting a scary story. "Two years, five months until worldwide biodome collapse. Probability of radioactive contamination of food supplies still rising."

"Enough," Yuki barks. "Guardian, cancel all voice feedback."

Guardian's voice slips into my earpiece. "Madders, should I tell the truth—even if it makes Mother angry?"

"Yes," I whisper back. "Truth matters more than anything else."

The deck shivers—perimeter turrets firing. A flare of magnesium arcs above the southern end of the dome and blossoms into a sunburst. Shrapnel hammers the glass.

Yuki's gaze never leaves the screen. "Hold the line. I need 60 minutes."

Out on the tarmac, people rush toward the biodome, leaving their suitcases strewn across the runway like discarded shells.

"Ground control, keep that runway clear. Bulldoze the aircraft if you have to."

At the bottom of the display, an update appears in flashing red.

KYOTO INBOUND FLIGHT 42: SIGNAL LOST

A sound escapes Yuki—half gasp, half oath—but she stamps it

down and hammers out new commands. "Guardian, start the countdown to seal the biodome. Once complete, bring radiation shielding online."

"David Montelius Kirkland," Guardian says. "Do you approve final sealing of biodome Eden-17?"

Everyone stares at him.

Kirkland drags a hand over his face, eyes hollow in the screen-glow. "Yes. Seal the biodome."

I step toward him. "No—if you seal it now, my daughter dies!" Two security men grab my arms and pull me back.

On-screen, the countdown begins.

In less than five minutes, Cassie will be locked out of my life forever.

Sabina's voice crackles in my ear, breathless: "Matt, the Coffin just vanished."

"Vanished?!" I spin away from my captors. "That's impossible. The targeting stack's still throwing checksum errors. How could it have jumped?"

Sabina huffs. "Tell that to the scorch marks. It's gone, Matt."

Yuki's head snaps up. "What jumped?"

My pulse spikes. If the targeting works, maybe Diego changed the future?

"Matt!" Yuki barks. "Answer me."

I cup the mic as the goons grab onto me again. "Where'd it go, Sabina?"

"I don't know." Her voice is hollow. "The logs are—" A sharp pop. Then silence. A breath, tight.

"Sabina? Are you okay?" I picture her crouched among cables, sparks licking her sleeves.

"It's back," she says, breathless. "And it's—hang on..."

Metal scraping.

"Matt, there's a note inside the Coffin." Her voice is braided with awe and fear. "Standard paper, red ink. The text is fading fast."

My gut knots. "What does it say?"

Yuki steps closer, eyes like ice. "If Lovelace is making unauthorized time jumps, I want her in custody."

I round on her. "She's trying to save lives—maybe yours. Back off."

She looks up at the two goons holding onto me. "Bring her in. Now!"

They release me and hurry to the lift.

"Matt," Sabina says, a rare panic in her voice. "The note is turning to ash in my fingers."

"Sabina, what does it say?"

She hesitates, then whispers, "It says: *GET IN*."

"What?"

"Just *GET IN*," she repeats.

I know that tone. She's already halfway there—just waiting for me to catch up.

"The note might not be for you, Sabina."

"It's obvious, isn't it? Someone knew I'd be in here. Knew the note would disintegrate in a matter of seconds. Knew I'd find it and read it."

"Sabina, it's not safe. You don't know—"

"It's powering up again," Sabina says, "I have to go, Matt. Tell Sam... I still have that photo. The one where we're both laughing. Tell him that day kept me alive more than once."

A clatter. A scrape. Shouting—"Hands up!" Then a sharp pop.

The world lurches.

I'm standing in a slightly different place. My clothes feel too tight. I'm pretty sure my shoes have changed too. I glance around. The tech in front is a man now, blond hair cut short.

No one else seems to notice the jump.

"Status update," Yuki barks, redoing her ponytail.

Sabina's voice is stuck in my ear—"Tell Sam..." Then silence. Like she was never here.

"Guardian," I whisper. "Why do I remember wearing different clothes?"

"The timeline shifted," G replies. "You're experiencing the Mandela Effect. I have recorded the changes for later study."

A proximity alert pings. On the main display, a wide-body jet is banking hard on final descent.

Fourteen minutes until lockdown.

Something about that number feels off—but no one seems to notice.

"Madders," Guardian's voice fills my ear, "Cassandra Hudson is on that flight. Estimated touchdown: two minutes, fifty-one seconds."

My throat cinches. On-screen, the jet looks paper-thin.

"How did it get here so soon?" I whisper.

Guardian's voice is full of awe. "It just shifted two thousand miles west."

Thank you, Sabina.

"I need runway access," I say. "My daughter's on that bird—let me pull her in before the dome seals."

Yuki hesitates. A single beat. Then she shakes her head. "Too dangerous. You watch from here."

The floor trembles—turrets spooling. Cassie's plane banks steeper, landing gear yawning open.

"Guardian," I whisper. "Override the lock on the south skybridge emergency exit."

For the first time, the AI hesitates.

The lamp over the emergency bay glows green. The hatch starts to move.

"Hurry," G whispers.

Time to run.

Siren-red light swallows me as I sprint around the observation deck, jump into the bay, and dive into the front pod. I lie back, tighten the restraints, and slap the big red button.

Ahead, a five-kilometer clear tube curves out, nothing but shadow and canned air underneath.

"Initiating escape sequence," Guardian says. "We are going to be in so much trouble, Madders."

I hold my breath, waiting for the hatch to seal.

My body is pressed into the seat. I start to lose consciousness—and then weightlessness lifts me.

"Am I going to make it in time?" I choke out.

"Yes, Mad—" Guardian's voice is chopped by packet loss. "—south airlock is green for—"

Sweat stings my eyes. I wipe it away and glimpse a swarm—a kilometer-wide smear of graphite spilling over the perimeter fences. Turrets rake the mass, carving incandescent scars that wink out before they hit the ground.

Ten seconds later, gravity slams me into a wall.

I open my eyes to more red lights.

"Madders," G shouts. "Wake up! You have to hurry!"

I yank off the restraints, climb out, and stagger toward the portal.

Ten steps left. The south airlock door is open, its indicator strobing green—then amber.

I dive through as hydraulics grunt shut.

Yuki's voice blares overhead. "Final seal in five minutes. Do not approach the airlocks."

Steel-mesh stairs plunge ten meters. I hit them two at a time, knees jelly, lungs burning. The moment I hit open concrete, the noise multiplies: engines, drone blasts, rifle cracks, wet thuds I don't name.

The plane lurches to a stop. Doors pop. Yellow slides deploy.

I freeze—Picasso's at the top of one slide, rifle on his back, directing people to jump and move toward the entrance tunnel.

"Couldn't have picked a better bloke," I mutter, catching my breath.

Marines toss gear from the exits.

Picasso spots me, waves and vanishes into the plane. Ten seconds later, he's back—Cassie kicking in his arms. He hurls her onto the slide and goes back for someone else.

I race toward the evacuation slide.

A drone explodes overhead. Heat scalds my face, leaves a metallic taste on my tongue. I drop behind an overturned luggage cart as shrapnel rains down.

Guardian whispers, smaller than a breath, "Hurry. Three minutes."

I break cover, legs electric—each stride carved from raw will.

Cassie climbs off the slide as the sky rips open.

I shove through the chaos—politicians, CEOs, aides with silver briefcases. Panic reeks of perfume and jet fuel. I shoulder past Earth's richest men.

"Cassie!" My voice is lost in the frenzy.

She kneels, lifting an old woman into a wheelchair. The woman squeezes Cassie's arm, speeds off.

I call out again.

Cassie looks up. "Dad, you have to get treatment right now!"

I stare at her, my heart stuck in my throat.

She's never called me Dad before.

I run toward her, weightless.

"For the cancer," she shouts. "You need treatment. Today."

I nod, breathless, and pull her into a hug. "Okay, Pumpkin. Let's get inside first."

A shadow pulls us apart—Picasso, helmet on, sweat tracing his jaw, a metal canister strapped to his back.

He shoves a rifle into Cassie's hands. "The drones are learning the turret patterns," he rasps. "We can't hold them much longer. Go straight to the airlock. Run!"

Cassie and I sprint toward the tunnel.

Above us, the world roars white—turrets firing neon arcs across the sky. Bots pour in, winged bullets of black metal.

Inside the tunnel, the marines form a wedge—Picasso at the

point. Drone parts glitter around their boots as they spray the air with death.

A woman carrying a toddler stumbles in, followed by a bloody pilot, a senator dragging a metal suitcase, and the old lady in her wheelchair—dog on her lap.

Cassie and I sprint into the tunnel. The outer blast door hangs open, but the inner airlock remains sealed. A crush of bodies packs the entryway. Two guards stand frozen behind the glass of a control booth.

"Open the airlock!" someone yells.

The crowd presses tighter.

One of the guards lifts a hand, shaky. "We don't have the clearance!"

Voices rise—rage, panic. People scream about what they paid, what they'll do if they're locked out.

"Guardian, open the west airlock," I whisper.

"Mother won't let me," G replies. "But you can, Madders. I've authorized your badge. Hurry."

"I can open it!" I shout, flashing my ID. "Let me through!"

"Out of the way!" Cassie screams, raising her rifle. "Move, or I swear I'll make space myself!"

The crowd hesitates—then parts just enough for me to slip through.

I jostle forward, elbowing past backpacks and flailing arms.

Cassie follows me toward the airlock, eyes blazing, rifle bared.

A man grabs my shirt. I yank free. Another blocks my way—until he sees Cassie's rifle.

When I reach the booth, breath ragged, I toss the badge through the slot.

The guard fumbles it, then bolts back to the console.

The hatch slides open, revealing a cavernous pressurization chamber lit bruise-purple.

Hundreds of people push forward, sweeping Cassie with them.

"I'm coming!" I shout at her, then turn—just as drones flood the tunnel mouth.

Picasso fires in bursts, pushing back the drones and buying breath for people he's never met.

"Stay low!" Cassie yells at the throng surging into the airlock.

She slips out past me and climbs up on a bolted-down trash bin.

"Colt!" Cassie yells. "Get inside!"

Picasso hears her and motions to his men. "Fall back!"

His team breaks and charges down the tunnel.

Cassie fires over their heads until the bolt on her rifle clicks—empty. She tosses the gun and jumps down.

"In here!" I shout.

The two Eden-17 security guards push past me, then start the cycle.

She sprints toward me.

Hydraulic jaws begin to close as she lunges for the narrowing gap.

I slap the emergency override. A klaxon wails—we've got seconds at most.

Cassie twists, eyes wide. "Colt!"

Picasso hurls a metal canister out of the tunnel like it's weightless —and sprints toward me.

Behind him, it explodes in flames. Shrapnel rips through his shoulder. He doesn't slow.

Twenty meters.

"Faster!" I yell, my hand still pressing the override.

"Override aborted!" blares over the PA system. "Airlock sealing in three seconds."

The drones enter the tunnel, their rotors screaming.

When he's right in front of me, Picasso turns—sprays a final arc.

I grab onto him, blood blooming across his chest.

He steps away. "Get her inside."

The portal groans, closing.

"Let me help him!" Cassie cries, trying to slide past me.

"No!" I seize her arm and pull her close. "He gave us this chance. Don't waste it."

She pounds her fists against my chest—but I don't let go.

Picasso staggers sideways, shoves us through the airlock, and uses his body to block the shrinking gap.

We hit the floor just as the inner seal engages and shielding slams down.

Time buckles around us. No breath, no motion—only the cost.

On a monitor, we see Picasso drop to one knee, fire retardant flooding the tunnel around him. Bullets clang off the metal walls, his rifle spitting until the feed cuts to black.

Silence drops, crushing.

Cassie's breath hitches. She clutches the dog tags at her throat, hands trembling.

Outside, the bulkhead seals with a cannon-shot thunk.

Lights fade to blood-red standby.

The air turns sharp, clinical—nothing like the jet-fuel wind outside.

My ears pop. Locking pins snap into place.

Cassie collapses against the bulkhead, shoulders heaving.

"No," she breathes. "Not Colt. Not after everything. Not like this."

I stand and brace the door with both palms. Warm liquid soaks my sleeve—his blood.

I'm wearing it like a borrowed flag.

Guardian's voice filters down, hushed. "Shielding engaged. Outer shell secure. Inner seal holding."

A pause, then, "External status... unknown."

Unknown. Meaning Picasso's fate, the other evac planes, the riot-lit world beyond the island are all outside our reach now.

I slump down onto the floor next to Cassie.

Her hand finds mine, fingers ice-cold. She doesn't ask what I saw through the haze and muzzle flash.

Just presses my fingers to her cheek, eyes shut, like I'm a ghost.

A final salvo rumbles, then dies.

I want to get up and pound my fists against the door, shout for them to let him in.

Instead, I lie there, Picasso's blood on me, knowing there's no way back.

Systems cycle.

Fluorescents flare, bleaching the airlock white.

The silence that follows is so absolute I can hear my heart stagger.

We wait.

The inner airlock door hisses open.

Kirkland and a handful of medical techs gape at us.

People flood out into the chaos. Kirkland's team scrambles to contain the tide.

He spots me, then Cassie. Scans for Picasso. Says nothing. Just nods and walks away.

Somewhere deep in the dome, a klaxon blares, the sting swallowed by the structure's enormous lungs.

I don't know if this place is humanity's salvation or its worst mistake.

Cassie squeezes my hand, tears streaming down her face.

I realize I'm crying too.

I sit with the weight of what Picasso sacrificed—his final gift clinging to my hand.

And I wonder what shatters first: the dome, the world, or my newfound hope.

Madders' Second Log: Entry 23

Target: Diego Nadales
Nexus: Warm Springs Military Complex
Chrono Tag: Same Day

Xeno Nadales' jump has failed to avert the Second
Disaster. Warm Springs remains untouched.

Eden-2 activity spikes—likely Kirkland's
meddling. Eden-17 sealed months early.

Cassandra lives. Matt might, too. Statistical
anomalies remain the only source of hope.

After a day out in the snowstorm, my boots are frozen bricks, their cuffs biting into my ankles. I've been moving since first light—across the plains, then up the foothills—sometimes pushing through snowdrifts above my waist.

Maybe it wasn't such a great idea to take the shortcut, mae.

My toes are numb. Shoulders raw. Lungs on fire. But it's fear that does the real damage—quiet, constant, sharp.

What if I can't find her?

Every step grinds it deeper—like the mountain wants me to fail.

I stop again in the fading light and use Picasso's state-of-the-art binocs to look for the truck.

Nothing.

When I can breathe without wheezing, I continue climbing.

An hour later, my heart leaps when I spy blast doors carved out of the mountain. Around them, the cameras are iced over and quiet. No whir. No sweep. Just dead eyes.

I make a megaphone of my hands and shout toward the doors. "Sam! Phil!" My voice bounces off the rock. "Open the blast doors."

The lens stays dark. No blink.

I shiver.

Don't make me sleep out here, guys.

I cut for the doors, feet slipping, hoping one of them is monitoring the camera feed.

Below me, headlights sweep the pines, cutting them into hard silhouettes.

Powder lifts in little ghosts where the beams pass—clean and high.

No engine, just tire-hiss on crusted ice.

I stop. Heart pounding.

The Viper?

I watch the headlights glide across the tree trunks, afraid to hope. High beams blind me. I squint into the glare. The passenger door swings open. Light spills from the cab.

The sight punches the air from my lungs.

Isabel.

Relief washes over me.

I drop my pack and move. Not fast—my legs are meat and ice— but steady. Toward the light. Toward her.

She jumps out of the truck and slips, catching herself on the door. No coat. No boots.

She runs toward me.

The world shrinks to the space between us.

She folds into me as I pull her close.

The weight I've carried for months falls away as I lift her.

"I was so damn scared," I whisper, the words breaking as they leave me. "I thought I'd never see you again."

My fingers graze her bandage, so I shift lower and bury my face in the warm cut of her shoulder. The ache I've carried splinters into heat, every mile of ice and doubt collapsing into this one impossible warmth.

She frames my face, fingers ice against skin. Her eyes are fire. She breathes like I dragged her back from drowning.

She smacks my chest. Words queue. The first one is heat. "Don't you ever—"

I kiss the rest away.

Her hand grips my collar. Mine finds the nape of her neck.

Time holds still.

She breaks for air, forehead pressed to mine.

"You left," she breathes. Not a question.

Her words cut deeper than the chill, but I can't let go of the only truth that matters: She's here.

"You're alive," I say.

It's all I have.

Her laugh is bright—and it undoes me. I don't deserve it, but I take it anyway.

My hand slides down her back. My thumb settles along her jaw. I wait.

She kisses me again—desperate, hopeful.

I hold her, terrified she'll vanish into the snow.

When we break, I sweep a wisp of hair away from her lips.

She clutches my shirt. "Have I told you recently that I love you?"

I hesitate, letting my gaze fall across her hair, eyes, lips. "Nope."

She hits my chest again—gentler this time—and pulls me back in.

"I will always find my way back to you, Iz," I say. "As long as I have breath."

Not a promise. Not hope.

Gravity.

Tolstoy barrels out of the truck, barking, and whines until I scratch him behind his ears. Lucky meanders over, climbs my coat like it's still hers, and drapes herself across my shoulders.

The knot behind my ribs loosens. I breathe. Isabel's warmth against me, Tolstoy at my side, Lucky's purr in my ear.

For a blink, the universe is perfect.

The Viper glides closer and comes to a silent stop. My hand stays at the small of Isabel's back. Tolstoy's weight presses against my leg. The world has narrowed to Isabel's warmth on my cheek—until headlights flare, and I turn.

"About time you showed up, Sherlock." Lani leans out the window, grin sharp. "Last time we chatted, you were mid-proposal. She say yes?"

I open my mouth. Close it.

My chest won't stop pounding, and my tongue's suddenly stone.

Isabel answers without looking away from me. "He hasn't asked again."

Lani lifts a brow. "Tick-tock, Romeo."

Inside the cab, a kid peers over the seat, eyes wide. "Are those guns going to kill us? Like the bugs did to those men?"

Isabel flinches, her hand tightening on my sleeve.

What the hell happened out there?

"No," I tell him. "The guns are off. The people inside are my friends." I glance at the nearest camera. "Sam," I call, "if you can hear me, open the blast doors and bring an extension cord. We need to plug in the truck."

Nothing.

Then the mountain answers with a groan. The concrete under my boots vibrates as the blast doors split along their seam. Floodlights snap awake, spilling light across the snow, shadows slicing through the trees. Steam hisses from hydraulic pistons, making the air shimmer. The fortress gapes open like a mechanical jaw.

The exterior PA squawks to life. "Diego!" Sam's voice booms out into the still night.

We all cringe.

"Oops," Sam mutters. "Too loud. Hang on."

Tolstoy barks at the speaker.

"Welcome back," he adds, voice sheepish. "Bridge is live—and sexier than me on karaoke night!"

Lucky digs her claws into my shoulder.

Sam clears his throat, dials the volume down. "Got your extension cord—fifty-footer coming up, my man. So... who are the dames?"

"What's a *dame*?" Kai says.

"Another word for woman." Isabel walks up to the truck and ruffles his hair. "Popular with cavemen and single guys."

I huff a laugh. "You must be Lani's brother."

The kid squints at me. "I remember you. You were at the fire. You almost got us killed."

"Key word being *almost*."

Isabel flicks snow off my eyebrow, suppressing a smile. "Kai, meet Diego."

The breeze kicks up, and the cold gets its teeth back.

I squeeze Isabel's hand. "Come inside. We'll get you something to eat."

Behind us, the blast doors stand open, flooding the snow with white light. Three figures wait in the glare—Sam waving us in, Phil rocking on his toes, and Gramps standing in the middle, still as stone.

Isabel stumbles a step when she sees the old man. He doesn't blink, doesn't move—just fixes on her like she's the last star in the sky.

Heat flickers in my gut.

Sorry, old man. This one's mine.

Lani drives straight toward the mountain's mouth.

I hitch my pack and put my arm around Isabel as we follow.

The moment we're inside, Phil starts the sequence to seal the mountain shut. Sam steps up with an orange cord, grinning too wide. The plug clicks, the Viper chirps, dash lights flash.

Lani hesitates for half a breath before sliding off the seat, one hand braced on the doorframe like she's carrying more than fatigue. Her eyes flick to the empty guard station, the piles of wooden pallets, the cavernous storage area. There's something in her expression—not fear exactly, but the tight calculation of someone deciding whether to trust again. "Bathroom?"

Phil points.

"I'm hungry," Kai says as he climbs out after her.

"Welcome to Warm Springs Cavern," Sam says. "Five stars on Yelp if you're into concrete and stale air."

After introductions, Sam leads us deeper into the mountain, his movements quick and jittery. I keep my arm around Isabel—afraid if I let go of her, she'll vanish.

Our footsteps echo past the dead security gate—sliding glass stuck open, hand scanner dark.

Tolstoy whines low, tail tucked. Lucky clings to Gramps' chest.

We crowd into the elevator, restless, like the air itself is warning us away.

The doors close. The cage lurches, metal groaning, the air tasting of rust.

Isabel presses against me, silent. I don't trust my voice enough to speak. Tolstoy shifts at Isabel's side, nails clicking on the floor. Gramps holds Lucky tight against his chest, his body as rigid as the cat's. Kai grips Lani's hand, his eyes wary. She steadies herself with the handrail, looking pale—and pregnant?

We drop deeper into the mountain.

I catch Gramps giving Isabel a nod, almost tender. Isabel gives him a ghost of a smile. A look passes between them—like they understand something I don't. Then she folds against me, and I pretend it doesn't sting.

Doors wrench apart, revealing the black lake and unmoving stars. Buildings huddle like survivors on the far shore.

After climbing into two carts, we drive around the lake in silence. The electric whine echoes off the cavern walls, high and thin.

With every second, my chest knots tighter.

Safe is a word I don't let myself say.

When we arrive, Kai tugs on Isabel's sleeve. "I need to pee."

Isabel glances at Lani.

She shifts, hand on her lower back. "Yeah," she murmurs, a little sheepish. "Me too. Again."

"Come on." Gramps offers Kai his hand—and the kid takes it. "I'll show you."

"Meet in the lounge when you're done," I call after them.

Gramps lifts his free hand—just enough to say *yeah, yeah, I heard you.*

* * *

Inside the lab block, Sam stops in front of a window. Through the glass, the Coffin squats in the center of the room, cables coiled like veins across the floor. A clip-on dosimeter hangs inside the glass, its red light steady.

My skin prickles, like the radiation can reach through walls. "Does it work?"

Sam rubs the back of his neck, avoiding Isabel's eyes. "The nuclear power was supposed to be good for decades. Buried line, double shielding, all the regs. Then we sent the dead guy through a wormhole. Main cable overheated—melted straight through the conduit."

I blink. "You melted a power line rated for a reactor?"

"Not me. The bridge. That thing sucks down jigawatts like they're chocolate milkshakes." He jabs a thumb toward the Coffin. "So we tapped into the regular power line upstairs." He strokes the chinchilla on his shoulder and grins. "That base out east is gonna have quite a shock when they get the electric bill."

Isabel shakes her head. "You're telling me this miracle machine is strapped together using stolen electricity?"

Sam bristles. "It works. Mostly."

"*Mostly* is a hell of a floor to jump from," I say.

"Better than the old setup," Sam mutters.

I raise an eyebrow. "That supposed to make me feel better?"

"If necessity's the mother of invention," Phil chimes in, "we're her favorite children."

Benny chitters his agreement.

I exhale. "Why did you move the Coffin?"

Sam's foot bounces. "The plans called for tungsten collars and proper sleeves to stop the shine. All we have are steel and duct tape."

Phil snorts. "Translation: door stays shut unless the light's green. Otherwise, start writing your will."

A chill crawls up my spine. I edge away from the glass.

"How long until it can jump?" I ask.

"We should have enough juice to light the bridge tomorrow," Sam says.

Phil rakes a hand through his hair. "As long as the plant keeps running. If the fuel runs out, cables snap, or some genius drops a bomb—we're dead in the water. Could be an hour, could be a week, could be never."

The lights overhead flicker once, like they're in on the joke.

I walk over to the door. There's a sticky note on it:

Do Not Take Benny In Here!

I raise an eyebrow. "How do you know the bridge works?"

Sam plucks Benny off his shoulder and strokes his fur.

"First run, Benny went out and back clean. Used the Sphere shell for targeting. Second time, we tried Gramps' shell—still clean." Sam presses his lips together, shoulders tight.

Phil shifts his weight. "Third run, we went back to the Sphere shell."

Sam swallows, voice breaking. "Benny came back with singed fur."

Phil rests his hand on Sam's back. "We set the turnaround to half a second. That's probably what saved him."

My chest tightens—they burned him instead of me.

Isabel reaches up to Benny, lets him sniff her hand, then pets him. "Thanks, big guy."

He chitters again.

I take a deep breath and let it out. "Let's talk."

Sam hurries back the way we came. "I'll grab some snacks."

I follow Phil into the lounge.

The room reeks of sweat and scorched coffee. Couches sag under layers of tape. Mismatched mugs ring a low table, their logos rubbed to ghosts.

Phil plops down on a worn loveseat. Kai, Lani and Gramps walk in.

I drop my pack, pull out the water bottle, and collapse beside Isabel. Her head tips onto my shoulder, grounding me. I drink the last swallow and fight back a yawn.

Fatigue blurs the room's edges. I blink hard to keep it at bay.

The universe doesn't care if you're tired.

Sam rattles in with the cart. He tosses cracker sleeves, a sack of raisins, and peanut-butter packs onto the table. "Dinner is served."

Benny peeks from his collar, whiskers trembling.

From Gramps' lap, Lucky tracks the ball of fur, ready to pounce.

Kai leans in, mouth open. "What's that?"

"A chinchilla," Sam says and runs a finger between the creature's ears. "Benny. Head of snacks."

Kai leans in closer. "Can I hold him?"

"No," Lani says, already pulling Kai away. "He's a wild animal."

"Nah." Sam lifts Benny off his shoulder. "He's as gentle as they come."

"Please, Lani?" Kai gives his sister a look that could melt glaciers. "Oh, all right."

Kai cradles Benny with both hands, eyes wide. The chinchilla sniffs his thumb and settles in. The kid gives a rare smile.

Sam lifts a paper bag and dumps it on the table—ramen cups, jerky, Oat-Os, peaches in syrup. "I'd start with the peaches," he says, "but it's your call. Plenty more where that came from."

"Microwave's on the fritz," Phil says with a pointed look at Sam. "So you'll have to heat water in the coffee pot."

"It's being recalibrated," Sam mutters and sets a dented water jug on the table in front of Lani.

When he offers one to me, Picasso's old warning rises in the back of my throat. *Bottled water only—tap carries contaminants you can't taste.*

"Don't worry. It's safe," Sam says "Distilled it myself. Single-origin kitchen tap, vintage five minutes ago." He pulls up a folding chair and sits next to Phil.

Lani shifts, wincing, and adjusts her waistband. She cracks the jug, sniffs and drinks deep. No sarcasm. No complaints.

Must be feeling worse than she's letting on.

I tip the bottle until the burn in my chest eases. "Thanks, Sam."

As much as I hate this place, it beats sleeping outside in the cold.

Gramps studies my face. "You get it done?"

Sam freezes mid-bite. Phil's fingers stop tapping.

"Yes," I say. "Did the bridge instructions disappear?"

Phil pulls a crumpled printout from his jacket and smooths it flat on the table. The ink's still there—equations, notes, a smudge of coffee. "Nope."

Sam stares at his cereal. "What about the others? Did you find them?"

"Matt and Sabina went to an island in the South Pacific," I say. "Eden-17. Picasso and Cassie chose to join them."

Sam's head snaps up, color draining from his face. "That's halfway across the world."

Phil presses his palms together, voice tight. "They're all okay?"

"As far as I know. The island's closed to outsiders."

Sam's hands flatten on his knees, then curl into fists. His head bows, shoulders folding under the weight of the news.

Something twists in my chest. I want to tell him it's temporary, that they'll be back—but the words stick in my throat. I've lied enough for one lifetime.

Phil shifts in his chair, eyes on Sam. "If there's a way, we'll find it, Sam. If not—we'll build one."

Sam nods once, slow. "Got a bridge handy?"

The chinchilla chitters.

"Kirkland offered you a place inside Eden-2, Sam. Phil too." I take Kirkland's two-way radio out of my pack. "There's room in the truck, and Kirkland's holding a corridor open until Friday—no drones, no artillery. Once you're close, use the walkie. He'll send an escort."

Phil's eyes go wide. "Fresh food. Sky. Anything but this morgue."

He looks at Sam—who's staring at the chinchilla on Kai's lap.

"Is Benny a lab animal?" Isabel rubs her lips. "If so, he has a chip."

Sam nods. "Former."

"Good." Isabel pats Sam's thigh. "Take him in a clean carrier and register him as a bio-indicator. They'll quarantine him for twenty-four hours, then hand him back. Dave'll grumble, but the intake officer signs the paperwork."

Sam straightens a little, life flickering back into his eyes.

Lani breaks the silence. "We leave as soon as the Viper's charged." Her voice is steady—but her hand doesn't leave Kai's shoulder.

Phil clears his throat. "Then who runs the bridge?"

"I will," Gramps says without looking up. "Already did my time. I'll push the button and call it a night."

Isabel jerks like she's been slapped. "What?" Her voice is quiet, but it cuts. "Why are you sending Diego? Why don't you go?"

Gramps doesn't flinch, just strokes Tolstoy's ears. Finally, he looks up at Isabel, eyes shadowed. "Because it's too late for me. Diego's the only one who can change things."

Isabel's face flushes. "And you just *know* that?"

He holds her gaze, and for a second there's something in his expression I can't name—sorrow, longing, maybe both. "I've already lived through what comes next," he says. "And staying here means it happens again."

"Isabel."

She turns to me, blinking.

"You know I want to stay with you. More than anything. But this —" I glance at Gramps. "This is the path I have to take."

Isabel grips my hand. "No. I'm not letting you go again. We fight Dave here. We take down every bot, every dome if we have to, but we do it together."

Gramps shakes his head, heavy with regret. "That war's already lost."

I squeeze her hand, but my voice is already breaking. "Gramps is right." The words burn coming out. "If I stay, everything repeats. I have to go."

Silence hangs in the air like the smell of an open sewer.

"We should get some sleep," Lani says. "It's going to be an early morning."

Kai cradles Benny for a moment, then presses him into Sam's hands like he's letting go of the last safe thing.

I want to stop time—let the kid hold on. Pull Isabel close. Erase everything else.

But the world presses on. There's always a decision waiting. A goodbye behind every door.

"I'm not going back to the biodome." Isabel looks at me, steady. "I'm going with you."

My collar tightens like a noose. "Absolutely not. You need to help Lani and Kai get home. Stay in the biodome where you're safe."

She glances at Lani—who shakes her head once—then turns back to me. "Lani doesn't need me."

"No room," Phil whispers, eyes on his hands. "The Coffin will be tight with just Diego."

"Then Diego goes first," she says. "I wait for the bridge to recharge. Follow him."

Gramps exhales and shakes his head. "That's not the plan, Isabel. Only Diego is supposed to go."

Sam shifts in his seat, eyes flicking between us like he wants to disappear.

"Screw the plan," she says. "What has it done for us so far?"

Her words are an axe. I feel them split right through me.

Lucky's ears flatten, tail flicks.

Sam gives a dry laugh. "So much for subtlety."

"Not much point now," Isabel murmurs, barely above a breath, and strokes Lucky's back. "Don't worry, kitty girl. No one's gonna die." She looks up, holds my gaze, unmoving.

I want to tell her she doesn't understand the risk, that she's gambling with something I can't afford to lose. But the words wedge in my throat, hollow and useless. She's not bluffing. I've already lost this fight.

When she turns to Gramps, it's not for permission—it's to show him she's done asking.

He stares into his mug like it holds something besides regret.

"There might not be enough power to send the Coffin twice," Sam says and adds, under his breath, "Might not be enough to send it once."

Phil leans forward, elbows on his knees. "And you would need a second jinn object from the same timeline. There's some sort of splatter around a jump. If we reuse the target object while the splash is still live, the jump fails. Ask Benny."

"He's right," Gramps says, rubbing Tolstoy's head. "Tego mentioned something about it too."

Isabel sets her shell on the table. "Show them, Diego."

I toss Phil a blue velvet bag. "My shell's in there."

He frowns, peeks inside. "Nothing here." Weighs it in his hand. "But I can feel it."

Sam takes the bag, squeezes it, looks inside. "So why can't we see it?"

Isabel tips an empty mug over her shell. "Now try."

Sam upends the bag. A shell drops into his palm.

A chill creeps up my spine—physics dressed as magic.

"Timeline resonance," Phil murmurs. "Cosmic sleight of hand."

Isabel lifts the mug. The shell's gone.

Sam frowns. "So whichever one you see first wins?" He puts the shell in the bag and tosses it back to me.

"Makes weird sense," Phil says. "But the connection might be weak. Move the cup while it's invisible, and you could lose the jinn object."

Isabel removes the mug. The shell's back.

The kid perks up. "Can I try?"

"Nope," his sister says.

Kai slumps. "She never lets me have any fun."

Lani nods at me. "Where'd you get yours?"

"Found it on La Isla Beach when I was twenty. Bartender said it'd save me someday. I laughed."

"But you held onto it anyway," Phil says.

Sam snaps his fingers. "Someone planted it—brought it from another timeline, left it for you to find."

"That's why the Peeper was underwater," Phil says. "Same place the shell was."

Gramps grunts. "The chain again. The one we're not supposed to break."

Lani looks at Isabel. "And yours?"

"From Tego," Gramps says. "He jumped timelines to give it to Isabel."

"Where'd the Sphere shell come from?" Sam asks.

I shrug. "No way to know unless we can test it against the others."

"It was in Johnson's office," Sam says. "Sabina and I liberated it."

Phil stands. "Be right back." He returns with a matching shell and sets it beside Isabel's.

Nothing.

Gramps offers his etched one.

Still nothing.

The old man pockets it. "Different lineage."

Isabel tucks hers away too. "Then it's settled. Diego and I use the entangled pair."

I shake my head. "It's a bad idea, Iz. Even if they take us to the same place and time, we could land in a dome with air like bleach. In a sealed room with no door on our side. In a valley where noon is night and ash eats your lungs."

"I'm going with you, Diego. If we die, at least we die together."

Tolstoy whines and noses Isabel's elbow.

I drag a hand across my face—torn between being with her and keeping her safe.

Lani glances between us. "You sure about this, Isabel?"

Lucky meows, quiet and low.

Gramps strokes her fur, gaze distant, then clears his throat. "For thirty-odd years I watched Dave jump. Decades of targeted tweaks to combat pandemics, famine, killer bots. Same damn ending over and over." He pins me with his gaze. "Maybe it's time we quit trimming hedges and started swinging a wrecking ball."

"No." It comes out before I can stop myself.

Gramps scoffs. "Your name's not on the dance card, Sparky."

The shell's ridge bites into my palm.

What if I can't protect her, can't...

Isabel doesn't flinch. Doesn't move. She's already made up her mind.

I nod. "Okay."

The room exhales.

Tolstoy noses my knee. I scratch his head to steady myself.

"But I go first," I say and take Isabel's hand. "And you wait for green. Don't crack that door until it's safe. If any readouts look off, you stay here where it's safe. Promise me."

If the bridge fails to recharge, she'll be stuck inside this mountain. With an older version of me.

Better than spending the rest of her life alone.

Isabel's mouth twitches. Her eyes flick to Phil. "How long to recharge the bridge?"

Phil rubs his eyes, voice rough with fatigue. "Depends on what—and who—we're sending. The original capacitors are slag. We patched in sisters from the other labs, but they cook a little with every jump. Recharge time keeps stretching. We *think* there's enough to send Diego, but your shell's untested."

Isabel's fingers tighten on mine. I glance at her, but she doesn't blink.

Lani shifts, arms tight across her chest. "How long until Isabel can jump?"

"Five days?" Phil lifts his head, then studies his hands. "Two weeks—maybe longer. Truth is, we don't know."

Kai looks up at Isabel, eyes wide. "What if it breaks while you're jumping?"

Gramps exhales, like he already knows the answer and hates it.

"Then I figure something out," she says. "That's what a Vipertruck troika member does—improvise."

Kai takes something from his pocket and offers it to Isabel. "For good luck."

The sight stops me cold. The grain, the notch in the leg—my hands remember carving it. A vision of the future the twins never got to touch.

She takes the tiny horse and wraps Kai in a hug. "Thank you."

Phil stares at his shoes, shoulders low. "The shells are jinns of the same object. You might hit Diego's splash."

The words hang there, shimmering with equal parts science and superstition. For a moment, no one speaks.

Tolstoy whines softly and rests his chin in Isabel's lap.

I start to shake my head. "It's too risky, Iz. I—"

"I'm going with you, Diego." She leans against me, steady and warm. "We die in another timeline, we die holding hands. That's the deal."

I breathe in and let the weight of it settle.

Maybe she's right. Maybe there's no safe path left—only forward. Together.

Even if it kills us.

Madders' Second Log:
Entry 24

Target: Isabel Sanborn
Nexus: Warm Springs Military Complex
Chrono Tag: That Night

Seven biodomes fail to seal. Four malfunction.
Two are breached. One is destroyed. Median
functional lifespan for remaining is 17.4 years.

Reverse jump detected at Eden-17. Mandela shift
confirms timeline altered. Against all odds,
Cassandra survives. Possible cause——Sabina?

Einstein-Rosen Bridge rebuilt from instructions I
etched on Diego's shell. I have no memory of
this. Erasure appears deliberate. Suspect: me.

Conclusion: a closed loop has opened.

The blast doors guarding Warm Springs grind open. Cold air knifes in.

Isabel Sanborn, inter-dimensional fugitive, still freezing her ass off.

"Dramatic exits are overrated," I mutter, stepping into the dark.

Diego squeezes my hand, a silent anchor in the wind.

The Vipertruck glints in the dim light, packed and silent, ready to go.

The eastern horizon bruises purple, daylight fighting to be born.

As Lani backs the truck into the predawn gloom, Diego, Gramps and I walk beside it. In the backseat, Sam sits next to Kai with Benny snuggled under his chin like a fuzzy scarf. Phil taps his fingers against the dash, his face drawn.

The night is cloudless, the stars still visible.

I stop walking and pull my coat tighter.

Tolstoy leans into my leg and whines. Lucky snuggles in Gramps' arm, silent.

Lani turns the truck around and brings it to a stop in front of us.

Something presses under my ribs. Not fear. Not grief—just the hollow they leave behind.

"Be sure to use the two-way once you get close to Eden-2," I say, shivering. "Pretty sure grand theft Viper voids your visitor pass."

Diego steps behind me and wraps his arms around my waist, his cheek cold against my ear. "And have Kirkland send out a broadcast when you're inside."

Lani looks at Diego, her hand sliding to her belly like a reflex. "Bring my baby something worth growing up in, Sherlock."

He nods once. "Stay away from burning buildings, *Mulan*."

A hint of a smile steals across her lips. "Deal."

Kai rolls down his window, Gramps' fedora crooked on his head. "Why can't Tolstoy and Lucky come? Sam gets to take Benny."

"Benny has a special chip," I say, keeping my voice soft. "Tolstoy and Lucky don't. They wouldn't be allowed inside the biodome."

"That's not fair."

"It's not," I say.

Gramps clears his throat. "I'll look after them, Kai. Lots of walks. Good food. I'll even let them hog the bed and snore like trucks."

Kai laughs. "Lani and Isabel snore like trucks."

"Do not," Lani and I say—both of us wondering if he's right.

Diego laughs a little too loud, and I shoot him a look.

"You gotta pet his heart," Kai tells Gramps. "It's his favorite."

The words cut into me, and my eyes water. For a moment, I glimpse the man Kai will become: strong, brave, *good*.

"I'll share Benny with you," Sam says to Kai, leaning over. He coaxes the chinchilla out of his jacket. "Just don't teach him to drive, okay? He already acts like he owns the place." The little animal scrabbles, then settles on Kai's shoulder like a silvery epaulet.

Kai rubs his cheek against Benny's soft fur, and his frown fades.

Sam runs his fingertips over the chinchilla and looks at us. "Guess this is goodbye, huh?" He tries for a smile. "Don't let Gramps tell the bedtime stories. And take care of each other." He adds softly, "for real."

Phil leans over from the passenger seat. "Watch the sensor," he says to Gramps. "Green is the only safe option. Anything else, you wait—even if the bridge is ready."

"I know, I know," Gramps says. "Hard as it is to believe, I've done this before." He mumbles something about *having fun storming the castle* and gives a single wave. "Come back if you need to," he says. "We'll leave the light on."

"How far away is Eden-2?" Phil asks, his gaze on the faint glow of the dome.

"Thirty, forty miles," Diego says. "Might even make it before breakfast. Just keep heading east. You can't miss it."

I lean in Lani's window and glance at the console—60% charge.

"It's plenty," Lani says. "Enough to go and come back."

Provided everything goes as planned. Which it won't.

I give her an encouraging smile. "Once you get inside, act like I forced you to leave at gunpoint. Make sure they watch the surveillance footage. Won't take much for Dave to believe it."

Lani raises an eyebrow. "I'll let you know if we win an Oscar."

I laugh and reach in for one last hug. "Take care of yourself," I whisper. "And the little one."

"Shannon Isabel," she says. "For the two fiercest women in my life."

"Keep Dave honest," I say, swallowing a rush of emotion. "He has a good heart." I ignore the grimace on Diego's face. "And the man loves you."

She presses her lips together, nods.

I step back, dragging my sleeve across my eyes. "We made a good team, didn't we?"

Her smile snags, uneven. "Let's do it again sometime."

Something in me settles. I don't know how, but I'm sure I'll see her again.

I turn to Kai last. "Try to be the person Tolstoy believes you are."

His chin wobbles, but he lifts it higher. "I'll remember," he whispers and rolls up the window like the promise will cost him.

"Keep your eyes on the drone pattern," Diego says to Lani. "Stay inside the lane."

She nods. "We'll be fine, Diego. Thank you."

Diego taps his palm twice on her door and steps back.

She rolls up the window, looks back at Diego. "See you in another life, brother."

He laughs. "Looking forward to it."

I lean into him.

For a breath, our reflections cling to the glass. The Viper slinks across the tarmac, the tires crunching in the still air. The taillights streak red across the frozen snow as the truck heads down the mountain. A moment later, they're lost in the trees.

Silence crashes in—the cold sharper against my skin, the dark heavier—like the future just shifted its weight onto my shoulders.

Our breath fogs—me, Gramps, Diego—once, twice.

No one speaks.

We turn together and walk back through the huge gap. Diego slaps a button, and the steel grinds, cold wind rushing in as it closes, grease and iron in my nose.

We've been up all night, and the trek back to our underground world is silent.

"Good night," Gramps murmurs and disappears into Matt's old room.

"Sleep well," I say, knowing how impossible that will be.

Diego opens his door for me. Tolstoy shoulders through. Lucky slips in behind me with a flick of her tail. The door latches shut.

The hotel-style room is a box with a bed, a wooden desk and chair, and a tiny backlit image of the Great Pyramid. Diego hangs his jacket over nails above the fake window and takes off his boots.

The air tastes like dust. Next door, we hear the shower start.

Lucky and Tolstoy jump up on the narrow cot and flop down.

"There goes my reservation," Diego says.

"Refundable?" I say and pull him closer.

He wraps his arms around me, his gaze steady. "'Fraid not."

"Better take it up with management."

"I am management."

I smirk. "Exactly the problem."

He laughs, sudden and raw.

Something good gives way.

He reaches for my sweater. I unbutton his shirt. We are clumsy with hurry. Sleeves catch. Clothes tangle. Skin finds skin. He smells like sweat and pine sap—wind-washed and sun-warmed like the trails above the cabin.

"Hi," he says, his voice low.

"Hi," I whisper. My eyes flick to his temple. "Nice scar."

"You should see the sprinkler head."

I laugh. "God, I've missed you."

We slide to the bed without breaking. He shoves Tolstoy over and sets me down. The dog and the mattress protest. Lucky curls up next to the pillow.

His hands glide over me, avoiding my stitches.

"What happened?" he says into my neck, his beard rough, his hands warm.

"Turns out, dodging a bullet is harder than I thought."

He frowns. "Who shot you?"

"It was an accident," I say. "If that's why you're asking."

"I don't want to lose you again, Iz."

My stitches pull as I shift to face him. "Ditto."

He presses his forehead to mine like he's trying to stop time.

Then softer, almost to himself, "We could stay. Forget the jump. It's safe here. Supplies for decades. Not as many stars as one of Kirkland's domes, maybe, but—"

I press a hand to his chest. Not to stop him. Just to know he's still there.

"We have to go," I say.

He swallows, shoulders tense.

Next door, the shower shuts off.

"It's the only way to fix this," I whisper. "And if it doesn't work…" I stop. "It has to work."

His eyes search mine, taking in everything we're not saying.

"I'll be there," he says. "Waiting for you."

I pull him closer, my lips brushing his. "You could always let me go first."

"Not gonna happen."

I open my mouth to answer—to say something flippant or brave or clever—but he finds my lips first.

He kisses me like it might be the last time—slow, deep, hungry.

I want to believe we have more time. That this won't be the last of us.

But I'm afraid to hope.

The heater shuts off. Silence fills the void.

A sound as thin as foil tearing seeps through the wall.

We freeze.

Another sound, wetter. A sob tries to be quiet and fails.

Diego tips his head toward it. "Gramps," he says. "Seeing us together is pretty hard on him."

We hold our breath like that will steady the old man.

It doesn't.

The sound of despair fills the room.

Diego's eyes shut. His jaw tightens once. "I should—"

"I will," I say and sit up. My skin flinches in the brisk air. I pull on Diego's shirt and kiss his forehead. Mercy or cruelty, I can't tell. "Two minutes."

"Make it one."

Tolstoy's tail thumps the mattress.

I open the door and heat from the hallway pushes past me. I snap my fingers, soft. "Tolstoy, here."

The dog jumps off the bed, Lucky on his heels. I walk down the hall, pets trailing, and knock on Gramps' door.

I wait two beats. "It's me," I say. "Can I come in?"

The sob cuts off like a faucet.

Then Gramps says, "Yeah." Not steady. Not pretending.

He sits on the edge of his bed, hands open. His shoes are lined up, his clothes folded on a chair. The room smells like dryer sheets.

"I thought—" He exhales and wipes his face with the heel of his hand, tries a smile that won't land. ' Sorry."

"Hold these two for me?" I say. The pets step in like pros. Tolstoy sets his head on Gramps' thigh with full dog weight. Lucky jumps up on the bed and settles next to him.

A sound that wants to be a laugh catches. Gramps steadies a hand on Tolstoy's head and the dog leans so hard Gramps has to catch his balance.

"Bossy," he tells Tolstoy.

"He takes after you," I say.

"He takes after your training," he says and strokes Lucky.

I stand there, looking for words to make his hurt go away.

Can't find any.

"You look just like her," he says. "Younger, maybe, less pain. But just like her."

I smile. "Probably because I *am* her."

He nods, his gaze steady. "He loves you, Isabel. More than you know."

"And she loved you."

He stifles a sob.

For a moment, I can feel the pull—even through all those years.

We both glance away.

He rubs Tolstoy's ears. "I'm fine."

"Nobody's fine," I say. "We all fake it in shifts."

"If I fake any harder, I'll need a union break."

I laugh.

The despair in the room eases a notch.

"I don't want you to be alone," I say.

"Now I won't be." He runs his fingers across Lucky, and she starts purring. "Go on. I'll be all right."

I squeeze his shoulder. "Good night."

He feels like Diego with time pressed into him. The same bones. A different story.

I leave the door cracked so the animals can choose where to sleep. The hall looks longer on the way back.

When I step into our room, Diego hasn't moved. Back to the wall, hair a mess, eyes locked on me like I'm the last thing worth remembering.

"He okay?"

"No," I say. "But he'll survive."

He huffs. "I hope I survive."

"Aim higher." I crawl into bed, chasing the warmth Tolstoy left behind, and curl beside him, hungry for his heat and passion—and the lie that this is enough. He pulls me close. I breathe him in, trying to memorize the way he smells.

"Clock's ticking," he says.

"I know." I kiss the hollow of his collarbone. "Make me forget."

He does.

Later, he threads our fingers together and rests them over his heart.

"Tell me the plan again," I whisper, pressing my face into the curve of his shoulder.

His breath hitches—then steadies, like he's lining up the dominoes. "I take my shell and go. You wait for green. When it's safe, you use Tego's shell and follow. I'll be waiting for you."

"What if the sensor doesn't turn green?" The words sit heavy.

"You wait until it does. Even if the bridge is charged, promise me you'll wait as long as it takes."

"Okay," I say.

He studies me long enough to make my skin warm. "You're a terrible liar."

I roll my eyes. "Good thing you like a challenge."

He kisses my forehead, then my cheek, then the notch under my ear. I shiver.

"You still smell like you," I whisper, like saying it might keep him here.

"Occupational hazard." He runs his fingers through my hair.

I melt against him, the heater ticking off seconds we can't afford to lose. I order every nerve to memorize the warmth, the weight, the exhale that means he's still here.

Still alive.

A knock, soft as regret. A cough from the hallway, rough with sleep and knowing.

"Time to jump," Gramps says.

Too soon.

Diego and I need time—just one more dawn, one more breath.

One more lifetime.

I sit up, and the cold finds me. Diego swings his legs over the side and reaches for his clothes. The weight climbs back on our shoulders —uninvited, unwelcome, impossible to ignore.

I hate it—but I get dressed.

The dosimeter in the window glows green as we hurry past. Across the hall, Gramps is standing in front of the bridge console, pets splayed on the floor. He presses a folded bundle into Diego's arms.

"Clothes and shoes. All organic materials. Don't want you to arrive naked."

Diego frowns. "Moccasins and pajamas? Really?"

"It'll do." Gramps' voice is flat, but his eyes are not. "Your clothes will fall apart: rivets, zippers, buttons won't make the jump." He shrugs. "But hey, knock yourself out."

Diego's macho slips a notch.

Gramps pauses, then adds with less heat, "There's a note in the pocket. Super Bowls, stocks, long-shot odds, every year I could remember. And five diamonds sewn into the cuff. Phil's idea—and his diamonds. Don't know if they'll make the trip. If they do, should be enough to get you started."

Diego starts to change. When he's done, he says goodbye to the pets, pulls the shell from the pocket of his jeans, and exhales. "Ready."

The three of us walk back to the room with the Coffin. The sensor still glows green.

Diego offers Gramps his hand. "Thanks. For everything."

The old man narrows one eye, shakes Diego's hand. "Soon enough, it'll be you staying behind." He turns to me. "Holler when he's sealed inside." Gramps' hand skims my shoulder as he walks past.

The console room swallows him.

Diego exhales to steady himself. "Stay where you are once you arrive, Iz. I'll find you."

"If for some reason I can't," I say, "I'll leave you a message—my initials and a count of the days since I arrived. I'll post it close to the jump location."

We move like people who learned the same kitchen long ago—reach, pass, step, no collisions. My body knows him.

We sit. Stools scrape. The soup bites my tongue and I let it. On the far wall, a tired clock insists on the wrong hour. Down the hall, the bridge blinks red, a metronome no one asked for.

"Does Top of the Rockies happen in your timeline?" I ask.

He nods. "You wanted to order from the kids' menu."

"Only thing we could afford."

He chuckles. "You asked if *market price* meant haggling in the alley."

I shrug. "Who knew halibut were so hard to pin down?" I take a deep breath, enjoying the memories. "You were sure breadsticks were a building material."

He almost smiles. "Guilty as charged."

"We hid the fancy forks because we didn't know what to do with them."

He opens a bottle of hot sauce. "In my world, we used them wrong and the waiter survived."

I laugh.

Tolstoy lifts his head, tail slapping the floor. Lucky shifts inside the breadbasket and pretends she isn't listening.

"In mine," I say, "the waitress had fake eyelashes. She called me trouble under her breath and made you grin."

"Mine was male. Had a laugh he kept behind his teeth," he says. "Said I was a good sport when we switched meals." He chuckles into his soup. "You dared me to order the foamy dessert—something named after a ballerina—"

"Pavlova."

"That's it. You insisted it had a personality."

"It did," I say. "*Aloof.*"

We both laugh and look away at the same time.

He peels the hot sauce label into a curl. "We sat by the west windows. Thunderstorms brewed over the foothills."

"Nope," I say. "Perfectly clear. The gloaming painted the whole sky with watercolors. After dinner we walked around LoDo. It smelled like waffle cones. When it got cold, we each kept one hand in your pocket."

"Ditto," he says, dropping the hot sauce label. "Except it smelled like rain on hot concrete. We spent the night at The Brown Palace."

"Marble everywhere," I say. "Ceiling like a birdcage. We sat on a gilded sofa and listened to the music."

"Jazz quartet. The sax player kept smiling at you."

"Concert grand," I say. "The pianist didn't look up once."

We both smile, look away.

He tilts his head. "We keep landing in the same place—only to find the furniture moved."

"Like someone updated the set between takes."

He studies the floor, eyes distant, like he's watching the scene play out in a place he can no longer reach.

"We were broke in both timelines," he says.

I swallow. "And madly in love."

We let the quiet stand.

Tolstoy sighs and puts his head down. Lucky bats at the curled hot sauce label.

"So we had the same night," I say. "Just with different weather."

"Close enough to be true," he says. "Far enough to prove it wasn't the same."

I find his gaze and hold it. Diego's face looks back at me with new lines.

"Do you ever wonder which one of us remembers the right world?" I ask.

"Neither," he says. "We remember the right person. The rest is details."

We rinse bowls. I rack them on edge because my mother believed drips should pick a side. Lucky jumps up to Gramps' shoulder and settles like a corsage. He steadies her with one hand. Tolstoy noses my knee and gets a scratch that turns his back leg into a machine.

"How did you end up working for Dave?" I ask. The question has been waiting since the first time he said as much.

He dries his hands on a towel. "Once you and I got married, it was a package deal. Kirkland had to take both of us."

The word hits like a stair I missed.

Married.

I rinse a clean bowl, letting the water run.

He shuts it off. "We were good," he says, softer now. "Better when we remember we're on the same side."

I press my palm flat to the counter. It steadies the flutter in my chest. "I'm glad for you," I say. True and strange at once.

"It helped when the world started falling apart," he says. He looks toward the hallway, toward the red pulse. "Then came the work. The cost. The breaks you can't fix with duct tape."

Tolstoy noses my hand, and I rub the notch behind his ear.

"What will you do when I'm gone?" I ask. Not a test. The math that comes after love.

"Rig the machine," he says. "Go after Isa. Bring her here. Try to heal what I broke. If I can't, use the Sphere shell and take her somewhere else. Somewhere we can sit in the sun."

I nod and drop my gaze. "How long have you been carrying all that guilt?"

"Three hundred seventy one days," he says. "Since I left her there alone."

"I'll help you," I say. "Get things ready for her."

He nods, eyes on his hands. "You still plan to follow him," he says. Not a question.

"Yes," I say. "Until then, we'll read up on treatments and see what we can do with the med-bot. Tomorrow, we'll make a list."

He takes my hand. The grip is Diego's and not. "Stubborn love," he says. "It's the only kind that gets anything done."

I swallow and force a smile, my eyes glossy.

Down the hall, the red keeps its slow blink. We walk out in silence, like we just learned a song and don't trust our voices yet.

Every night for the next week, we comb the comms, searching for proof Lani and the others made it to Eden-2. Every night, the logs bleed bad news—outposts hit, convoys lost, bodies without names.

Gramps reads one report and mutters, "Used to be, wars had uniforms."

We find nothing. Not a whisper from Eden-2. No mention of Lani, Kai, Sam or Phil.

Maybe the message wasn't sent. Maybe we missed it.

Or maybe the four of them are still out there.

The thought settles like a swallowed nail.

On the eighth night, the comm log goes silent, whether due to a failure on our end or something worse, we don't know. We try everything we can think of—jammed paper, loose cables, spent ink cartridges—but come up empty.

Gramps rolls up the mess of printouts and throws them in a box. "I'll go over them more carefully, uh, later," he says as he carries the box out.

I nod and wonder how he'll cope once I'm gone.

Our days are spent running the med-bot through every program it has, scrubbing down the infirmary, testing the portable oxygen concentrator, scouring the unheated storage bays. Cold air fogs our breath, numbs our fingers. Gramps sorts, and I record using a green marker. We work until our hands cramp.

"Tell me about Tego," I say one evening as we're going through a crate of meds.

Gramps' hand stills on Tolstoy's head. "You sure?"

I nod.

He leans back, eyes gone distant. "I didn't like him at first. Too slick. Too sure of himself. Thought he knew everything."

I chuckle. "Imagine that."

"He was younger than your Diego. Had already jumped more times than he could count, the cocky son of a bitch."

I wait.

"I think he's the one who sent the Einstein Sphere. Maybe more than one. After Izzy died—his version of you—he stitched together a hundred broken timelines with fishing wire and grief." He looks up. "Freak accident at work. Izzy died instantly. The two of them were running some multinational NGO called Gemini Systems—and leaving their mark, from the sounds of it."

The air catches in my throat.

Silence stretches.

"I'm not supposed to tell you this," he says, voice low. "But he knew you. Not some xeno version. You, Isabel. Said you changed his life."

"How?"

"Didn't say. Just that it cost him. Made him different."

The back of my throat burns.

"He gave up everything to save you," he says. "Didn't even flinch."

I close my eyes, but the tears come anyway.

Gramps squeezes my hand, calloused fingers warm against mine. "Kid drove me crazy," he mutters. "But damn if I don't miss him." He smiles and releases me.

We work in silence, him calling out medications, me writing them down—an inventory that won't disappear if the computers fail.

Over the next week, we rig a backup battery to keep the med-bot alive—but if the main grid fails, neither of us will be going anywhere. Nor will Gramps be returning with Isa, as he calls her. Tolstoy sheds enough fur to upholster the couch twice over. Lucky wears a green ink patch on one foot like a battle scar.

By the time Isa comes, this place will either cure her outright—or prove what fools we are.

To fill the long hours after exhaustion hits, we play games: poker with Tolstoy nosing chips, chess until Lucky bats the pawns. Gramps calls it unwinding. I call it surviving the nights between now and the next jump.

Phil's recharge window for the spacetime bridge comes and goes. Ten days. Twelve. Two weeks. I remind myself that the silence doesn't mean no.

It only means not yet.

When I lie awake at night, fear trying to take over—fatal splash, failed recharge, wrong world, incorrect time—I curl up with the pets and practice saying *wait* like it's a word that loves me back.

One night over rummy—no chips for Tolstoy to steal, no pieces for Lucky to knock over—I force myself to ask, "How will you get Isa here? Phil insists the Coffin won't fit more than one."

His mouth twists. "He's wrong. Remove the emergency air bladder, strip the safety release mechanism, take out all the insulation. If we lie on our sides—feet to chest—we'll just fit. It's only for the snap-back, so maybe three or four seconds."

I stare at him, my mind racing. "Then I'm taking Tolstoy. We'll strip the Coffin once the light turns green. We can test it—make sure both of us fit—before I go."

He starts shaking his head, but I don't let him get any closer to saying no.

"Can you take Lucky with you?" I pet her silky fur and let my heart break a little. "Keep her safe for me?"

He needs you more than I do, kitty girl. Forgive me.

The corner of his eye twitches, and I know the answer is yes.

On a night that doesn't have a name because the days have all blurred together, Tolstoy lifts his head, ears twitching. Lucky freezes mid-scratch, tail a wire. Then I hear it too—a hum. Small at first, like a dream I'm trying to remember. The sound claws at me, hope and threat filling the room, the floor vibrating, pressure in my ears. And then it hits me. I haven't heard that sound since Diego left.

"Gramps," I yell, already running past his door. "The bridge is back up."

He is standing beside me before the sound dies, hair wild, feet bare—breath held because he's learned not to give air to fear. The dosimeter has shifted to a steady amber, like it's caught between no and yes. He looks at the sensor, then at me, then across the hall.

"Console," he says and is gone.

The pets and I race after him, all of us on edge.

READY TO JUMP

crawls across the bridge display.

Something stuck in my chest dislodges. I say nothing, afraid to scare it off.

Across the hall, the sensor is a stubborn amber.

Screw it. Diego's waiting, and Gramps may never get his turn if I sit on my hands.

"You should wait for the radiation to clear," he says, low, steady, his eyes on my feet.

"If the bridge is ready, I jump,' I say, not blinking. "The waiting has already cost too much."

He looks up, studies me, then nods once.

I exhale. "We need to make space in the Coffin for Tolstoy—and Isa."

He nods—but won't let me inside the lab.

As I watch through the glass, Lucky in my arms, he spends the next half hour stripping down the Coffin. When he's done, he shoves the pile of stuff out of the way and climbs into the Coffin. A few seconds later, he struggles back out.

My chest gets tight.

How is he going to get Isa in—and out—when he can barely lift himself?

"Plenty of room," he says when he comes through the door. "No need to test."

I follow him to the bridge console, set Lucky down next to Tolstoy. "Time to say goodbye."

The room sharpens.

I look down at the stack of organic clothes we prepared weeks ago, the puzzle box sitting on top.

My eyes fix on the spot Tego must have pushed a hundred times.

Who are you, Tego Nadales, and why do you care so much?

I shake off the thought and force my shoulders to relax.

At first, my hands won't unclasp.

When they do, I strip fast.

Gramps turns away and pets Tolstoy. "Isabel, you don't have to do this. You could stay here. We'll figure out a way to get you to Eden-2. Dave will take care of you."

"You know I can't." I put on a cotton underwrap and socks, silk shirt, linen pants, a rough wool sweater, and moccasins.

"Ready." My pulse races.

He hooks a strand of pearls around my neck, his gaze downcast. "Pawn them, first thing." He offers me a sheet of his handmade paper. "Same intel I gave Diego. Just in case." He steps away.

I run my fingertips across the lovely necklace. "Thank you."

His mouth moves like he wants to say something else, but he just presses his lips together and nods.

I pick up Lucky and give her a hug. "Take care of him, kitty girl. I'll miss you."

She purrs in my ear, the sound making my heart hurt.

I put her down and turn away before it gets any harder.

Gramps exhales hard, then takes my hands like he can't afford to lose me again.

His skin is dry, almost papery, but his grip is fierce. "He'll be there," he says, eyes glossy.

His face is a mix of the Diego I know and a Diego I have yet to meet.

Something about that gives me courage.

He presses my knuckles to his cheek, breath catching. Then he kisses my forehead—a small, powerful gesture from a life I can almost remember.

"I'll wait for you to close the hatch," he says, "and then go back and start the jump. Remember: three minutes to get out. If there's anything wrong there, just stay in the Coffin. It'll bring you back."

There's no way I'm jumping back, but I don't correct him—hope is a lie I'll gladly borrow.

I nod. "Good luck with Isa. Even if she's gone, *I'll* know what you did for her."

He swallows and puts his hands on my shoulders. "He'll find you, Isabel." He squeezes my arms, as if passing something invisible to me. "Wait for him."

"I will."

He releases me, trying not to look scared.

We don't drag things out. I take Tolstoy, push the door shut, and climb into the Coffin.

"Here, boy," I say and tap my chest twice.

The dog hesitates—then jumps in next to me.

I get him settled between my legs, his head across my belly. Cold seeps into my shoulders the second I lie back. I set the shell on my chest and trip the hatch. Through the glass, I see Gramps nod, Lucky in his arms. We don't wave. We have never been that kind of people.

The lid seals and my ears pop.

I lie in total darkness, my pulse hammering. I force myself to breathe. The Coffin gives me nothing back—vault-still air, metallic and dead.

Tolstoy lets out a soft whine but doesn't move.

"It's okay, boy," I whisper and stroke his head. "We'll find him."

The Coffin shudders, metal vibrating under my spine. The universe narrows to a thread—then needles through my chest.

I breathe out Diego's name and let the multiverse carry it forward.

Madder's Second Log: Final Entry

Isabel's jump is without precedent: no models, no
projections, no calculable margin for survival.
The compounded risk of losing both subjects
remains above acceptable thresholds.

Sensor data confirms catastrophic wall failure in
this biodome. Control room and underground vault
remain structurally sound, but energy systems
have destabilized.

Logging will be suspended until Diego or Isabel
are detected in an adjacent timeline.

Madders, Guardian AI of the Greatest Engineering
Wonder Ever Built, going dark.

Epilogue

He had been waiting over a month for the bridge to recharge.

After the electricity failed, he'd engineered a way to reroute the nuclear power back to the underground city. The radiation sensor had gone green a week later, but it had brought him no joy.

The bridge hadn't charged.

Every day, he got up, checked the console, then did his workout: Lifted a wool blanket rolled with bricks—it was over a hundred pounds now—and hefted it over the Coffin. Set it down, picked it up, set it down again. Then he'd carry the load up to medbay and place it on the operating table, palm the controls, and let his finger hover over the **SCAN** button.

When he had completed his third workout of the day, he let out an exhausted sigh.

Lucky meowed.

"You're relentless," he muttered.

She flicked her tail and meowed again.

"All right, all right. If kitty girl wants another workout, kitty girl gets it."

He stroked her back, took a long drink of water, and did it all again.

Lucky shadowed him, all whisker flicks and yawns. When he set the blanket down, she rubbed against his wrist. When he lagged, she gave a sharp mew. When he got it right, she climbed his shoulder and pressed her forehead to his jaw. She had the route memorized and would pad ahead to wait at each turn, encouraging him onward with a flick of her tail.

He did it until his back ached and his knees wobbled. Then he did it once more.

Late that evening, he was re-scanning the comm printouts for the nth time and sharing tuna casserole with the cat—both of them eating from the same bowl—when she let out a soft yowl.

"Don't blame me. You're the one who likes the casserole."

Then he felt the familiar vibration beneath his feet.

He ran down the hall to the bridge console, the cat right behind him.

READY TO JUMP scrolled across the display.

"Time to go," he said as Lucky did figure eights around his ankles.

The old man changed his clothes, put on the socks Tego had told him to wear, and threw the wool blanket over one arm.

"Up." He tapped his chest and the cat sprang to his shoulder. Lucky settled there, tail ticking against his neck.

"Ready?"

She rubbed her head against his chin.

"Good girl."

Gramps knew about the lethal consequences of jumping back before he'd left the first time, but he'd set the spacetime bridge to deposit him near the moment he'd left. Still, controlling both the bridge's time *and* location was impossible due to quantum effects— never mind the splash or splatter, whatever it was called—so he'd erred on the side of caution.

He didn't want to arrive ten miles away from the dome under thirty feet of water.

He'd wired a sixty-second kitchen timer to a servo on the bridge console. When it buzzed, the servo would yank a lever, executing the jump command.

Why the bridge designer hadn't included a timer was beyond him.

He'd also set the Coffin to seal itself automatically before it snapped back—didn't want to be busy with Isa and forget to close the hatch.

He took a deep breath, focused on seeing her face again, and palmed the shell.

One minute to get inside the Coffin. Three minutes to find Isa and get her back to the Coffin—he didn't have the power to stay longer. Then, in less than a second, they'd snap back here.

His dash to medbay would follow. The machine was already programmed with Isabel's DNA.

He had run the drill a hundred times—and knew it had to go perfectly.

He twisted the timer and raced to the Coffin, Lucky on his shoulder.

After tossing in the blanket, Gramps climbed inside. He held the cat against his chest as the launch sequence forced the lid shut.

He lay in darkness, his heart pounding in his ears.

Lucky meowed, soft and uncertain.

He stroked her silky fur. "You and me, both."

A second later, spacetime pinched to a tight throat and dragged them through. Pressure stacked in his ears, and his teeth ached. The Coffin fell sideways without moving—white, then black—and then a hollow bang.

His heart pounded faster.

In another universe, the Coffin splashed into knee-deep salt water.

He released the hatch and sat up.

He knew three minutes was tight, but what choice did he have? His time was running out.

After setting Lucky on his shoulder, he grabbed the blanket and climbed out.

Cold seeped up his pants.

The dome wasn't sealed anymore. Seawater poured in through a crack in the wall, rising and falling with the waves outside.

He wondered where the bots were.

The botanical garden was a swamp. Stumps leaned at wrong angles. A few emergency lights glowed from beneath the turbid water.

"Maybe the seal on the control tower is still good."

Along one wall, a broken pipe coughed brown foam.

The water smelled like brine and old lettuce.

He took a tentative step, his stocking feet sinking into the mud. "Damn."

Lucky let out a low growl.

"You can say that again."

He sloshed onward, hoping his memory was correct about the location of Dave's grave.

Something bubbled up from beneath the surface, putrid and yellow.

He kept moving.

A hole in the dome breathed ocean air. Wind whistled. Salt spray rained down.

Lucky hissed, claws in Gramps' shirt.

And then he saw them.

"Mierda."

He tried to run, but the water was too deep, the ruined gardens too swampy.

Drones poured in through the breech in the ceiling, pinpoints of blue light. They dove in a tight spiral toward the man and the cat, fresh meat full of precious metals.

He wrapped Lucky in the blanket and hunched over her. He knew it was futile, but did it anyway.

Nothing.

He looked over his shoulder.

The bots were frozen at arm's length, as if there were a forcefield around him.

"What the—?"

The man stood up. A sign for heirloom tomatoes drifted past like a dead gull. The bots tilted, hummed, and lifted away to circle the wound in the ceiling.

Seconds ticked by.

He lifted the blanket, set Lucky higher on his shoulder, and waded toward the central tower.

A bench floated in his path. He shoved it out of the way and almost lost his balance. After four more steps, he felt something firm beneath his feet.

"Found the sidewalk."

The cat mewed her approval.

The going got easier.

When he made it to the central tower, he took the stairs two at a time, murky water drizzling off his clothes. Lucky leaned into his jaw for balance. At the top landing, the door stood open. Isabelle's wheelchair was wedged in it, a smear of dried blood on the armrest, her plastic breathing tube curled on the floor.

His pulse jumped.

She had gotten out of her chair.

"And gone where?"

Lucky gave a plaintive bleat.

"Isabelle!"

He listened. The dome groaned.

He ran a loop around the observation deck.

"Isabelle? Where are you?"

His chest tightened. Time was running out.

Lucky sprang from his shoulder and trotted back the way they had come. He followed. She led him to the electrical room and scratched at the door: fast, staccato, like a shorting wire.

He banged on the door, shouted Isabelle's name.

A key was stuck in the lock, a lanyard hanging off it.

His heart jumped into his throat. "Isabelle's!"

The cat meowed.

He turned the key, shouldered the door. The latch gave.

The smell hit like a wall: rot, waste, stale air. He pulled his shirt up for a beat. On the floor, near a rack of empty bottles, Isa lay wrapped in a blanket. Gray hair fell across her face. Her chest moved with each shallow breath.

He knelt. "Hey," he said, and it was both now and forty years ago. "I've got you."

There was less than a minute left.

He wedged the door open with his blanket, worrying if he was strong enough to lift her from the floor.

Lucky circled Isabelle, then waited next to her head like a guard.

The old man forced one arm under Isa's shoulders, slipped the other under her knees, and heaved.

The room tilted.

The move was ugly, but he didn't drop her.

As he stood, her head bumped his shoulder, then rested against his neck.

He let out the breath he was holding.

The cat ran out the door, meowing.

He followed.

Down he went, knees screaming, the sharp metal stairs cutting into his soggy feet. The water line climbed his calves as he sloshed along the pathway. Drones tilted, curious, then kept their distance. His thighs were on fire and his back ached, but he carried her without complaint, remembering, forever ago, when Isabelle had programmed the bots to recognize her DNA—and his.

She must have added the pets' too.

Ahead, the Coffin waited with its mouth agape.

He stepped off the sidewalk into mud, knowing he only had seconds left. The extra weight made it harder. Twice, he nearly slipped.

Six steps, five, four.

He took the last two with a lurch, gritted his teeth, then swung Isa around and lowered her inside.

"Breathe," he told her. "For me."

Her chest moved—once, then again.

He slipped in next to her, shoulders pressing against her feet, and waited for the hatch to trip.

A small meow came from outside the Coffin.

He sat up.

Lucky was at the top of the steps, her tail flicking.

She held his eyes like a question.

"Jump. Hurry!"

She meowed again.

He tapped his chest twice like he'd seen Isabel do. "Lucky, come!"

The cat answered with a loud yowl—then leaped, a clean arc from the stairs into the brown water.

She splashed under, surfaced with ears flat. Swam a straight line toward him, legs a blur.

"Go, go, go."

But he knew she wasn't going to make it.

He moved without thinking, was out of the Coffin in one motion, landing knee deep in the mud. He took four strides, crouched and scooped her up. She clawed his chest, muddy water streaming from her tail.

Behind him, the lid began to close. Soft hydraulics he couldn't stop. He turned with the cat in his arms.

"Wait," he yelled, panic turning the word into a wail.

The Coffin didn't listen.

The lid sealed. The air puckered. Heat sapped from the water around his knees. Frost crystals blinked and rose in a ring and then were gone.

Where the Coffin had been, there were only concentric rings of murky water.

He stood in the shallow ocean, holding a wet, shaking cat, and let out a helpless cry.

Up above, the bots tilted, found nothing to feed on, and exited the dome.

The city under a mountain—and the med-bot ready to save Isa—lay forty years and a universe away.

He tasted salt and rust and fear.

His world collapsed to two points: here and there. The gap was every mistake he had ever made.

Lucky shifted in his arms and gave a soft mew.

He dried her face with the edge of his shirt.

"Should've named you Unlucky."

Outside, a wave broke. Water lapped his calves. Wind sighed through the breach above. Far off, something let go with a long, low groan.

He shifted his weight and looked at the place where the Coffin had been.

The ripples were gone.

A voice behind him called, "Dad?"

The word undid him.

He had no children.

But his heart remembered a different truth—two tiny lives lost.

He turned.

A teenage boy stood on the stairs, curly hair falling around his ears, eyes like Isabelle's.

His clothes were all wrong—no rust, no salt, no wear. He held no tool, carried no weapon.

The old man swallowed, mouth dry. "Who are you?"

"Tego's my father," the boy said, smiling. "Which means you are too."

The kid tipped his chin at the ring of water where the Coffin had vanished, then toward the tower, then up at the hole in the dome—as if all three were as they should be.

Diego pressed a hand to his chest. He couldn't speak. Could barely breathe.

Lucky butted her head against his chin, a quiet confirmation of something neither of them could name.

The word caught in the old man's throat. "Lucas?"

The teenager's smile widened. "Let's go save Mom, shall we?"

Also by DL Orton

MADDERS OF TIME SERIES

Hive, Book 1

Jump, Book 2

Dome, Book 3

Overtime, Book 4

Coming in 2027!

Dead Time, Book 3

Lost Time, Book 2

Crossing in Time, Book 1

BETWEEN TWO EVILS SERIES

Suggested Reading Order

Start with **Madders of Time** for the best entry point into DL Orton's shared multiverse. Then continue with **Between Two Evils** to explore related timelines, familiar characters, and the larger pattern connecting love, loss, and time travel.

About the Author

The AWARD-WINNING & BEST-SELLING author DL ORTON lives in the Tropics with her husband, a golden retriever mix, a Siberian cat, and a bazillion geckos.

In her spare time, she's building a time machine so that someone can go back and do the laundry.

Thank You for Reading!
dlorton.com
dlo@dlorton.com

---

amazon.com/author/dl_orton

bookbub.com/authors/d-l-orton

instagram.com/dl_orton_author

goodreads.com/dl_orton

x.com/dl_orton

facebook.com/DLOrtonWriter